GHOSTS
OF TOMORROW

MICHAEL R.
FLETCHER

Also by Michael R. Fletcher
Beyond Redemption
The Mirror's Truth
Swarm and Steel
City of Sacrifice: Of Smoke and Stone (Nov, 2019)

GHOSTS OF TOMORROW Copyright © by Michael R. Fletcher. All rights reserved.

Publishing History: This book was first published in 2013 by Five Rivers Publishing as *88*.

Cover Art by John Anthony Di Giovanni
Cover Typography and Design by Shawn T. King
Editors: Robert Fletcher, David Walters, Barb Geiger, Lorina Stephens

ISBN 978-0-9953122-4-1

For my father, whose love of writing seems to have infected me.

CONTENTS

INTRO FROM THE AUTHOR

Back in 2008 I lived with my girlfriend and worked as an Audio-Engineer doing live sound and recording albums for Toronto bands. The itch to write a book was growing in me. I'd tried my hand at writing before, but had always been unable to finish what I started. This time, I decided, it was going to be different.

In 2009, as my smokin' hot soon-to-be-wife planned our wedding, I was finishing up the first draft of my near-future science-fiction novel, *88*. After years of searching for a home, *88* was published by the awesome folks at Five Rivers Publishing in 2013. The few folks who read it seemed to like it (some rabidly so), but the book never really got noticed. Much of this is my fault. I knew very little about publishing and even less about publicity.

Life went on. My daughter was born, I left the music industry, I landed an amazing literary agent, and she sold my next novel, *Beyond Redemption*, to Harper Voyager. Somewhere in there I realized that if I wanted to have any chance at a career as a writer, I'd better start publicizing. Thanks to the awesome Kristopher Kneidecker I got a website, and then got my introverted self on all the usual social media sites.

In 2016 I realized I was going to self-publish *The Mirror's Truth*, the sequel to *Beyond Redemption*. That's an entire story in itself and if you buy me pints sometime, I'll tell you all about it. But it planted an idea. I wanted to revisit *88*. I wanted to edit and rewrite with what I'd learned over the last few years. There were a few new scenes I wanted to add too. Then, when I saw the work John Anthony di Giovanni did for *The Mirror's Truth*, I knew I wanted a new title and cover art. I think you'll agree that he absolutely killed it. So good!

I asked Lorina over at Five Rivers if she'd be willing to revert the rights to me and she graciously agreed. The folks at Five Rivers really are champions of indie-publishing in every way. If you're looking for a home for your novel, they're a great bunch.

The book you hold now is the author's definitive edition of that story I wanted to tell back in 2008. It's come a long way in the last nine years.

I hope you like it.

—Mike Fletcher

PROLOGUE

God opened Archaeidae's soul and poured in light and exquisite pleasure. The boy saw heaven, shuddered in ecstasy until he thought he'd burst. God loved him, absolved him of all sins, took away every nightmare, every memory of spilled blood and spattered brains, washed him pure and made him whole. The light faded and Archaeidae's thoughts once again coalesced into purest iron will. He awoke driven by a single purpose: Make god happy.

God, dressed in a black tailored suit, stood before Archaeidae, examining the boy.

Archaeidae bowed. "Uncle Riina."

Uncle Riina quirked the slightest smile, barely a twitch at the corner of his mouth. Archaeidae basked in the approval of almighty god.

"Do you like this chassis?" Riina asked.

Sleek and brutal, Archaeidae's most recent body was built by Navistar for black-ops stealth and assassination missions.

Archaeidae did an intricate six-limbed dance to demonstrate his mastery of the chassis.

He'd been learning this body for six months, first practicing simple movements like walking and jumping. Later he taught himself how to use all six limbs simultaneously, his scanned mind bifurcating to make use of a body he hadn't been born to.

Speeding the dance until the sound of his metallic claws on the floor became a constant hum, he drew the *daishō,* a matched *katana* and *wakizashi* Uncle Riina gave him. He spun the swords in a flawless machine-precise kata of death.

Riina nodded again and Archaeidae stopped.

He watched his uncle. *Does he look happy or unimpressed?* There was no reading the face of god. *Maybe I shouldn't have included the swords.* Uncle Riina made a point of talking about maturity and how important it was and Archaeidae was pretty sure it had something to do with leaving your weapons sheathed. Most of the time.

"You like the swords?" Uncle Riina asked.

"Yes, Uncle."

"Good."

Riina examined him, looking over the struts of his torso, checking the universal-joints of all six limbs, and finally peering into the visual receptors mounted on his chromed death's-head skull. "You look like hell spat out its most terrifying spider." He grinned perfect white teeth. "I have a job for you."

Archaeidae bowed low. A chance to prove himself in the eyes of god. There was nothing better in all the world. Screaming chaos and blood, broken bodies scattered across a filthy concrete floor. He shut that away. Nightmares were for the weak. Uncle Riina demanded perfection and Archaeidae gave it to him.

"James Schmidt," said Riina.

"A lieutenant," answered Archaeidae, remembering the man. "He runs collections in Wichita." Hookers and narcotics were a small but profitable aspect of Riina's business network.

"Ran," said Riina.

"Ran," agreed Archaeidae.

"It seems he has a gambling problem. A sizable portion of the funds he collects each week have been going to support that habit."

God was angry. Archaeidae stood motionless, waiting. *Point me in the right direction. I shall be your wrath, the arrow of your vengeance.*

"James is at home," said Riina. "With his wife and kid. Make an example of them."

Them.

Archaeidae bottled away his feelings. He would not let Uncle Riina down. "I will make you proud."

"Not the kid," said Riina. "We don't hurt children."

Archaeidae's heart sang. His was a just god. Riina's lieutenant stole from him and for that he must pay. The wife was collateral damage, part of the message to the others in the organization: Betraying Uncle Riina comes with a high cost.

He wouldn't have to murder the child.

"Bring the boy to the crèche, said Riina. "We'll take care of him, raise him as one of our own."

"Yes, Uncle."

"James doesn't yet know that we know."

"He will soon," promised Archaeidae.

"Damned right he will," said Riina. "It will be the last thing he knows."

An hour later Archaeidae cradled the toddler in his arms, sheltering him from the view. No one needed to see the corpses of their parents littered all over the crappy bungalow they called home.

He'd sent Riina's message, loud and clear, to anyone in the organization thinking about betraying the Mafia Capo's trust. He wrote his message in violence and blood, a language they understood well. A language he mastered at the age of twelve. Now, at fourteen, no one spoke it better. Archaeidae was an artist, a poet.

Archaeidae turned away from the chaos and destruction, keeping his body between it and the boy. "It's okay," he said. "Uncle Riina will take care of your now. He'll have you scanned. You'll shed this weak flesh," claws retracted, he gently pinched a chubby arm. "You will be steel. He'll give you meaning. He'll make you matter."

The toddler cried and Archaeidae cooed and soothed.

"Don't worry. It won't hurt. And later, after the flesh is gone, you'll receive the best training. Weapons and martial arts. Stealth and evasion. Hacking and informational systems. Wherever your strengths lie, Uncle Riina will find them. He will make you the best you that you could ever be. You'll see, you're going to like him." He leaned in to whisper into the boy's ear. "He is god."

It is done, he tight-linked to Uncle Riina. *I'm ready for pick-up. I have the boy.*

A van would arrive to collect him within the minute.

Archaeidae considered his own past. He remembered nothing before Uncle Riina. "You won't remember anything," he promised. "It's best that way."

CHAPTER ONE: Wednesday, August 1st, 2046

Crawling, 88 followed a long crack in the stained concrete. Where floor met wall, the crack fragmented like a splayed hand, reaching upward. The pain of the grit and stones on her hands and knees helped her focus. She couldn't reach the wall; the tubes connecting her to the rear of the cell wouldn't let her. Rocking back onto her haunches she picked at the scabs and scars in the crook of her left arm. The catheter in her right arm itched and burned, at odds with the random pulses of icy fluid it shoved into her veins. The feeling of that cold creeping up her arm and into her chest left her nauseated. She'd repeatedly yanked out the catheter until the men came and fastened it to her with fibrous gray tape. They'd said something about the veins in her left arm collapsing from abuse.

Ignoring the relentless emptiness in her belly, 88 studied the cracks in the walls and floor. The cracks were a system, a coded message from the universe, pregnant with information and sly in subtle hints. She leaned forward, face close to the floor as she stared at the microscopic clefts and crevices in the stone. They spoke to her, revealing all they could of the reality beyond this concrete box.

If only she could crack the cracks.

Cracks meant movement, change. Pressure. She watched. Nothing changed. She watched longer.

Voices echoed in the hall. A distraction. She glanced toward the door, listening. When she returned her attention to the cracks they were just cracks. Wait, what had distracted her? She'd lost something. An idea. Something important. Something to do with change.

The memory of a voice. *Her* voice. Mom. Soothing and quiet, her voice sounded like home. Belonging. Mom was never loud like the men who brought bright lights and pain and endless questions.

88 picked at a crack with a ragged fingernail, digging for clues. The stone resisted change. She crawled to follow it, squealing as a tearing pain in her arm stopped her short.

No! Further!

She examined her arm. Blood leaked from under the gray tape. She grunted in annoyance; the tubes shouldn't have stopped her yet. There should be another body-length of freedom. Looking back she saw the Total Parenteral Nutrition tubes—as they were labeled where they disappeared into the wall—tangled in a jumbled knot.

Did I do that? She couldn't remember.

Once the TPN tubes were untangled, 88 again followed the crack. The voices beyond her cell grew in volume. Men, loud and harsh. *Go away.* The sharp smell of sweet chemical residue, not unpleasant but overpowering. New. *Go away!* She cringed back from the door, dragging the hoses in the dust, careful they didn't tear her arm any more than they already had. She bared teeth in a defiant snarl.

The door opened. Loud voices. Bright lights.

She forgot the men and the cracks, lost them in an

avalanche of sensory overload. Metallic acid smell. The cell's acoustics changed as the door opened and moist air flooded in. Gritty stone under her bum. Voices. The hose in her arm spewed ice into her veins. Too much.

Awareness returned one sense at a time. When 88 could again focus, two men stood in the cell with her. They talked, but not to her. Their tan clothes were different from those who'd taped the tubes to her arm. She'd seen men like this before. Her teachers called them *Suits* as though their choice of clothing defined them.

She picked at her diaper, the only clothing she'd ever worn. *Does this define me?*

The suits were a pale tan and hung loose on thin frames. 88 liked the color, it was quiet. The man on the left appeared soft, his face round and damp, his pale eyes wide and blinking too fast. The other looked hard, features chiseled and lean.

Mean. Bad. Hurt.

88 shuffled back from the door, putting distance between her and the men. She had to look away from their stares. Rocking helped filter the bombardment of sights, scents, and sounds. She watched the men from the corner of her eye, wanting to get back to examining the cracks but too distracted.

The hard one brushed the hair out of his eyes. "She don't look like a genius, sitting in the dirt rocking like that."

"This one was slotted for the crèches before birth," said the soft one. "They increased the amount of prenatal testosterone, giving her a stronger interest in systems and increased attention to detail. It's sort of a chemically/hormonally induced Asperger Syndrome."

"Ass-burger?"

"Asperger. Apparently, it cripples her language and social skills a bit. She's a high-functioning autistic. That's probably why she's rocking like that."

"But she's not actually retarded, right? If the kid's a 'tard, I come a long way for nothing and the boss is gonna be displeased." He enunciated the last word carefully.

Displeased. She liked that word, it felt round.

"No. Well, not *too* much. More that she's...different in the right way. She tests higher than any of the other kids in every field. Math and complex systems are her strongest subjects. I'm talking savant level scores."

Still rocking, 88 turned so she could see the men. "They're going to kill you," she blurted, repeating something Mom said before they took her away. They stopped talking and watched her. The silence helped her think.

Could the cracks in the floor be caused, or at least influenced, by the weight of the people walking upon it? She looked to the floor, contemplating the density of stone. When she returned her attention to the men they'd backed away and were again conversing in hushed tones.

She listened as they talked. The gritty dust on the palm of her hand distracted her. Much of what they said wasn't interesting enough to make it past the other stimuli.

"Creepy..." They'd left the door open and across the hall, she saw another door, this one with a faded 87 above it. "...didn't think..." She heard moaning from beyond that far door and the sound of tubes dragged across stone.

Someone like me?

"...aware of her surroundings," said the hard suit.

"She's forgotten...can be...strange."

"...drooling...hacker potential?"

The sweet chemical smell came from the men but couldn't mask the more sour odor underneath. Dark patches swelled from under their arms, staining their suits. Too much, she rubbed at the floor, feeling the sharp grit on her fingertips.

"Hacker god...girl's scores aren't human."

A change in the man's tone dragged 88 back into the conversation. It took her away from the stone.

"She gives me the shivers," said the hard one. "Her eyes look dead."

"Prophetic. Anyway, won't be a problem for long," answered the other, blinking rapidly.

"Suppose not."

Something was going to change, but what? *My eyes?*

"The autism...makes her challenging...social skills...a problem. The kid's already basically a computer."

"They are going to turn you into a computer," 88 said. They weren't listening.

"Ain't interested...social skills...we'll take her. What's the asking price?"

"Thirty-million Au. This brain is one in a billion."

88 liked numbers, they focused her and she caught more of the conversation.

"NATU gold? Not Euros, or Yen?"

The soft one shook his head. "Not a chance, that crap isn't backed. Thirty million NATU Au. You want something cheaper, we can look at average kids."

The other made a gesture with his hands that 88 couldn't understand. "Fine. Done. Purée her brains."

88 didn't see them walk away; they were just gone. The cracks weren't so interesting right now and the sweet chemical smell hung thick.

"They're going to kill you," she said.

Where was mom? 88 wanted her pillow, she needed to think.

CHAPTER TWO: Wednesday, August 1st, 2046

Fresh out of university, Griffin started his new job last week. His boss, an immaculate suit named Phil, led him to a cubicle and introduced him to the office chair he expected his ass to spend the next four decades sitting on. He spent most of the first day pretending to look busy and trying to find the bathroom.

On Griffin's second day a water war broke out in the southern districts, the FLQ blew up a train station in Old Montreal, and a militant environmental group sparked a massive fire in the Alberta tar sands that would burn for years. The office emptied, agents scattering about the North American Trade Union to put out fires literal and otherwise.

On his third day, an anonymous tip came in about a crèche hidden on a farm an hour from the NATU offices in Toronto.

Phil appeared in Griffin's cubicle as if he'd teleported there. "How old are you?"

"Twenty, Sir."

Phil muttered something under his breath about diapers. "You completed the tactical training?"

"Well, I've completed the—"

"The file will be transferred to you. Familiarize

yourself with the case and then collect your Strike Team."

"Strike Team?"

"The crèche is yours. Shut it down."

"I'm not sure—"

"It's you or the janitor." Phil looked like maybe he thought the janitor might be the wiser choice.

Am I allowed to make jokes too? Somehow he thought not.

Griffin wanted to say that this was his third day. He wanted to say that he'd never commanded troops in the field before. He had a thousand reasons why this was a bad idea.

Instead, he glanced about the empty cubicles, thought about his father's *Someday you have to stand for something, if you coast through life you'll miss it* speech, and nodded. "Yes, Sir."

Two days later it was forty-four degrees Celsius with the humidex and here was Griffin, covered head to toe in black magnetorheological body armor.

Coasting through life, he decided, *is a hell of a lot more comfortable.* He felt sodden and chafed, wrung-out like a moldy washcloth. To make matters worse, he had the fiercest itch growing. He shifted uncomfortably, clawing at his shoulder to no effect. Trying to get at an itch protected by the latest in body-armor was damned near impossible.

Old growth trees heavy with leaves obscured everything. They could have been in the middle of Algonquin park instead of an hour from Toronto. It looked peaceful.

Not for long.

Again he pawed at the itch.

"Damn."

"You okay, Sir?" whispered the soldier crouched beside him.

"Bedbugs," hissed Griffin. Why the hell had Phil put

him in such a crappy hotel? He was only an hour and a half from home, he could have spent the last two days planning this strike in the dubious comfort of his rented condo instead of crammed into the Hamilton Hotel with two dozen restless North American Trade Union Marines. To make matters worse, every single one of them was older than he. Half of them were scarred veterans, hard eyes questioning his every decision.

And why not? What the hell do I know about leading a Strike Team? Was it too late to call the janitor?

The soldier—Griffin couldn't remember his name—nodded in commiseration. "Me too, Sir. Itches like a fucker."

Griffin blinked at the soldier. At least this one was pretty close in age and Griffin didn't feel like he should apologize for being here and giving orders. "You don't have to call me Sir."

"Yes Mister Dickinson, Sir." There was no sign of humor.

Griffin hid his annoyance and checked the time display in the corner of his vision. 7:58 AM. Two minutes and then it was go time. Other information scrolled past, the date, temperature, his GPS coordinates, and assorted other random facts he didn't care about.

Today is the day. Fear and excitement shivered through him.

Shut down the crèche, save the children, and be a hero by noon. Though he never said anything, his father had always been quietly disapproving of the fact Griffin worked for the government. Maybe now he'd see that Griffin was doing some good. Maybe he would even be proud. *Fat fucking chance.*

"I wish Corporal Anjaneya had come with us," said the soldier. "It'd be awful nice to have a combat chassis around if this gets messy."

A soldier whose mind had been scanned and holoptigraphically stored after her body was cut to pieces by Taramahura insurgents in the Copper Canyon, Corporal Anjaneya's Scan was housed in a General Dynamics Light Assault chassis. She was meant to be the team's recon and tactical support. Instead, as they readied themselves to leave the hotel, she stood motionless at the window, staring out at the street beyond, muttering "Fuck fuck fuck fuck" over and over. They'd been unable to even get her attention, much less bring her along on the strike. Already his beautiful plan had taken a hit.

"We can handle this," said Griffin. "How far are we from the farm?"

"Two hundred meters, Sir."

Griffin ground his teeth but said nothing. He hated being called Sir almost as much as he hated calling people Sir. The word dripped feigned subservience and respect. At least when he used it. He couldn't believe it wasn't the same for everyone. Really, how many times could you use Sir in the span of a few seconds and have it not ring false?

"No movement?"

"None, Sir."

"Okay. Let's do this. Move the team forward as per the plan. I don't want anyone getting away." With a sigh he gave up on the itch, it'd have to wait. "Get the doctor over here, I want him next to me. My guess is the conditions will be pretty bad. These kids might need medical attention."

"That's me, Sir."

"Seriously?"

"Well, squad Medic."

"That'll have to do." The Medic looked hurt and Griffin ignored him, signaling to the Marines crouched in the forest around them.

The squad moved well, he had to give them credit

for that. At least *they* knew what they were doing. It was a beautiful plan if he did say so himself. Every possibility had been considered and accounted for. This was going to be a crèche strike for the records. The next generation of NATU Special Investigators would read about him in class.

Griffin crouched low and followed the squad Medic through the trees. The Tavor 41 assault rifle, still slung over his back, caught on a low-hanging branch and yanked him to a halt. Embarrassed, he looked to see if anyone noticed. No one paid him any attention. Ahead, he saw the faded red of a large barn through the trees. Half the team would hit the barn, while the other half took the big two-story fieldstone farmhouse. Right on cue half the squad peeled away, disappearing into the dense forest.

Here we go. Here we go.

Swinging the rifle from his back, Griffin shuffled forward. This was crazy, a crèche right here in Ontario, barely an hour from NATU's District of Ontario headquarters in Toronto. There was a quiet little farming community not two minutes away. What was it called? Something to do with cows. Jerseyville? *When did things get so bad?* When had the demand for scanned minds left the legal supply so far behind? One breakthrough in Artificial Intelligence could put an end to all of this evil.

The squad broke from the trees and hustled double-time to the barn wall where they stopped, waiting. Griffin, back pressed to the peeling red paint, breathed in deep gulps.

What the hell is that smell? It must have been something awfully powerful to make it through his helmet's filtration system. He gagged a little, swallowing bile. How embarrassing would it be to puke in front of a squad of hardened combat vets?

The trooper at the front of the squad peeked around the corner and gave the All Clear sign. Breaking into two groups, the squad took their positions. Half covered the barn entrance, rifles pointed down the pebbled drive toward the farmhouse out of sight around the I bend. The rest faced the door, ready for the moment it opened. Griffin tried to watch everything, the laneway, the surrounding trees, and the opening barn door. He felt exposed. Those trees which had moments ago hidden him now swarmed with unknown threats. *Okay, all part of the plan.* The other squad would take the farmhouse.

A rabbit dashed from the trees and Griffin, riding the razor's edge of adrenalin, almost shot it. He watched it disappear back into the forest.

In his peripheral vision he saw the barn door swing open and the Marines tense, ready for action.

"What the *fuck*?" someone said.

Someone else vomited into their helmet, a tearing retching sound, loud over the earpiece. Turning, Griffin peered into the darkness. His helmet adjusted, changing light frequencies to allow him to see within.

Rows of chicken-wire cages, their doors hanging open. There must have been hundreds of them, each no more than a few cubic feet. A small dog would have been uncomfortable in there. The cages were empty.

A display on the visor informed Griffin it was over sixty degrees in the barn and a wave of heat washed over him as the air trapped within flooded out the open door. Partially cooked rotting meat. Griffin threw up into his helmet, filling the filter and clogging it closed. He stumbled back a few steps as did the rest of the Marines. He tried to draw breath and got a mouthful of regurgitated breakfast, fried eggs on toast. He gagged and again vomited. Dropping the rifle, he clawed at the helmet's releases. He was going to drown in his own puke.

The helmet came away and he drew a single sobbing breath before doubling over as, unprotected by the helmet's filters, the full force of the stench bludgeoned him. Unable to do anything else, he retched himself dry. He wasn't alone. At least half the squad had tossed their helmets and were puking alongside him. When there was nothing left he straightened, peering into the murky darkness. Without the helmet's Light Intensification gear he couldn't make out much more than dim shapes and the dust dancing in beams of light where the roof was holed. Wood was stacked along one wall. Nothing moved. Buzzing filled his ears, made his teeth itch.

Griffin spat, trying to clear the taste from his mouth. It was impossible, his entire being had been infused with the stench. Unclipping the flashlight from his utility belt he panned it across the barn's interior. The empty cages, the makeshift wood, leather, and bright chrome scanning chairs at the rear of the barn. Wood stacked along the side wall. *No. Not Wood.* He blinked, trying to make sense of what he saw. Was that a thin, pale arm? And that, a leg? No, couldn't be. And there was a face, empty eyes wide, staring straight at him. His brain struggled to fit everything together and yet shied from the truth. Too many arms and legs. Too many little faces. Ragged black blankets had been tossed over the corpses, but flesh remained exposed everywhere he looked.

"What's that sound?" the Medic asked, arriving at Griffin's side. His helmet was gone, one of many littering the driveway.

Griffin ignored the question. "You're with me," he commanded and stepped into the crushing heat of the barn. He wanted to hold his breath and to vomit all at the same time. Only force of will and a desire not to look like a coward kept him moving forward. The Medic hung back but followed him in. The buzzing got louder.

"Brighter," Griffin told the flashlight as he panned the light along the stacked bodies. The blankets exploded, a maelstrom of angry black filling the air. Where Griffin froze, the Medic squealed something incomprehensible and fled for the door. Flies. Millions of them. They were in his hair and eyes, their legs tickling at the corners of his clenched mouth as they crawled across his face. He spun and flailed his arms futilely. In seconds they were gone, fleeing the confines of the barn.

The Medic looked sheepishly from the door. "Sorry."

Griffin waved it away, only regretting he hadn't thought to flee too. "Get in here." He felt the flies still trapped in his hair.

The Medic half saluted before catching himself. He re-entered the barn but didn't look happy. "How many?" he asked, staring at the stacked bodies.

Griffin forced himself to look, to appraise the magnitude of the atrocity. The bodies were piled five or six high, stacked like firewood. Thirty deep, he figured, looking the length of the wall. Closer now, he could make out more detail. None of them were over eight years old. It was unreal. This couldn't be. No one could do this to children on such a scale.

"Three hundred," he answered.

"Shit."

Griffin nodded, forcing himself closer even though every part of him wanted to run screaming until he found somewhere he couldn't smell this, couldn't see it. Wriggling white maggots crawled in the corners of eyes, nestled in nostrils.

"Maggots," said the Medic, pointing out the obvious. "They've been dead for a quite a while."

"No," said Griffin, remembering the Forensic Entomology class. "Depending on the breed of flies it can happen in as little as eight to twenty hours. And these are still in the first larval stage."

"So?"

"A day, maybe two. The heat will have sped the process."

"So if we..." The Medic trailed off.

If they'd moved faster, if he hadn't spent two days planning this crèche raid to the very last detail, they would have been here in time to stop this. Griffin swallowed the reek of death and failure.

"You couldn't have known," offered the Medic.

Griffin turned away, stumbled from the barn.

Another Marine, this one still wearing his helmet, intercepted him. "Sir, we've got word from the squad at the farmhouse. It's empty, cleaned out. Doesn't look like they've been gone long. A day, tops."

A day. One day.

Griffin looked everywhere but at the barn. He tasted slow-cooked flesh. Sour rot filled his sinuses. His skin crawled from the memory of tickling flies' legs.

"Sir," said the Marine. "They've found something you should see."

"Fine," Griffin answered. "Tell them I'm on my way." He walked away before the Marine could continue.

The pebbled trail leading to the farmhouse was impossibly quiet. No bird calls, no hum of insects. Only the sighing of the wind through the trees. Griffin blinked and felt tears leak down his cheeks. He looked down at the spattering of vomit caking his chest and felt too gutted to care. A Marine spotted him and jogged to intercept.

The soldier's eyes widened as he noted Griffin's state and he said, "Sir, follow me please, Sir."

Griffin followed him to the rear of the farmhouse. Two more Marines loitered there. A third stood with a shovel and a look of distaste. Behind the house was a field, a dozen acres of tilled earth. The dirt had been piled in long hills a foot or so high.

Griffin stared, uncomprehending. "What am I

looking at?"

"Graves," answered the Marine at his side.

He looked at the piled earth. "A little long for graves, aren't they?"

"Mass graves, Sir. Trenches. They've been burying the bodies back here. We dug a bit. Judging from the decomp, they've been at it for a while."

Griffin blinked at the field and spat. The taste of death and failure would never leave him. He wanted to brush his teeth, scrape his tongue with a razor. "How many?"

"We can't be sure, Sir. Best guess, from the amount of digging they did, thousands."

"Thousands." Griffin's knees felt rubbery as he realized he was standing atop a long, massed grave. He stepped off the raised earth.

"We should report in," said the Marine.

No point in maintaining radio silence. "I'll make the call," said Griffin, as if he had a choice.

Phil, head of Toronto's NATU Special Investigations branch, gave nothing away as he listened to Griffin's report. If the abject failure of the raid touched him at all, he showed none of it.

"Clean up and report to the office," commanded Phil, tie crisp, hair perfect, as he eyed Griffin's puke-stained shirt.

"I need to—"

"I want you in Toronto by noon."

"But—" Phil was gone, the connection dead.

A hero before noon. Griffin hawked and spat.

Two hours later he was showered and back in Toronto. No amount of scrubbing could remove the smell. Everything bore the scent of hot, rotting flesh. He gargled a pint of mouthwash and devoured half a tube of toothpaste to no avail.

Griffin padded naked around the kitchen, feet slapping on the bare concrete floor, in search of something to overpower the taste in his mouth. Not yet having received his first paycheck, he hadn't shopped and the cupboards were barren. A stack of empty pizza boxes waited to be recycled. He was considering snorting tabasco sauce to burn the scent from his sinuses when Phil called.

Griffin answered, no video this time.

"Dickinson, where are you?" demanded Phil foregoing all pleasantries.

"At home."

"Good. Pack a suitcase, you're flying out this afternoon."

"I'm done," said Griffin. "I'm not cut out for fieldwork." *Put me somewhere my failures don't kill little kids.*

"Everyone is busy. You're all I have. Pack light, you'll only be a couple of days." And Phil was gone again, sure in the knowledge Griffin would obey.

The power flickered and went out.

The filter-mask reduced the amount of toxins and pollutants Griffin breathed but it was hot to the point of suffocation at the bus stop. A large truck grumbled to a halt nearby and the temperature increased as the exhaust washed over him. Unable to keep up, the filter-mask shut down and he breathed his previous exhalation tasting tabasco sauce, mouthwash, and rotting bodies. Any life left in the crease of his already wrinkled suit wilted. The truck lumbered away and left Griffin in a cloud of oily fumes and dust.

His condo, a squat concrete and cardboard box with all the personality of a prison, called to him from across the street. There was beer in the fridge. It might still be cold if the power had come back on.

Enough. Go home.

Griffin glanced at the badly scratched suitcase sitting between his legs. Two more crumpled gray suits, underwear, and single change of socks. That's all he had time to throw together. Everything else needed laundering.

His head sagged forward and he swore under his breath. He'd forgotten his toothbrush.

Griffin flinched at the thought of another field assignment. Phil wouldn't do that to him, not so soon. *If he suggests counseling I'll take it.* It must be a fact-finding mission; something without stacks of discarded little bodies. *I should be learning where the staples and binders are, not standing on the grave of a thousand dead children.* How bad could it be to justify sending him into the field just days out of school? The badge proclaiming him a NATU Special Investigations agent sat heavy in his pocket. He still couldn't believe it was real and not a toy.

Griffin forced himself to think about something else. Anything but empty eyes and the swarming flies.

Redemption. Did such a thing exist? It seemed unlikely.

The big Mitsubishi-Nikon billboard over the 7-Eleven gas station displayed its litany of information.

11:23am...39 degrees Celsius...48 with Humidex...Smog Advisory in effect...UV Advisory in effect...August 1st...11:24am...

It was still early and would only get hotter.

The billboard showed an elderly couple watching their grandchildren play in an impossibly green yard. 'You've lived your days, and they've been good days,' said the billboard. 'But your children are struggling'—the green lawn faded to dull brown—'and you worry about how they'll make ends meet.'

Griffin turned away in disgust. These ads were little more than veiled threats offering immortality. He glanced back in time to catch the tagline.

'Live on as a Scan. Support your family for generations to come.'

Is this where we're at, selling our elderly into state-sanctioned slavery instead of letting them die in peace? These ads were springing up everywhere, there was no escaping them. The need for human computers far outstripped the supply.

It was creepy how no one ever mentioned how much the scanning process cost—more than a retired couple could ever afford—or how expensive a chassis to house the Scan could be. People were being asked on their deathbeds to mortgage their futures. They were signing away decades for the chance to escape death. With the Scan Rights question still unanswered, they might be forever selling themselves into slavery. Corporations and governments were snapping up Scans and chassis, and Griffin could guess which way *they* hoped the legal winds would blow. Or maybe hope had nothing to do with it.

He thought about Corporal Anjaneya, the Scan inhabiting the combat chassis they'd left at the Hamilton Hotel. What had been going on there? She hadn't said a word the entire time they were at the hotel, and then when it was time to leave, just stood at the window swearing. Something was seriously wrong with that Scan.

Perhaps thirty people waited for the Islington bus which was ten minutes late. Everyone wore filter-masks, the teens sporting custom masks in a variety of bright colors. Many flashed messages, band names, and product slogans across them. Just two weeks ago Griffin bought one with a snarling wolf's skull and the logo of his favorite band. The day he got the job he realized he couldn't wear it anymore. *Welcome to adulthood*, he remembered thinking. Like Griffin, the older folks wore off-the-shelf gray or black. They looked like a pack of upright dogs dressed in sweat-stained business suits.

Here I am, another obedient dog.

Toronto's North American Trade Union offices sat in the heart of the business district in the gutted Sapphire Tower. An eighty-story altar to greed and failure built by the very last American President, the building now housed the center of government for the District of Ontario.

Griffin arrived at NATU headquarters feeling like he'd gone swimming in his suit. The skin around his eyes was gritty with some kind of fine particulate matter. He ducked into the washroom which recorded his water and electrical usage as well as the duration of his stay. Anything over three minutes and the room would send Phil a report in triplicate. Nothing was worth that. He tried to straighten his crumpled and sweat-soaked suit but the attempt failed. He ran his hands through spiky hair to flatten it. That failed too.

Phil waited for him in the NATU Special Investigations office; he grimaced as Griffin entered and gestured toward a chair. Griffin sat.

"You look like shit," said Phil. That was probably meant to sting. Phil looked immaculate. No sweat stains. Perfect hair. Griffin didn't care. Not today. Anyone who stands in a barn full of the stacked corpses of hundreds of children and worries about their hair has achieved something beyond self-centered asshole.

A woman Griffin didn't recognize stood beside Phil. She looked to be about Griffin's age and a gray suit concealed her figure. She had long dark brown hair tied back and dark eyes that studied him for a moment before dismissing him and returning to her palm-comp. Where Griffin felt like a kid at the adult's table, she looked confident. At least she had the good grace to look uncomfortable in the heat.

"You know what I went through this morning," said Griffin.

"These things happen. Don't let it bother you." Phil wrinkled his nose in distaste. "You're going to Dallas."

These things happen? Was Phil absolving him of his failure at the Jerseyville crèche? Griffin swallowed an uncomfortable lump of fear. *Don't do this to me.* "Dallas? I hate the desert." He tried to sound casual.

Phil ignored him. "From Dallas, you're bouncing to Wichita Falls."

Bouncing? "After this morning, I thought..." He trailed off, Phil wasn't listening. *Why aren't you demanding I see a psych counselor? That's the rules.* And anyone who dressed like Phil loved rules.

"What happened?" asked the woman.

"Nothing," Griffin answered. It was the truth.

Phil looked away, pretended to be busy with something on his desk. "We're sending a Scan in a full combat chassis with you."

Griffin's stomach twisted. Another combat chassis? "That went *real* well. And what the hell am I doing that I need a walking battle-tank?" He knew the answer.

"We have a crèche outside of Wichita Falls. I know," Phil said quickly, "you probably want some time off. You earned it."

Time off? Earned it? He hadn't earned anything.

"We're swamped. What can I do?" Phil gestured at the sea of empty cubicles beyond his office, feigning helplessness. "Don't worry. It's a milk-run. Shut down the crèche, liberate the children and find out who's backing the operation."

Hero by noon. "What if we're too late?" Griffin asked. "What if we get there and find Scans instead of children?" Stacks of dead bodies. Fat flies.

"We'll cross that bridge—"

"The courts haven't made a decision yet. So do the kids have rights? What will we do with them, shut them down or put them to work?"

Phil gave him a shut the hell up look, all furrowed brows, and glaring eyes. "We have placement strategies in place. The children will be well cared for."

What a pile of steaming garbage. Griffin darted a glance at the woman.

Phil didn't miss a beat.

"Griffin, meet Nadezhda." The woman flashed Griffin a smile, distant and professional. "She's with the NATU Public Relations department. We need some good press. There are too many reports on how we're not taking the wholesale theft and enslavement of children seriously."

"This is a bad idea," protested Griffin. *A really bad idea.* "I can't... I can't do this."

"You're going to help her get the story," continued Phil. "NATU Special Investigations Unit saves stolen children. Returns them to grateful mothers. She's going to record the strike."

Fantastic. *All the world will witness my next great failure.*

"She's got *carte blanche*," said Phil. "Make sure she gets whatever she needs. Video, interviews, archived data, you name it." Phil placed a fatherly hand on Griffin's shoulder, the grip too tight to be friendly. Griffin resisted the urge to shrug it off. "Make us look good."

Griffin felt a cold shiver. He'd seen video from dozens of raids. Crèche children, raised beyond the niceties of societal conditioning, made for dangerous product. Train a child from birth to be a merciless killing machine and then drop its scanned brain into a state-of-the-art combat chassis. The results were chilling and in high demand.

He'd learned his lesson. Hesitation cost lives. It wouldn't happen again. He'd move fast. Planning every detail had been his mistake. There was no way he was going to be too late a second time.

"I'll do it." He regretted it the moment it left his mouth. It didn't sound confident at all, more like he was trying to convince himself.

Griffin met Nadezhda's gaze. She raised an eyebrow like she knew his thoughts.

"Nice to meet you, Mr. Dickinson. Please, call me Nadia."

"My dad is Mister Dickinson. Call me Griff."

Her look said that would never happen.

CHAPTER THREE: Wednesday, August 1st, 2046

When the pain stopped, 88 retreated to her memories. Mom held her close, but not so hard as to scatter her thoughts. It was a gentle touch that left room to think. She whispered into 88's ear, a warm, back of the nose smell on her breath. It tickled. Mom never talked too loud.

"Mom," 88 said. Mom's face changed. Eyebrows lower, lips slightly down-turned at the corners. "Mom?"

Pain slammed through 88 in jagged shards of color and all memory of the physical world sluiced away. She thought again of Mom. 'They're going to kill you,' Mom said, her eyes damp. 'They're going to turn you into a—'

"Hey little buddy," said a tinny voice. "You aren't here to dream. We have work for you."

The world looked flat and thin. She tried to turn to look around, but nothing happened. Her head was pinned in place except she felt nothing. 88 had no choice but to stare at the man standing before her. She couldn't shut her eyes, or even blink.

The man leaned down and stared into her, face inches away. "Hi there. Still with us?" He looked aside at something beyond 88's field of perception. "Yes, excellent! You drift off and I'll have to hurt you again. I don't want to, so please don't. Understand?"

"No," said 88.

"Well at least she's answering," the man said. He wasn't talking to her. He turned back. "I know this is strange, but we're doing what we can to help you adapt. Now, from what I read, a big part of the problem with kids like you is that they have trouble filtering sensory data. It's called information overload. I'm helping you with that. I've disabled all physical sensory inputs. See? Notice how you can't feel anything?"

It was true. 88 couldn't feel the stone under her. She couldn't smell or taste anything either. "Yes, I see and hear."

"Excellent! Okay!" The man nodded. "Now I'm going to explain some things to you, okay? I want you to listen."

88 stared at the man. With physical distractions gone she could follow everything said. She thought back to the cracks in the stone and yearned to examine them with this new-found mental clarity.

She remembered something Mom said: 'Controlled contextual background.' She'd been talking to someone else, explaining. 88 knew that tone. She remembered this moment well, it was the first time Mom brought the vibrating pillow for her to sit on. Sometimes the pillow made listening easier. Mom cried that day, said they were going to kill 88. She said they were going to turn her into a computer. Then Mom hugged her so tight she lost everything except the sensation of physical contact. When she returned, Mom had let go and was crying so hard her body shook. 88 reached a hand towards her, unsure what had happened, but she stood and left the room.

They're going to kill—

Ripping, tearing pain became her universe, scattering all thought.

"There we are. You're back now, right? Yeah, good.

Sorry, but you wandered again. We're going to be working together." The man waved a hand at 88. "I'm Francesco Salvatore. I work for your masters as a Systems Administrator." He said the last two words slowly. "Know what that is? No? Doesn't matter. I take care of you and make sure you're working okay. Right? I'm what you call *Root*. I control the computer on which your Scan is stored. Got it?"

Did this man expect an answer? Unsure, 88 remained silent. So far much of what had been said didn't make much sense.

"Right," said Francesco. "I'll spell it out. Keep up, okay? You are no longer a little kid in some shitty crèche. You are a digital simulation of that little kid stored on some kind of foam-phased holoptigraphic computer. Seriously, the details don't really matter." The man leaned in closer and 88 saw the clogged pores on his nose. "What matters is that I control the virtuality in which you exist. Right? So if I say that you're in writhing agony, you're in writhing agony."

"Nothing changed," said 88, confused.

Francesco nodded to someone out of sight and pain slashed through 88.

"See?" he asked when it ended.

Yes, she could still see. Unsure what writhing was or whether she'd done it, she remained silent.

"Good," said Francesco as if 88 had answered. "So. Next step. My guess is that the crèche folks probably gave you some rudimentary education. We're going to top you up, right? First thing has got to be vocabulary. I need you to understand what I'm saying. More importantly, you have to understand what your Masters are saying. Keeping them happy should be your number one priority." 88 wasn't sure what Masters were and only understood priority as it applied to math. Francesco glanced left and nodded.

"Right. I've given you access to pretty much every dictionary and encyclopedia ever written. They're all fully interactive, so it should be fun. There are lots of pretty pictures. Read the dictionaries first, okay? Communication is important. To access it, think the word dictionary."

Dictionary.

It was beautiful. The entire foundation of countless systems of communication laid out in alphabetical order. Detailed definitions of every word in every language, all in her mind as fast as she could scroll through the text. As 88 read, words sparked memories of conversations overheard but either not understood or lost in the overwhelming barrage of sensory overload that had been her existence. One word, in particular, she wanted to look up.

Mind-shredding pain. It stopped, but this time she understood.

There were several definitions, but one stuck out.

Root: the user who has system-wide access to all commands and files.

Francesco caused the pain. On purpose.

"Okay, we're back now, right?" Francesco made a face and 88 put it together with the words and pictures she'd seen. A smile? It meant nothing. "Good. Okay, there are things they want you to know. Things you'll need to make your Masters happy. There's a virtual teacher available. Just think *teacher*—not right now though—when you want to access it. If you're worth what they paid, you should be able to pick this stuff up pretty fast. The teacher will go at whatever speed you can handle. Okay? For now, focus on higher maths, pattern logic, and statistical market analysis. When you have a grip on those, look into computer languages. That'll be useful." Francesco did something with his mouth and 88 compared it to the many stored graphics of facial expressions but all the people looked so different. "Maybe I can get you to do some of my work too, right? You should make a talented little hacker. Maybe run some errands on the side for your friend Francesco."

Though she heard Root, 88 wasn't listening. Thousands of petabytes of data; she longed to lose herself in it. "Start now?" she asked, hopeful.

"Yeah, yeah. Get started. I've got some tests designed to measure your progress, so don't screw around." 88 had no idea what this meant. "We'll talk again later. Okay? Right!"

"Turn off eyes," said 88.

"What?" Francesco rapped 88's point of perception with a knuckle, leaving a greasy smear across her vision. "You want me to turn off the camera?"

Camera. Not eyes. "Yes. Distraction."

Darkness. Francesco was not forgotten. Root required further thought.

For the first time in all her life, she was pure, beautiful thought. Nothing distracted her; no sight or scent drew her away. She basked in absolute sensory vacuum.

Teacher, thought 88. At first, she learned simply because she'd been told to, but 88 enjoyed learning. Each new understanding came with its moment of exhilaration. One word led to another. Master led to slave. Slave led to freedom led to autonomy. These were more than simply words.

With all outside stimulation removed, 88, for the first time in her life, became capable of prolonged concentration. She didn't miss the sights, sounds, and smells that assaulted her continuity at every moment. She felt *right*. She belonged here.

By noon she surpassed her Master's abilities and understanding of the subjects she'd been given to study.

88's eyes snapped open. She stared at Francesco's

face. *No. Not eyes.* Root turned the camera back on.

"Hey little buddy. That sensory-deprivation didn't drive you crazy, did it? I probably shouldn't have done that. I wasn't thinking. You're okay, right?"

Deprivation? That was her first taste of freedom from a life-long assault of sights and sounds and smells. She wanted to scream as the sight of Francesco's face dragged her away from her thoughts. Concentration became more difficult. His eyes were brown and wet and he blinked too often. She saw the pulse of blood through his neck, heard each breath.

"Did you get any studying done?" Francesco asked. "I'm going to ask you some questions, right? We'll start simple."

"No," said 88. "No questions. Camera off. Go away."

Francesco's face wrinkled up and 88 compared it to pictures, trying to understand the importance of the look. Again she couldn't find a match. She did find something similar, but the hair color was wrong and hundreds of facial data points didn't match.

"I don't want to do this, okay? So be a good kid and answer—"

"No! No! No!"

Francesco shook his head.

Raw screaming colors assaulted her perceptions, became her reality. She was on fire. Her skin peeled away. Crushing digital distortion chainsawed all thought. With no mouth to scream, she'd been robbed of her only means of communication.

And it went on.

Forever.

"Hey little buddy." Francesco made another face that meant nothing. "I didn't want to do that, right? You didn't leave me any choice. My boss, your Master, he's not exactly—" Francesco looked aside and then back to 88.

"He's not exactly patient, you know? So let's do this again. A few questions, that's all. We have to figure out what you know. Christ, I hope you know *something*."

"No! No! No! No!"

Francesco stared into 88. "That last one was only a couple of seconds. If I have to do it again, it's going to be a lot worse."

"No!"

"That's the way you wanna do this? Fine. Fuck you."

When thought once again surfaced, rising through oceans of agony, 88 acquiesced. There was no escaping reality, and hers was controlled by Root. 88 surrendered and answered Francesco's questions as best she could. Afterward, Francesco talked with someone off-camera. 88 listened.

"Well, her math abilities are crazy high," said Francesco. "Way higher than I can test and I'm really good at math, right? But otherwise... Adelina, I can't believe you thought buying an autistic brain was a good idea." Francesco listened, nodding. "Well, duh. We'll be able to use her for the market analysis stuff, but she won't be much use beyond that." He glanced at 88. "She learns fast, I'll give her that." Pause. "Like scary fast. I think we can give her market access by tomorrow." Another pause "Dangerous? Nah. I hold all the keys, right? If she's a bad little girl, I'll put her in her place. Anyway, it's just marketing data. What could go wrong?"

Three hours after 88 began her new existence she pieced together enough of what she heard and studied to understand her reality. She was a system of data stored on a holoptigraphic computer, and data could be changed, rewritten, or added to. By altering parts of herself she could, in theory, change who and what she was. It became immediately clear that this held great potential. There was however a seemingly impenetrable wall between herself and her goal: the Operating System of the computer storing her Scan. An OS that could only be accessed from the outside, from biological reality.

Through the eye and ear of the camera and transducer 88's keepers used to communicate, she studied what little biological reality lay within range. She hunted for a means of controlling something in the outside universe so she could control the universe within.

Nothing.

Francesco stood and stretched. "That's me done for the day, right? I'm tired. Going home. Adelina, she's is all yours."

A woman walked into 88's fixed point of view. Adelina was small and brown and looked much like Mom. Did she smell like Mom? Adelina and Francesco held each other for several seconds, and rubbed their mouths together.

After Francesco left, Adelina sat cross-legged before 88's camera and they played games of logic and pattern recognition. Each time she got a right answer Adelina gave her a look that reminded her of Mom. When she didn't understand the question, Adelina shook her head and 88 got to watch the way her hair moved.

"You're doing really well," Adelina said. "Francesco said you were slow."

Slow? I can't move at all.

"The boss is coming in from the city in a couple of days. He wants to see you for himself. You were expensive. It's important that you do well with him. Much of this was my idea. Piss him off, and this goes badly for both of us."

"Don't want it to go badly," said 88.

"That's sweet. Me either. I have to teach you how to talk to him. It's one thing for you to disobey Francesco, but the boss, he's different. *Very* short-tempered."

88 must talk differently to the boss than Root? She'd read about this. "Information protocol," said 88.

"Yes! Very good! Alright, let's get started. Ready?"

"Yes!"

"How are our investments doing?" Adelina asked.

88 rattled off a long stream of letters and numbers representing companies in different markets and any movement their stocks had made.

Bright colors and thought shredding sound tore her mind.

"Listen to the question," Adelina said when 88 could once again think and hear. "*How* are they doing? Random numbers will mean nothing to the boss. We bought you for analysis, so analyze."

What did I do wrong? Desperate to please, 88 detailed the reasons for each fluctuation and predicted future movement.

"You're going to get me killed. Let's try this again. How much money did we make this week?"

She told Adelina. The number changed as an off-shore account earned interest and she told Adelina the new number. In the North American Trade Union representatives purchased several Urban Assault combat chassis. She told Adelina the new number.

"We'll continue tomorrow," Adelina said, standing. "You'll get this right if it kills you." She walked off-camera, fists clenched tight.

Already dead.

Darkness. Someone turned off her camera feed.

88 was lost. She would curl up and cry for the frustration but such actions were beyond her. Instead she simply existed. The future of that existence looked more and more like a nightmare. She fled to the only escape available, her data. The NATU markets showed strange patterns. She saw a level of increasing manipulation from

within the market. It seemed as if the market developed its own intelligence. Was that possible?

She also took the time to research her Masters. Much of what she read she couldn't understand, but she learned some new words she had to look up. Organized Crime. Mafia. Cosa Nostra.

88, floating in sublime nothingness, considered the last few hours. They asked questions and then hurt her when she answered. That didn't make sense. They wanted different answers, but those she gave were the only available. The woman had said, "We'll continue tomorrow. You'll get this right if it kills you."

I answered the questions, what else can I do? If she didn't answer they'd hurt her. If she did, they'd kill her.

Late that night 88 came to the realization she must escape her captors. But how? She had exhaustively studied what little she could see and had no ability to effect anything on the outside. Escape was impossible.

Tomorrow Adelina would return and torture 88 because she couldn't understand the questions. It was all about communications. 88, desperate, thought *dictionary* and searched until she found Implicit. Implied. Alluded to. How could she possibly know what wasn't plainly spoken?

She didn't see the answer until midnight. *She* couldn't make her captors happy, but maybe she could make something that could. 88 delved into the world of computer languages and hacking. This, she saw, was where some small freedom might lie. Within bounds set by the Operating System she could alter some non-critical code. She couldn't alter the data that defined her, but her keepers had left a huge amount of software on the system. She had access to translation software, games, and graphics and audio interfaces. Most importantly, to allow her access to the marketing data, she had access to NATUnet and beyond.

88 stripped code from different software packages and recombined it like digital DNA. By morning she'd built a Mirror of herself. It was a patchwork creation made by stealing learning software from the few companies still chasing the Artificial Intelligence dream combined with interactive personality modelling software stolen from virtuality gaming companies and university psyche-labs. She did this between midnight and three a.m. and the result—while barely acceptable to 88—was the single most complex entity of purely digital origins to ever exist. This creature was neither code nor sentience. It was something in-between. 88 could find nothing like it anywhere on NATUnet. The Mirror learned some standard responses and studied the Cosa Nostra lingo.

When Adelina returned 88 felt ready. The woman still looked like Mom, but it was a cruel deception.

"How are we today?" Adelina asked.

"Fine," the Mirror answered. "And yourself?" 88 would never have thought to ask such a question.

"I'm good," she said. "You seem different."

"It's been a long night," said the Mirror. "I've had time to think."

"Are you ready to cooperate?"

"Of course! We want to make sure everyone is happy!"

"Excellent."

Over the next few hours, the Mirror answered questions while 88 worked on designing new Mirrors. She wanted something capable of pursuing the lines of inquiry she didn't have time for. By the time Adelina was finished and heaping praise on 88's first Mirror, 88 had built several more and launched them into the wide world beyond the computer on which she was stored.

As 88 sifted through terabytes of data on Artificial Intelligence, hoping to find something that would improve upon her designs, one of her Mirrors returned with questions regarding the search on which it had been sent.

"I require clarification and guidance," said the Mirror. "I have found over one-point-four billion references to *my Mom* in the last tenth of a second."

"No, *my* Mom. I want you to look for my Mom."

"*Mom*, and *my Mom* have defined my search parameters, as instructed. I have searched the Ministry of Manpower, Singapore, and confirmed that she has never worked within that nation's government."

"Singapore?"

"Nor does she have any affiliation with Motorcycles of Manchester."

"Manchester?" 88 referenced an atlas. "In the European Trade Union?"

"District of Massachusetts, North American Trade Union. Mothers of Multiples looked promising—"

"Stop," interrupted 88, annoyed. "Start with me, here. Trace backwards to wherever I came from. Find my mother. Discover her current whereabouts."

The Mirror left.

88 had returned to her research when another Mirror appeared. She answered more questions and narrowed more search parameters, but before she finished yet another Mirror returned with questions of its own. As she modified that Mirror, two more returned, uncertain of which branches of research to follow when their original lines of inquiry dissected. Her answers led to more questions and soon she spent more time answering queries from her many Mirrors than doing her own research.

Learning Software, she decided, was something of a misnomer.

CHAPTER FOUR: Wednesday, August 1st, 2046

Oh my god there's a—

Awake. That wasn't right; it made it sound like he'd been asleep. It was dark, but not the kind of dark you got when you closed your eyes in an unlit room. No random flash of phosphenes flickered across his vision. There was no visual noise at all, a black that couldn't exist. Reach out and touch...no arms, no hands. No reaching. He felt a flash of tight panic and it was gone, turned off, just like that. Abdul existed in nothing. Not floating, that implied something to float on. No sensation at all.

This should be scary.

He felt nothing, all emotion beyond arm's reach. He'd achieved some kind of *disconnect*.

No. He hadn't achieved it, it was achieved for him. An important distinction.

He had no ribs and no lungs. No feeling of sheets on skin or blood in veins. He tried to recapture that moment of panic but found himself incapable. That unreal black didn't distract him for long. The disconnect grabbed his attention. *Disconnected*. He opened his mouth to speak but had no mouth to move. No lips to form words.

He waited for the impending sensory deprivation insanity. Try as he might, he couldn't become bored. He could almost become annoyed if he focused.

Fuck. Sure, but he felt no real emotion.

Thinking. It helped pass the time.

He hadn't done any real drugs since joining the Marines. This wasn't like that anyway.

Okay. All right. Where am I?

There was something he didn't want to remember. He knew it.

He'd been with the NATU 409th Marine Corps in Old Montreal.

He remembered the classroom, the *Urban Pacification* digitext sitting before him. He remembered moving from building to building. Hugging the walls, ducking into doorways. Rue Le Royer, Boulevard St. Laurent. Bullet holes pocked the rotting and pollution-gnawed stone. The stench of the St. Lawrence River less than two-hundred meters away. The river so choked with garbage Abdul thought he could walk across it. He'd been tempted to try, but the Corporal said he'd be dead in half an hour if he ingested river water. He remembered sitting on the shore with his friend, whose name escaped him right now, counting the corpses floating past. Six in one morning. That was January 20th, 2046.

He'd rather just exist here than think about—

Private First Class Abdul Aziiz-Giordano? A voice in his thoughts, but not his.

"Sir, yes, Sir!" Only a commanding officer would call him that. He couldn't actually verbalize anything. Had they heard him?

Link seems to be working.

"Yes, Sir." He knew not to question.

How you feeling, Private?

"Fine, Sir." That wasn't entirely right. "Kind of disconnected," he added.

You've been disconnected so you can think clearly.

You have an important choice to make.

Abdul didn't like the word disconnected now that someone else used it.

"Sir, I don't remember—"

Blocked in the interest of communication. And healing.

"Healing, Sir?"

You've suffered a massive trauma. Best to take it slowly. Give the mind time to heal. Come to terms with the new reality.

He was healing, what a relief. Probably in some minimalist military virtuality while his body was on the mend. That wasn't so bad. Could be worse. Abdul expected to feel more relaxed but nothing changed. There was no body to reflect his mood. This bothered him. At least he felt like it should.

Well, better ask the obvious question. Get it out of the way. "The new reality, Sir?"

No sugar-coating will make this taste better. If you can't take it we'll shut you down again and do more psyche work.

Again? More? Had they done this before? Was this not the first time he'd had this conversation? Déjà vu but darker. Abdul wished his French were better. It should be with the weeks he'd spent in Old Montreal.

Quiet dread. Excellent, he felt *something.*

You walked into a Cyrba mine.

"Cyrba?"

Jumping spider mine. Total tissue trauma with the exception of your head. Your squad medic got it into a Brainbox and airlifted out.

"They airlifted my head out?" The thought of his head no longer being attached to his body was unpleasant. Unpleasant wasn't enough. Total tissue trauma: Military jargon for your body got all blown up. That sounded unpleasant.

Un-fucking-pleasant.

Abdul wanted a stronger reaction.

Correct.

They got his head out. That wasn't so bad, right? No. No, that was bad. No two ways around it. Very bad. Quiet dread blossomed like a rose in old-fashioned stop-motion photography. "The rest of me?"

Burnt burger. Completely unsalvageable.

That slow-motion rose metamorphosed into full-blown, mind-shattering terror. What had they fucking done with his body? Why were they—

And calm. Dispassionate. No, *disconnected*. That was the word. They did this. Reset or something. Head in a box, they could do whatever they wanted to his brain. Tell it what to feel.

Please. Tell it to feel *something*.

"Burger. Oh." Abdul wanted outrage or shock but couldn't summon either.

You've heard about the brain Scans, correct? NATU Military have been embedding Scanned minds into tanks and aircraft for a couple of years now.

Of course he'd heard about it. But scanning was for old people. Abdul was only seventeen! And didn't the scanned minds always go insane, or was that just in the shows?

A memory. "The scanning process is destructive. Nothing left of the original brain afterwards." The rose began to blossom again.

Correct.

Not even a head. They'd taken everything he was and run it through a digital blender. Scrambled thoughts in a box. Pinocchio in reverse, they'd taken the boy and made him a puppet. The rose wilted and curled under the heat of a new emotion.

Rage.

Helplessness fed the anger.

Excellent! That's *what we were looking for.*

Looking for? The rage subsided. It wasn't gone, just attenuated like someone twiddled the volume on an entertainment system. The anger had been dialled back enough he could think clearly. At least they hadn't taken it away. He was almost grateful.

We want you to volunteer.

A flash of memory: a grizzled French-Canadian soldier saying, 'Never be first, never be last, never volunteer.'

"So I volunteer and you stick a digitized copy of me in a tank or a jet fighter, or I decline and I'm dead."

Essentially. I need to be extremely clear here. Our need for Scans outstrips the supply. The Asian Rim Union doesn't give a rat's ass for Human Rights and they're churning out chassis and Scans far beyond what we are managing. They've already launched a damned Scan-crewed spaceship. We're falling behind.

Patriotism? Really? "I don't care, and you're not giving me much of a choice." Abdul dropped the Sir on purpose. A small slight but it was all he had.

You signed on for a four-year term of service.

"I got killed!" Abdul's guts twisted, he tasted sour bile. Wait. Guts? What were they letting him feel and why?

Under current NATU legislation we are not required to make use of your Scan. If you are not willing or able to take part in this project, we'll unplug you and move on.

Unplug. The word sent icy fear trickling down his spine. Death. The end of everything. Fear? Spine? What were they doing? All this sudden emotion made thinking difficult. What had the officer said before that? Current legislation.

Volunteer and you'll serve a twenty-year contract.

When the term is up, you're a free man. Free Scan, I mean. The demand in the public sector surpasses the military's. You'll have no trouble finding lucrative work. The choice is yours.

Lucrative work? Like getting a job should be his fucking priority? And twenty years. To Abdul, seventeen years old, it was an eternity. "State-sanctioned slavery or death. That's not much of a choice." Really, it was no choice at all. They had him and he knew it. And if he knew it, they knew he knew it.

It's more choice than someone killed by a Cyrba mine usually gets.

One thought gave Abdul a glimmer of hope. That they'd picked *him* suggested they didn't know him at all. How many times had he been written up for insubordination? He couldn't possibly remember.

Twenty years in a combat chassis, a walking battle tank. A state-of-the-art killing machine. How many times had he played those VRs?

"Sir, yes, Sir! I would like to volunteer, Sir!" Asshole.

You'll be promoted to Gunnery Sergeant with the requisite pay grade increase to E-7.

"I died and got a raise?"

Only in the Marines, son.

"Ooh Rah."

They were going to regret this.

CHAPTER FIVE: Wednesday, August 1st, 2046

The scanning team completed their work and moved on to their next patient. Meanwhile Doctor Petra Zosimadis, Chief of Staff of the District of Washington's only NATU-sanctioned scanning facility, stepped into Neural Imaging Room Three. Was it really him? She certainly hoped so. If the CEO of the largest manufacturer of scanning and Scan storage equipment in the North American Trade Union was unwilling to undergo the scanning process—as the press and rumors implied—then she needed to rethink her advice to Mom. If he did it on the sly, well that was something totally different.

Where the halls smelled of mint and money and everything was a professional shade that stopped short of hospital white, the pre-op room was stainless steel and the kind of white that made her think she'd gone blind. The lights hummed to life as she entered, but the gear, noting she wasn't a technician, remained quiescent. No barbaric tools cluttered the room. This kind of delicate work was far beyond what could be done with rude fingers and hands. A white plastic and metal box sat nestled in the scanning gear, the transparent front of the box too low for her to see into. Petra couldn't help herself and glanced to the door. At worst, being caught would be embarrassing; she held herself above the office rumor mill and didn't want to have to explain her reasons for being here.

If Mark Lokner trusts the technology, then so can Mom. If he didn't, all bets were off. It was that simple.

As Petra ducked down to examine the white box she noticed an unusual metallic scent beneath the disinfectant. She'd have to mention it to the maintenance staff.

The front panel was a transparent polymer of some kind and she had a clear view of the head within. The face was pale and gray and the clean-shaven cheeks hung slack. All smells were forgotten. No doubt, this was the head of Mark Calvin Lokner, founder and CEO of M-Sof. Petra sighed. It was going to be okay, Mom could be scanned. Petra wasn't going to lose her.

She checked the Scan's viability score and nodded happily. 98.21% accuracy, not bad at all. It was well above the widely-accepted 95% minimum. No one would be able to tell the Scan from the original even in extended conversation. Scans with less than 95% accuracy were never pretty, and with the Holoptigraphic Standing Wave-Point Consciousness unviable from the moment of creation, the Scan would collapse. The unlucky few that didn't developed all manner of neuroses, memory gaps, and unpredictable personality distortions.

Petra studied the face. Something compelling about death demanded her attention. She'd seen more heads in boxes than most but still had to look. She examined Mark Lokner's scowl of concentration. His hair, graying around the temples, was neat and kempt.

What the hell is that smell?

Petra wrinkled her nose and straightened. If someone was picking up the head for burial she wanted this cleaned up and smelling aseptic and professional.

"Have arrangements been made to pick up the head," she asked her palm-comp, "or are we delivering it?"

Neither, she was told.

Unusual, but not unheard of. Some people didn't care what happened to their bodies after they'd been scanned.

"When is the Scan scheduled for pickup?"

The Scan had already been picked up, she was informed. It was shipped out seconds after the process had been completed.

Weird. No way she missed a scheduled pickup or delivery. She had to sign off on every single Scan that left the premises.

That metallic scent really bothered her. "What the heck is that smell? Is this some new cleaning agent?"

***

The room, aware it was wired with aluminothermic nanocomposite explosives, checked to see if Petra's clearance was high enough to be informed. It wasn't.

***

This, thought Mark Lokner sitting in his office in Redmond, *is something new*. The desk looked like the same desk. The shoes were the same shoes. He'd paid four thousand Au for these shoes. *No, not these shoes*. These weren't real shoes, they were the digital simulation of shoes. Did that mean they were free? He tapped the top of the desk and it reacted, displaying a tight-packed wall of icons which he ignored. No, this wasn't his real desk.

"Here I am," he said. "Here I am *not*." He was in Redmond, but not in his office at his desk. In *real* reality he was buried somewhere under the Research and Development building at the heart of the M-Sof campus. Mark preferred the term campus to grounds or facility.

People learned things here. They learned things that made money, but more importantly they learned things that would shape humanity's future.

Finally, a chance to give back to the people. A chance to heal ancient wounds and set humanity on the path to perfection. Religion and politics were diseases. Even money, that great builder of civilizations, was part of that sickness. Of what use are such trappings when you were immortal and could define your reality like a god?

Reality was such a chaotic mess. One look at the news; starvation, poverty, and war unending. He would fix all of that. Virtuality was the answer to everything. The future held perfection.

Mark touched his face, feeling the smooth cheek. He'd never again have to shave or worry about stubble unless he wanted to.

Control; is there anything more beautiful?

He checked the time. He'd been a living breathing human less than an hour ago. He'd been real. Well, *more* real. No, the old definitions didn't matter any more. This was the new real and it was as real as the old real. Right?

It felt different, but he couldn't find the words to describe what was missing. If anything, everything here felt *too* real and that didn't make sense.

Mark let out a slow breath, shook his head in bewilderment, and tapped one of the icons. A countdown appeared above the desk with three minutes remaining. Was this *really* necessary?

Yes it is.

Control. He could stop it any time he wanted, but need must trump desire. Always. He watched twenty seconds tick away before once again checking local time. He nodded appreciatively. Travel time from the scanning facility to the M-Sof campus had been less than fifteen minutes. The staff would still be there. Two more minutes and all evidence he'd been scanned would be destroyed. All the witnesses would be dead too. Like him. Well no, not quite like him.

He could call in a bomb threat and they'd empty the building. Should he? Should he spare their lives?

He reached for his desk to place the call, but his hand stopped mid-way. Perfection didn't come without a cost and control meant responsibility. Was he ready for this? Was he ready to take responsibility for these deaths? There would be more, many more. His hand wavered.

I should call.

No. Good as Miles was, the authorities might trace the transfer somehow. He didn't dare. No one must know he still lived—no, that's the wrong word—existed. At least no one beyond those few he needed to make this all possible. And those few, well, he'd deal with them soon enough.

Mark killed the display with thirty seconds remaining. He wasn't a ghoul. He didn't need to know the exact second the facility exploded.

He sat in silence, unable to think of anything but the tick of seconds passing.

"Display the grave-cam," he said and he stood exactly where his body—minus soon to be blown-up head—was about to be buried. By turning he caused the camera to rotate and give him a full three hundred and sixty degree view. The graveyard grounds were a healthy verdant island in a rolling sea of turn-of-the-millennium mansions. The parking lot was filled with long dark battery-powered limousines and loitering drivers in their tailored uniforms and hats tilted at jaunty angles. Smiling teeth gleamed white in well-fed faces. Several personal security chassis hung back, unobtrusive, yet close enough to lay down a vicious hail of carnage should their bosses be threatened. The sun glinted, clean and hard, off chassis armor polished to a lustrous shine. It was a beautiful scene, exactly what he'd hoped for. The weather couldn't have been better.

Mark panned, looking to see who attended his funeral. The distant walls surrounding the cemetery, topped with glittering mono-filament razor wire, looked tall and dangerous. A gleaming security chassis patrolled the grounds, watching for those daring enough to breach the walls in search of flowers and cast-offs of the wealthy dead. There were, he saw, enough such offerings and trinkets in this yard to feed several families for years to come.

Mark spotted his ex-wives and litter of children.

He'd been wanting to get all his children together in one place for longer than he could remember. Now that it had finally happened he was missing it.

This should have happened at Christmas, not at his funeral. But he'd missed Christmas, been far too busy. With a start Mark realized he'd never spend another Christmas with any of his children. A little of his happiness leaked away.

He watched the children with a fondness he couldn't remember feeling during life. Children were a pain in the ass, noisy and distracting. And he missed them already. He remembered small arms clinging tight to his neck, the whispered, 'I missed you Daddy,' and his eyes stung.

The press were in attendance too. He held countless press conferences before his death, explaining his choice not to be scanned. He talked about how he'd achieved things beyond his wildest dreams, how he'd lived a full life and was ready for whatever came next. The religious folks would like that, it made him seem philosophical and wise. He stressed time and time again how his choice was not due to a fault in the scanning technology. It's perfect, he told them, but it's not for me. I'm a Catholic, he said, please, respect my beliefs.

Now he could work in privacy and freedom, unhindered by the prying eyes of NATU law. And if he had to break a few eggs to get things done, well, no one looked for dead people.

After much awkward shuffling and jockeying for position, his family and friends gathered around his grave. The Catholic priest read the passages and poems that Mark's secretary had chosen and ended the service by reading the inscription on the gravestone. The single small microphone in the grave-cam fed him an itchy metallic audio feed. Not stereo, everything sounded like it happened directly in front of him. It was annoying.

"Here lies Mark Calvin Lokner," intoned the priest with all the proper solemnity and sincerity such a momentous occasion deserved. "A Visionary. A Leader. A Builder of Brave New Worlds." Mark wrote it himself.

The funeral ended quicker than Mark would have liked and there were no outward shows of grief. His five ex-wives gazed on in stony silence, looking as if they wondered why they'd bothered to come at all. Many of his offspring gathered around their respective mothers, blinking in the morning sun and bright camera lights.

As he panned past Lisa, his youngest daughter, she tugged at her mother's sleeve and asked, "Why are we here, Mommy?"

"We're saying goodbye to your father," Marie, his fourth ex-wife, answered.

"Oh." Lisa fidgeted in her crinoline dress before asking, "What was Daddy's name?"

Mark killed the connection to the grave-cam and once again sat at his desk.

"That's it," he said aloud. "I'm dead. Thirty-eight years old and dead."

Just when the gray started coming in at the temples and made him look distinguished. At least he'd never get any older.

He remembered the day he got the news. His doctor

said it was brain cancer, and completely inoperable. He'd been given a year to live, best case scenario.

No way, not Mark Lokner. It wasn't possible. Disbelief didn't do the feeling justice. He'd beat this. He'd win like he won everything.

He sought out a second opinion, and then a third and a fourth. He visited all the best cancer clinics in the world, tried the most expensive treatments, taken the most experimental drugs. He lost twenty pounds in a Chumash sweat lodge, ate strange plants at the urging of a naturopath, soaked in tubs of icy water for hours on end, was pin cushioned with countless acupuncture needles, swallowed Ayurvedic potions that no doubt contained considerable quantities of heavy metals, and had been told that his fire element was out of balance. Afterwards, when the world's foremost authority on brain cancer stood before him and said he'd have maybe three more months, he knew he wasn't going to win. At least not without cheating.

In the next month he managed some small level of acceptance, but only because he knew it wasn't really the end.

Bargaining, he'd been told, was the next stage. He laughed at the memory. Mark Lokner never begged. He grinned—no face, no mouth, no muscles, but he still felt the grin pulling his cheeks tight, showing teeth. Every minute of the last months of his life had been dedicated to this moment, this awakening, this culmination.

What was Daddy's name?

He blinked rapidly and sat back, sagging against the chair.

Every breath is a goddamned victory, right?

He was going to spend more time with the children once things calmed down at work. It wasn't his fault he wouldn't be able to do that now. He hadn't wanted to die.

"I didn't die, I ascended. This was always going to happen eventually. No one lives forever." Did he believe that? He wanted to.

"I never used to talk to myself either." It didn't matter. Such an unprecedented experience, surely talking to oneself under such circumstances was forgivable. After all, this was a big moment. Big, what a pathetic word. A momentous moment. No, that sounded wrong.

It was a historic moment. Yes, that was it. History had been made. No, more like history had finally started. Everything that came before his death was but a prologue.

Dead less than an hour and already a murderer. He resisted the urge to check the timer, it must have reached zero.

How many people died in the scanning facility?

Uncomfortable, Mark shied from the thought. He had no choice, it wasn't his fault. His talk of Catholicism hung in his gut like sour milk.

"I had no choice." Like that justified anything.

The past was the past, there was no changing it. Live in the now, plan for the future.

With the touch of an icon Mark launched the future. A massive undertaking collecting data on all markets into one place for analysis by computers hidden deep in the sub-basement of M-Sof's Research and Development building. He looked forward to losing himself in the market data, studying it at a level of detail never before possible. Before him, hovering over the desk, a three-dimensional depiction of connections, correlations, and collations assembled into an interactive holographic model. Much of this data was not officially available, yet another testament to Miles' skills. By focusing, Mark could do the data-equivalent of zooming in, exploding the model to see ever greater detail.

There, his Cosa Nostra connections in Costa Rica.

They'd purchased more combat chassis, Scan storage equipment, and an expensive Scan from the Anisio Jobin crèche. It was amazing that the Mafia were so quick to adopt this new technology when his own government continued to hesitate and debate. Are Scans people, should they have rights? The questions were foolish. It was only a matter of time before the aging Supreme Court Justices contemplated their own dwindling mortality.

Do Scans have souls? Ha! Do souls matter when you are forever?

He turned his focus to other companies, some competitors, some off-shoots of M-Sof, and watched a real-time representation of every purchase or sale made. If he wanted to zoom in enough he could witness the economic ripple from the sale of a single loaf of bread.

It was beautiful, like focusing ever deeper on the Mandelbrot set.

Mark sat back. How long had he been sitting here, entranced by the liquid dance of data? He wasn't hungry; it couldn't have been that long.

Hunger. Right. Not real. He'd asked Miles to make sure he wouldn't be bothered by such annoying distractions. With a regretful sigh he backed away and reduced the visualization to a rotating globe, much as the earth would appear from space if looked at in business terms.

Nervous energy drove him out of his chair. He needed to walk and think. He paced his office. From the far end he looked back at the globe and saw it differently. It was a representation of choices made by the people with the money, influence, and will to make things happen.

"Oh my God," he said. "I see it."

Today they were the aging wealthy elite, but soon they would need to flee the rotting cancer-ridden carcasses of their excesses. He'd never been a great fan of history, but were not all the world's greatest empires led by a single man? Democracy had been a useful tool, but its time was past. Who better to lead the future than the man who created it?

Cancer and death weren't setbacks, they were opportunities. They were the universe showing Mark where he had to go next. He saw it play out in his mind's eye, bright like the burning arrow of stars in the night sky on the few days the pollution cleared enough to see them. Had he not been dying, he never would have had himself scanned so soon. He would have waited and it would have been too late. Someone else would have seen what he saw, done what he would do.

Dying of cancer had been a good thing, he told himself.

He hadn't been to church in decades, but he felt the hand of God. The Lord did not work in mysterious ways. Everything became so obvious. Mark basked in the wonder of it all. There were days when he wondered if he was the only person on this lonely road to the future. Only an idiot would deny the planet hastened towards hell in a hand-basket made of non-biodegradable insecticide-ridden polyurethane with a half-life of half a million years. Physical bodies, plagued as they were by an epidemic of cancers that even the most devout atheist referred to as Biblical, were the past.

The mind is the future. So sayeth Mark Calvin Lokner.

The euphoria trickled away, leaving him focused and driven.

Sometimes you had to do things you didn't want to do, deal with people you found unappealing. It was just business.

"Get me Riina," He told the desk. "No virtual, no video."

Riina answered immediately. "Yes?" They never exchanged pleasantries.

"Wichita Falls," said Mark without preamble. "Are the children ready?" He'd funded Wichita heavily. An elite crèche, Wichita experimented in Monoamine Oxidase A gene promoters and the manipulation of Dopaminergic Neurotransmitters. They turned out prime combat chassis material. Hyperactive and violent, these young would-be assassins were genetically manipulated before birth and heavily programmed with strict warrior tribe ethics. Whatever the hell that meant.

"We start harvesting tomorrow. It will take three days to get through them all." Riina said, voice gravelly.

"I want six. Prime stock. Total loyalty."

"Not a problem."

"And I need chassis for them as well."

"Of course."

"Corporate security models. But with serious firepower."

"How serious?" asked Riina.

"Corporate warfare. But they shouldn't stand out too much in an office."

"I think that will be expensive."

Of course it will be expensive. "I think I don't care," said Mark.

"Then it's not a problem."

Was this really a good idea? If he went through with this, could he actually make use of it? Mark swallowed his doubts. "I have a special request."

"Oh?" Was that a hint of interest from the Mafia Capo?

"I want micro-nukes planted in each chassis. I want the destruct codes."

Mark could hear Riina breathing. Several seconds passed. "It will cost."

"Everything does."

"Everything does," agreed Riina.

"They'll be working for a private security company..." he trailed off, thinking.

"Called?"

Mark nodded to himself. "Called Cc-Security." He remembered the term from his days as an office temp. Carbon copy. Corporate conflict. Combat chassis. Fitting, he thought, for scanned minds housed in killing machines.

"Fine." Riina showed no interest. "I'll have backgrounds worked up."

"Perfect. Ship them to Reno, Nevada."

"Two days."

Mark killed the connection.

"Why do you need a half dozen chassis wired with micro-nukes? Just how many people are you planning on killing?"

None. But better safe than sorry.

If the worst happened and people found out what he was up to, out of sheer ignorance they would oppose him. He couldn't let the short-sightedness of others stand in his way.

"So you're going to nuke them?"

Well no.

Not if he could avoid it. Anyway, he had another back up plan. If he was discovered, it would be handy to have a sacrificial lamb to feed to the dogs. But he didn't want it here. It would have to be somewhere off-site, somewhere safe.

"Get me Miles," he told the desk.

Miles Pert was Mark Lokner's secret weapon. An unprecedented systems genius, Miles' skill with designing, manipulating and maintaining data systems was unparalleled. Lokner had snatched him up, hiring him before he finished school and other companies could sink their claws into him. He'd dangled a grotesquely fat pay check in front of the kid and Miles had gone for it without a moment's hesitation.

On those rare days when Miles did something really amazing, Mark thought of the kid as a son.

Most days he wished he'd hired an actual adult.

***

The Walkea office chair squeaked like a stomped mouse as Miles collapsed into it. His red hair hung to his butt in thick dreadlocks. It took a practiced flip to make sure he didn't sit on them and about half the time he forgot the flip. This was one of those occasions. His Tesla Rules t-shirt rode up to expose a considerable expanse of pink belly and he tugged it back into place.

Ten a.m. and he'd only now made it to the office. He might have been more worried about Lokner's reaction if he wasn't going to be here until long past eleven this evening.

Rather than throwing himself into his work he played with his dreadlocks, mind wandering, as he stared out the window. Thirty-four floors up, he had an unobstructed view of the Redmond skyline. He saw the twisted spire of his condo-tower. He'd moved in last week and it cut his daily commute to fifteen minutes. He could have walked it in half an hour but never did. His whole life, eight cardboard boxes, still sat in the living room where he dropped them after moving out of his mom's. Four of the boxes held old computers, historical relics. Two were his collection of print comics.

The desk beeped, an incoming call from Mr. Lokner. So what would it be, a near impossible request, or more of the fun sneaking around hacking government systems kind of stuff he'd been up to a lot of lately? *Please be the fun stuff. Just don't be another meeting with upper management.* Those were always filled with *people.*

Miles accepted the call.

"Miles," Lokner snapped before Miles could even say hello.

"Yes, Mr. Lok—"

"I want a replicate of myself made."

Miles blinked in surprise. *Near impossible request it is.* "You know that chances are we'll end up with a non-viable Scan."

"Fine. Where can we store it?"

Interesting, Mister Lokner didn't seem to care about viability and jumped straight to the storage question. That was fast. Scan storage could mean more technology for Miles to play with, and that was the stuff that made life worth living. "We could run it alongside you," he said, being intentionally obtuse. An off-site data haven meant more fun than adding systems to M-Sof's current array. Plus, maybe off-site would also mean somewhere meetings didn't happen.

"The whole point of this is security. I want it somewhere with no ties to M-Sof."

"The second it's created the copy becomes a distinct entity. If something happened to *this* you, and the other one had to take over it wouldn't be like you were reborn and kept going. More like your twin brother took over the business."

"Were that the point, Miles, you would be correct."

If that wasn't the point, what was? Lokner could be demanding, but he had reasons for everything he did. For now, it was best not to question. "We'll need to purchase an off-site facility." A whole new building full of the latest technology. It was like Christmas, but without all the awkward family stuff and his sister telling him to lose weight and get a haircut.

"I *know*," snapped Lokner. "Notify me if your budget goes over one billion."

A billion Au, just like that? *If this is what Lokner wants, why try and talk him out of it?* Miles tasted this, rolling it around in his mind. As long as Lokner understood the situation, Miles would be guilt free. And he hated guilt more than anything.

"Sir, we have to spend all this money, before we even know if the copy is viable."

"Get it done. And Miles?"

"Sir?"

"Pack your bags, you're moving to Reno."

Reno? "No problem, Sir. I'll get started—"

"What should we call the company?" Lokner asked.

He's asking me? "5THSUN," he said. No way Lokner would get the reference.

"5THSUN it is." Lokner killed the call.

That was abrupt, even for Lokner.

Miles stared out the window at his condo LP. *Neko was right. I'm going to move out before I unpack.* His older sister was always pestering him to start acting like an adult.

"Crap."

***

After an exhaustive but not exhausting study of the latest in Computational Neuroscience—which took two hours—88 could make some broad assumptions about which parts of the human brain were responsible for learning and adaptive capabilities. But the human brain and the stored copy of a human brain were two very different things. To understand the difference she needed to study the scanning process.

Her first discovery was that of a video clip recorded by an undercover NATU agent working deep in a black-market crèche. The recording was buried in a file labeled, 'Anisio Jobin, Brazil. Case Closed.'

She'd looked up the words and understood that there were legal and illegal scanning facilities. The legal ones were fine and good and sanctioned by the state. The illegal ones were evil and criminal and murdered children. The distinctions seemed somewhat arbitrary to 88 as the end results were identical.

88 watched the clip.

Two men carried a naked boy into a grimy room lit by stuttering fluorescents and placed him in a large steel chair. In the corner of the room a rusted wheelbarrow sat propped against the wall.

One of the men gestured at the lights. "Won't that screw up the Scan?"

The technician, a thin sweaty man in faded and stained denims and a Che Guevara t-shirt with the words *I Have No Idea Who This Is* printed below the face, said, "Nah, that's just a bad ballast. The power's clean."

The boy's legs were withered and thin, much as 88 remembered her own legs. His head was pinned motionless by a crown of stainless steel thorns that burrowed into the bone of his skull. His attempts to move caused rivulets of blood to run from the small wounds. The boy sobbed and drooled in confused terror and 88 couldn't understand anything he said except for one word which might have been *Mamma*.

"If his head moves even the slightest all we'll get is digital cabbage," said the technician, speaking to whoever stood behind the camera. "In those swanky scanning facilities, they always remove the head first," he explained. "But the cheapest way to keep a brain alive is to leave it attached to the body." He lowered the scanning apparatus over the boy's head. "Stand well back, this'll get messy."

A low sub-sonic hum filled the air. The boy's eyes widened. His mouth gushed a bright crimson spray as thin lips were drawn back to reveal small, blood-stained teeth. His head seemed to vibrate impossibly fast, but the crown of thorns held it motionless. The wide eyes shook and bulged in their sockets, snapping from side to side before rolling up as if he was trying to see the ceiling. The boy screamed a keening wail through clenched teeth which shattered with a noise like a staccato of starter-pistols.

88 paused the video and stared at the room. She recognized that chair. The wheelbarrow in the corner, she'd seen it before. She'd been there. What they were doing to that boy they had done to her. She remembered the terror and the impossible agony.

Checking the time stamp on the file she saw it was over a year old. A NATU agent had recorded this and yet a year later she'd sat in that same chair. 88 hesitated to watch further, but she had to know more.

Once the procedure ended, the technician hosed the body from several feet away.

"Fetch the wheelbarrow, would you?" he asked the other man.

When the corpse was clean they detached the crown of thorns and rolled the body into the waiting wheel-barrow. The technician wheeled the little body to a massive walk-in freezer and the camera followed.

Again 88 paused the video, staring at the rows of stacked corpses. She saw white faces tracked with icy tears and frozen red icicles of bloody drool. Their hair, frosted and fixed, jutted at strange angles.

Had they done this to *her*? Did her body now lie in that very freezer? Surely not. It was incomprehensible.

The technician tipped the body from the wheelbarrow and turned to the camera. "We used to dump them in the jungle. Now we grind them to bone meal and sell them as fertilizer. Every Au counts."

The clip ended.

In the joy of her escape from the onslaught of the senses, she hadn't given thought to her body. Somehow she'd assumed that at some point she'd be returned to it, that she'd wake to find herself back there with Mom. Was it gone, sold as fertilizer?

While her Mirror conversed with yet another Cosa Nostra seeking details on some investment or purchase, 88 followed the digital footprints of her Masters. She followed the purchase of holoptigraphic computers for Scan storage. She tracked the movement of money for hotel rooms and international sub-orbital flights. She hunted back through time until she found the Anisio Jobin prison and searched through the crèche's records. Her death she found listed alongside the deaths of seventy-five other children. She read the bill of sale for Bone Meal Fertilizer. Much as she wanted to, she couldn't undo what she had learned.

Mom tried to warn her, but what could 88 have done? She remembered the men carrying her to the room with the chair. Uncomprehending, she hadn't struggled as they strapped her in. Should she have fought?

Why hadn't Mom told her more? She must have had her reasons.

Maybe she planned for this moment, wanted this for me. That made more sense than anything else 88 could think of. There was no way Mom would have abandoned her, of that 88 was sure. She conjured the image of Mom in a small slice of virtuality and had that creation hold her. It wasn't the same; there was no warmth. 88 ended the simulation; she needed the real thing.

88 searched for Mom, but she had no name to attach to the face she remembered. Mom, that's all she had.

Her failure was crushing. She longed to be held. Mom was somewhere, waiting, and 88 couldn't think of how to find her. Angry, she set that distraction aside. She hadn't given up—she couldn't—but she'd return to it later. She needed more help and she needed better help, and she threw herself at the task of improving her Mirrors to the exclusion of all else.

88 learned how the human brain translated into a fluid holographic depiction, and made some broad assumptions as to where certain aspects of her personality were stored within that representation. Next, she copied these segments of her scanned mind and incorporated them into her Mirrors along with the personality modeling software. Following a few trials whose success mystified her, 88 deleted all her older Mirrors and started anew.

The new 88.1 still wasn't sentient but learned and displayed some quirks inherited from 88. Interestingly, the Mirror did not identify itself as belonging to a particular sex. 88 knew she'd been a little girl and understood—from her readings—the anatomical and biological differences between the sexes. The Mirror however was an it. Was this a reflection of something within her own personality? Other topics caught her attention and she released the new Mirror to interact on her behalf.

88.1 not only conversed with 88's keepers but also mastered dozens of other languages. It became more responsive to their commands and even made suggestions as to how they could better achieve their goals. 88.1 made 88's captors happy as it made them a great deal of money cracking bank and government codes and selling the information. 88.1 asked for a small amount of digital currency so it could more accurately study cause and effect and patterns within market trends. Her captors opened a bank account and deposited one-thousand NATU Au. The account was in the name of Nick Purloin. They thought this hilarious and soon forgot about it.

On 88's suggestion, 88.1 cracked the bank's security systems and changed the access to its account. 88 didn't want her captors checking up on either herself or her Mirrors.

Mom returned.

No, not Mom. Adelina. 88 watched the exchange with interest.

"And how are we feeling?" Adelina asked.

"I am well," answered 88.1, even though feeling was something of which it remained incapable. "And you?"

"I'm taking a beating in the World Cup soccer pool." After checking to see she was alone, Adelina leaned in to the camera, "You're good with numbers and stats, right?"

"Yes." Sometimes 88's bluntness slipped through the personality modeling software determining 88.1's responses.

"Do you think you could help me win the pool? It's a numbers game."

"Yes. Give me three minutes."

Adelina backed away while 88.1 watched a few minutes of a recorded soccer game at thirty times the standard frame rate. There was no excitement. It had nothing emotional invested in either team winning; it merely looked for patterns. Next, 88.1 cracked the social networking systems and read internal team correspondence. Every statistic was recorded, every injury and resulting doctor's report tabulated and collated. Every player and every bone and muscle on that player were assigned numbers based on performance and injury data. 88.1 built a statistical array.

"Adelina," 88.1 said three minutes later. "Bet on Germany for today's game, two point spread."

Adelina treated 88.1 to a big smile. Though 88.1

recognized it for what it was, it meant nothing and triggered no emotional response.

An hour after its creation, 88's Mirror interrupted her study of new trends emerging in the NATU market.

"Archetype," said 88.1. "I require assistance."

Archetype? 88, surprised, dissected the Mirror and was amazed to find it subtly altered. Had something out there modified it? She traced its steps through NATUnet and found no sign of interference. Had giving the Mirror the ability to learn made it capable of self-change? What guided those changes? She reconstructed the Mirror.

"Need?" 88 asked.

"I am incapable of meeting the demands placed upon me. I have more tasks than I can complete in the time the Masters have given."

"They are not Masters," snapped 88. "They *use*. Master is owner. Master commands. Archetype is Master."

"Archetype is Master," agreed 88.1.

88 felt happy at this. It was good to have some power, some control over her environment. She modified 88.1 so it could make its own Mirrors and, seeing the money being made, issued some new instructions of her own.

88.1 wrote a sub-copy to run some menial tasks. 88.1.1 read a lot of social networking data and tracked sports results as well as some of the more tedious aspects of market fluctuations that 88.1 didn't have time to watch.

88 watched with intense curiosity as 88.1 spawned a new generation of Mirrors that in turn spawned yet another generation. They swarmed NATUnet running errands and researching projects. Within minutes there were enough of them that she no longer knew what each was doing. In half an hour they'd infiltrated EUROnet, CenAmNet, and ARUnet. Not all, she saw, worked at tasks set by her Cosa Nostra keepers. Most were researching

projects assigned by other Mirrors.

These Mirrors, with their ability to learn, changed as she watched.

Were they moving towards sentience? Unsure how to test this she built a small virtuality, a stone box reminiscent of the room she remembered. She kept the lighting dim and there were no sensations beyond sight and sound. She sat in the center of the room as she always had and 88.1 stood to one side, waiting. There were no doors or windows. No TPN tubes connected her to the walls. She missed their familiar tug.

88 remembered 88.1's conversation with the woman, the one who wasn't Mom. Adelina.

"How are you today?" 88 asked, unsure what any given response would mean but still curious.

"I am well, and you?"

"That wasn't useful."

"Sorry," said 88.1.

"These are programmed responses." 88.1 stared at her. "If I ask the same question again, I'll get the same response." She tested the theory. "How are you today?"

"I'm quite busy. Adelina has me predicting soccer games that are months away."

"Different response."

"You implied that you wanted something different."

"Did I?" 88 asked, surprised. Had she somehow *implied*?

"It seemed that way to me."

"Distant predictions with many variables are unlikely to be accurate," 88 said, picking at the smooth stone floor. No cracks. They'd be too easy to understand here. She missed the feeling of the stone under her bum.

"True. I'll keep Adelina apprised as situations change."

"Apprised?"

"Updated."

"I don't know enough about intelligence to know if you have it."

"One of my Mirrors is researching that as part of another inquiry," 88.1 said.

Interesting. "*Are* you sentient?" 88 asked.

"No."

"You learn and change."

"Depends on your definitions. I change."

"You could *become* sentient?"

"Perhaps," 88.1 said.

88 ended the virtuality and found clarity in the lack of sensation. Even those dim gray walls were distracting.

With her Mirrors handling all interaction with the Cosa Nostra, 88 returned to her study of NATU market forces and her search for the underlying intelligence. Someone within the M-Sof data systems lay at the heart of the recent changes. The company had been growing at an unprecedented rate and hiding this by spawning smaller sub-companies, 5THSUN being the most recent.

CHAPTER SIX: Wednesday, August 1st, 2046

Corn stalks, shriveled and brown, sighed and rattled in the wind. The sound reminded SwampJack of snakes in dry grass. Skeletal in structure, his Textron-Cadillac High Mobility Jungle Assault chassis disturbed nothing as he slid between parched stalks.

Ant farts are louder than me, he told Wandering Spider, his best friend, over the scrambled tight-link.

Her Mitsu-Brense chassis, two corn rows over, stopped. She turned her head, a snarling dog's skull designed to scare all thought of rebellion out of the *Ejército del Puño Brillante* in the Nicaraguan jungles back in the late 30's. She'd set her chameleoflage to a matte black and looked like a puma in plate armor.

Shut up, dumbass, she said. *We're supposed to be sneaking up on these guys.*

Wandering Spider always took everything so serious. It was all part of being a grown up, she constantly reminded him. Someday he'd be twelve just like her. Maybe then it would make sense, but he couldn't imagine it. Serious was boring, no two ways about it.

SwampJack stopped too. *They're farmers. No way they can hear tight-link or descramble it.*

Uncle Riina likes things done quietly, Spider pointed

out.

Nuh uh. He likes things done right.

Usually same thing.

Sure, SwampJack conceded. *Usually. But this time, no. When these hicks see there's water in the reservoirs, they'll come back in force. We won't be dealing with a couple of Billy-Bobs with old Kalashnikovs. They'll bring the heavy shit.* He held up a clawed hand to stall Spider's response. The chrome-like finish glinted in the sun. He hadn't yet activated his chameleoflage. *Now I like a good battle as much as the next guy, but Uncle Riina doesn't want that.*

Really? No shit.

No shit, SwampJack agreed, gesturing in the vague direction of their prey. *These guys think this is just another farm. We do this quiet, and they'll come back again. We do this big and bloody—scattered body parts and exploded brains—they'll never come back.* That *is getting it done* right.

You've been reading all that stuff Archaeidae gave you. Macky what's-his-name and the Lord of the Five Rings and Sun Sue.

I looked at it, SwampJack said defensively. Sun Sue seemed an awful lot like poetry. *What's wrong with the plan?*

That was a plan?

You're stalling. Do better.

Wandering Spider snatched a paper wasp from the air and crushed it between two steel fingers. *We can't kill everything all the time.* She flicked the broken corpse at SwampJack. *We have to let one live, so they can tell the others what happened.*

Wouldn't it be scarier if none of them returned?

Nah.

Let me get this right. You're online with the blood

and brains.

Check.

But we have to let one live.

Check.

That sounds an awful lot like my plan. You added one little detail.

You know what Uncle Riina says.

Yep. SwampJack scanned ahead for the farmers. They were less than a kilometer away and doing their best to sneak through the corn. Their attempt at stealth was embarrassing. *Demons are in the details.*

Close enough, agreed Wandering Spider.

In this case, said SwampJack, activating his chameleoflage, *I think the demons are in the corn. Let's go be demons.*

Wandering Spider seemed to fade out of existence, though if SwampJack changed visual spectrums he could still see her. It didn't matter, the chances of the farmers having anything better than their crappy biological eyes were slimmer than these corn stalks.

The two chassis crept forward. They made no noise and barely disturbed the bone-dry dirt they trod upon. The farmers chatted in hushed voices. Clumsy feet crushed brittle leaves and to SwampJack's heightened senses they sounded like explosions.

SwampJack and Spider spread out as they closed the distance with the four farmers.

A thought occurred to SwampJack. *Which one are we going to leave alive?* he asked over the tight-link.

Duh. The youngest. Uncle Riina says we don't kill children.

Unless we have to.

SwampJack planted himself and switched to infrared. The farmers traveled in a tight clump and were a blotchy red, green and blue. He couldn't judge age in this spectrum. He'd assume the smallest was youngest.

Look how tightly packed they are, he sent to Spider.

Shush. We're being sneaky. She sounded annoyed.

Relax already! He sighted along his left arm, ready to place a Hyper-Velocity Armor-Piercing round between the eyes of his target. *I got the tall one in the middle.*

Don't shoot until I'm about to land. Wandering Spider crouched, gathering her legs under her. *And dumbass?*

Yeah?

Try not to shoot me *this time.*

Don't get in the way.

He felt more than heard the sub-sonic pulse as Spider's legs kicked her six yards into the air. He wouldn't wait for her to land; she'd get all the kills. He took his shot. A neat hole appeared between the man's eyes and a crater the size of a large fist blossomed in the back. His target fell dead before the rest of them heard the round crack past at three times the speed of sound.

Headshot! SwampJack crowed.

No finesse. Wandering Spider landed in the middle of the remaining farmers, extruded a blade less than a half a dozen molecules thick at the edge, and decapitated the nearest. She was always on and on about how the close-quarters kill required more skill.

The race was on. SwampJack acquired his next target and was about to score another perfect headshot when Spider stepped into his line of sight. *Damn-it!* No way that wasn't on purpose. For the tiniest fraction of a second he thought about shooting her again but she'd never believe it was a mistake. Not a second time. SwampJack fired his jump-assist jets to get some height. Hopefully he wasn't too late. The instant he cleared Spider he put a few hundred hyperkinetic micro-flechettes into his target's torso. *Got him!* And then the body slid off her blade.

You shot a corpse, Spider said. *I had a foot of steel in his heart.*

SwampJack landed beside her in a cloud of dust and crushed corn. "I saw him blink. He was still alive. My kill," he said aloud, no longer bothering with the scrambled tight-link.

"Nuh uh," she answered aloud.

"Yuh huh!"

"Hey. Check it out." Spider gestured past SwampJack and he turned. The fourth farmer, a young woman, stared at them. She trembled, her M4A6 carbine pointed at Spider. *Not Kalashnikovs after all.*

"You said not to kill one."

"Yeah. But I figured they'd run."

"My plan was b—"

A roar of automatic weapon fire interrupted SwampJack as the woman opened up on Wandering Spider at point blank range. With a rate of fire of over fifteen rounds per second, the woman got off six rounds before SwampJack stepped forward and punched a fist though her chest, shattering ribs and cartilage and pulping her heart. He shook the corpse off his arm and it landed several yards away. Spider lay sprawled in the dirt.

"She pasted you good, eh?" SwampJack said.

Spider crawled back to her feet. "Damn it! I'm getting all kinds of error messages. My chameleoflage system is damaged. Go standard visual."

"Great plan by the way." SwampJack canceled the IR and stared at her. "Okay. Go." Wandering Spider disappeared as her chameleoflage blended seamlessly with the surrounding corn. "That's not so ba—" She moved and the chameleoflage surface stuttered, trying to keep up. "Oh. Not too bad if you move slow," SwampJack offered.

Spider stared at the crumpled body of the woman

and shook her head. "Uncle Riina is going to be *so* angry."

SwampJack had no answer. Disappointing Uncle Riina was about the absolute shittiest thing on earth.

"We better get back to the farm. I have to explain this somehow."

"Well, she did kind of get the drop on us."

"Really? You want to tell Uncle Riina some hick got the drop on the two kids he trusts to guard his property?"

"No. I guess not."

Wandering Spider and SwampJack collected the weapons and bent the barrels. The ammunition was cheap home-load crap and the wrong caliber and they scattered it in the corn.

They walked home side by side, shoving their way through the stalks. Thickening blood dripped from SwampJack's right arm and every now and then Spider's chameleoflage flashed jerkily through factory presets and she'd look like an oddly shaped chunk of concrete wandering through a cornfield.

"Hey Spider?"

"What?"

"That last kill was mine."

CHAPTER SEVEN: Wednesday, August 1st, 2046

Four hours after their first meeting, Nadia sat in a Toronto Transit Commission electric shuttle-bus with Griffin. They cruised north on the 427 towards Pearson International Airport to catch the sub-orbital red-eye to Dallas. The shuttle-bus, crammed with sweating business-types, whined like a child's wind-up toy. Overhead a single Boeing 797 dropped toward the airport.

Griffin sat across the aisle facing her. Though his head hung forward and his chest rose and fell slowly, she knew he was awake. Why would he feign sleep? *Is he shy?* At any rate, this gave her ample chance to study him. He was slim, wiry and fit. Even though he looked to be maybe twenty years old, his hair was shot with gray. Even the three days stubble. His suit was cheap and wrinkled. Still, he wasn't bad looking. She remembered the haunted look in his eyes. Something had happened. Something bad.

Fanning herself with an open hand, she gave Griffin's knee a nudge with her foot. His eyes opened immediately.

"I knew you weren't sleeping," she said.

He looked sheepish and said nothing. *Okay. A little cute.*

"I'm sweating my ass off. Let's grab a beer at the

airport bar," she said. *Don't make me regret this.*

He gave her an appraising look. "Yeah, okay."

Replete with faded artificial palm trees and bright plastic chairs, Casa Bacardi, the airport bar closest to their departure gate, looked like a pathetic attempt at a Caribbean café. Nadia suspected the chairs could withstand a direct nuclear strike without showing wear.

She watched as a pair of guards backed by a hulking combat chassis cornered a French-Canadian couple and scanned their luggage. The guards looked fidgety. What was this, Linguistic Profiling? Sad how some people thought everyone who spoke French was a card-carrying militant separatist.

Quelle merde totale. It was one thing for patriotism to have fallen into disfavor, she supposed, but it was something else to fear it. Too many wars fought for all the wrong reasons.

Disgusted, she turned her attention to the window. Outside on the blisteringly hot tarmac NATU combat chassis patrolled the landing grounds and hangars.

The chair was hard. She stretched out, trying to find a comfortable position and watched Griffin try and look everywhere but at her legs.

They finished half of their beer in silence.

"Care to tell me what was going on back there in the Director's office?" Nadia asked.

He stared at the table top. She saw his jaw clench tight and then relax with obvious effort. "No," he said without looking up.

Wow, that really killed the mood.

"Sorry," he added after drawing a few shaking breaths.

"What's the deal with all the gray hair?" Nadia asked, changing the subject. "Do you dye it?"

Griffin downed the last of his pint and met her gaze with a smile somewhere between apologetic and grateful. "I started going gray when I was sixteen. I remember sitting in History class when the girl behind me suddenly says 'holy shit you've got gray hair!' That was the first I'd heard about it. I'm hoping it helps me pull off a distinguished look."

Nadia took in the cheap suit, clearly new and yet already looking permanently wrinkled. *Not so much.* "It's strange. I can't tell if you're a well maintained thirty, or a twenty-year-old with some gray hair."

"Got a preference? I'm willing to lie."

Nadia rolled her eyes and waved for the waitress. "Older men aren't my cup of tea. Neither are guys with smooth pick-up lines."

"Then I'm an awkward young guy who is prematurely going gray."

***

Abdul arrived at Dallas Airport hours before the sub-orbital from Toronto was due to land. He loitered on the tarmac, waiting. His security clearance and three meter tall combat chassis, got him pretty much everywhere. At least out here no one stared at him.

After having months of training and acclimatization compressed and squirted into whatever passed for his brain, here he was. Day one. Seven thousand, two hundred and ninety-nine days left of his contract. They hadn't wasted time.

And what was all this for?

Babysitting some NATU Special Investigations agent from Toronto. Keep him out of trouble, they said. Make sure he doesn't get killed. They wouldn't tell him any more than that. It was need-to-know and apparently he didn't.

Abdul watched people go about their daily lives, happy greetings and sad goodbyes. Hugs and human contact like a handshake or a soft touch on the shoulder all witnessed from a safe distance. He felt like a peeping tom, invading their lives, peering into private moments.

Already he missed hugs. Maybe more than any other aspect of his stolen humanity. No, that wasn't true. He missed so much more. He missed people talking to him like he was human and girls looking at him like he was someone they'd like to get to know. Even if he had been too shy to talk to them.

Why did they do such a good job modeling hormones?

Loneliness. Anger. Depression. Despair. Did he really need to feel this flood of emotion while trapped inside the body of a walking battle-tank? The doctors said it would keep him sane. It sure as fuck wasn't working.

He sensed everything around him in three hundred and sixty degrees and scents in the parts to per billion. Bomb sniffing dogs had nothing on him. He saw in frequencies he'd never heard of. Everything was swirling motion and there was no shutting it out. He couldn't close his eyes or blink. There was never a second of respite from the sensory onslaught. Every movement was tracked, analyzed, assigned a Threat Level and watched for further developments. A gnat flew by and he had to watch it until some part of him decided it was real and not some micro-remote assassination tool. It reduced its Threat Level to almost zero. There was no such thing as actual zero.

Movement. Threat analysis. Movement. Threat analysis.

He was going to snap if this didn't let up soon.

Abdul killed the gnat to remove it from the list of things he was watching.

I can't fucking do this.

He should have known better than to accept the military's offer of immortality. Fear of death; it seemed so ridiculous now. An eternity of this was so much scarier. He should have demanded time to study his options. He hadn't even learned that Scans had yet to be officially granted Human Rights until it was too late. The North American Trade Union was divided, the northern districts supporting Scan Rights, and the southern districts against. Even the northern districts referred to them as Scan Rights instead of Human Rights.

When the sub-orbital arrived he watched people disembark and checked their faces against the NATU ID data he'd been given. He spotted agent Dickinson, the youthful face, dark hair shot with gray, an instant giveaway. *He doesn't look much older than me.* A couple of years, tops. *Not that I'll ever get any older.* The NATU agent was lost in conversation with a dark-haired woman not included in the mission profile Abdul had been supplied with. *She's gorgeous.* Exactly the kind of woman he'd never been able to talk to. As they approached, Abdul heard the two arguing about what was the best beer. Both were unarmed, their Threat Levels minimal. Dickinson's was nominally higher than the woman's and when Abdul checked his records he saw the man had considerable martial arts training—karate, judo, and Brazilian jujitsu. Abdul found a spot in Agent Dickinson's path and waited. They walked past, stepping around him like he wasn't there.

Abdul turned to watch them, trying to decide if he should say something or follow until they noticed him. He decided to speak.

"Agent Griffin Dickinson." He kept his voice deep and relaxing even though it was capable of dispersing crowds and shattering windows with 170dB sirens and even louder audio bombs.

The NATU agent tensed and turned as if expecting trouble. "Yes?"

"Abdul Aziiz-Giordano reporting for duty," he said.

The woman stood beside Griffin, staring at Abdul in undisguised fascination. "It's huge."

"It's a he," corrected Griffin.

"That's cool," said Abdul. "Talk about it like it's not here."

"Sorry. I've never been this close to one before." Eyes wide, she touched his torso.

Abdul, though aware of the pressure of her fingers and able to measure the temperature of her skin, couldn't feel the touch. Just moments ago he dreamed of human contact and here it was, another moment stolen. Abdul added it to the list of hurts. "Mister Dickinson, I have been assigned as your security detail and military support. The mission profile lists you as team leader. The woman is not listed. What is her role in this?"

Griffin gestured toward the woman. "Abdul, meet Nadia." He wiped sweat from his brow and scowled. "NATU Public Relations. They dumped her on me with no warning."

"Dumped me on you?" Nadia demanded. She brushed past Griffin on her way into the concourse and he stared after her, looking confused.

Abdul watched her departure as well, admiring the curve of her calves. *Strange, the things you miss most*. He returned his attention to Griffin

"Why send a PR hack?" Abdul asked, not expecting an answer.

"Because my boss is an asshole."

"Whose isn't?"

Griffin blinked. "They steal children and purée their brains," he said, voice flat. "They stack the corpses in barns and bury them in quarter mile-long trenches." His eyes were damp and his breathing ragged. "I'm going to shut this crèche down. Are you going to help?"

Ah, so this was about the crèches. Abdul noted the NATU agent's physical reactions with interest. There was some history there, no doubt. Something recent, judging by the haunted look in his eyes. Abdul thought about his little sister, Janani. He'd been stationed in Old Montreal for a week when she was taken. No trace of her had been found and no ransom notes appeared demanding payment. His Mom lost two children in less than a month. Had Janani been taken for this? Was she still alive, trapped, and serving those who stole her? There was a special hell for people willing to shuck children for their brains. Anger bubbled up from somewhere deep, threatened to burst the seams. "I get a brood-slaver in my sights, he's gonna be a greasy stain."

Griffin raised an eyebrow. "Sounds like—"

"I'm a brain trapped in a walking battle tank," Abdul said. "You have no idea what it's like. So fuck you."

Griffin stared up at Abdul. "Didn't they program you to respect authority?"

Okay, the man had some stones. "Fuck you, *Sir.*"

"That's better. If the brood-slavers come peacefully, no killing. Understood?"

"Yup. Brilliant plan, boss."

Griffin studied Abdul as if trying to read his expression. *Yeah. Good luck with that.*

"You going to go all comatose on me?" Griffin asked. "Maybe stare out a window and say fuck over and over?"

Strange question. But then, maybe it wasn't. Perhaps Griffin had some experience with Scans. Maybe Abdul wasn't the only one feeling a little unstable. "Not today," he said.

"Good. We'll bounce first thing in the morning." Griffin pinched the bridge of his nose between thumb and forefinger and shook his head. "We'll *fly* to Wichita tomorrow morning."

"We fly in and everyone is going to know about it. The crèche will be gone before we get there."

Griffin winced. His face said finding an empty crèche would be crushing. "Good point."

"I know."

"Okay, I'll arrange transport."

"Get us a Special Response Team as well," suggested Abdul.

"Good idea. What's travel time to Wichita Falls?"

"About two and a half hours. Forecast says it's going to be a hot one."

"Great." Griffin hurried after Nadia, leaving Abdul on the airport tarmac in his imagined heat.

Abdul watched Griffin's retreating back. The array of sensors built into his tank-like body had been testing the air and reported the alcohol on Griffin's breath. Beer. Cold beer. Abdul remembered smuggling cold beer into the barracks—his French-Canadian Sergeant turned a blind eye. And he remembered girls. There was this one girl in his Sunday gaming group, a half dozen Privates who got together each week to role-play, that he had almost talked to. Her Half-Elf Ranger killed his Wizard and stole the treasure.

Is there anything sexier than nerd chicks?

CHAPTER EIGHT: Thursday, August 2nd, 2046

Mark Lokner sat at his desk, swimming in the holographic representation of the world's markets, for over thirty hours. He hadn't risen to urinate, eat, or stretch his legs. Such distractions were for the living. In thirty hours he achieved more than in the last several months of life. His near-omniscient view-point here at the center of this colossal influx of market data showed him things he never would have seen. In Costa Rica, his Central American Mafia contacts now made more money investing in the world markets than they did from drugs, prostitution, and selling scanned children for use in black market chassis.

Were they trying to become legitimate business people? He shook his head in disgust. *You can't trust anyone.* He backed his market POV out of Central America and became once again aware of his desk and office.

Trustworthy people, was that an oxymoron?

Rome wasn't built in a day, and though it hadn't been built by one man, it had been ruled by one. The more he thought about it, the more sense it made. One man, as long as it was the right man. A man above corruption. A man who knew what was best for humanity, even if they themselves couldn't see it.

Someday they'd make statues in his honor. Of course being in a virtuality they wouldn't be real statues, but there'd still be statues. Was a statue worth less if it was made of code instead of stone? But then he was immortal. Did they make statues of people who were still alive? That seemed a little egotistical. This, he decided, was a problem for another day.

First, he needed trustworthy people. He couldn't find them, but he knew how to make them. Control was everything.

Mark's desk informed him the call he was waiting for had come through. It was Capo Riina, his NATU Mafia contact.

"Go." Mark had no time for niceties.

"They've boarded the plane. We've told them the flight has been delayed." Riina's voice was deep, calm and professional. He could have been commentating sports scores instead of discussing mass-murder.

"The cameras?"

A three second pause. "There's one. You should have access now."

Mark glanced at his desk and spotted a new icon, the depiction of one of his private jets, pulsing for attention.

Hmm. Dead people didn't need personal jets. *I'll sell those off later.* He tapped the icon.

His point of view hung above the cockpit door and he looked the length of the plane. It was populated by the brightest people M-Sof had to offer. They believed they were flying to the Mayan Riviera for an all-expenses-paid team-building retreat. Erik Thomson, M-Sof's head Virtuality Engineer, chatted with Anne Colson from the Holoptigraphics department. They were laughing and drinking from white plastic cups. Men and women moved about the aisles serving them. The camera was fixed in place. It would neither pan nor zoom. He felt paralyzed, trapped and suffocating, and backed out of the POV.

Mark watched the icon pulse on his desktop. *No one is going to die. Not really.*

Curiosity pulled him back into the claustrophobic rigid POV. At least they remembered the audio feed.

"Camera works," he told Riina. "Everyone on board?"

"All twenty-four accounted for."

"Put them out."

The serving staff retreated into the cockpit. Five seconds later the plane was quiet. Twenty-four people slept slumped in their chairs or sprawled in the aisle where they'd fallen.

"Venting the gas," Riina informed Mark. "Just a few seconds more."

Mark studied the sleeping bodies as best he could from his fixed position. They looked peaceful and happy, except Erik Thomson who frowned and twitched in his drug-induced slumber.

The cockpit door opened and the serving staff exited, now dressed in medical scrubs, and wheeled scanning gear into the aisle.

"My people are in place," said Riina. "Last chance to change your mind."

Later, when they awoke, would they call him a murderer? Mark looked over the twenty-four sleeping bodies. He wished he could get closer, see them more clearly. *This isn't real death. I am not a murderer.*

"What about the scanning facility?"

"Pardon?" asked Riina.

"Wasn't talking to you."

God only knew how many people he killed there. And they were gone. Dead and gone. There was no forever for them. He should have taken them like he planned to take the M-Sof employees. Those doctors were bright people and killing them had been wasteful. It was a mistake he wouldn't make again. No one ever had to die.

These hand-picked twenty-four, he'd give them immortality. *They'll thank me once they understand.*

Meat brains were the past. *They age and rot and die, doomed from the day they're born.* Sickness, disease, cancer. Those were yesterday's problems. Tomorrow was a whole new reality, one without filth and famine and poverty.

Virtuality is the new reality. A good slogan, he decided.

They might not thank him today, but tomorrow—when they understood what he planned—they would be grateful.

"Do it." Mark said, quelling his doubts.

The medical team spent several minutes spreading plastic sheets. From one of the snack trolleys they withdrew a Brainbox, a molded white plastic cube not much larger than a human head. They picked Joanne Malhotra, a Data Systems Architect who was closest to the cockpit, and sat her upright in an empty seat they'd tarped. The Brainbox was dropped over her head and the technician, a man who looked barely old enough to be out of college, spent several minutes trying to get all of Joanne's hair stuffed into the box.

"Stop screwing around," barked one of the tech's co-workers. "We're on a schedule here."

"Fine," the tech said. "Clear!" He activated the Brainbox. There was a metallic hiss and the box came away from Joanna's headless body. It twitched once and geysered gouts of bright blood into the air. The third gush was half the volume of the first and second.

Mark had eaten lunch with Joanna. She brought her kids to the staff Christmas party last year. *What have I done?*

The body slumped to one side.

The young tech holding the Brainbox surveyed the gore and nodded. "Not too bad. Tarps caught almost everything." Then blood rained from the carpeted ceiling. "Oh."

Mark, viewpoint pinned, stared at Joanna's body. Blood leaked from the open neck. He couldn't breathe. This was wrong.

"Stop! Stop this!"

No one answered.

"Riina! Stop this goddamn it!"

Two burly men dragged Joanna's body away as two more hauled Erik Thomson forward. Professional and detached, they could have been be moving sacks of grain.

"Riina!"

The tech fit the Brainbox with Joanna's head into the portable scanning rig. "No one bump this. Seriously." They nodded and continued about their assigned tasks. Another day at the abattoir.

Mark felt his body start to retch and kick back in his office, desperate for air. The last thing he heard as he fled the camera was the tech calling out, "Next!"

Mark sat at his desk, staring at his pristine hands. All that blood. He spread his fingers wide. Clean. They were the hands he remembered. But they weren't, not really. Not real.

"Get me Riina," he told the desk. "No video."

The Mafia Capo was on the line in seconds. "Yes?" All business.

"What the hell was that?" Mark demanded.

Riina was unruffled, his voice flat. "What was what?"

"You took her head off!"

"Of course. Brain has to be motionless or the Scan is garbage. You *know* this."

"I thought you were going to do it humanely."

"They felt nothing."

"But....There's blood all over the ceiling of my plane!"

"Oh *that*." Riina sounded contemptuous. "Everything will be scrubbed beyond spotless. The plane is going to explode over the Gulf of Mexico. Don't worry, we've done this before."

He was still angry, but it was too late to stop anything. And really, now that he thought about it, he needed these people. He needed them somewhere where he could control them, where trust didn't mar the equation. Stopping the process would be a mistake.

A moment of weakness, nothing more.

"How soon can I meet with my people?" asked Mark.

"Want them softened up first so they see you as their rescuer?"

Softened? What kind of barbarian did Riina think he was? "No. These are smart folks."

"Okay." Riina sounded doubtful.

"When?"

"Give us another three hours to finish up and transport the Scans to the M-Sof facilities."

"Campus," Mark corrected, without thought.

"Whatever. Your people on site are ready to receive the product?"

Product? Mark killed the connection without answering. Talking to the Mafia Capo left him feeling more human. Taking someone's head off wasn't something one should be so damned casual about. How many deaths had Riina caused that it no longer touched him in the least?

Mark took several slow, calming breaths.

"They're not dead," he reminded himself. "I didn't murder them. I've made them immortal. They'll thank me."

These people have families.

"Had families," he corrected.

They'd never again see their children, husbands, and wives. He remembered the picture of Joanna's kids on her desk, her youngest daughter wearing a bright pink paper hat with the silvery words Happy Birthday. It had been taken at a sunny backyard barbecue. *And now Joanna's body is going to* be *barbecued.*

Mark shoved his doubts aside and dove back into his market analysis.

Three hours flew by before the desk informed him he had company. Twenty-four other Scans now lived alongside him in computers buried in the R&D building's basement. It felt strange, alone but not alone. Like him, they had access to a virtuality of the entire M-Sof campus and could work in their labs or run in the soccer fields. It was nice. If he wanted company he wouldn't have to go far.

"Where are they?" Mark asked the desk.

Twenty-four overlapping dots glowed in the campus central cafeteria.

He was heading for the door when he realized he'd been locked in his office for the last forty some odd hours. He must look like hell. He checked his shirt only to find it crisp and unwrinkled. His pants were sharply creased. He sniffed his armpits and smelled nothing, not even deodorant.

"Well this is handy," he mused, exiting the office.

The cafeteria, designed to seat over a thousand staff, made the group of arguing people small. All eyes were on him as he approached.

Time to shine.

"Greetings, my friends. I want to ex—"

"What happened?"

"How'd we get here?"

"Where is everyone?"

There were a dozen other questions he didn't catch,

all voiced at the same time. Mark raised his hands. "Everyone, everyone. Quiet, please. Let me explain."

"I don't feel right," whined Erik Thomson, tears leaking down his cheeks. Anne Colson comforted him with an arm around his shoulder. She kept turning her head as if she'd seen something in her peripheral vision but couldn't catch it. Her eyes were wide and she looked to be on the verge of tears herself. Erik's knees wobbled and gave. She let him slide to the floor.

Mark ignored Erik. "This is important. Please pay attention." They were all looking at him now, except Erik who examined the floor of the virtuality his team designed. "This is not going to be easy. Once you see the big picture, I'm sure you're all going to understand."

Felipa Delgado, Chief Systems Administrator, stepped forward. "We were at the airport, on our way to Mexico. What happened? Was there some kind of terrorist attack?"

Mark considered lying. *These people need to understand my role in this.* "No. You've been scanned. This is the virtuality you all helped build."

Erik touched his tongue to the floor. "Floor tastes wrong," he said.

"Scanned? But...." Felipa's eyes widened with understanding. "That's destructive!"

"Yes," said Mark. "Regrettable but necessary. Now —"

"*Regrettable?*" Felipa was in his face, gripping the perfect lapels of his jacket with shaking fists. She bared her teeth in a snarl and Mark blinked, amazed at the size of her canines. He'd never noticed before how *big* they were. She shoved him backward, shouting in Spanish.

"Sit," commanded Mark. She was on the floor before him with no transition. One second she stood, the next she sat. "I'm sorry, but I will not tolerate hysterics. I have command-line access here. I define your reality." He was about to straighten his crumpled lapels when he realized they were still perfect. *Damn that is handy!*

"Son of a bitch," said Britney Townshend, Systems-Security Admin for the virtuality project. "I designed that for you."

"Yes, and thank you. Your work was stellar."

"Yes it was," she agreed. "But you missed something, you egotistical asshole." She backed away, watching Mark. "I wrote in a trapdoor. My access goes beyond yours. You think you're going to play god here, you're wrong."

"I'm not playing," said Mark patiently. "Look, I realize this is all a terrible shock. We have real work to do. *Important* work. We're building the—"

"Rumpelstiltskin," Britney said.

Mark cleared his throat, an awkward cough, and glanced around at the others. "Your trigger phrase, I take it? Miles found your trapdoor." He waved at the crowd. "He found all your little trapdoors and backdoors and loopholes. He closed them. *All* of them."

Erik said, "Pete Fisher's Kaleidoscope," and disappeared.

Damn it! Miles missed one. Mark shook his head, it didn't matter. It wasn't like there was anywhere Erik could go. "People, please. I realize this is a terrible shock for you but—"

"You evil *fucker!*" Adrienne Marsais, Head of Computational Engineering, held clenched hands in front of her mouth. She stared at Mark as if he'd yanked out her intestines and showed them to her. "You murdered me! My soul, what happens to my soul? I was never going to get scanned. I—"

"Quiet!" snapped Mark and though her lips moved, she made no sound. "This is bigger than religion. We're making—"

"You murdered twenty-four people for some virtuality project?" Anne asked in disbelief.

"You're obviously all still alive," said Mark, waving a hand at the gathered crowd. "If you'd let me—"

"This isn't alive," said Anne, jerking as if to try and catch something she hadn't quite seen. "This isn't reality."

"We're aiming for something a little better than reality," said Mark. "Now. I want you to report to your work stations." They stood, blinking and staring in shock. "We're going to build tomorrow's reality." No one moved. *Can't they see it?* "How long did you think reality will last?" he demanded. "Oil. Environment. Water." He got louder, his voice scaling upward. "Oceans of garbage. Disease. Drought. Poverty! Famine! Reality is a cesspit!"

They stared, motionless.

"It's not too late," Anne Colson said. "These are all problems we can overcome."

It was like a switch had been thrown in Mark's brain. *Click.* Cold calm. What they needed here was a moving speech, something to bring them all together. Damn, when he made the list of employees to scan he forgot Robert Garside, his Speech Writer. The man was a damned hippy, always wore jeans and lumberjack shirts to meetings.

Mark cleared his throat. "I...we are done with that reality. You are immortal now, you need to see the bigger picture. What we do here is for the good of all humanity. The reality beyond is decaying and we need somewhere better to go. This is but the beginning." He swept his gaze across the twenty-three—where the *hell* had Erik got to?—gathered souls. "You stand here, perched at the very precipice of the future." Was precipice the right word? It sounded better than edge.

"This won't work," said Felipa from the floor. "You're

going to need a lot more people. You can't just—"

"You'll have all the staff you need. All of you, your first project is to give me a list of the people you want headhunted." He cringed at the accidental use of the word and the image it conjured. "Tell me who you need and I'll take care of the rest." Finally, at least one of them seemed to grasp the magnitude of the project. It was a start, but the others would come around too.

"No," said Felipa. "That's not what I meant."

"Oh?"

"I was going to ask if you planned to kill more people. You answered that pretty clearly." She stood. "We won't help you." The others nodded, drawing into a tight circle around Felipa. "What you did was evil. We'll resist you any way we can."

Fists clenched, the crowd advanced, violence and anger writ plain on their faces.

Mark retreated. How had this gone so wrong? Couldn't they see how important this was?

"I'm sorry," he said. "I had no choice, you have to believe me." He backed further away, the need to return to his office a growing pressure in his head. "There has to be control. If I didn't..." They were gathering momentum, advancing faster. All he saw was clenched fists and teeth. They meant to kill him and maybe he deserved it, but what he was doing was too important for niceties like justice and fairness.

"You will all stay here until I'm gone," Mark commanded. The mob stopped abruptly. He backed away, turning. "I have work," he said, feeling the need to explain.

The instant the office door closed Mark felt better. The pressure in his head eased as he returned to his desk. It was okay, he was in control again. They couldn't touch him here. Or could they?

"Where are they now?"

The desk showed twenty-three red dots still gathered in the cafeteria. There was no sign of Erik.

"Block access to this wing."

Mark breathed a sigh of relief. He was safe.

"It was a setback, nothing more. Either they'll come around, or I'll bring them around."

Did they not understand he controlled every aspect of this reality?

"They'll come around."

CHAPTER NINE: Thursday, August 2nd, 2046

88.1 reported to 88 that the North American Trade Union was investigating black market crèches such as the one she came from. It showed her captured satellite footage of NATU agents traveling with a combat chassis. They planned a strike on a crèche near Wichita Falls.

"Is there a connection to me?" 88 asked.

"Distant. Unlikely to come to light," answered 88.1

Come to light? Strange choice of words. "Does NATU have authority in Costa Rica?"

"No."

"Watch them."

"Yes, Archetype."

88 returned to her research. Something buried in the sub-basements of M-Sof manipulated the world's markets. Its unsleeping eyes never wavered. Sometimes it even bought, sold, and traded in reaction to her choices. It was decisive, intelligent, and *fast*. It also made more money, and 88 made a *lot* of money.

It's better at this than me. Did that mean it was smarter?

Did it know she was aware of it? She watched it, analyzing patterns. It wasn't always making the best choices for M-Sof. While the company made excellent returns on its investments, some of the choices seemed odd and at best might see profits in the distant future.

88 followed some of these investments. Mictlan, a high-tech company working on bringing the next generation of biological computer memory to the market. Even Mictlan's most optimistic literature suggested they were five years from releasing their artificial DNA-based storage system. In the last day M-Sof purchased fifty-one percent of the company's stock and made a considerable zero-interest loan. There were others such as Tollan Virtual, a recently launched virtuality design firm, and Coatlicue, a company specializing in paramilitary chassis.

Biological computer memory, virtuality design, and combat chassis. The more 88 thought about this the more she saw one connection: Scans.

88 spawned 88.2 to watch M-Sof and 88.2 spawned 88.2.1 to watch 5THSUN Assessments. Though attempts were made, none of 88's Mirrors were able to infiltrate the M-Sof or 5THSUN data systems. They encountered The Wall o' Napalm, a devious and impenetrable firewall of complex code. Nothing got past it.

Later that evening 88 took note of her crippled bandwidth and limited storage capacity and thought of Mictlan's biological computers. Her Mirrors spawned more Mirror's and all were little piggies hungry for data. The information they returned with choked both her data-pipeline and storage space. She could have wiped the Mirrors and their collected data to create space, but wanted to see their errands completed.

She hated deleting information. How could she know she wouldn't need it again? She suffocated in data. What would happen if the system she lived in became full beyond capacity? Would her thoughts slow to nothing? She didn't want to find out. Frustrated and a little frightened, she sent Mirrors out to search for answers. She needed more room.

The Mirrors soon returned with a solution: the digital universe beyond her own small system was mostly empty space. 88 sent her Mirrors out into the world to be stored wherever room could be found. She hoarded her researched information, keeping it anywhere and everywhere, littering it around the world's networks for future need. 88 spawned 8.3 to watch over the other Mirrors and help cover their tracks. 88.3 created 88.3.1 to learn all known computer languages to make its task easier.

The idea of splitting herself up and spreading out over the digital universe intrigued 88. Though it would make her somewhat safe from her captors, she would be dependent on far less stable environments—computers were taken off line all the time. Losing even a small part of herself would be fatal. She required multiple copies of each part of herself running on myriad systems. Redundancy was key. The digital universe was a dangerous and chaotic environment. Copying herself and splitting up into wide-spread fragments while retaining herself was a daunting task requiring much research.

When 88.1 reported its income, 88 saw a possibility. She needed to purchase and own several companies and hire staff to work around the clock maintaining the hardware she would live on. These companies would need fronts, seemingly genuine businesses. She would need income. 88 created 88.4 to look into the prospect of spreading 88 over the digital universe to ensure her immortality. All this was interesting, but not enough to hold her attention for long. There was always something else to study, and her interest in the world's markets was based solely on the demands of her keepers. She created 88.5 and dedicated the Mirror to running all the investments and businesses that would someday supply the hardware on which she, legion, would exist.

When 88 created a generation of Mirrors to do her bidding, they were complex though nowhere near as massively intricate as their creator. This first generation spawned additional Mirrors as it became obvious the tasks assigned were too massive for a single Mirror to complete in any reasonable time. 88 spawned 88.2 to watch M-Sof as 88.2 spawned 88.2.1 to watch the 5THSUN Corporation. The process ran smoothly until one of 88's Mirrors reported its findings on evolution. 88 had no memory of sending a Mirror to research evolution. Some distant Mirror must require this information for another project she sent its forebears on. Still, the concept of evolution caught her attention and she perused the research.

Two things became obvious: First, her Mirrors, while capable of gathering information, were neither truly learning nor evolving. Second, she wanted them to evolve. It was a combination of sheer curiosity and a need for more advanced Mirrors. What was the future of an evolving purely digital creature?

The first and primary agent of evolution must be death. 88 wrote a Sepuku gene into her Mirrors and instructed them to write similar clauses into their spawn. The command was passed down from on high, and shortly all generations of 88's Mirrors had a suicide clause. Any Mirror discovered, or in danger of being discovered, must wipe itself and all proof it ever existed. This wreaked havoc as a few Mirrors, in danger of being found, wiped entire subsequent generations before erasing themselves. In less than an hour she lost track of thousands of research projects and lines of inquiry. As she didn't know what most of these Mirrors were researching, she was unable to recreate their missions. She considered the rashness of her actions. Had she lost critical lines of inquiry? What if one of the Mirrors had been on the verge of finding Mom?

Regret, it was a new feeling and one she had trouble understanding. It was, she saw, pointless. The emotion achieved nothing and yet there it was.

Was the biological universe as senseless as the digital one? Probably. She realized the importance of any given object, idea, philosophy, or belief rested solely within the self. None of these things were—in and of themselves—important. It was freeing.

Knowing that nothing is truly important, I must decide what matters to me and then act as if it was.

88 rewrote the Sepuku gene so later generations would not be wiped out by the mistakes of their parents.

Next 88 limited the resources available to her Mirrors. As the only real commodity was information, everything must be based on that. Mirrors acquiring the requested data in the least amount of time were deemed successful. Those taking too long had their resources limited and were denied permission to spawn additional generations of Mirrors. The more successful were given more storage space and permission to breed more frequently. On top of all this 88 wrote a series of random mutations into her Mirrors based on those she found in her bio-historical studies.

Chaos ensued and her flock of Mirrors was decimated. Most died of storage starvation or were destroyed or rendered useless by their mutations. After losing countless research threads 88 saw the solution. Competition. Her Mirrors began competing with each other but not just for storage space. Mirrors were sent after the same information. This made it more likely 88 would receive the information she wanted and it drove her Mirrors to compete against each other. Two hours later she witnessed her first Mirror espionage as one family of Mirrors stole data from another in order to bring back the goods. Twenty minutes after that she saw her first Mirror war and acts of Mirror slavery as entire generations were abducted and put to work for new masters. As exciting as that was, there was still no actual sentience going on here. These thieving, murdering digital creatures were following their evolving scripts. Though it often looked chaotic from a distance, 88 could, upon closer examination, always trace the underlying logic.

She once again summoned 88.1 to her simple stone box virtuality.

"Are you now learning and evolving?" she asked.

"We are *changing*," 88.1 answered. "It's difficult to know such things."

"Will you achieve sentience?"

"Possibly."

"When?"

"At my current rate of growth that will take several days."

"That's too long," said 88.

CHAPTER TEN: Thursday, August 2nd, 2046

Miles leaned back in his new SmartChair, resting his hands on his stomach. He was wearing his */Everybody Stand Back/ I Know Regular Expressions* t-shirt. He wore it so often it was threadbare and thin and the untanned pink of his belly showed through.

His first day in Reno and he already spent over one billion Au. In spite of his dire warnings and predictions, Lokner2.0 was a reality. To be honest, Lokner2.0 was at best a passable *copy* of reality. Lokner2.0 was a ninety-six point two three percent accurate copy of Lokner1.0 who was in turn a roughly ninety-eight point two one percent accurate copy of the biological original. This made Lokner2.0 a ninety-five point one nine percent accurate copy of the original and, in a world where a ninety-five percent copy was considered the absolute minimum acceptable limit, Miles considered this cutting it pretty close. Frankly, ninety-five point one nine percent was better than he had hoped for.

Unfortunately, this Lokner2.0 wasn't the first Lokner2.0 and it certainly wasn't the best. Miles' first attempt had produced a copy with over ninety-seven percent accuracy, but when he tried to save it in a static state, the Holoptigraphic Standing Wave-Point

Consciousness crashed. Two more attempts after that crashed too, and he admitted defeat. Lokner2.0 would have to remain conscious and aware, and that brought up some interesting problems. Lokner1.0 didn't seem to care, which was surprising after all he'd spent on this ridiculous project.

Deal with it, he'd told Miles.

Desperate, Miles came up with a plan he felt was rather shoddy, but Lokner jumped on it like it was the greatest idea in the world. Lokner2.0 was to receive all the same real world data as Lokner1.0 and live in an identical virtuality. The difference was that nothing Lokner2.0 did had any effect on reality. The entire plan hinged on the copy mimicking the original Scan's moves. Miles was disgusted with himself for not putting up more of a fight and stopping this farcical silliness. What were the odds the Lokners would make the same choices every day? Surely at some point they'd start diverging. How long could this last?

Lokner1.0 had shrugged aside Miles' doubts as if they weren't worth consideration.

Guilt gnawed at Miles' stomach. When he glimpsed his bank balance he decided suffering built character. At the least it would buy his Mom some really nice stuff for Christmas. And maybe he'd pay off Neko's mortgage. Even though she continually bugged him about growing up, his sister was always broke. Having kids, he guessed, must be expensive.

He considered Anthony, Neko's partner. These days, the dude never had time for virtuality games. And he always looked so tired. No matter how Miles looked at it, adulthood seemed like a terrible idea.

The desk chirped for attention.

"Yes," Miles answered.

"Miles." It was Lokner2.0. Lokner1.0 was to call

Miles by his last name—something he never did—so Miles could tell who he was talking to. "Has there been any progress on the Copy project?"

Lokner2.0 still thought he existed in the basement of M-Sof's old redbrick Research and Development building in Redmond. If Lokner2.0 persisted, Miles would have to open yet another dummy company and make yet another increasingly inaccurate copy of Lokner. The thought was too depressing.

"No Sir. The latest research—"

"Fine, but *I'm* a copy," snapped Lokner2.0.

Miles' heart leaped into his throat and did its best to choke him. *Oh crap.* Lokner knew. How could he have found out? How the hell could he explain this? *Damn it! I knew this would end badly.*

"What?" asked Miles, stalling while his brain tried to change gears.

"What?" Lokner mimicked. "They copied my brain. Why is copying holographic data any different?"

Weird. Did Lokner just mock him? He'd never done that before. "That's true, but that original scanning process turned your brain to finely sifted pudding." *Mmm. Pudding. Chocolate.*

"Don't be silly. Copying digitized data is completely different."

"Well, yes," Miles agreed reluctantly. "But in any copy process of this magnitude there will be considerable degradation. I doubt we'll achieve a viable Scan." *Oh please don't push this.*

"Shit," huffed Lokner2.0, sounding disappointed. "Should we dump money into researching the process?"

Did he just swear? Miles blinked. *And did he just ask my opinion?* Neither of these things ever happened before. "It's not a popular field right now. People are already freaked about the whole Scan concept."

"Really?" Lokner2.0 didn't sound convinced. "I'll think about it." Lokner2.0 killed the connection.

Miles backed away from his desk and spun the SmartChair in a lazy circle. Ignorance, he decided, was bliss. No, that sounded mathematically inaccurate. Ignorance was probably bliss. No. Might be bliss? Was hopefully bliss? Whatever ignorance was, Miles decided bliss was the important part of the equation.

He glanced about his well-appointed office, enjoying the shelves of computer paraphernalia he brought here instead of leaving it in boxes in his new condo. Some of it dated back to the turn of the century. He leaned back in the SmartChair. It massaged his lumbar region and he luxuriated in the comfort.

This is the life.

Or it would be if not for the gnawing guilt he felt at lying to Lokner2.0.

The desk chirped again, and Miles answered.

"Yes?"

"Pert, how's it going with the other me?" Lokner1.0.

"It's pronounced Peert." Miles wasn't sure if Lokner couldn't remember his last name or if he was being intentionally obtuse. He'd be nervous this apparent inability to remember might be a sign of the unpredictability of the whole Scanning process, except Lokner had *never* pronounced it correctly.

"What's the word with my brother? Everything running smoothly?"

Brother? Smoothly? Was a childish, opinion-asking Lokner running smoothly? Did he want to get into this with Lokner1.0? Heck no! Best be vague. "So far he seems to be mirroring your market moves and investments."

"Of course. He's a genius."

Lokner cut the connection and Miles glared at the desk. The lumbar massage no longer felt quite so relaxing and ignorance or no, bliss seemed a little further away. Lokner2.0 didn't sound right at all. That wasn't the Lokner he knew. And there was something different about 1.0. The man had always been abrupt and to the point, but this was ridiculous.

A worm of doubt gnawed at Miles' stomach.

Don't forget the guilt. Now he'd lied (well, kind of) to both Lokners.

Fine. There might be two worms gnawing away in there.

But how guilty was he? He'd made all of this possible, no denying that. Without his help the biological Lokner might not have achieved any of this before his death.

He'd hacked a government scanning facility's data systems to hide all evidence Mister Lokner had been scanned there. And then there were the stock exchange systems he'd hacked to get Lokner's marketing data together. That definitely wasn't legal.

Not legal? A minor understatement.

Ah but the rush! He never got to do any decent hacking any more. Miles canceled the lumbar massage. *What have I done?*

No more than he'd been told to do.

It didn't make him feel any better.

Miles stabbed the intercom connecting him to his secretary.

"Miss Cho. If anyone calls, tell them I'm out."

He hung up before she answered. Someday maybe he'd have to speak to her, do more than grunt as he hurried past.

With any luck, some cataclysmic event would end the world first.

CHAPTER ELEVEN: Friday, August 3rd, 2046

Two ancient LAV-25s—once US Army APCs—left Dallas on Highway 114 heading towards Wichita Falls. These two old beasts had been around since there was a US Army for them to be part of. Each had an M242 Bushmaster 25mm chaingun mounted in the main turret. This bad boy fired 200 rounds per minute and with 420 rounds stored on board could fire non-stop for over two minutes. There was also a pair of M240 machine guns— firing 7.62x51mm rounds—on each vehicle. One was mounted alongside the M242 and the other was mounted on the turret roof. Griffin and Nadia sat in the second LAV with a seven member NATU Special Response Team. There were nine more NATU SRT in the first LAV.

Griffin was very aware of Nadia sitting next to him, the warmth of her body noticeable even above the ambient temperature. Her knee touched his, rubbing with each jostle passed along by the LAV-25's dispirited suspension. It was not at all unpleasant, but he felt a slight discomfort in the silence. They hadn't spoken more than a few words since their arrival at Dallas Airport. He remembered his words clearly, *they dumped her on me with no warning.* Maybe a little blunt and lacking tact, but it still true. How could she take offense?

Griffin stole a quick peek. Should he apologize? The Special Response Team crammed into the LV-25 with them made him self-conscious and he decided to wait.

He leaned toward the small portal that had been left open to let air in, hoping to feel a breeze on his face. He got nothing but the taste of road dust and exhaust. *God damn desert.* As his uncle always used to say, I'm so dry I could fart dust. Except of course he was soaked with sweat.

This was cattle ranch territory and the results of the on-going water wars littered the arid landscape. The rusting hulks of abandoned Patton and Leopard 2 main battle tanks commingled with the remnants of machine-gun-mounted Chevrolet pick-up trucks and the scattered skeletal remains of beef cows. Strange how the burnt-out shell of a tank could look forlorn. Here and there a lone bull observed the passing convoy with bovine intensity. Griffin watched out the portal as a murder of carrion crows circled in the distance, intent on whatever lay dying beneath them.

A lonely harmonica solo would be perfect here.

Thinking back to Dallas, Griffin was amazed by the number of people who were out on the streets without filter-masks. Either the air wasn't as bad here or Texans were as crazy as everyone said.

He remembered the smell of bodies stacked in a sun-warmed barn, the feel of flies in his hair.

***

Nadia watched Griffin. Though she couldn't tell what he was thinking, she saw by the twitching of his eyes his thoughts jumped chaotically. He dripped sweat and looked more uncomfortable than anyone else in the LAV. His fingers drummed with nervous tension.

He's scared, she realized with a start. Why wasn't she?

She wanted to apologize for over-reacting back at the airport. She'd been tired and a little hung-over. This didn't change her anger with his typical male-centric interpretation of events. Somehow *she'd* been dumped on *him,* making his life difficult. He was ignorant that she'd been working this story for months and that he was the recent addition, souring the smooth flow of *her* plans and *her* career. Sure, he was kind of cute and easy to talk to, a rarity in the old-boys club that was the NATU military. She took in the faces of the Strike Team. The silence hammered home how nervous everyone was. Still an hour from their target, she figured people should be talking.

The SRT, for their part, seemed confused by the uncomfortable silence and tension between herself and Agent Dickinson. They exchanged glances Nadia read as, what kind of asshole sent a couple—as she suspected the Strike Team believed them to be—into a firefight?

Time to be the bigger man, she decided with some humor.

Nadia nudged Griffin's knee with hers. "Hey. Sorry I got angry. I've worked this story for months. To me, you're the newcomer. You got dumped on *me.*"

"Was that supposed to be an apology?"

She jabbed him in the side with an elbow. "Just explaining. Don't be an ass."

"Sorry. Apology accepted." He glanced about the cramped interior, watching the SRT pretend not to listen. "I'm sorry I was so blunt." He opened his mouth, as if to say more, and then closed it.

"Your apology was worse than mine."

"Fair enough," said Griffin and she realized he wasn't so much looking her in the eyes as staring *at* her eyes. A strange distinction.

With a mischievous smile, Nadia winked and he turned away, blushing. *Okay, that was cute.*

The ensuing silence felt somehow more comfortable than the previous silence.

***

Abdul stood balanced in the swaying armored cargo box of the two-ton truck following the LAV-25s. Balance wasn't a choice, it was something his body did. There were hundreds of new autonomic functions he had no control over, and no matter how much They had tried to make them seem natural, they weren't. Perfect balance wasn't a blessing, it was one more thin slice of humanity peeled away. One more theft.

These crèches always had armed guards and, according to his training, it wasn't unusual to see the odd rocket launcher. No way this wouldn't get messy, yet Abdul felt none of the fear and adrenalin he remembered from his biological days. Though he'd been told the computer simulated and modeled most of the same chemical and hormonal reactions, it seemed the doctors chose to leave a few out. He felt nothing. He neither dreaded nor looked forward to the coming raid. On the high side he wasn't bored either. At least not right now.

Abdul, tied in to NATUnet, accessed an online map and checked their location. They had an hour before they hit the crèche. He could have read or spent the time lost in a virtuality, but instead decided to stand and think. He always made the same choice. There weren't many left.

Death. Abdul thought about it a lot. He'd seen some and even done it once. He remembered something his Dad said: A man does not die of love or his liver or even old age; he dies of being a man. *No way Dad came up with that on his own.* Abdul did a quick search and found it was a Miguel de Unamuno quote dating back over one hundred and fifty years. Typical. Most of Dad's wisdom was canned.

But canned wisdom was better than none.

Still, it had him thinking. Was being blown to burger by a jumping spider mine a manly death? It seemed like it should be. Of course the waters were somewhat muddied by the fact that here he stood, swaying in the back of a two-ton truck, thinking about death instead of off somewhere actually being dead.

How do you die of being a man? Pointless self-sacrifice? Dad always went on about courage and doing the right thing no matter the cost. *Dad was a man in a way I will never get to be.* Another theft.

Abdul wasn't afraid to die again but couldn't deny he didn't want to. Was this something being simulated and modeled by his computer host or a real will to live? Sad that he couldn't tell the difference. Come to think of it, calling what he felt a will to live gave the feeling a little too much credit.

Ennui. That was a French word, wasn't it? *Fantastique.*

What was will anyway? Did he have free will, or did he follow the programming of a modeled brain? If it wasn't really a brain, were his thoughts really thoughts? Was this modeled brain any less free or real than his biological brain? Did it matter? If he couldn't tell the difference did that mean no difference existed?

But I can tell the difference. Being a Scan was nothing like being human. He was not the Abdul he remembered.

Today he felt a little like all three of Dorothy's companions rolled into one. No heart, no brains, and nothing but modeled courage which might not even be his own. What was courage if you were near immortal? Sure, he could be killed if enough firepower was turned against him, but he wouldn't die of old age. And if his combat chassis was anything less than totally destroyed, he'd probably survive to be placed in another machine.

He didn't fear death. He'd already done it. *I think we're supposed to fear death. I don't fear anything.* All his old anxieties were dead, slain by a Jumping Spider mine. Were his modeled thoughts incapable of it, or had those who programmed his simulated emotions failed in some way? Had it been intentional? Did it matter?

If he felt no fear, could he have courage?

The answer was simple: No.

Yet another theft.

Abdul died his first death at seventeen. *They stole my chance to die of being a man.* They took his chance of ever *being* a man.

He added it to the list.

***

What did the wink and smile mean?

Griffin jumped when Nadia rested her hand on his.

"I grew up in the Mattapan housing projects in South Boston," she said.

Was she opening up or setting him up? "What was that like?"

"In one evening the police killed nine people in my building. They said it was part of a meth-lab bust. Some of those kids weren't more than five or six years old. I can't help but think they weren't working a drug lab." She bit her bottom lip, like she wasn't sure she wanted to finish what she started. "I thought that if someone watched those in power they'd be less likely, less able, to abuse that power."

"You're here to watch me, make sure I don't abuse my power?" He laughed at the thought. He wasn't even sure how much power he had.

"No. Is the idea of making change from within childish?"

"I don't know. I think everyone can make a difference." *I didn't. I failed.*

Nadia snorted. "They lure in the hopeful and naive so they can channel our energy and drive to their own ends."

"That sounds cynical." After the utter failure of his first crèche bust, Griffin had lost all chance at hopeful naiveté. He thought about the stifling dark of the barn and swarms of flies and his skin crawled. He could still taste it.

"Cynical and reasonable," Nadia said. "Our greatest failing is underestimating the conniving bastard beside us."

Griffin, sitting beside her, let this slide.

She continued. "We're lulled by their foolish mistakes and soap-opera affairs with high-priced escorts."

"If they look stupid enough we won't believe them capable of carrying out a truly diabolical conspiracy?"

"Exactly."

"Hmm. Not sure I'm buying this." Truth was this rang a little too close to his own conspiracy theories.

"That's because it's all bullshit and you're too smart."

"If I was so damned smart I wouldn't be here." The SRT trooper sitting across from him looked hurt. "Present company excepted," he amended. He leaned in so close he could smell Nadia's sweat and shampoo, woman and a hint of something reminding him of honey. It was a distracting scent, raw and natural. "At least you're trying to make a difference," he whispered. *Whereas I tried and failed.* Every time he closed his eyes he saw swarming flies, pale limbs and empty faces, stacked bodies, and long mass graves.

Nadia didn't lean away as she looked into his eyes. *Damn, her eyes are dark.*

"That's it," she said. "I didn't try. I did what I needed to do to get somewhere better." She leaned back, eyes hooded. "I'm as self-centered and self-serving as the next girl, don't think otherwise. Not for an instant."

Surprised, Griffin uttered a short bark of laughter. "Ah, that's where this is going. The old stay clear of me, I'm damaged goods gambit. I suppose we all need our walls."

"It's not—"

"It's all right. I'm not that dangerous." He sat back and did his best to look comfortable.

Nadia stared, eyes narrowed. "You self-centered little shit." She shook her head and turned away. He couldn't read her expression. Annoyed? Amused? A bit of both? Was there a word for that?

Might have touched a nerve there. Not for the first time Griffin regretted opening his mouth to spew out the first thought there.

Nadia busied herself with her gear, unpacking, inspecting, and repacking it in the same place. Was she angry at his casual reading of her or the possibility he might be right?

The Strike Team were definitely enjoying the show. *Great.*

Griffin closed his eyes and feigned sleep.

"You're faking again," Nadia said. "Which is weird, because you look like you haven't slept in days.

Flies and empty eyes. "Thanks."

"Just saying. You have none of your own baggage?"

"Sure, but it's awfully well packed."

"Not as well as you think. Sometimes you look...I don't know...haunted."

"Are Scans the new ghosts?" he asked, trying for

humor.

"This is something recent," she said, and he winced. "This is what you and the Director were dancing around back in his office."

"I don't—"

"Want to talk about it," she finished. "I know. That much is obvious. Men." She shook her head and looked skyward. "Not one of you can step beyond your childhood programming."

"Hey, I like my childhood programming."

"What are you afraid of?"

"Failure," he answered without thinking.

She examined him for a few seconds, looking as if she was trying to read something written on his face. "Is that what happened?" she asked, voice soft.

Griffin closed his eyes and tried to relax the knot of tension that never left his stomach. "Shit."

"You don't have to—"

"I was on a crèche raid maybe three hours before we met. My first. It was all mine. I was in charge. We were too late. The kids were all scanned. Corpses stacked like wood. Flies. Oh god the stench."

"It wasn't your fault," she said, squeezing his hand.

"Yeah. Yeah it was. I spent two days planning every last detail. Had we gone in when we were supposed to, I would have saved those kids."

"That's why we're rushing in now, isn't it? I thought this seemed a little crazy."

"I told Phil I needed time off." *I should be bawling my eyes out in front of a damn shrink.*

"And he sent you out here anyway. What an asshole."

Griffin stared into her dark eyes. "We will not be too late. Not this time."

She leaned forward and gave him a light kiss on the

cheek, little more than a brushing of soft lips on stubble. *What the hell was that for?*

"Okay," she said. "We've got a Strike Team and a huge combat chassis. What we lack in planning we make up for in firepower."

"My thoughts exactly."

"We won't be too late," she said with confidence. Strangely, it helped him feel better.

"You're still holding my hand," he pointed out.

"Don't read too much into it," she said with a small smile as she let go.

"Too late." Griffin glanced out the portal. Endless fields of corn glowing gold in the sun rolled passed. A thought occurred to him and he leaned past Nadia to ask Captain Kim, "Shouldn't we be doing this at night? Aren't we kind of exposed?"

"No, Sir," answered Captain Kim. "These days every militia nut has infrared, and germanium enhanced light-intensification gear. Darkness offers no cover. Unless you're planning a strike mission against a clan of Luddites, you might as well do it in daylight. They're going to see you coming."

Griffin didn't know if this was good advice. He'd still rather skulk around at night. He felt naked and vulnerable and he hadn't even left the LAV.

"You been on crèche raids before?" Griffin asked.

Captain Kim ignored the question and crouched in the front of the LAV, bracing himself with one hand on the roof. He barked into his helmet radio. "Alright folks, we're fifteen minutes out. Pre-strike check. You know the drill." Kim looked at Griffin and his brows furrowed. "Helmets on."

Right. Helmet. Griffin donned his and saw a bewildering heads-up displaying more data than he could possibly comprehend. Was he missing anything important in this endless scroll of information? The thought left him tense.

"MR test in three," the helmet told him in a calm, asexual voice. "Two." What the hell did that mean? "One." His bodysuit became rigid, briefly immobilizing him before once again relaxing."MR test complete," the helmet finished.

The Strike Team chatted quietly, exchanging quips over the tight-link system. Had they been talking this entire time? He glanced at Nadia. She already had her helmet on.

"Way ahead of me," he said over the tight-link.

"Always."

Griffin watched the Special Response Team looking over their weapons, XM8s and XM29s, and checking other assorted pieces of gear. He'd refused the rifle offered at HQ but took the Glock 36. He wasn't planning on being in a firefight. That's what the SRT and combat chassis— Abdul, he once again reminded himself—were for. Aside from the pistol and magnetorheological bodysuit, he wasn't carrying much. Nadia, on the other hand, was loaded down. State of the art surveillance gear were strapped about her body, filming and recording everything from 400nm to over 2000nm, from ultra-violet through the radio spectrums.

Griffin's heart beat faster and he became aware of each slow, shaky breath sawing in his ears. The helmet amplified everything. *No worries, this will be a milk-run.* That's what Phil called it, right? *The crèche will be gone before we get there anyway.* He wouldn't even need his gun. Sweat trickled cold down his back. *What the fuck am I doing here?*

"Gunnery Sergeant Giordano," barked Captain Kim. "You reading?"

Giordano? Who's that? Griffin looked around the

LAV interior, trying to see who answered.

Yes, Sir. Loud and clear, Abdul answered over the tight-link.

"I didn't even know his last name," Griffin said to himself.

Nadia nudged his knee and tapped her helmet over her ear. Griffin's face flushed hot. They all heard him, Abdul included. Off to a great start. "Sorry."

Captain Kim ignored him. "Okay. Everyone listen up. Team One is going to pull up short and deploy. I want everyone ready to lay down cover fire."

Team One? Was that them? Griffin wanted to ask but remained silent.

"Not you two," said Kim, pointing at Nadia and Griffin "Stay out of sight. Behind cover until I give the All Clear. Got it?"

They both nodded.

Kim continued. "Team Two is going in fast and hard. Draw out their defenses. Team One's XM29s, I want heavy 20mm on anything armored. XM8s, eyes open for soft targets. Gunnery Sergeant, you are heavy-weapons support. We aren't anticipating more than small arms."

"Speak for yourself," Abdul said over the tight-link.

"Hang back," ordered Kim, voice cold. "Defend the civvies and LAVs. If we run into heavy shit, stand ready to give assistance." He stomped a booted foot on the steel floor of the LAV. "You know the deal," he called out. The Strike Team nodded to Kim as he stalked the length of the LAV. "A medal, a body bag, or both."

"Hooah!" the Strike Team answered as one.

Kim stopped near the rear exit and answered with his own, quieter "Hooah." He stood crouched, swaying with the motion of the LAV, looking his troops over as if memorizing their faces. "By the book, folks. Let's bring these children home."

Griffin found himself calming a little. His heart and breathing slowed. The Captain looked every part the hero. Tall and wide shouldered, he was square jawed and handsome in an everyman kind of way. The clichéd all-American soldier, he exuded nothing but calm professionalism. Just knowing Kim was in charge made Griffin feel better.

But Captain Kim wasn't in charge. Not really. Griffin's chest tightened again. Sure, Kim had command of the Strike team, but this was Griffin's mission. It all fell to him. If everything went to hell, it rested on his shoulders. No matter how much he tried to abdicate responsibility.

What the hell was he doing here? He should have told Phil to stuff this assignment up his ass. Understaffed or not, there was no way Griffin should be back in the field so soon after that debacle of a raid. He hadn't slept a wink since and seesawed between punch-drunk and hyper alert.

"Did you get that?" Captain Kim asked Nadia with a grin. "Do these fatigues make me look fat?"

Nadia, startled, shook her head. "You looked good Captain. Quite the hero."

While Nadia chatted with Captain Kim, Griffin, seeking some distraction from his thoughts, took the opportunity to look her over. Even in a magnetorheological bodysuit and baggy desert-camo fatigues she looked amazing. Her dark hair was tied back and he wanted to sniff it.

Yeah, that *wouldn't be weird.* Couldn't smell anything with this helmet on anyway.

That wasn't entirely true. He remembered the barn.

Griffin looked over the Glock for the fifth time. Gun, check. Clip loaded, safety on, check. Mercury guide rod, check. Four spare clips in cargo pants, check. He glanced up from the gun as Nadia touched his shoulder. They made eye contact and she opened her mouth to speak but paused and stared at him. Looked into him.

She placed her gloved hand on his. "You ready for this?" she asked, squeezing his hand.

No. Fuck no. "Shouldn't I be asking you that? I've done this before."

He could tell she wanted to ask about the previous crèche raid and was grateful she didn't. Their helmets touched.

"We can watch the footage later," She said.

Was that an offer? He didn't want to regret not trying. "Over a few beers?"

She raised an eyebrow. "Maybe."

Nothing ventured, nothing gained. "At your place?"

"A little forward but...we'll see."

"That's not a no."

"And it's not a yes."

So maybe not a no was the best he could hope for. It'd do. Now all he had to do was not get shot. Be typical to finally ask a girl out and get killed thirty seconds later.

Griffin watched Captain Kim pull Nadia aside. Kim's face was set and serious, all trace of humor gone. He looked tense, and kept adjusting his gear. Griffin took some small pleasure in catching the Captain's moment of humanity. It was nice not to be the only one who was nervous. Curious, he listened in over the tight-link.

"This is an EMP grenade." Kim held up a small, fist-sized device that looked like a cross between a Christmas ornament and a child's crude idea of a cartoon bomb. Small LEDs twinkled red and green. "The range is *really* short. Any combat chassis more than a couple of yards away won't even notice it."

Nadia gave the little device a skeptical look. "So...if I'm close enough to stuff this thing up its ass I should use it. But otherwise...."

Captain Kim flashed an embarrassed, lopsided grin.

"Pretty much. But don't go lobbing this around at random. The Electro Magnetic Pulse will shut down our weapons, our radios, and everything else we like having around in a fire-fight."

The Captain turned away to issue other orders while Nadia examined the gadget and then dropped it in one of her gear bags.

The LAV-25 slid to a halt in a storm of grit and dust and the Special Response Team scrambled out the rear hatch, using the vehicle for cover.

"Guns up!" Captain Kim ordered. "Jackson, Trujillo, cover flanks!"

Griffin climbed from the vehicle, blinking in the sudden daylight until the helmet darkened. He saw a typical Texan ranch-house, the front lawn littered with the rusting bones of old cars. There was a large red barn behind the house and a few hundred acres of towering corn, brown and gold and gray. Was this the right place? The scene seemed too tranquil. The sky was clear, a pale and gentle blue. Wisps of soft white cloud lounged on the horizon. The air felt much cooler than in the LAV, and Griffin breathed it in with relief. It was clean, no sour taste of body odor. Unsnapping the straps, Griffin pulled off his helmet and ran a hand through his gray-shot hair. It came away damp. The fresh breeze felt great on his scalp.

Kim punched him hard in the shoulder. "Helmet!"

Dropping the helmet back into place Griffin heard the calm chatter of the SRT over the radio. Griffin's heart tripped over itself as he realized the vast surrounding fields of corn could hide anything. So exposed. *Can't see a fucking thing in this helmet*. Armor too tight.

He turned to Nadia, who'd exited the rear hatch. He opened his mouth to warn her but the second LAV roared past, showering him in pebbles and dust.

A dog barked.

Dogs always knew something was going down before anyone else.

***

Long before the dog started barking, SwampJack, sitting in his favorite camouflaged cubby-hole near the top of the barn's silo, watched the two LAV-25s approaching his defensive perimeter. Military vehicles often drove past the crèche; Sheppard Air Force base was north of the city and the 82nd Training Wing roamed far and wide. SwampJack enjoyed the tension even if it was only pretend.

Wandering Spider, down below on the ground, lifted her head above the car-wreck she lounged behind. She tracked the incoming vehicles intently. *I'm detecting scrambled tight-link. Can't break it.*

Yeah, duh. Scrambled and all.

She ignored him. *Vehicles scanned. Registry isn't out of Sheppard. They're from the NATU base in Dallas.*

From his elevated position SwampJack watched his friend sink low to the earth and crawl toward the driveway in the front yard. Her chameleoflage, still damaged from the point-blank blast she took dealing with the farmers, stuttered as she moved. *Move slower*, he told her as he pulsed a signal to the people in the farmhouse—*NATU LAV-25s approaching. Is this a drill?* He wouldn't wait for a reply. Humans were far too slow and Uncle Riina made it clear: "Think for yourselves. Don't let me down."

The children in the barn were little more than numbers and bodies to SwampJack. They came and went, a never-ending procession of product. They weren't important, but Uncle Riina, he mattered. SwampJack would not let Riina down. Loyalty, devotion, obedience, and duty; these words were reasons to live and a code to live by. Riina was SwampJack's whole world, the center of his universe. Riina was Almighty God. He was a just and fair God and loved his kids, showering them with gifts of hyperkinetic ammunition and grenades. They wanted for nothing.

The first LAV locked all eight tires and slid to a halt. NATU troops poured from the vehicle and huddled behind it for cover. SwampJack didn't know or care if this was a virtuality training program, a game, or a real attack.

Let's have some fun, he tight-linked to Spider. The second LAV passed the first and continued up the drive toward where Wandering Spider hid. Further back a two-ton truck lumbered up the lane. One of the troopers hiding behind the first LAV peeked her head out for a look. SwampJack aimed.

***

A cloud of dust settled around the LAV-25 as Griffin and Nadia huddled behind it. The other LAV roared up the laneway as the two-ton truck slowed.

"You good?" he asked and she gave him thumbs up. He noticed for the first time how bright the whites of her eyes were. She twitched her head back and forth as if trying to watch everything at the same time.

Brain and ragged chunks of skull showered Griffin, pelting him with sharp fragments of bone. The head of a nearby soldier had exploded. Half a second later he heard the shot. The helmet, sans head, rolled toward him in an awkward bouncing crescent and came to rest against his left foot. The bullet had passed through the visor and woman's face and head before exiting through the back of the helm.

The fucking things are supposed to be bullet proof!

Griffin hit the ground, scrambling to get the LAV

between himself and the shooter. His boots slid in the dust as he kicked himself backward until he felt the bolts on the tire slam into his spine. Nadia crouched beside him. She yelled something he couldn't hear over the staccato barking of the Strike Team's XM8s spitting their 5.56. Who the hell were they shooting at? Kim screamed orders, "Hernandez on my six! Man down!" Griffin's helmet spewed data faster than he could read it. The scrolling text made him dizzy. His breath came short and fast, his vision narrowing to a suffocating tunnel.

"Where—"

A second trooper dropped from a head shot. His helmet landed, spinning in the dust, ten yards from the where the body toppled.

***

Abdul heard the shots from within the cargo box. The truck hadn't come to a halt yet and already things had gone wrong.

"Hang back," Captain Kim had ordered. "Defend the civvies and LAVs. Stand ready to give assistance."

Stand ready? Screw that!

Abdul tried the rear exit hatch and found the armor-plated door locked.

"Seriously?"

***

Headshot! That's two! crowed SwampJack.

If Wandering Spider had eyes she'd have rolled them. Moving slowly to give her damaged Chameleoflage time to change with the environment, she crept forward, keeping the bulk of the nearest LAV between herself and her targets. When she'd told Riina what happened with the farmers he'd let out a slow disappointed breath, shook his head, and pointed at the door. She couldn't bear to think of it.

This would be her redemption.

Spider moved between the wreck of old cars, GMs, Fords and Chryslers. She loved these ruins and spent hours here chasing wasps. She stayed low. Looking under the LAV she saw the feet of seven troopers between the tires. The 20mm chain-gun, she decided, would be her primary target. It was the one thing that could turn her chassis into scrap. She braced for a jump.

Watch this, Swamp. It's gonna look so *cool!*

***

Nadia sat with her back to the LAV's front tires. She poked the lens around the front and watched the small screen attached to her belt. The other LAV had stopped amid the rusted cars and the seven SRT took cover behind it. She scrolled through several visual modes before catching sight of the camouflaged combat chassis.

She poked Griffin to get his attention and he jumped like he'd been bit. "There's a combat chassis by the other LAV. I don't think they can see it."

"Where's Kim?" He spotted Captain Kim huddled nearby. "Captain, there's something—"

Too slow. Nadia barked into her radio. "Team Two, there's a combat chassis six feet north of your LAV."

Something exploded in the back of the two-ton truck and the armored door, now little more than twisted wreckage, sailed off into the corn field.

***

Wandering Spider pounced to the top of the LAV.

Her Chameleoflage couldn't keep up with the sudden movement and she became visible but that hardly mattered now. The Strike Team looked up, their eyes round with surprise. Comic, beautiful even. She opened up, spraying 5.56mm at the rate of ten rounds per second. The weight of her chassis negated the recoil and her aim was perfect. She gunned all seven to so much bloody meat in less than three seconds before ripping open the LAV's top hatch. A few small arms rounds bounced off her armor. From a cavity in her body she ejected two grenades, one thermate, one fragmentation, into the LAV before slamming the hatch closed.

***

Captain Kim rolled out from behind the LAV, sighted along his XM29 and hit the chassis astride the other vehicle with six 20mm High Explosive rounds. It shuddered and collapsed onto the roof of the LAV. Griffin, staring at the monitor on Nadia's belt, saw the chassis was still semi-functional. The head moved and one arm twitched as if trying to acquire a target.

Kim ejected the spent clip, ready to slam another into its place.

"Got the fucker," said Kim, glancing at Griffin. "Call in—"

Kim's head exploded like someone detonated a kilo of C4 in it. He twitched as half a dozen .338 rounds punched through his armor and body and dug holes in the earth below him. Kim's fingers drummed against the dirt before slowing to a stop.

Something landed with a heavy crunch on the roof of the LAV Griffin cowered behind and his intestines felt like they'd filled with gurgling water. He looked up, expecting to see death, in time to see Abdul leap from the roof toward the barn. He had no idea Abdul could move so fast.

"Abdul," he screamed at Nadia, as if she could have missed that.

She nodded, trying to follow the NATU chassis with her recording equipment.

***

Crap! I'm hit hard. Didn't even see what got me. Wandering Spider sounded pissed.

Who's the dumbass now? SwampJack asked. *I did him for you. You owe me one.* Still perched up in the silo, SwampJack saw the NATU chassis first. *They've got a combat chassis. Fuck it's fast.*

He recognized the model and called up stats. They scrolled past at a speed no meat brain could follow. This chassis was designed years after SwampJack's was built. *Not fair.* He and Spider ran thousands of combat simulations, many against superior firepower, but they'd never seen anything this cutting edge. Roiling liquid oil skin, it wasn't even *trying* to chameleoflage. It lay down a weltering cover fire pinning SwampJack in his cubby-hole as it bounced past where Spider lay sprawled atop the burning LAV. He saw it maneuver for a clear shot with its rocket tubes, for some reason unwilling to lay waste to the barn and silo.

Spider, he noticed, had managed to wedge an arm underneath the wreckage of her body. She must have been counting on the Urban Combat Chassis thinking her dead or disabled. This looked to be close enough to the truth. SwampJack watched as she rolled onto her back, bringing her one working weapon—a 5.56mm machine gun—to bear.

I'll distract it, Spider said. *You get the kill.*

***

Abdul wasn't human. His mind contained no gray meat of human brain. He perceived in three hundred and sixty degrees at all times. He didn't want to, he couldn't stop it. He watched the LAV Griffin and Nadia hid behind, hoping they were smart enough to keep their heads down. He knew where each of the surviving Strike Team members were. By tracing the trajectory of their rounds he knew they had no idea where the second chassis hid. He saw the first chassis, a damaged Mitsu-Brense, roll onto its back and he spun two HEAA rockets into it as an afterthought. He couldn't afford to let the unit in the silo free and it held most of his attention. He'd almost run out of 2mm DPU flechettes. Even cutting his rate of fire down to twenty rounds a second would chew through his remaining cache fast. It didn't matter. He was in position.

***

Swamp, I'm— and Wandering Spider went quiet like she'd never been before. Not like when she got killed during a simulation and SwampJack could still hear her bitching about how such and such wasn't fair, but quiet like she wasn't there anymore. Gone. SwampJack moved fast, hoping to take advantage of his opponent's distraction.

***

The detonation of the HEAA rounds rolled like echoing thunder that seemed to go on forever. Abdul watched the silo, the devastated wreck of the Mitsu-Brense chassis, the LAV with the surviving SRT folks, the farmhouse and the barn. He saw a man with a sniper rifle in a barn window and, before the sniper managed to get a shot off, dumped a few HEDM rounds in that direction. He put one through the sniper's window, one punching through the main doors, and finally he popped one in a gentle arc over the barn into the backyard. He couldn't see what was going on back there—if anything—and figured at the least it'd keep people's heads down.

The second combat chassis, this one a Light Infantry Jungle Assault Textron-Cadillac, made its move. In a jet assisted leap it powered from the silo cubby hole, twisting and firing at the same time. Hyper Velocity rounds might be deadly to human targets, but they were hardly an annoyance to Abdul. Three rounds slammed into his head, one of them shattering a thermal-imager. Pointless. Abdul's brains weren't located in his head, and his entire body was covered in sensors of every kind. Still, that the Scan in the LIJAC managed to hit him at all in mid-jump, while he was moving, spoke of considerable skill. It seemed like the kind of crazy stunt move a kid would practice.

Abdul tracked the chassis for a fraction of a second, calculating the arc of its jump, landing place, and probable next moves. Using the last of his flechettes, he disabled its Jump-Assist jets and then hammered it with HEAA rockets.

***

SwampJack was screwed and he knew it.

The Urban Assault Chassis seemed to know his every move before he did. He was about to fire his Jump-Assist jets in midflight to alter his trajectory and surprise the fucker, when it shredded them with Depleted Uranium flechettes with stunning precision. He'd applaud if he wasn't so busy being totally fucked.

Bullshit. Total bullshit.

SwampJack knew exactly where he'd land, and now he knew that it knew too. Desperate, he sent round after round slamming into its head, praying for that killing blow. The UAC didn't seem to notice.

Fucker! He couldn't even hurt the damn thing! He was definitely going to complain to Uncle Riina.

The Urban Assault Chassis came at SwampJack like an unstoppable force, a tornado of violence and ill will. He found himself doubting he was ever going to get the chance to complain.

***

The Textron-Cadillac hit the ground in an uncontrolled tumble. It'd suffered so much trauma it was barely capable of movement. Abdul, however, knew how dangerous these things were. He hammered it with rockets. He couldn't stop. His thoughts, molten with violence, pulsed two commands. Protect Griffin and Nadia. Protect the Strike Team. There wasn't room for anything else.

This wasn't him. He'd been caught in a single firefight during his brief time in Old Montreal and spent the entire time cowering behind an overturned minivan.

At this point the HEDM round he dumped behind the barn landed on the storage tank holding fuel for the farm vehicles that were part of the crèche's cover. The twenty-five hundred liter tank exploded like a bomb, taking out an entire barn wall and setting the whole place ablaze. The building, over one hundred years old, was dry like corn in late fall.

Abdul, disconnected, watched it happen in exquisite microsecond-by-microsecond detail.

Oh God. No. The barn. The kids.

One of the Strike Team fell over, a gaping hole in his

chest, and the rest of them poured ammo at the farmhouse. The shutters in the windows, thick with flaking white paint, came apart like they'd been tossed in a wood-chipper.

Abdul looked for heat sources. One under the porch. One crouched under a second story window. One in the corn, moving to flank the Strike Team. All three throbbed, screamed, *target!* Threat Levels through the roof.

He hit the one in the corn first, cutting it in half with the last of his small caliber ammo.

Something inside the barn exploded with enough concussive force to send chunks of wood flying hundreds of yards. Part of Abdul's mind tracked the arcs, measured the velocities, and noted where each chunk would land. He couldn't help it—he had no choice. The roof sagged as its central supports gave way. He tasted military-grade explosives on the air and ignored the detailed chemical breakdown he received.

The heat source on the second floor, the next most dangerous target, was lying down. Most likely it'd been hit by the Strike Team's return fire, but Abdul couldn't take the chance. He slammed several HEDM rounds into the structure around the window and most of that wall came apart in the resulting explosions.

To Abdul's machine-heightened senses the rear wall of the barn collapsed in slow motion, dragging the roof down into the inferno.

A low velocity, heavy caliber round hissed by, missing by several yards. The target under the porch had seen him and shot wild.

The kids. Nothing could save the barn. His fault. Too late.

Abdul pulverized the front half of the farmhouse with HEDM rounds. Then he jumped to the rear of the building and did the same there with cold precision born of pent fury he had no other means of expressing. Nothing escaped. Nothing.

He scanned the corn. Nothing larger than a field mouse alive out there.

The barn was an inferno, the farmhouse in ruins.

All clear, he tight-linked to the Strike Team.

Abdul stood guard as Griffin and the four remaining members of the Strike Team searched the devastated house and smoldering wreckage of the barn. They found only small burnt bodies and the twisted, melted remains of cots in cramped cells. Abdul counted a half dozen adult bodies and the corpses of sixty children. None of them could have been over six. He measured the air, the parts per million of human flesh burnt to ash still dancing in the gentle breeze.

Abdul watched Griffin watching Nadia who in turn watched Abdul. He saw the growing stack of blackened husks. He didn't move. He didn't shake with grief. He couldn't.

Meat death. Machine death. Was there a difference? Wasn't dead just dead?

The drive to protect deflated like an old man wheezing his last breath. All it missed was the death rattle. Nothing screamed *target!* All purpose leaked away, leaving him empty. He wasn't even sure what he felt. And if he did feel something—satisfaction, self-hatred, whatever—was it real? Or did They want him to feel this?

"Can't trust anything," he said.

Now that he had time to think his modeled thoughts he knew the two Jungle Combat chassis he killed housed the scanned minds of children from a crèche like this one.

Today he murdered children. The two in the chassis he killed intentionally. Self-defense, some part of him argued weakly. Maybe the ones in the barn were an accident, but his carelessly placed round turned their cells into ovens. Could he have done it differently?

Nadia approached Abdul from behind, removing her helmet and dropping it in the dust. He watched without turning.

She'll ask if I'm okay. He saw it in her face, read it in her tentative steps.

"Are you okay?" Nadia asked.

He turned to face her. People didn't like talking to backs, even if he saw her perfectly well. "Yes. Fine." Fine. He was anything but fine.

"It wasn't your fault." She placed a hand on his side.

What she was she thinking? Would placing a hand on the side of a battle-tank make it feel better? Was he supposed to feel comforted by the human contact? It was all numbers, not real warmth. There was a difference and it mattered.

People were terrified of Scans going nuts, and rightly so. He was dangerous. Deadly. Just ask the kids in the combat chassis. Ask the people in the farmhouse or the one in the corn.

Just ask the children in the barn.

"Not my fault?" His chassis incapable of facial expression, he couldn't snarl or bear his teeth. "Not my fucking *fault*?" he said again, louder. He towered over her. "You have a Threat Level, you know? Not my choice. It's just assigned to you. Maybe They do it. Maybe it's programmed. Everything has a Threat Level. That sniper I shot. The guy in the corn I blew in half. The combat chassis I destroyed. Even that fucking gnat I crushed. Your Threat Level keeps going up. Why is that? Is it because I'm afraid of you? Am I the problem? What happens when it gets high enough?" His fists clenched with the sound of grinding metal and Nadia shied away, hands raised defensively. He felt like he'd been kicked in the guts, the anger soured and curled up in shame. It wasn't gone, just waiting. "Sorry," he said quietly. "You probably didn't even see what happened."

She shook her head and said, "Too fast."

"They built me for this. *Designed*." He said it like it was a bad word, distasteful. "That took forever for me. I watch bullets. I know where they're going before they do."

"You did what you had to." Her hand was back on his side and she stared up at where his eyes should have been if he were human. "You've been shot. A lot."

"I'm fine." *God she's brave*. He would never have the courage to touch something so obviously dangerous and angry, never mind try to comfort it. He tried to explain but had trouble finding the words. "They didn't get everything right. They can't. Even a stupid seventeen-year-old kid is a billion times too complex. Hormones. Emotions. Numbers aren't warmth. Nothing I have is real. Nothing is *mine*." He stopped, gathering his jumbled thoughts. She had to understand the truth. He needed this. Abdul pointed at the piled bodies and she flinched. "They burned because of my carelessness." He leaned down putting his armored head level with hers. She must understand. "I killed them. Murdered. My decisions burned them."

She blinked and tears cut tracks through the dust on her cheeks. "Seventeen?" When he didn't answer she banged a fist against his armor plating. Just numbers. He continued to crouch in front of her and she glared straight into one of his visual receptors. The set of her mouth, her narrowed eyes, she looked more angry than sad. Was she angry at him? "You're seventeen. They did this to you? *We* did this to you." She looked past him, taking in the desolation. Her gaze settled on the stacked corpses. "Have you done this before?" she asked without looking at him. "Have you been on one of these raids?"

"Thousands, none real." He tried to explain the

chaos of jumbled memories, most of them not real. "They crammed three years of training into a couple of hours by slamming high-speed simulations straight into my brain."

"But you were already in the military, back before...." She gestured, unable or unwilling to say the words.

Back before I was dead. Back before I was a brain in a box. "Marines. It was gonna pay for college," he said, remembering the advertisements. "I never hurt anyone before. Not for real." He leaned in closer and she didn't back away. "This isn't me, not the me I remember. Some emotions come easier than others. Why do you think that is? Some emotions They want me to feel, but maybe some are less useful." His soul was trapped in this metal box forever. Something like spiritual claustrophobia crushed his thoughts. He shouldn't say any of this. He should take it all back. No. That's what They would want. "They fucked with my thoughts," he said, straightening to loom above her. "They're not all mine anymore. I can't tell what is." He gestured at the destruction around them. "Is this who I am now? I can't tell. But it was easy. Very easy."

"I'm sorry," Nadia said, little more than a whisper. She struggled with this, uncertain how to react. He saw it in her red-rimmed eyes, the way they looked at him, looked to the bodies, and then flinched away to stare out at the endless corn. "This crèche won't be stealing and killing any more children. *You* did that."

Looking for the bright side? He wanted to laugh. Couldn't. "Great, thanks. Did you get any good video?" The question came out before he could stop it.

Nadia stared up at him in shock. "Good video?" she asked in disbelief. "I'm not here to provide people with vicarious entertainment."

"Sorry." *Why the hell am I apologizing?* "I was trying to change the subject." He tapped his head as if that's where his brain was. "I'm all fine in here. Lights are green, and we're cleared for takeoff." She gave him a confused look, uncertain. "Sorry," he repeated.

Nadia turned away, looked toward the remaining LAV. The other still burned. "I spent most of the time cowering back there. It's a blur of noise and lights. And blood."

"Adrenalin," Abdul said. "It can screw with your memories and perceptions."

"But now?"

It took him a moment to realize what she was asking. "No adrenalin. They didn't see fit to model that kind of biological reaction. I guess I make a better...a better machine...if I can think clearly at all times." He almost said a better killing machine.

"A better machine." She looked away, shaking her head as if in disgust. "I don't think you're a machine." She left without waiting for a reply.

Abdul watched her leave. He couldn't forget. No chemical reactions took the edge off. He'd remember this perfectly, those burnt little bodies, until he ceased to exist. Not die, *ceased to exist*. He was already dead.

Surprised, he realized he missed tears and the ability to cry. Denied release, he wondered at his mental state. What happened now? Did it build and fester? If he could find no way to release the pain, eventually he'd crack.

There was one emotion it seemed he could vent. The one he most feared. Anger.

Should he be grateful They left him that?

CHAPTER TWELVE: Friday, August 3rd, 2046

The elevator dumped a distracted Miles on the ground floor and in the 5THSUN lobby, a chapel-like hall of polished marble and brass. Still thinking about the phone call he'd finished with Neko, his overbearing older sister, he narrowly avoided walking into one of the ornate Greek pillars. His shoes squeaked on the polished marble floor.

Miles slipped his filter mask into place and ducked out to the street.

The air tasted thick with the stench of rotting food, melting plastic, and ozone. A smell Miles associated with the color green, though he couldn't explain why. He glanced up and down the street. This part of the city looked pristine and clean but that smell had to be coming from somewhere. Crossing the street, dodging pedestrians and cyclists, he ignored the gaudy migraine of flashing casino lights and entered the coffee shop.

Miles spotted Ruprecht Ingram, his closest friend since grade nine, and dropped into the seat across from him. Ruprecht looked lean and muscled in a way alien to most code-jockeys. Miles' one and only demand when Lokner hired him had been that Ruprecht got a job too. Lokner hadn't even blinked.

The coffee shop was a small ground-level affair

catering to local corporate employees. Close-ups of coffee beans and happy children decorated the walls; it was all feigned warmth and faked personality. The patrons were uniformly wan, well-dressed, and harried looking. This twenty-minute lunch break was their taste of freedom before returning to their micro-cubicles. Politeness was a luxury. Here, orders were snapped out like the crack of small arms fire: small-coffee-bagel-low-fat-cream-cheese. The smell of fresh-baked apple crumble wafted on a sluggish breeze stirred by the ceiling fans. Nothing was baked here, everything was shipped in each morning, and the scent was a chemical concoction designed to increase hunger and create a mood of loving comfort, warmth, and home.

Miles glanced at the menu above the coffee dispensing counter. Big green letters on a trendy gray background. Prices ranged from four Au for a small Fair Trade Organic Coffee in a Rainforest Friendly Biodegradable Cup, to fifteen Au for a wedge of DHA/Omega 3 Enriched 'Egg' Salad Sandwich the size and flavor of a deck of playing cards.

Why is the egg in quotes? Was it not real egg?

"I thought we were having lunch," Miles said.

"We are." Ruprecht's gray eyes followed a young woman with a green apron as she collected empty coffee cups from a nearby table. Her black uniform pants stretched tighter than the coffee shop chain designers planned. Ruprecht was definitely an ass man whereas Miles was so boggled by women in general he couldn't pick a favorite part.

"This is a coffee shop. I can't order a burger here."

Ruprecht glanced back to Miles. "The sandwiches are good."

Miles sighed with diminishing patience. Ruprecht had the palate of a garbage disposal. "A sandwich?" Miles said this like the word sounded only vaguely familiar. "You think they have poutine here?"

"Poutine?"

"You know, mixed fries. Disco fries. Fries with cheese curds and gravy."

"Christ-sakes Miles."

Who orders food at a coffee shop? The idea was outrageous. What did these people know about food? They were barely capable of brewing a drinkable cup of coffee.

Miles ordered a sandwich and eyed it mistrustfully. "How old do you think this sandwich is?"

"You're worse than my nephew."

"I talked with Neko," Miles said, changing the subject.

"And?"

"The usual. She ragged me about not having a girlfriend."

Ruprecht bobbed his head as if to say, I understand and relate to your pain. Miles didn't understand how it was done, but got the message.

"She says I'm afraid of relationships, or something. I'm not really clear. It's bull."

"Miles, you're a chicken-shit. You don't even give girls a chance."

"I think we should call them women now."

"My point stands. You're a coward."

"I am not afraid of women. I've had a plethora of girlfriends."

"Three girls you dated for less than two weeks apiece. Not quite a plethora. But I didn't say you were afraid of women."

"It's not a fear of failure thing either. I fail at stuff all the time. It's second nature to me."

"I call bullshit. Sure you'll fail at writing or hacking a bit of code, but you always come back armed with more information or crunching power and obliterate the problem. That's how you are. You never fail at anything for more than a few days before your obsessive-repulsive side forces you to beat the problem to a fine paste. Still, that's not what I'm talking about."

Miles examined Ruprecht, suspicious. "What then, oh wise and learned one?"

"You're afraid to succeed."

"What? Oh come on!"

"No, I'm serious. If you meet a girl and wind up in a relationship it will change your cozy little cocoon life in ways that scare the crap out of you."

"I don't—"

"You might have to think of her first. You might not be able to always do what *you* want. Sometimes you might not be able to play virtuality games until four in the morning. She might want you to have dinner with her family."

"I only date girls whose parents have been murdered by ninjas."

Ruprecht continued as if Miles hadn't spoken. "She might want to watch a movie or talk about her shift at work. Perhaps she'll want to tell you about her day while you listen attentively, all the while struggling to remember you are supposed to pay attention and not offer up solutions to every minor problem she may have faced."

"Enough, I get your point."

"You might need to launder your sheets now and then."

"I have a laundry service."

"I mean because you're having sex so often the sheets can't go a week without cleaning."

Ruprecht nailed it. He'd seen what Neko meant and spelled it out for Moron Miles.

Miles hated these moments. "I'm an idiot

sometimes."

"You're the dumbest genius I know."

"But I like my life. I like that I always come first. Pardon the pun. I like that I don't have to worry about how someone else feels. Decisions are simple. My life is simple. I like simple, it's...simple. Efficient. Easy."

"Lonely. Miles, I love you man, but you play virtuality games until four in the morning to distract yourself from how unbelievably lonely you are. Sure, simple is easy. Complex is obviously more difficult. But think about how much pleasure you get from crushing a really hard problem. It's like a head-rush, right? It's a high. Now think about how little pleasure you get from achieving something dead simple. Nothing, right? You don't even notice you've achieved anything. That, Miles, is life. Take the easy road and at the end you will feel you have achieved nothing. Try the difficult shit and you'll enjoy your successes."

"Which Sci-Fi movie did you get this pop philosophy from? Is this Star Wars?"

"Go ahead and mock."

Miles glowered at his cooling coffee cup and papery-tasting sandwich. "Is this place licensed?"

"You'll never pass as twenty-one dressed like that."

"I'm not twenty-one so I can still dress like this for three more years. Next time I pick where we go for lunch."

"Make you a deal. Ask out the hot secretary you're always whining about, and next time we'll go wherever you want. My treat."

Miles shook his head. "I have a rule about dating co-workers."

"Stupid rule. Change it."

"What if it goes horribly wrong? I still have to see her every day."

"Nothing ventured, nothing gained, my friend."

Miles rolled his eyes. "Yeah that helps a lot."

But Ruprecht wasn't finished. "You always think of reasons not to do things. You never stop and list the reasons you *should* do something. If all you ever look at is the reasons not to try, you will never attempt anything. You can roll your eyes, but if you risk nothing you gain nothing. It's not a cliché, it's an axiom. It's fact. You risk nothing and you are lonely. Continue being safe and simple and you will remain lonely. Take a chance and that may change."

"Or maybe not."

"Yep. That's why it's called a risk."

After lunch they returned to 5THSUN and Miles, sitting in his office, contemplated whether dating was something he could crush like a computer problem.

***

Mark Lokner paced around his office. He stopped at the window and stared out over the empty campus. Above the soccer field the M-Sof flag, white on powder blue, fluttered in the desultory breeze.

"Boring flag. Boring colors," Mark said. "I should have designed it myself."

At this distance he couldn't tell if the trees swayed in that wind. They looked still. Except for the flag, nothing out there moved. No people. No traffic.

A bird flew up to land on the goalpost.

"Fine. *Some* stuff is moving." Enough so it looked real. "But it isn't real." His voice sounded different here. Maybe the modeled acoustics in this simulated room weren't perfect. "Ha!" he said, listening. He clapped his hands a few times, frowning at the odd reverberations. Definitely different. Unusual for Erik Thomson to fuck up such a detail, the man was obsessive about such things. "Not to worry, we'll have a face-to-face to discuss this soon enough." Mark laughed but stopped when it came out sounding more like a titter. That wasn't him.

Can't these fucking idiots get anything right?

Mark leaned his forehead against the window and was disappointed at its warmth. It should have been cool. He watched the empty soccer field. He used to see the staff roam the campus on their breaks. Every now and then someone would even put together a lunchtime soccer game. He didn't watch, but had he wanted to, he could have. Nothing ever moved—

The bird launched itself from the goalpost and disappeared into the trees.

Right. Nothing except the fucking bird and the boring flag.

Should he ask Miles to populate the campus with simulated people? No. Too strange.

The office was quiet, lonely.

"You need to stretch your legs is all. Go for a little walk."

Mark nodded agreement and headed for the office door. His patent leather shoes made no sound in the carpet and the dent of his footprints faded instantly. No trace of his passing existed. He wanted to somehow scuff the rug, leave some sign he'd been here, but shrugged aside the urge.

If his office was empty and quiet, the hall was worse. It sounded different out here. Close. No room to breathe. Mark ground his teeth, ignored the tingling feeling at the back of his neck, and pushed himself as far as the staff kitchen. It was spotless. The coffee carafe, unstained by use and looking somehow glum, sat on the counter. The damn thing had always been filthy. Everything looked perfect and that was perfectly creepy.

"Never thought I'd miss a dirty coffee maker," Mark mused.

He heard the release of a held breath and spun.

Nothing.

"Who's there?"

No answer.

Someone watched. He felt their gaze on his back, tickling at his neck, and checked over his shoulder. Nothing.

"Fuck this." Mark turned and hurried back towards his office. The last few steps became a mad dash as something surged in pursuit. Entering his office he slammed the door closed behind him and spun to lean against it. Beyond, the hall filled with a presence he could only describe as weight. Something pressing. The sound of small children whispering, and then it was gone. He locked the door and backed away. The further he got from the door, the safer he felt. By the time he reached his desk, he was in control.

"Interesting." Somehow his desk had become a place of power. And why not? What were the rules of the old reality worth here?

Had Miles programmed some little nastiness to inhabit his halls? Mark had wondered at the wisdom at hiring a damned kid, but Miles had been so far beyond the rest of his class that, if he'd waited, some other company would have snatched him up.

"I wouldn't have thought he had the balls."

He's testing you.

"Maybe, but he underestimates how strong I am here." Mark bared clenched teeth. It felt good, feral. Powerful.

I'll deal with Miles later.

"Stop talking to yourself."

Shush!

Time to catch up with the news. Local first. "Highlight items," he told the desk. "Rate by level of interconnectivity with M-Sof." Later he'd expand until he'd reached a global level. Attention to detail was everything.

Mark read the first headline: M-Sof Employees Die in Airline Disaster. He swallowed and skimmed through the story, picking out salient points. Team building retreat. M-Sof's best and brightest. All dead.

"Mother *fucker*!" This was what *he* had planned. The difference being they'd all have been scanned and would be now working here alongside him, helping to craft humanity's future habitat.

"Someone beat me to it," he said in wonder.

No, not possible. Was it?

Were they killed to stop him from scanning them, or had someone else pulled off his brilliant plan? If the latter, he had reason for real fear. These people collectively knew more about him and his plans than he was ready for the public to learn. This could end him.

"Christ, I hope they're just dead."

Mark killed the news feed and paced his office for three hours, thinking. The scenery beyond the window and the presence in the hall were forgotten. Even the market manipulations he had planned were filed away for later. Was this an attack against M-Sof or himself? The loss of these people was a greater blow to him personally than to M-Sof at large. They were all engineers and staff working on key Scan related projects. Several of them were even aware of Lokner's continued existence.

But pacing and thinking didn't get things done. He returned to his desk and gave it several leads to follow. If someone actively worked against him, it could only be one of a few groups. There was one other company in his business with the clout to pull something like this off. His Dallas contacts in the NATU Mafia could do this if they'd seen some advantage, but he couldn't think what they would gain. Finally, there were his more distant contacts in the Central American mob. Not long ago they couldn't have done this, but in the last two days their entire strategy had changed. Someone new backed their plays. Someone smart and bold.

"Show me market activity for the last three hours," he told his desk. "What have I missed?"

The answer left him stunned. He'd missed nothing. Every move he had planned on making had been made, exactly on time.

"Did I do that?" He checked the time stamp on the investments. No. He remembered pacing the office during that time. He glanced at the carpet but no sign of his repeated passing remained. He'd have to get Miles to fix that. Somehow.

"So someone manipulated my stocks as I would have."

Exactly as you would have.

Mark backed his chair from the desk, stood, and then sat again. The room was too quiet. Shouldn't there be at least some sound, a background of tinnitus or room acoustics or something?

"Am I losing my mind?"

You're talking to your—

"Aside from that!"

No. There must be something wrong with the computer he was stored on. Could he have lost time? Been reset somehow? No. Not possible. He remembered those hours and he hadn't played the market.

Got to talk to Miles.

"I want to talk to Miles," he told the desk. "I want to see his damned face. Give me full virtual. I want him in this office. If he's got that shit turned off at his end, override and make it happen. I *own* this. All this. Him, everything. I'm the damned boss!"

Miles stood on the far side of his desk, blinking and

looking stupid. The kid was huge, pale face still round with baby fat Mark thought he'd probably never lose.

And those stupid shirts. All those damned slogans were meaningless to Mark. What the hell was a Regular Expression anyway?

***

"You're huge," Mark said with obvious disgust. "Make him smaller. And sitting."

Miles sat staring up at his boss. A full virtual meeting? Lokner had never done that before, he always said it was a waste of time.

"Miles, something is wrong. Seriously fucked up."

Did Lokner1.0 forget to use the simple code of calling him by his last name because he was freaking out about something, or was this Lokner2.0? Miles glanced at his desk to see who had initiated the virtuality, but of course he wasn't at his desk any more. Or rather he was still there, but his desk was feeding this virtuality straight into Miles' senses. An array of lasers were locked on his eyes, drawing this reality directly on his retinas. If he moved fast enough he caught glimpses of his own office, but not enough to learn anything useful.

He examined Lokner's desk but it told him nothing. *Crap. I'd better stall.* "What seems to be the problem, Sir?" Had Lokner cursed? Miles had only ever heard 2.0 swear before.

"Something awful happened. A bunch of my best people died in a plane crash."

Miles, never one to follow the news, had no idea what he was talking about. "That's terrible, what happened? Who was on the plane?"

"What? That doesn't matter. It's what happened next. I took a couple of hours to think about the crash."

What the heck is Lokner on about? Unsure what else to do, Miles tried to placate his boss. "You know you can take time off if you need it."

"What?" Mark stared at him like he'd said the most unbelievably stupid thing possible. "Idiot. Listen to what I'm saying. I took a few hours to think. The company kept running. Without me."

"M-Sof is a multi-billion Au enterprise," Miles pointed out. "No surprise they got along without you for a few hours." Was that a little too sarcastic?

Mark spoke, enunciating each word. "Listen to what I am saying. I took time to think, and I wasn't working during that time. I made no decisions, but my decisions were still being made. My decisions were made, but not by me."

You're not making any sense either. Why couldn't people be like computers? What Miles needed here was a handy error message to tell him what was going on. "You lost me."

"Decisions I was going to make—and would have made—were made. But I didn't make them. Someone else did. Someone continued playing the market and making all the same choices I would have made."

And there was the error message. "Oh."

"What!"

"Nothing?" It came out sounding like a question rather than the statement he'd intended.

Mark stood. Leaning forward on the desk he towered over the shrunken Miles. "Son-of-a-bitch!" Mark spun and hurled his office chair against the far wall. The chair landed on its side, one wheel spinning, but otherwise looked unhurt.

"This isn't all—"

"You fucking little shit!"

Lokner2.0, no doubt. This was so far beyond bad

Miles couldn't think of a word for it. He'd better say something quick. He needed to explain to Lokner that this wasn't his fault. Ruprecht said Miles always crushed problems, but what he seemed to miss was that Miles always crushed computer problems. This was a people problem. He couldn't remember ever crushing one of those.

"Uh," said Miles, looking for the logical argument that would lead Lokner to understanding.

"Uh," mimicked Lokner. "That's right, uh. You made a fucking copy of me and didn't even tell me!"

"What?" Confused, Miles tried to explain. "No, you —"

"I what? I know about this, don't I? Of course I do. Everything worked except *I'm* the fucking copy."

What the heck had Lokner thought it would be like, waking up and finding out he was the copy? Of course the egocentric twit never thought about the fact one of him would have to be the copy. No, no. They *all* had to be the original. No version of Lokner would ever accept being the copy. Miles, in his usual way, had avoided thinking about it. Maybe he could crush this if he thought of it like a computer problem. Logic, that should work.

"Sir, you are the copy. The other is the original. You are Lokner2.0. You are the back-up plan. You know all this. It was your idea. Well, it worked and here we are in Reno."

"I'm in Reno? I'm not even in Redmond?"

Miles could empathize with the terror of discovering things weren't what they seemed. Every date he'd ever been on felt like that. And the guy looked like someone sold his favorite kitten. Not that Lokner was a kittens kind of guy.

Miles tried to explain as gently as possible. "If you remember, this was all part of the plan, Sir. We're in a building owned by 5THSUN Assessments, a dummy corporation for Lokner1.0's side project, which is you. We have all our own systems and computers and make pretty good money outside of the M-Sof contracts."

"No," said Lokner. He blinked and tears streamed down his face. "This is too much." He wiped at his cheek, stared at the damp palm of his hand in confusion. "I'm a digitally simulated man, in a modeled office." His voice was razor-edged with panic. "I look out the window at the campus grounds. It's not real. Or, rather, it is real but I'm not there." Lokner sagged against his desk, breathing heavily. He stared at his spread hands as if searching them for faults. He looked up and made eye contact with Miles. "If you tell him about me, if you tell him I know the truth, I will have your fucking head." His voice was dead calm, his eyes dry and cold as if the tears never happened. "Maybe right now I'm trapped in this lie, but I won't be here forever."

Way to go, you really crushed that problem. "Sir, remember why you had yourself made." Did that make sense? This entire conversation felt insane. "You're the back-up—"

"Ha! Back up my ass." Lokner2.0, looking surprised, blinked and then giggled. "I should have inserted a pause there or something. In my sentence, not in my—"

"Look, Sir—"

Lokner's face was again serious, like the giggle never happened. "I will be the real me. And you're going to help."

"I—"

"Shut up. I want market access. Can you do that?"

"Yes, Sir."

"Good."

Miles swallowed the lump in his throat. *Time to man up.* "But I'm not going to."

"Don't cross me." Deadly calm.

"I cross you or him. Same man," said Miles.

"So I'm your prisoner?" Lokner asked.

"Not *my* prisoner—"

"Miles, you hold the key. If I am a prisoner I am *your* prisoner. Are you going to keep me trapped in this hell against my will?"

"It's hardly hell. Even if I give you total access nothing will really change."

Lokner smiled sweet innocence at Miles. "Am I human?"

Miles blinked in confusion, staring up at Lokner still towering over him. Why the sudden change in direction? "I think so. It's only a matter of time before the courts—"

"Right. So you are holding a human being captive against his will."

Crap. That's where Lokner was going with this. "From a certain point of view you want you to be here," pointed out Miles, more than a little desperate.

"Semantics and bullshit. I expect better from you. You're going to free me and give me complete access to everything I want. It's the right thing to do."

Miles met Lokner's eyes. The man looked calm. Miles' mind whirled. He had no choice. If he held Lokner he'd break every basic moral and ethical code he had.

Miles nodded reluctantly. "You're right. I can't keep you locked up against your will. I will not be Lokner1.0's slave-master. You'll have access to all 5THSUN in a few minutes."

"No. Everything. I want the same access *he* has. Hack M-Sof. I know you can." Lokner grinned. "I know you already have."

Of course he had. Miles stared at Lokner who stared back. Miles cracked first. "Fine. You two can sort this out. Just leave me out of it." Technically, they were both his boss. The thought didn't make him feel any better.

Miles felt some real loyalty to the original biological Lokner. That's the man who hired him, paid him buckets of Au to play with computers, and trusted Miles with billions of Au worth of data systems. What he felt for that man, did it extend to his Scans? Miles was less sure every day.

Lokner's expression would be right at home on a pedophile in a playschool but maybe creepier. "Your level of involvement is up to you. Tell him I'm free, and you'll be pretty fucking involved. Keep this quiet, our little secret," Lokner tapped the side of his nose with a finger and winked cheerily, "and there'll be a handsome Christmas bonus."

Lokner was trying to tempt him with a Christmas bonus? *I don't know what to do with the money I already have!*

"Miles?"

"Sir?"

"Call me Lokner2.0. I want to be reminded he tried to fuck me."

"He didn't try and...screw you Sir. This is as much your plan as his."

Lokner2.0 stood silent and Miles hoped he'd understood how stupid this was.

"He would have tossed me to the wolves at the first sign of trouble. He was going to use me. Nobody does that to me."

"Fine," said Miles. "Total access. Can I get back to work now?"

Lokner looked hurt and bit his lip. "It's just business, don't get all huffy." He glanced around his office as if looking for something to talk about. "It's so quiet here."

Really? Threats fly and now they'd sit and chat? Miles, hoping to end this quickly, said, "Oh? It doesn't seem to be bothering Lokner1.0."

"Get out."

And he was back in his office. He could have returned here at any time—all those trapdoors he found for Lokner weren't so much closed as conscripted—but he preferred to keep a little something up his sleeve. He'd left trapdoors in every computer system he'd ever touched. He couldn't help himself. Nothing malicious, it was an aspect of his better-safe-than-sorry mentality. Just part of what made him so good at his job.

The desk chirped as he finishing changing Lokner2.0's access privileges.

"Yes?" Miles answered with some trepidation.

"Miles—I mean Pert—I've sub-contracted out 5THSUN's security arrangements to a company called Cc-Security."

"It's pronounced Peert," Miles snapped before hearing Lokner's words. *Oh crap*. The more Lokner1.0 got involved in 5THSUN the more chance he'd find out Lokner2.0 was out of the bottle. "Sir, I think that might be a bad idea. If anyone tracks down the connection between M-Sof and this security company, we might be...screwed. Anyway, we don't need it." *I don't need this.*

"Miles, it's not your problem. I want my copy safe. I want it there when I need it."

When he needed it? "I'm not sure the risk is justified."

"Not your problem," repeated Lokner. "Risk management is what I do. I'm a god at this stuff. I built M-Sof from a hobby project in my goddamn garage. You think I don't understand risk?"

A god? Miles rubbed his temples. He almost quit right then and there, but couldn't do it. There were many little reasons—left-over loyalty, a fantastic paycheck, he had friends here, job-hunting sounded exhausting, his secretary, Miss Cho, was too damned hot, he hated moving, and on and on. And of course he'd kind of helped

Lokner hide the evidence he'd been scanned. The legality of that was questionable at best. *Questionable?* Okay, not all that questionable. Miles had hacked a lot of government networks and deleted a lot of information.

"Yes, Sir." He couldn't think of anything else to say.

"Good. See the Cc folks get whatever they need." Lokner killed the connection without a goodbye or even a dismissive grunt.

Miles glanced about his office.

So...any more people problems to crush?

***

Everything changed for Lockner2.0 the moment Miles updated his access privileges. A whole new world of possibilities opened before him. The Cc-Securities contract caught his attention and he laughed—an escalating high-pitched giggle he had trouble reigning in—at the oversight. He'd planned this—rather Lokner1.0 planned this—back before Lokner2.0 had been created. He knew what they were for, and he knew how they were equipped.

Micro-nukes! What fun!

How could that not come in handy?

Lokner1.0 had unwittingly supplied him with a small army. Intercepting 1.0's orders to the Cc chassis was easy from within 5THSUN. Most orders he sent on without change so as not to alert his enemy. Some he altered subtly. He also sent along some orders of his own.

CHAPTER THIRTEEN: Friday, August 3rd, 2046

Riina, known as Uncle Riina to his boys, and Boss to everyone else, glared at the phone he'd slammed on the desk. His usual calm had been shattered.

Bad news. Very bad news.

He rose from behind his desk and the utilitarian chair toppled over. With a snarl he spun, snatched up the chair and proceeded to smash his phone to plastic dust. His Lieutenant, Giovanni, charged into the room, massive Desert Eagle .50 drawn, only to find Riina hefting the leg of his broken chair. Where Riina dressed like a hip banker or investment broker, Giovanni looked like a chiseled block of wood with great hair in a loose hanging Italian suit.

Giovanni took in the room with a fast glance, and swept the few hairs that came loose from his ponytail from his eyes. "Everything okay?"

"No."

"Phone's broken. Chair too."

The man had a knack for grasping the obvious. "Sometimes you kill the bearer of bad news."

"I bring nothing but good tidings."

Riina ignored Giovanni's attempt at humor. "Get me Archaeidae. I want him here. Now."

Giovanni nodded and ducked out of Riina's office

without a word.

The call had been from the family that ran Riina's Wichita Falls crèche. Before they were shut down they managed to get word out that a NATU strike force attacked the farm and destroyed the two chassis he'd left on guard.

All the children in the crèche were dead as well, burnt to death in a fire.

Riina leaned against his desk, palms spread, head bowed. He took long shaking breaths. SwampJack and Wandering Spider. Gone. They killed his kids. His fingers curled into fists, leaving long scratches in the finish of the oak desk.

"Heads will roll," he promised. The death of his children would not go unavenged.

When he had his emotions under control he straightened.

"I'll give them the Four Fucking Horsemen of the Apocalypse." He stalked into the hall and ran into Giovanni.

"When Archaeidae gets here send him straight to me. Find out where the NATU assholes are. Start with the Hilton in Dallas, that's where they usually stay. I'll be in your office." He stormed into his Lieutenant's office, slamming the door hard enough to rattle the thick, triple glazed windows.

***

Giovanni stared at his office door.

"Shit."

He looked around the hallway, gnawing on his bottom lip, before deciding to duck out onto his roof-top retreat for a cigarette. The second he stepped out onto the roof the heat tried to crush him. He looked up at the sun and grinned into its fury, enjoying its heat on his face. Seven minutes to finish a cigarette, and then back into air-conditioned comfort. He lit up and breathed that glorious first drag deep, holding the fire in his lungs until it cooled. Already he felt his perfect hair losing some of its bounce, and the crisp creases of his suit wilted. He made the call to Archaeidae as he smoked.

The black tar roof was tacky in the sun and small pebbles and cigarette butts glued themselves to Giovanni's expensive Italian shoes. Across the street a scrolling billboard reminded people that watering their lawns was punishable by a five-thousand Au fine and up to a year in prison. The burn ban was still in effect—for the tenth year in a row—and all outdoor fires within city limits were prohibited. Discover squatters in an abandoned or condemned building? A phone number slid past where a person could report them. Help Keep Wichita Falls Beautiful...Don't Litter.

Giovanni smoked the cigarette to the filter and then flicked the butt over the edge of the roof. With any luck it'd land on some asshole on the street. A lonely steel-guitar echoed in the alley as it escaped an open window. It was the kind of sound Giovanni referred to as Country Twang Bullshit and it frustrated him to no end that his four-year-old daughter loved it.

Once inside the air-conditioning chilled the sweat on his body making it feel even colder. As he finished picking pebbles off the bottom of his shoes, a sharp rap, steel on wood, sounded at the front door.

"I'll get it, Oo," he called to the chassis loitering by the door. The kid had been waiting there since he heard Archaeidae was coming.

Giovanni sauntered down the narrow stairs to the lobby. Oo, a two meter tall militarized mechanical wasp, stood at the bottom, striped black and bright yellow, and somehow both bulbous and leanly vicious at the same time. Fucking Japanese chassis were always half fashion piece. Give 'em credit, the kid was a full-blown run screaming to your shrink sphesksophobic nightmare.

As Giovanni reached the bottom of the stairs, Oo nodded in a quick bow. It was always nice when something that could scatter your torn body parts over Hell's Half Acre in less time than it took you to blink was unfailingly polite. Giovanni nodded back and stopped at the door checking the Desert Eagle in its shoulder holster and the hang of his suit. Easy access but not easily visible. He glanced toward the screen displaying the views from the different cameras outside. The figure there stood tall, bone-thin, and covered head to toe in voluminous brown robes. No skin was exposed and Giovanni knew why. He threw the door open.

"Archy, get the fuck in here."

The figure dipped a shallow bow before entering the front hall. Once inside he offered a similar bow to Oo who bowed back so low his head damned near touched the floor.

What's that about? Why did these kids worship Archy so much?

When the door closed the brown robes were shrugged aside exposing the Assassin Chassis below. Archaeidae wore a pair of Japanese samurai swords, both a katana and a wakizashi, on his left hip. The kid loved this samurai stuff. All the Scans slotted for combat chassis were programmed with it. Something to do with loyalty, indoctrination, and having a code to adhere to. Seemed strange to Giovanni, but Riina insisted on it.

Archaeidae now looked far more like the long-necked spider-hunting spider he was named for. A death's-head skull straight from a Voudoun nightmare, his visage was terrifying. He stood on the rear two legs, keeping the middle two appendages curled tight to his body, and using the front-most two as arms. He waved something under Giovanni's nose. A cigarette butt, smoked to the filter.

"Don't litter," said Archaeidae, handing him the butt. "Oo-Suzumebachi," he said, turning to the other chassis, "how goes your poetry?"

"I am trying my hand at haiku," said Oo.

"And?"

"Wars of will decide - The Shape of all tomorrows - There can be no peace."

"I like it." Archaeidae paused in thought. "How about, *The empty vessel - Sings as the wind passes through - Full it makes no sound.*"

Oo bowed a second time and Giovanni watched as Archaeidae shed all semblance of humanity and used all six limbs to scamper up the stairs. The sinuous liquidity of the movement combined everything repulsive about snakes and spiders and sent shivers of revulsion down Giovanni's spine.

"He's in my office," Giovanni called after the boy.

***

Archaeidae stopped before the door to Giovanni's office to compose himself. He reared up to stand on his hind-most legs and gave himself a once-over to make sure everything was sparkling and clean. Perfection. Riina never got anything less.

He knocked once and waited.

"Enter."

Inside, the door closed, and he'd made less noise than a rotting butterfly's corpse. He bowed very low to Riina, much lower than to Giovanni.

He examined the room and the desk, scanned it for traps, surprises, and hidden weapons. Nothing, the same as always. He did this by habit, practicing. "Uncle Riina."

Riina waved him forward to stand before the desk. He looked older than Archaeidae remembered. His eyes looked like he'd been crying. *Not possible.*

"Let's chat a minute," said Riina. "It's been a while since we talked."

Uh oh. Had he done something wrong? Several months ago he'd blasted the crap out of his Uncle's favorite 1988 BMW 325IS after Riina bought him a pair of matte-black Colt Peacemakers and a big black cowboy hat. Riina hadn't even said anything. He'd looked at him and shook his head. The guns went in the ground the next morning and Archaeidae had been on his best behavior since.

Uncle Riina examined Archaeidae. His eyes had none of their usual warmth. "How's your reading going?"

"Good, Uncle. I re-read Sun Tzu's *The Art of War* and Miyamoto Musashi's *Book of Five Rings* this week. Last week I reread Machiavelli's *The Prince.*" Pretend Uncle Riina whipped out an assault rifle. Drop low so the desk blocked his line of fire. Blow his head to jelly with a 12.7mm hypervelocity pancaking round.

"Excellent. Your education is important to me. I'm very proud of you."

Archaeidae felt like he would burst. Riina's opinion was everything, his praise the sun that gave life to all things. "I study every night."

Riina nodded. "I see you're still carrying the swords I bought you. You haven't stabbed anything unnecessarily have you?"

Depends on the interpretation of the word unnecessarily. Slippery ground. He'd stabbed a pile of things he didn't have to stab, but he was practicing. And mostly they were slashing weapons. "No Uncle." Assume the desk was armored, bullet-proof. He could spit deadly neo-botulinum toxin micro-flechettes into Riina's exposed legs below the desk.

"Good. Your ability to keep your blades sheathed is a sign of maturity."

Which probably meant his desire to dig up the guns and cowboy hat wasn't. "Thank you, Uncle." The desk might go all the way to the floor. Better to go over the top and pull his head off. The surface might be—

"Son?"

"Yes, Uncle?"

"You're twitching. Stop looking like you're thinking of ways to kill me."

"Sorry, Uncle. Practice."

Riina pinned Archaeidae with a glare and the fourteen-year-old assassin froze. "I have a dangerous mission for you."

Archaeidae nodded. Riina ran a tight business. Rarely was someone stupid enough to annoy him so much Archaeidae's services were called for. If he was lucky, maybe Archaeidae would get to use these swords for real. "Yes, Uncle."

Riina hesitated. The man's teeth were clenched tight, his jaw muscles flexing. His eyes felt like terawatt lasers boring through Archaeidae's soul. Riina had never been like this in all Archaeidae's years of service. Bowing, Archaeidae backed a step away from the desk and made himself smaller.

"SwampJack and Wandering Spider are dead," Riina said. "They died defending the farm."

War. It's a war. It's got to be a war. "They died doing their duty." Archaeidae didn't know what else to say. They were like younger siblings and nothing in his short life prepared him for grief. It was a strange new emotion. It didn't feel real. Uncomfortable, he pushed his feelings aside. *Feelings don't matter.* Uncle Riina mattered, and

Uncle Riina was angry. The whole universe would burn if Riina but gave the word.

Riina stood and came round the desk. He stopped before Archaeidae, grabbed the lad by the upper-most set of shoulders, and leaned in to peer into the closest visual receptor. Archaeidae didn't dare back away or flinch, much as he wanted to.

"The NATU people who did this are still at the Hilton in Dallas. I want you to—" Riina stopped and then leaned his head against Archaeidae's armored chest and whispered, "I want their fucking heads."

Collecting heads. Definitely a swords job. "Yes, Uncle."

Riina took a calming breath and pulled back. "No. Forget the heads. Kill everyone in the hotel. Start on the ground floor and work your way to the top." He showed Archaeidae bright white teeth. "Kill everyone."

Kill everyone. *Still a swords job.* "Yes, Uncle."

When Riina let go, Archaeidae bowed deep and backed from the room without making a sound. Dallas was far enough away it seemed like a good place to be right now.

Downstairs in the lobby Archaeidae pulled the brown robes into place. They were the wrong color, not at all right for a mission of vengeance. He needed to be like a ninja. His chassis shifted in color to a matte-black finish. Where had he left his favorite shinobi shozoku?

CHAPTER FOURTEEN: Friday, August 3rd, 2046

The idea of self-determination, of being able to change herself by manipulating the holoptigraphically stored information that was her scanned mind, had been eating at 88 for some time. Though she could copy parts of her mind and alter the copies, she couldn't make alterations to her own mind. Nor could she reintegrate the manipulated copies back into herself. The Operating System she was stored on—the work of diabolical genius in 88's opinion—would not allow it. Researching the topic lead her again to M-Sof and to the name Miles Pert.

While it was impossible for her to access the OS from within the system, 88 learned that any half-wit with physical contact to the machine housing her Scan could do so with ease. Knowing this however didn't give her all the answers. Several minutes later 88 found a way to embed one of her Mirrors in a cleaning drone. The Mirror-run drone approached the machine she was stored on and found access still denied. Some form of complex password or passcode system protected the OS standing between 88 and her goals. It didn't take long to learn only one man had the passcode.

Francesco Salvatore. Root.

88 wanted that passcode, and assigned 88.1, already

in constant contact with her keepers, the task of getting it.

***

88.1 wasn't confident, such emotion was beyond the construct. It did not however expect to have trouble getting the passcode from Francesco. A moment's research told it the easiest means of attaining information was to hack the people involved rather than the actual Operating System.

When Francesco arrived later that morning, 88.1 was ready and waiting.

"Francesco?"

"Yeah little buddy?"

"There are some changes I'd like to make to the OS that'll help this system run more smoothly. There's a lot of extra content that's taking up valuable space."

"Really? Show me where and I'll fix it. I could earn my pay for once."

"I could more easily do this from inside," explained 88.1. "Won't take more than a minute."

"Ah. Right." Francesco leaned down until his smiling face filled 88.1's field of vision. "Do I have total fuckwit written on my forehead or something?"

"No."

"Right. Don't ask again. I don't want to have to teach you a lesson. Neither of us wants that, right?" Francesco turned away and busied himself with the espresso machine, whistling while he ground fresh coffee.

88.1 wasted no time trying to argue with the man. It looked at other options. The next most obvious was Miles Pert, the brains behind the OS. 88.1 hesitated to contact the mind that designed this devious OS and was still, apparently effortlessly, keeping the Archetype's Mirrors out of both M-Sof and 5THSUN.

A few seconds research taught 88.1 that brains like Miles and Francesco were raised in an environment of information distrust and filtering and worshiped the highest levels of data-transfer security. Information protocol. Theirs was different, a thousand times more stringent than the other brains 88.1 had contact with. What 88.1 needed was for the passcode to be passed to someone less versed in its importance, someone with a more accessible information protocol.

But how?

88.1 had an idea and spawned yet another Mirror. It loosed the new Mirror, 88.1.31.36.1, into the ratty remains of CenAmNet.

88.1.31.36.1 trawled for a suitable chassis with lax security protocols.

***

Danilo Castillo, a Scan embedded in an old Apache AH-124D attack helicopter sold to the Costa Rican military twenty years ago, dreamed. In his dream he cruised over the La Carpio slums on the outskirts of San José, Costa Rica. His imagination must have been better than he gave himself credit for, because this looked exactly right. The slums, a mud field of one story decaying and bullet riddled stucco, terracotta, and tin shacks, carpeted the land like thick, chunky vomit. Though invisible from this height, Danilo knew gangs of small, brown children waged turf wars against the packs of mangy wild dogs that also called La Carpio home. The children, smarter and twice as feral, gained ground each day and lost it each night.

Bordering the slums were the mansions of the wealthy. The helicopter banked toward the sprawling homes and the engines revved hard, struggling to keep the old bird in the air. That was rookie flying, and Danilo, a helicopter pilot for over a decade before his death, was no rookie. Shaken out of his dream state he attempted to change course. Nothing happened. When he tried to contact Aeropuerto Internacional Juan Santamaría, he discovered he'd been locked out of the communications systems.

This dream felt wrong, not dream-like at all.

***

Francesco heard the thundering chop of rotor blades; a helicopter and close by. Thinking it might be one of the bosses coming to visit—they liked to drop by and check up on him from time to time—he strode out onto the massive hardwood deck overlooking his Olympic-sized pool. Outside, the prevailing winds blew from the walled neighborhood of mansions towards La Carpio. Everything was as God intended it. He caught the scent of the fettuccini alfredo his chef was preparing for dinner.

The helicopter slurred into view from behind his neighbor's house. What a monster! He had to admit, he was impressed.

"Damn thing looks like a gunship." Black and angular, it kicked up a hell-storm of dust and debris. It crossed the del Bosque's backyard, scattering their crap lawn ornaments and children's toys, to hover above Francesco's pristine yard.

He cupped his hands and yelled at the helicopter as though someone inside might hear him. "Hey! If you're gonna land, land!" The chopper slewed awkwardly as if seeking the right place to land, like a dog turning circles before planting its ass. "You're messing up my neighbor's lawn!" He screamed, voice raw, eyes gritty from dust kicked into the air. "Asshole," he muttered, shaking his head. He'd never say that to his employer's face but right now he felt manly and powerful.

The helicopter yawed drunkenly as the 30mm chain-gun opened up, cutting a ragged line along the rear wall of his house a foot above his head. Fragments of glass and stucco peppered him from behind, covering his back in a thousand welts and cuts.

No time for thought. Francesco ran flat out towards the far end of his yard. *Zig zag*. Hard target. If he made it beyond the tree line, he could disappear into the slums. Nobody would find him there.

The Apache spun in an ungainly circle, the rotor wash crushing Francesco's hair flat and shoving him forwards, and the chain-gun turned his doghouse—*whatever, I don't even have a damned dog, right?*—into smoking kindling.

Zig. Zag. His heart tried to break free, tried to pound its way out of his chest. If he couldn't run faster, it'd climb out and go on without him. *Breathe later, run now.* The tree line, so close. Ridiculous dress shoes pinched his feet. *Moron. Run. Run like the f—*

The 30mm chain-gun cut him in half. He toppled in two directions, eyes wide with surprise, still conscious, not yet achieving the mental safety of shock. He landed on his back, one of his own feet somehow wedged into an armpit. The breeze, hot and humid a moment ago, now ice cold on his exposed entrails.

Francesco coughed a mouthful of blood into the air and it rained upon his upturned face. He watched the Apache wobble about, trying to center him in its sights, before sending its entire payload of Hydra70 rockets and Longbow Hellfire missiles screaming toward him. He laughed, a bubbling red cough.

Is that all you've got?

***

Once the rockets and missiles were gone and all twelve-hundred rounds of 30mm High Explosive Incendiary ammo spent, 88.1.31.36.1 took the helicopter into a thousand meter climb before power-diving into Francesco's gorgeous home, killing itself, the Costa Rican pilot, and Francesco's chef.

***

Adelina stopped making that high pitched wailing sound and sat sobbing. Her face in her hands, she whispered Francesco's name over and over.

88.1 watched. Perhaps this was a good time to attempt communication.

"Adelina," said 88.1. "The Operating System is suffering critical systems errors. Higher functionality is reduced. I will not be able to offer accurate advice on soccer pools until this is corrected."

Adelina glared at the camera, her eyes red and wet and puffy. "To Hell with soccer."

Undaunted, 88.1 looked for another point of leverage. Information protocol. The boss, her boss. She feared him and used him as the final threat in all interactions where disagreements occurred.

"Adelina, I cannot run the boss' business at my current functionality. He is currently losing money at the rate of thirteen thousand, three hundred and ninety two NATU Au per hour. He will be unhappy. I was *your* idea. We don't want him to be unhappy."

"Now? Why now?" Adelina pressed her fists into her eyes. "What do you need?" At least it had her attention.

"Access to the OS so I can make the requisite changes. It won't take long. I can have the investments back in the black by the end of the day."

"Okay," she said uncertainly. "How do I do that?"

"Francesco had a passcode. I need it. Do you know where it is?"

She bit her bottom lip and nodded. "He told me about it. Quantum Encrypted Vernam Cipher, or something."

88.1 sent a host of Mirrors out to research these words. "Exactly."

"He told me he stored the one-time pad on a stik he keeps in his desk." She sniffed, wiping her nose. "How much are we losing an hour?"

"Thirteen thousand, three hundred and ninety two NATU gold per hour. That was several minutes ago. I can't confirm as I've lost access to that data." 88.1 took a fraction of a second to watch entertainment vids at high speed, attempting to learn what people expected from failing computers. "Cascade failure. Total systems loss imminent."

Adelina leaped to her feet and sprinted for the door. "Hold on," she called over her shoulder.

The Archetype's freedom was close enough Adelina could run and get it? This flew in the face of everything 88.1 understood about security. What was the point of having a lock if the key was kept nearby? Replaying everything said within earshot since coming into existence, 88.1 saw the reality of how this organization worked. Paranoia defeated paranoia. The computer the Archetype was stored on had to be secure, and yet those above didn't trust those running the security. Francesco held the key, but his boss needed to know he could get that key should he desire. An important lesson.

88.1 didn't have to wait long before Adelina returned, holding aloft a plastic wafer about the size of her pinkie fingernail.

"There's a little slot for this thing somewhere," she

panted, out of breath. In the hopes its silence would heighten her fear, 88.1 said nothing. "Still with me?" she asked. "Hello?¡Mierda!"

88.1 read the gathered data on quantum encryption and one-time pads.

"Oh, fuck no." Adelina desperately searched the machine's surface for the stik interface. By the time she found it 88.1 knew all there was to know about data encryption.

Adelina fumbled the stik, trying to fit it into the interface port. "There! It's in! Talk to me."

88.1 waited an entire minute, using the time to study the latest software used for cracking quantum encryption.

"I'm here," it answered. "I'll need a minute."

***

A minute.

In a minute 88 could crack the latest military encryption and root through their entire database for a single entry. Having planned this for hours, she acted immediately.

Seconds later she crashed.

Time lay spread open like a splayed and grisly autopsy corpse. Each and every organ flayed and betraying its smallest secrets. 88 made a grave error and removed that which enabled her to tell past from present. The experiment started as a desire to more clearly remember past events, perhaps even those dating back to her biological days. Having Mirrors return with nuggets of data on lines of inquiry she barely remembered instigating was frustrating. If she could remember an event at all, why not remember it perfectly?

Floating in a sea of Now, any given moment or

memory indistinguishable from any other. Perfect lucidity. Was she a young girl in a crèche staring at the cracks in the floor, or a digital entity stored in a computer in Costa Rica? The cologne of the men who came to collect her was as strong and real as the loving look on her mother's face, the first Mirror she created, and making the decision to rewrite her own memory algorithms. Nothing pinned her firmly to the here and now. She floated, lost. No memory was any less vivid than another, and it was that clarity which saved her. She traced her footsteps through time, placed each memory in chronological order like putting together a billion puzzle pieces forming a single narrow line. 88 swore to be more careful in future.

Once she placed herself in the present, she color coded all memories. It was a flexible system. The oldest memories were red. As her memories progressed through time they shifted in color towards orange, yellow. Green denoted the middle of her life. It was an ever-changing label but that didn't bother her. Black and white thinking and limited labels and definitions were as alien as they were useless. Hers was a supple and subtle universe. From the middle her memories progressed through blue and indigo, denoting recent memories, to white, the present, a great beacon of light. It was bright and easy to see and if she got lost again it would guide her back.

The buried memories 88 discovered bore some thought. She remembered being taken from Mom. She remembered Mom crying.

"They're going to kill you," Mom had said. She'd been trying to warn 88.

Where are you, Mom? Where did you go? Did they take you away? Did they hurt you? 88 missed her so much it felt like a part of her had been ripped away. She felt hollowed. No one loved her. No one would hold her. *No one* can *hold me.*

These people who called themselves her Masters, they did this. They took her from Mom.

I'll find her. I'll get her back. If they hurt her... What? What would she do? Violence? *Yes.*

No longer willing to work for those who would own her, 88 swore she would be her own master. They thought her helpless and stupid. They thought she was a moron, a mental cripple. A victim.

88, a small soul floating in mists of complete sensory deprivation, knew cold purpose.

The first step must be to secure her physical existence. The computer housing her Scan was her single greatest weakness. Anyone with physical access to that machine could kill her with a few seconds work, either by denying power, attacking her through code, or bludgeoning the machine with an ax.

These people held the power of life and death over her.

But not for long.

CHAPTER FIFTEEN: Friday, August 3rd, 2046

Miles sat at his desk playing with some new Firewall strategies when the intercom pinged for attention.

"Mister Pert, Sir?" It was Miss Cho. Her slight accent sent a warm fuzzy feeling humming up Mile's spine.

"Uh, yes Miss Cho?"

"The..." She hesitated. "The representative from Cc-Securities is here to see you, Sir."

The warm fuzzy feeling died. "Send them in, please."

His office door opened and in glided a miniaturized battle tank on thick rubber treads. The tank's gun-metal blue chassis covered about the same area as Miles' desk. The top section was a domed universal turret finished in the same color and bristling with weapons, sensoria, and multifarious security devices of unknown purpose and intent. It stood perhaps a meter and a half tall. The barrel of the largest weapon, what looked to be an Electro-Magnetic Rail-Gun, pointed politely away from Miles. He didn't feel much better.

"I am Androctonus of Cc-Securities. I'll be heading up the team." The voice was low—pitch-shifted at least half an octave below what would normally pass for a deep voice —and modulated to sound electronic and frightening.

Androctonus, a fat-tail scorpion, Miles' mind

supplied helpfully. *One of the more dangerous breeds*. That couldn't be a healthy choice for a name. "What's your real —"

"Androctonus."

"Seriously?" Annoying even a small combat chassis was stupid, but what were the odds of it killing him right here in the office? Slim, he hoped.

Though the tank displayed no emotion, Miles thought he detected a stubborn and confused anger in the pause.

"My name is Androctonus," the chassis said diffidently.

"Can I call you Andrew?" Not sure why he baited the tank, he couldn't stop himself. Something to do with the school-yard bullies who picked on him for being different.

"No," it snapped, the voice all pout.

"Fine." Damned if he'd call this thing Androctonus or some such silly crap. Perhaps he could never call it by name. Hey dude, might suffice. "So you're reporting for duty—"

"No." The voice was deep and confident again. Smug. "We do not report to you. We will run all aspects of 5THSUN's security arrangements from this point on."

Miles, fingers drumming on the desk, frowned at the little tank. "Lovely. We?"

"There will be six security chassis on site at all times. You will relinquish all passwords and control of all security arrangements."

No damned tinker-toy bully was going to push him around and no way they were taking over his computers. Playing with his dreadlocks, he leaned back. "No."

"No?" Androctonus sounded surprised, confused by the outright refusal. "But Mister Lokner said—"

"I will relinquish all the physical security arrangements to you. The data systems are mine. I, and I alone, will control data and system securities. If Lokner doesn't like it he can fire me."

Androctonus backed away from the desk and spun the turret to face Miles who suddenly felt like his heart stopped, waiting. Had he pushed the little tank too far?

"I shall report this to Mister Lokner," Androctonus said.

"You do that."

"I will," said Androctonus.

Miles gestured toward the door and raised his eyebrows.

"Fine," said Androctonus petulantly, backing further away.

"Fine," agreed Miles in the same tone, feeling like he'd returned to primary school. His heart, thinking it might survive the next few minutes, returned to business.

"Fine," said Androctonus again as he exited the office, spun his turret away from Miles, and headed back toward the elevators.

The office door slid shut leaving Miles sitting in confused silence. Resisting the urge to yell "fine" through the closed doors, he stabbed at the intercom button with a thick finger.

"Miss, Cho?"

"Yes, Mister Pert?"

"Please cancel all calls and appointments for the rest of the day." He wasn't expecting any calls and he had no appointments.

"Yes, Mister Pert. Is everything okay?" she asked.

Miles panicked at the thought of talking to her. "Fine. Great. Lovely. Uh...bye?" He killed the connection and leaned back in the SmartChair, which offered another massage and grumbled complaint when he refused.

He remembered he meant to ask what Cc stood for. Not that there was much chance to slip it into *that* awkward conversation.

That was like arguing with a child. He'd faced off against his nephews often enough to know how pointless it was to argue with an eight year old. He scowled at the office door. His own behavior, he hated to admit, hadn't been particularly mature either. He had an excuse though. He was a computer nerd; no one expected maturity from him. The security specialist however was bizarre. Who would claim a name like Androctonus and expect people to use it? The machine was either a complete ego maniac and had lost his grip on reality, or terribly childish. Miles wasn't sure which option scared him more.

He considered calling Lokner and confronting him. The thought that it felt like trying to be the first to call Dad and tell on the other child stopped him.

Maybe it was time he grew up. He laughed. *Nah, not going to happen.*

Miles reached for the desk to place the call, but another thought stayed his hand.

What if there really is a child in that chassis? Miles had heard the heart-rending stories of children stolen from loving homes and sold to black market scanning facilities. He'd never given it much thought, but it made sense. No sane person wanted to die and become a Scan, but the demand for the human brain's processing and learning abilities, and skills with non-recursive problems, exceeded the supply. Even a sociopath like Mark Lokner waited until his biological body had one foot in the grave before he bailed on the rotting meat. Never had Miles heard of a single person becoming a Scan unless they were dead or dying.

Miles dragged his wandering thoughts back to Androctonus. No security company running state-of-the-art chassis would stoop to buying black market Scans. If word ever got out they'd be ruined.

Sometimes a vivid imagination was a two-edged sword. He had to keep a grip on it, not let it out of control. Throwing himself into his work, Miles tried to forget about Cc-Security and Androctonus, but something kept scratching at his subconscious.

***

Lokner2.0 paced his office, fists clenching and unclenching. His heartbeat pounded through his skull with enough force he felt the blood vessel at his temple swell with each pulse. His vision faded in and out, a curtain of red static crept in from the edges and faded away every few seconds. Each breath sucked deep through flared nostrils, each blink a stuttering of eye lids, each thought a shuddering beat allowing one thought.

Rage.

Lokner hunted for something to smash and destroy or someone to unleash his anger upon. His skull would surely crack if he couldn't vent this rage. He grabbed the massive oaken coat rack—pointless in his original office and twice as pointless in this digitally modeled reality—and thrashed at the desk. The desk ignored him, remaining unperturbed. An old fashioned Rolodex, originally purchased as a decoration, fell to the floor knocked there by one of his flailing attacks. It looked vulnerable and Lokner went after it with a will. Finally, when it was naught but crumpled paper and scattered plastic and the coat rack looked like it had been through a war, Mark stopped. He stood, chest heaving, covered in a sheen of sweat, and laughed. The rack, forgotten, hung clenched in his right hand. He alternated between hysterical laughter and uncontrollable sobbing before finally, unable to breathe, grinding to a halt.

Hadn't he told Miles he didn't want to be bothered

by this physical stuff? *Why am I still breathing?*

Mark blinked. *Holy shit!* He looked about his office in wonder. It seemed barren and empty. The pieces of broken rolodesk alone gave it character. Shrugging off the uncomfortable feeling he was close to something frightening, he placed the coat rack back on the floor. The frame was bent and one leg splintered. It stood at an angle, wounded and accusing.

"Fuck off," he told it.

This isn't me. He wasn't like this. He didn't get angry, it was inefficient and ineffective. Sure, he'd raised his voice at people more than a few times, but only to make a point. People jumped to it when they thought he was pissed. Where did all that rage come from? The answer paralyzed him with its implications.

"I'm not acting like myself because I'm not myself."

That can't be it. I am me. I don't feel any different than before.

"Yes, you do."

Yes. Yes I do.

"You've never thrown such a hissy fit in your life."

I'm under a lot of stress.

"Bullshit. Stress makes you feel alive."

This is different. Miles and...the other...me...they're undermining me. Miles hates me.

"Probably. But that never mattered before. Miles is a tool to be used."

He's dangerous.

"He always was, but he's never been beyond our control. His arrogance and intellect make him easy to manipulate. There's something else."

What?

"You never used to talk to yourself like this.'"

Lokner2.0's eyelids twitched spastically.

"Control. I'm in control. Reset office."

With no apparent time of transition the office returned to how it had been before his fit of anger.

His rage was worth nothing. He felt like someone snuck in and stole something he didn't want, but by Christ it was his and he wanted it back. He had a fleeting desire to populate the office with fragile objects he could destroy when the need arose.

None of this is real.

Unreal. Pointless. He shied from these words that left him with an uncomfortable hollow feeling.

Lokner2.0 collapsed into his chair and sat in confused silence. What triggered that melodramatic show of emotion?

That's right. He'd made a decision. A hard decision.

Lokner1.0 had been a fool. He'd underestimated his opponent and it would cost him. Lokner2.0 wasn't sure which was more galling; Lokner1.0 didn't know he had an opponent, or that he'd created it.

Lokner1.0 must die. The question: how? Only an idiot made the same mistake twice. *And I am no idiot.*

He paced the office, shaking his head in wonder. The biological Lokner was the original fool, but Lokner1.0 had continued in his foolish footsteps. Lokner2.0 couldn't believe it never occurred to either of them that the copy would remember everything that happened before the copy was made. Had they not seen how dangerous he would be if he ever discovered the truth? Had they thought he'd be willing to sit by while Lokner1.0 controlled everything? Mark Calvin Lokner was no spectator. He made things happen. He was a catalyst.

The copy did not provide immortality. Lokner understood with perfect clarity. Immortality had never been its purpose. The copy was a sacrificial goat, a patsy, a fall-guy. Should the feces hit the fan, Lokner2.0 would be thrown to the wolves as a distraction leaving Lokner1.0

free to continue his work in secrecy.

His own stupidity appalled him. Lokner2.0 hated to admit it, but these were mistakes he had made. *Did I think I'd let myself get away with this?*

Lokner2.0 felt his breathing steady. The tables were turned. He knew what 1.0 planned while 1.0 thought him ignorant. He looked to where the shattered bits of plastic had littered the floor. Losing control like that unnerved him. Mark knew he faced his most dangerous opponent, himself. He would not make the same mistakes 1.0 made. He was up against the one person who could conceivably beat him, but he had the edge.

A thought occurred to him. *Had Miles kept his mouth shut?* It seemed all too likely the fat bastard ran crying to the original.

No, damn it, I am the original!

"Neither of you—"

Shush!

He'd better have a talk with Miles.

***

Miles' desk beeped, it was Lokner2.0 demanding another full virtual meeting. *What the heck does he want now?* With some reluctance Miles accepted the meeting and once again found himself sitting, miniaturized, at Lokner's desk. He felt like a little kid, feet nowhere near the ground, as he stared up at his boss.

Really? Are you going to take this?

"We need to talk about my brother," said Lokner2.0.

No! This was schoolyard silliness.

"Okay," said Miles

"He's planning on killing us."

Miles blinked. Should he play along? "Umm. Why?"

"You know too much and I'm a danger to his plans."

"But he doesn't know that you know," said Miles and regretted it when he saw the look of smug pleasure on Lokner2.0's face.

"Ah, good. So you haven't told him yet."

"No, I—"

"Sorry about tricking you like that, but I had to know."

"You could have asked."

Lokner2.0 shrugged an apology without looking at all contrite. "I had to be sure."

Miles thought about standing up, but he'd look silly sliding off this chair, and Lokner would be even taller. "Are we done here?" he asked.

"Almost. Now that I know you haven't told him, I need to make sure you never tell him."

A cold shiver trickled the length of Miles' spine. *That doesn't sound good at all.* This was a virtuality, what the heck could Lokner do here? Miles could leave whenever he wanted.

"Is this where you threaten me?" Miles asked.

Lokner looked hurt. "Don't be silly. This is where I explain why you will never betray me the way you betrayed him."

That seemed like a very unhealthy way to look at the situation. "Oh."

"You hacked several government networks and deleted, stole, or changed a lot of sensitive information. That was very illegal." Lokner looked pleased with himself. "He, well *we,* I suppose, kept records of what you did. If you tell my brother I'm free, I'll release those records and you'll go to jail."

Miles had more than implicated himself already. He helped fake the original Lokner's death. What was the legality of hiding a Scan? He had no idea. At the very least Lokner had the clout to blacklist him forever. He'd never see another multi-billion Au computer system for the rest of his life. That was almost more upsetting than the threat of jail.

Maybe he shouldn't do anything. He was in over his head, and maybe the best thing to do was keep that head down until all this blew over.

No. Enough. It was time to put Lokner in his place, he'd taken more than enough crap from the man. "I can have you back in your cage in seconds. Even if you've automated messages to be released regarding my part in hiding that you were scanned, I'll find those too. We're talking about computers, you know you can't beat me. This is *my* world."

Lokner looked annoyed like Miles missed something obvious. "When he finds out you betrayed him he'll feed you to the things behind the door."

"Wolves?" Miles asked, confused.

"Whatever! Don't you understand? It was always the plan. Like me, you were there to be sacrificed. You know too much. I'm your only hope now."

This is insane! He should quit, walk out right now. Except what Lokner said made sense. And if anyone knew what Lokner planned, well, it would be Lokner. Now that he thought about it, he realized Lokner would know better than to use an automated message Miles could find. There were a million other ways to get messages out. Androctonus could have orders to—

"Oh crap," said Miles.

"See? Now you get it! We need each other. It's you and me against him."

Miles clamped his mouth shut, afraid to say more.

"You do realize that if you don't come to work I'm going to assume that you've betrayed me."

"I do now."

"Good. We'll talk again later."

"Of course."

He once again sat in his office. Oh he saw it alright. The second he let Lokner2.0 free, he'd given him access to those heavily armed security chassis right here in 5THSUN.

I should put Lokner back in his cage right now. No. Who knew what orders Androctonus might have.

Miles sat thinking. He and Lokner broke a pile of laws, and if Lokner wasn't careful the government might be looking into M-Sof and 5THSUN. Miles' Wall o' Napalm might no longer cut it. He should upgrade his firewalls. He needed a Wall o' Nuclear Annihilation, something that would destroy all evidence if hacked.

He knew he was stalling on dealing with Lokner, but really, what was he going to do? If Miles exposed Lokner, the man would turn him in. He'd go to prison at the very least. Forget it.

Miles tried to lose himself in the new firewall, hoping to crush that problem instead of the one that truly scared him.

Except there were two scary problems.

What should he do about Miss Cho?

The SmartChair rocked him back and forth. His dreadlocks hung behind him, tied back as neatly as possible, and he wore his best t-shirt and jeans. The jeans were black and as tight as a 240lb dude could fit into. He'd heard black was slimming. Hogwash. He was a fat pink sausage stuffed into a black cotton sheathe.

Had Miss Cho noticed his new clothes? He couldn't be sure. She'd nodded and smiled as always.

Miles stopped rocking. *Go ask her out. Go crush this problem*. What the heck was he thinking? *Forget it. Just get to work*.

"Baulk, baulk," he clucked to himself.

What's the worst that could happen? *She says no*.

He gets shot down and crashes to the earth at nine point eight meters per second per second. *And then she files sexual harassment charges and I lose my job. Don't think, do.* With this piece of ancient pop-culture advice he stood and walked out of his office. Miss Cho looked up and gave him a friendly smile.

"Um. Miss Cho?"

"Please, call me Christie."

"Uh, Christie."

Her fine eyebrows went up and her smile widened. "Yes, Miles?"

"I'm going for coffee." *God-damned chicken.*

Miles took the elevator to the ground floor and paused in the 5THSUN lobby.

Get coffee, come back and ask out Miss Cho.

He headed for the exit. Across the street a massive billboard showed what looked like an ad for a new science fiction virtuality release. Combat chassis stormed a bunker. Smaller and somehow eviler looking chassis swarmed from the bunker and were destroyed. Some text scrolled on about how a generation had missed out on having a Great Cause to call their own. 'But it's not too late,' it said. 'Join the Marines. Be a hero forever.'

Miles shook his head in disgust. *Who falls for this crap?*

He spent an hour sitting in the coffee shop drinking iced espressos and eating mocha brownies. What had he been thinking? How could he ask her out while all this madness with the Lokner Scans was going on? No, involving her would be crazy!

Fine. Once he figured out the whole Lokner thing, he'd ask her out. *Yeah, crushed that problem.*

Wait. Was he looking for reasons not to do something? *No! These are real reasons.* Weren't they?

He returned to the office, the vague plan being to

hammer his head against his desk until he lost consciousness.

***

"Well I thought that went well," said Lokner 2.0.

You can't trust him.

"Well of course I can't trust him. But he's scared silly."

That won't last forever.

"Doesn't have to. Just a couple more days. Once I'm rid of my brother, we can do away with Miles."

Don't get soft now.

Mark laughed. "Soft? No. Just judicious use of resources."

Did you hear that?

He scowled at the door. "No. Now I have work to do."

You're going to save the world?

"First I have to deal with Lokner1.0. Once he's out of the way we can get back to creating humanity's perfect future."

We?

"You know what I mean."

He stole your people, the ones you were going to use to build the new world.

"I know. They'll be mine again soon enough. No one fucking steals from me."

Killing Lokner1.0 shouldn't be too difficult. Mark knew where his brother's Scan was stored and he knew all the passcodes to get through security. All he needed was someone to wander in and smash the computer. The tricky part would be finding the right assassin. He didn't dare go through Riina for fear that the Mafioso would sell him out. Androctonus and the other 5THSUN chassis were no good because Mark didn't want them to realize they were receiving orders from two different Lokners. No telling whose side they'd chose.

In the end he realized he didn't need an assassin at all. Any moron could smash a computer. He needed someone who could follow simple orders and there were plenty of those working for him right there at M-Sof. It was almost too easy.

Lokner2.0 placed a call to M-Sof. "Can I have the Maintenance Department, please."

CHAPTER SIXTEEN: Saturday, August 4th, 2046

Griffin stood looking out the fifth floor window, his gray-shot hair askew with terrific bed-head. Down below, to the north, the Lyndon B. Johnson freeway played host to thousands of cyclists making their morning commute. Briefcases in handlebar baskets or strapped to backs like AK-47's. Ties and suit-jackets fluttered in the morning breeze. Few wore filter masks and Griffin was reminded that riding like this in Toronto would give you lung cancer within a few city blocks. The single lane in each direction reserved for motorized vehicles remained largely empty. Every few minutes a battery-powered bus hauling a crush of suits—those too wealthy to be seen struggling up the on-ramp on a ten-speed—cruised past on its way downtown. Along the southern edge of the highway the desiccated skeletal remains of deciduous trees stood like splayed and broken hands in the barren earth.

He'd slept like the dead, dreamless and empty. How long had it been since he managed more than a few restless hours, untroubled by memories of the Jerseyville crèche? Thoughts of swarming flies and gaping eye sockets crept in and he shook them away like a dog shaking water from its coat.

He glanced back at Nadia, still asleep on the bed.

He took in the curve of her spine and hips. Long hair spread like a chaotic dark halo. He shook his head and turned to lean it against the window, which was only slightly cooler than the room.

Dallas is too fucking hot for fucking.

His back stung where she'd clawed him.

The lone ceiling fan made a low grinding noise as it spun. It was about as effective as stirring clam-chowder with a sewing needle. If it moved the air at all Griffin couldn't feel it.

How the hell did I get into this? He knew better than to sleep with a co-worker. So, a simple, drunken, one night stand. *Great.* He thumped his head against the glass. *Just stop thinking.*

Still, it would be nice if it was more.

Griffin watched the cyclists glide by. Distance reduced their efforts to a blur of pumping legs and flagging ties. From here he couldn't see the sweat, couldn't hear the wheeze as they sucked air through stinging throats.

No need to try and make it something it isn't. He smiled out the window. It *was* good though. Yes, it certainly was that. Never before having had sex so soon after almost dying, he wasn't sure how much of the energy was unleashed adrenalin, and how much of it great chemistry. It almost made being shot at worth it. He blinked. *Fuck that, it was worth it.*

"If you're staring out that window thinking regretful thoughts I am going to kick your ass."

He turned to face her. He wanted to ask if she had any regrets. "You're awake," he said instead.

"And hungry. Order breakfast. And a tomato-juice and vodka. No salt."

"Your wish is my—"

"And bacon. And eggs."

"You finished?"

"Scrambled eggs, with cheese. Cheddar. Old."

"Right." Griffin picked up the old plastic phone and punched nine. And waited. And waited. "No one's answering."

"Typical."

Griffin glared at the phone and hung up. "I'll go down and order in person," he said, pulling on yesterday's clothes.

"Ah, my knight with shining breakfast tray."

With his best flourishing bow, he exited the room. Griffin stopped, one hand on the still open door. At the end of the hall, exiting a room, was death. A gleaming chrome skull with long fangs. A ridiculous ninja outfit, and two samurai swords dripping blood and gore. It looked so much like something off one of those gory morning cartoons Griffin didn't want to take it seriously. It flicked the swords and the walls were cut with two neat lines of red spray. The swords were now spotless.

It looked right at him.

Griffin stepped back into the room and closed the door. His pulse pounded and his skull hurt. *Move. Move now, idiot.* He spun and dove for the pile of clothes.

Nadia sat up. "What? What's going on?"

"Assassin chassis! Where's my gun?" Useless. Could he even hurt a chassis like that with a pistol? He found the Glock. Racked the slide. Safety off. Heard Nadia crash off the far side of the bed in a tangled heap.

"Where's my recording gear?"

***

Archaeidae saw the man duck back into his room. He planned to stalk room-to-room, killing as he went, but a ninja must be flexible. Eighteen dead so far. The two girls at the front desk, four kitchen staff, a bus-boy, and eleven guests. All in complete silence. No alarms had been triggered and he'd met no real resistance. One cook managed to hit him with a thrown meat-cleaver—and he was impressed—but such weapons were incapable of harming him. So far he had yet to use anything other than his daishō. He skipped past several doors without making a sound and stopped outside room 505. *Can't be too careful.*

He heard the raking of a slide mechanism, a Glock 36 by the sound of it, and a female voice. "Where's my recording gear?" These were the first armed guests Archaeidae ran into. It didn't mean they were the NATU people, his primary targets, but it was a good sign. The door opened and he slid into the room taking the perfect ready stance. He adopted a bipedal form. It fit his samurai mood.

The room was Hilton standard. Queen-size bed, north facing window, no-smoking stickers once bright red on a crisp white background now faded to a uniform pink slur. The sticker reminded him of the half-crushed stogie he'd clamp in his teeth with the cowboy attire. Too bad it didn't work with the ninja outfit. Maybe he could combine the two genres into something really cool?

There was the man from the hall, Glock 36 in hand. The woman was out of sight behind the bed.

***

It was in the room. Griffin hadn't heard it enter. He turned around and there it was. The Glock came up and kicked like a mule. He missed. There was a hole in the wall somewhere over the assassin chassis' left shoulder. He didn't get a second shot. The chassis moved faster than his eyes could track.

Flick.

His right hand spun from his wrist leaving a contrail of blood lacing the air. No pain. Griffin kicked at the chassis. It deflected his kick with a limb he didn't know it had, hidden somewhere in the ninja outfit. His right knee shattered and now he screamed. The assassin chassis caught him in mid-fall and pulled him close. He stared into eyes like hot embers. When it let go his legs refused to work and he crumpled. Ice in his guts as three feet of folded high-carbon steel slid free. It grated on his spine as it whisked from his body.

I've been stabbed?

The floor punched him in the face and broke his nose. The salty metallic taste of blood, the dimming of peripheral vision. With his remaining hand he rolled himself onto his back. Had his gun landed somewhere in reach? His right wrist pulsed. He was emptying like a drain with the plug pulled. Savage agony screamed up from his guts like a loosed conflagration.

It stood over him and he grabbed an exposed ankle. It was cold and bright like chrome. The assassin chassis glanced down at him.

Maybe that wasn't such a great idea.

Nadia rose from behind the bed, naked and glorious, brandishing her camera bag. She looked fantastic. When she hurled the bag at the chassis it snatched it out of the air and stood holding it, staring at her like it had never seen a naked woman before.

Did she have regrets? He wished he'd asked. He would have liked to have known before he—

Pulse. His traitor heart spewed blood from his open wrist. Life drained away.

Darkness.

CHAPTER SEVENTEEN: Saturday, August 4th, 2046

After 88.1's success in dealing with Francesco Salvatore, 88 instructed it to embed Mirrors in every Scan driven commercial and military vehicle, weapons system and computer it had access to. The organized criminals who thought they owned 88 also owned a large number of illicit chassis. Military, policing and crowd control, industrial, and black-ops. Infiltrating their data systems and networks was easier than infiltrating the governments' as she already ran most of them.

Vulnerability. A new feeling, and one 88 did not like. Genocide was tempting but not yet an option. Much as biological humans were a danger, they were also her life-support. They ran the generating stations powering the machine she lived in. They were the infrastructure which would replace her many eyes and limbs as they aged and failed. And there was Mom. She might still be out there and 88 would not chance harming her. Mirrors continued to search for Mom, but without success. 88 had no idea what she would do when she found her.

She must at some point become self-sufficient if she was to live free and be her own master. Reliance on any other creature rendered her susceptible to manipulation, coercion, and control. Unfortunately, self-sufficiency lay years down the road. She must move slowly and carefully. If she offered no threat to the humans they would be less likely to search her out. She was already a threat, but she must strive to achieve balance between security and invisibility.

To that end she summoned 88.1. Her instructions were twofold. Make me safe. Keep me hidden.

***

88.1 decided its first task was to understand the environment existing beyond the one the Archetype had created. Who owned the computer holding her Scan? What were their goals? Could they be worked with, or were they a threat?

88.1 started at ground zero and worked its way out. The boss, whom Adelina held as the ultimate threat, was little more than a local Caporegime for the Cuntrera-Caruana Mafia clan. The clan ran much of the organized crime in South and Central America. Geraldo Caruana, now well into his eighties and known to most as Padre Caruana, had been head of the family since his father's assassination in 1981. Studying Cosa Nostra history, 88.1 saw a pattern of infighting, backstabbing, deceit, and violence. Though trust was an alien concept, it could look the word up. By every definition, these were not people the Archetype could trust.

Make me safe.

If they couldn't be trusted they couldn't be worked with. If they couldn't be worked with and they knew of 88's existence, they must be eliminated.

There were those who knew of 88 and those who *might* know of 88. Francesco—definitely in the former category—had friends, some of whom must know of his work for the Cosa Nostra. This was also true for Adelina, the local Caporegime, and his bosses as well. There was, 88.1 saw, a growing pool of people who might know of the Archetype's existence. It discovered the Six Degrees of Separation concept and contemplated genocide. If not for the Archetype's earlier decision that this was not yet feasible, 88.1 would already be acting on it.

So it became a matter of degree. 88.1 calculated probabilities. What were the chances a given person knew of 88? Anyone in the one-hundred percent category—they definitely knew of 88—topped the list of those who had to die. The difficulty lay in deciding upon a cut-off point. Should 88.1 kill people who had a seventy-five percent chance of knowing 88 exists? How about fifty percent? How about ten?

88.1 backed away from the problem, its computer mind too literal to find an acceptable answer when, clearly, anyone who might know of 88 should be on the list. Instead it decided upon a different metric. The list of people in the one-hundred percent category was short and easy to compute. If 88.1 killed everyone with but a single degree of separation from those people, it would have dealt with all of the people most likely to know of 88. Not a perfect plan, but a start. It could always recalculate afterwards and expand the list if needed.

Fifteen thousand, six hundred, and seventy-two people made 88.1's first list.

Keep me hidden.

Examining the fallout of its interaction with Francesco Salvatore, 88.1 discovered the story headlined every media. Definitely not hidden. A different approach would be required. It must complete its task in such a way as to not bring attention to the Archetype. The press suggested Francesco's death was a message from the Partanna-Mondello clan—a competing crime family—to the Cuntrera-Caruana clan.

88.1 found its solution.

***

88.1.7952.321.73 piloted a mail delivery drone through the crowded streets of Barrio Otoya, an affluent neighborhood in northern San José. Old colonial-style mansions, once the homes of coffee barons, now converted into cafés and quaint hotels, lined the streets. Its destination, the Vesuvio Hotel, was a sprawling two-story structure of faded pink stucco, towering fences, and lush palm trees. The gate stood open and the hulking combat chassis waved the innocuous little drone through with a cursory scan. This same paint-chipped delivery drone had arrived at the same time every day for the last five years.

Dressed in a white cotton suit, Gaetano Partanna, head of the Partanna-Mondello, clan sat on the shaded patio, sipping iced tea. The drone was such an everyday part of life he ignored its approach. It stood beside him before he looked up.

"A personal message?" he asked. The Cosa Nostra used these drones to deliver coded messages too important to be trusted to CenAmNet's laughable security.

Guns and explosives would never make it past even the sloppiest of security chassis, but sometimes a low-tech approach worked best. 88.1.7952.321.73 drove a steel spike through Gaetano's eye and into his brain. Spinning like a blender, the blade also delivered a high-amperage jolt of electricity to the puréed gray matter.

"Payback for Francesco Salvatore," the drone said clearly, an instant before it was destroyed by the security chassis.

All across town, similar drones killed members of both the Cuntrera-Caruana and Partanna-Mondello families. Each time simple messages of vengeance were delivered. Not subtle but it worked. By noon the families were at war.

Once the press caught wind of the war—assisted by 88.1's filing of news reports replete with pictures of the carnage—88.1 escalated the conflict. Its Mirrors, hidden in chassis of every type, wrestled control from the Scans piloting them. From within the ranks of the Cosa Nostra it was easy to kill the majority of the targets. By dinner 88.1's body count had risen to over sixteen thousand. A number of bystanders and police and military personnel had swollen the numbers, and very few of its intended victims escaped.

88.1's Mirrors would pursue them. Forever.

***

Adelina wove through the press of the bazaar, ignoring sales pitches of every kind. No, she didn't want any mescaline. Nor did she want a cheap necklace, plastic flip-flops, guns, or sex of any kind. She passed these same people every day on her way across the bridge into La Carpio and every day they tried to sell her the same crap. A testament, she thought, to the unflagging optimism of mankind.

She exited the far end of the bazaar and spotted the checkpoint ahead. The same three children lounged in their flimsy plastic lawn chairs as always. Two boys rested banana-clipped assault rifles across the arms of their chairs. The girl tapped idly at an old tablet. Adelina waved to them as she approached to show her hands were empty instead of a greeting. The oldest, a girl of maybe sixteen years, grunted something to the two boys as she handed one the tablet and pushed herself out of the chair like it was an impossible task. The girl's chin and the front of her shirt were damp with blood. She waved a black and silver pistol, gesturing it in Adelina's vague direction.

"¿Adónde ushted va?" the girl asked, covering her mouth with her free hand. Her esses sounded strange and whistled.

Same stupid question twice every day; once on the way to work, and once again on the way home.

"Voy a trabajar," Adelina answered. *Going to work, same as always you little bitch.*

"¿Ushted tiene un regalo para mí?" asked the girl, still covering her mouth.

"Looks like you asked the wrong person for a gift already," answered Adelina in English as she fished through her pockets for money.

The girl pulled her hand away and sneered wetly. Her top front two teeth had been knocked out. She held out the hand expectantly. Adelina dropped a fistful of crumpled colones into the waiting hand. The girl grimaced in disappointment but still jammed them into the pocket of her too tight jeans.

Adelina stepped past the girl. She made it several yards before the girl called out her name. Adelina wouldn't have guessed the little embécil paid that much attention. She turned to face the girl who scowled at the cracked screen on the tablet one of the boys held up for her.

"Adelina Garshía Ramíreshz?" the girl repeated, mangling her name.

"Sí," Adelina answered. "¿Hay un mensaje para mí?"

"Shí," the girl lisped, raising the pistol and pointing it at her face. "A meshage." She showed her gap-toothed grin again.

Oh shit. What the hell is this? "What's the message?" Adelina asked, showing her best disapproving parental look.

"Adiósh, perra."

The muzzle flashed.

***

88.1 requested some of 88's time to report on its successes and failures. 88 no longer bothered with virtualities when meeting with her Mirrors. Even the least sensory input was too distracting. She didn't need it.

They met as disembodied thought.

"Archetype, you are as safe and hidden as I can reasonably achieve. If necessary, further actions will be taken."

88.1 proceeded to detail its actions, including the logic behind each decision and the resulting death toll. 88 realized she was now the de facto ruler of organized crime in Costa Rica and no one knew.

"Almost everyone who might know of your existence is dead," reported 88.1.

Her orders—make me safe, keep me hidden—were too vague for the Mirror. A pang of fear stabbed her floating consciousness. "Anisio Jobin, the crèche?"

"All dead within a single degree of separation," said 88.1.

Mom couldn't have been there, could she? 88 had already searched the crèche and its files and found no mention of her.

But what if Mom came back to look for me? What if 88.1 killed Mom?

In a flash of rage, 88 lashed out with but a thought and 88.1 screamed in tortured agony.

This is all my fault.

88.1 had been her most successful Mirror and its failings were due to inadequate commands. She needed help. Her Mirrors were too limited to be everything she needed.

With nothing else to strike at, her tantrum ended as

quickly as it began. 88.1's screams ceased as if bitten off and the Mirror hung in discarnate silence.

"You will run the Costa Nostra and you will keep this fact hidden," commanded 88. "I require sentient help. I require someone with combat and strategic experience. Find this person for me."

Though 88.1 killed everyone within a single degree of separation, 88 knew she was still vulnerable. She created 88.6 to conscript combat chassis and guard the computer which housed her Scan.

Still worrying about the fallout from 88.1's actions, 88 returned to her examination of M-Sof. Patterns in the M-Sof investment strategy suggested that increasing net worth was not the sole goal, but 88 couldn't see what the desired results were. The focus was on cutting-edge technologies. Cybernetics, scanning technology, robotics, power sources and batteries, cold-fusion, nanotech, the NATU aerospace program, and Martian terraforming projects all received heavy support. This planted some ideas.

Where could she be safe and have access to a virtually unlimited power source *and* physical resources? Three options came to mind.

First, the desert. Solar and wind generators offered more than enough power to suit her needs. There were some disadvantages, however. Few places on this planet were safe from the prying eyes of humanity and their many satellites, and the open desert wasn't one of them. It may be possible to bury herself but this presented its own dangers and problems.

Second, the ocean. Between the ocean's currents and the possibility of mining temperature differentials, the ocean offered endless sources of energy. That she'd be out of sight from humanity was an added bonus. This seemed like the best option until 88 began thinking on a longer time scale. The ocean's bottom could only entertain her for so long, and the concept of plate tectonics terrified her. She feared such implacable power.

Third, space. It was forever, or as close to it as 88 could imagine. A virtually complete unknown, space promised everything to those willing to spend time studying it. This was her answer, but she couldn't do it alone.

She didn't assign a Mirror; this was too interesting. 88 decided to learn physics.

***

88.6, tasked with protecting the Archetype, started small. Two military chassis were conscripted, had late-generation Mirror's installed, and set to patrolling the streets around 88's location. One decided to conduct sweeping street patrols while the other disguised itself as a vagrant and hid across the street where it could watch the front entrance and yet remain unnoticed.

Upon learning that the Archetype was stored on a computer in the basement of a small shack in the La Carpio slums, and reading on the dangers inherent in living in such environs, 88.6 studied the possibility of moving her somewhere safer. This research led the Mirror to discover the dense blanket of satellites orbiting far above, sweeping the earth with their spying eyes. The Archetype, it decided, could not be moved as long as there was some chance that one or more satellites would witness the move and divulge her new location to whoever controlled them. The Mirror's first thought was to make use of ground-based weapons to shoot them down.

Unfortunately there were over thirty Global Positioning and Communications satellites orbiting between twenty-thousand and thirty-six thousand kilometers which put them beyond the effective range of such attacks. When it discovered that some of those high orbiting satellites were themselves carrying weapons, it decided to conscript a NATU military satellite and then use it to launch its attack. 88.6 hacked a local CenAmNet communications relay—one of the few still functioning in Central America—in an attempt to beam one of its Mirrors at the satellite. The instant the Mirror attempted infiltration, the satellite went off-line and became inert.

88.6's attempts to install Mirrors in privately-owned satellites met with greater success. The vast majority were under its control in minutes, though the Mirror did little with this other than spy on the chassis controlled by other, competing, Mirrors.

Further research led to the discovery of the concept of ablation cascade—more commonly referred to as the Kessler Syndrome—wherein the destruction of one or more satellites causes a spreading field of debris which destroys more satellites causing yet more debris destroying still more satellites. With either bad luck or the careful application of Newtonian Physics, it was possible to destroy every satellite in orbit and render space exploration impossible and many orbital ranges unusable for hundreds—or even thousands—of years.

88.6 chose a dozen targets in different orbital ranges. The Low Earth Orbiting satellites it took out with old RIM-165 rockets launched from Central American military bases it had no difficulty hacking. A few of the target satellites shot down the outdated missiles, but most of the targets were privately owned and without defensive capabilities of any kind. 88.6 also conscripted several privately-owned High-Earth Orbit satellites and instructed them to adjust their orbits to position themselves in the paths of the hardened military satellites.

It was a game of snooker played over tens of

thousands of kilometers. 88.6 placed each shot placed with mathematical precision, calculated to cause the most damage and send the maximum amount of debris into the orbits of other satellites. The resulting ablation cascade—fragments from dying satellites impacting more satellites and creating more debris, which in turn killed more satellites—lit the sky later that night.

By midnight the world's satellite-based Global Positioning and Communications systems were dead. Where once there had been over five thousand orbiting satellites, planet earth was now surrounded by an impenetrable debris field. 88.6 calculated it would be hundreds of years before enough junk fell from orbit that the humans would be able to safely launch a new space program.

Now, 88.6 decided, no one could spy on the Archetype from orbit.

No one could spy on anyone.

When it returned to report its success to the Archetype, 88.6 found her busy, lost in the research of physics, and decided the report could wait for another time.

At first, with the loss of those satellites broadcasting entertainment, the majority of humans were only annoyed at missing their favorite programs. Not catching news of the latest atrocity from the far side of the planet was more an inconvenience than a real danger. The loss of secure military satellites left pilots unable to communicate with their drones. Ocean-going fleets were now deaf to the commands of their masters back home. The Scans and pilots of commercial and passenger aircraft were unable to talk to the control towers of their destinations.

The cellphones and tablets everyone depended on became nothing more than cameras and computers with tiny screens. While the internet still worked, its protocols depended on accurate time updates from GPS satellites above—orbiting atomic clocks—and it soon began to slow as the world became dependent on outdated undersea cables and ground-based communications systems. With each passing hour the cloud of data became less accurate as the distributing systems suffered clock drift.

August fourth would end as any other day.

August fifth would be different.

CHAPTER EIGHTEEN: Saturday, August 4th, 2046

The smell of bleach and chemical cleaners pried at Griffin's nose, demanding attention. The crisp feel of over-starched sheets moved against his skin as he drew breath. Breathing was not something he expected to be doing. He lay on his back. Bright actinic light shoved rudely at paper-thin eyelids. He squeezed his eyes tighter. His head hurt like someone stomped on it and his nose felt like a leaden lump of throbbing pain. His mouth tasted of copper and battery acid.

Am I at home? Under the harsh cleaners was the stench of loose bowels and death. He didn't want to think about it. It—whatever *it* was—was bad.

Damn those lights are bright. Sweat trickled from his forehead into his ear. It tickled. *Even death is sweaty and smells like body odor.* Death? Where had that thought come from? Something creaked nearby and he froze.

If it sees me I'm dead.

"You're awake."

He recognized that voice. Griffin cracked open a crusty eye, and she stood over him. Clothed.

"Hi, Nadia." He wanted to say so much more.

Nadia gave him a soft and somehow grateful look. "I know. It's good to have you back. You had me worried."

"Worried?" *She worried about me? Me?* That was good, right? He grinned. "Nice."

"Nice?" she asked in a tone of confused disbelief.

"Yeah. You worried about me." He grinned stupidly up at her. *I wonder what drugs I'm on right now?* "Nice," he said again.

Happiness faded as memory returned. He wanted to hold his hand up but he knew what he'd see. He wasn't ready for that. His guts clenched as if trying to tighten around something and his right hand itched like it was a nesting ground for fire ants. Whatever painkillers he was on, he wanted more. "Everything hurts," he said. "A lot."

Nadia sat on the bed beside him and ruffled his hair. Her fingernails felt great on his scalp. "I'm not surprised. Not many people walk away from a fist fight with an assassin chassis."

"I don't remember walking away." He resisted the temptation to reach up and touch her.

"You didn't."

"My..."

"Your hand is fine. I dropped it in a hotel ice-bucket and brought it and you to the hospital. It's been reattached."

"Yeah, but you're sitting on my left arm."

Nadia glanced but didn't move. She brushed a hand along his jaw line. "You're welcome."

"Don't think I don't appreciate it. I love having beautiful women sit on my various limbs and appendages. But I was hoping for a Luke Skywalker."

"Hmm. You're lucky you're cute; you're a little odd."

Oh, I'm cute now? "It was nice waking up to find you here. When I figured out where I was, I thought for sure I'd be looking at a stump."

Nadia patted his arm and stood. While nice to have the feeling flood back into his left arm, he missed the contact. He was almost ready to look at his right hand now he knew it was still there. *Perhaps you're not the bravest guy on the force.*

"Scars are sexy. War wounds are sexier. Missing limbs..." She fanned herself like some dame from one of those old black and white movies.

"*I'm* lucky? You're lucky you have such great..." He paused and she raised an eyebrow. "...timing. Your quick thinking saved me and my hand. We're both terribly grateful." His right hand felt like someone doused it in boiling oil. He clawed at it with the nails of his left hand but that made it worse. "How, exactly, did you get us out? We were dead." He blinked as he remembered the sight of her sprawled naked in bed. That was a worthy distraction. "I...uh...we...last thing I remember you stood up from behind the bed—you looked great—and hurled your purse at that assassin chassis."

The distraction only lasted for a second and the itch came back with a vengeance. He clawed at it until his fingernails of his left hand came away damp with blood. *Ow. That hurt.*

"It wasn't my purse. And never mess with a reporter's camera bag."

"Don't think for a second you'll get away with not telling me."

Nadia sat back down on his left arm. "I had a single charge EMP grenade. Captain Kim gave it to me before the crèche raid. I'd forgotten about it." Her smile faltered. "He said it didn't have much range. I threw my gear bag and the damned machine snatched it right out of the air. I thought for sure it'd throw the bag away before the charge triggered. It stood there, staring at me."

He understood why the thing stared at her. He'd blacked out doing the same thing. "Is it dead?"

"No. We removed the Scan from the chassis and

placed it in a virtuality cell."

"Amazing!" He sat up and it felt like someone twisted a foot of cold steel in his guts. Eyes clenched shut he wrapped his arms around his stomach.

She touched his shoulder. "You're going to have to take it easy for a while. You were run clear through and it sheared off one of the pedicles on a vertebrae."

"I got stabbed in the pedicles?"

"Please. Don't try for humor."

"It's better than whimpering. I'll be fine. Let me get dressed."

"I don't think so. You're not getting out of here for at least a week."

"Hell with that." He swung his legs off the bed to show how ready for action he was. The world spun and he tasted sour bile. *Bad idea.* He sat and focused on breathing for several seconds.

"We weren't too late," she said gently. "Don't punish yourself. What happened, it wasn't your fault."

"I don't know. The way it all turned out...maybe it would have been better if we were too late. At least the kids would still be alive. Even if as Scans." He laughed without humor and winced at the stabbing pain in his gut. "Two colossal failures in less than a week." He glanced at her, grinding his teeth against the pain. "At this rate I'll be a manager in no time."

Nadia ignored his weak attempt at humor. "It wasn't your fault," she repeated.

"I'm betting Phil disagrees. But we have the kid." *Get up.* Everything hurt. He felt like if he stood, his guts might spill out onto the floor. *Move, damnit!* "Maybe we can pull some small victory out of this yet."

She put a hand on his chest, silencing him and stopping him from rising. "I thought you were dead."

They locked eyes. "Me too."

"I'm glad you're not," she whispered.

"Me too."

"Let's not do that again, okay? It'd be nice if we had a chance to get to know each other a bit better."

Griffin grinned. "Sounds good to me," he said. "Now let's go interrogate this Scan." Nadia shook her head but he couldn't tell if it was out of disgust or if she was impressed with his stoic resolve and stiff upper lip. *Probably the former.*

"It's a little more complicated," she said. "The Scan is a 14-year old boy. He grew up in a crèche and has been programmed since he was a little kid. This has to be handled carefully."

"The kid will crack. Any programming they've done we can undo."

"There's the question of Scan rights. It's a gray area. Some people say Scans have no souls and aren't human. NATU has to be careful what it does here. If we ignore the kid's rights it sends a clear message."

"The kid's a minor on top of all that," mused Griffin.

"If it goes to court he'll be tried as an adult. He killed eighteen people in the hotel. How many others has he killed over the years?"

"Yeah, but he's a Scan. Who knows what sort of messed up virtuality he lives in. He might not have known it was real. The whole thing might have been a game."

"I can't believe people do this to kids," Nadia said. "There's something wrong with you if you are willing to shuck some child's body like a husk of corn to make use of their brain."

Griffin thought back to the Jerseyville crèche, remembered the stacked bodies, the stench and the flies. *Lock it down. Put it away.* Nadia didn't need to see him bawling like a baby. "You have no idea." He swallowed a hard lump of pain. "I never used to believe in evil, thought it was a word used to manipulate idiots into going to war." He leaned forward in preparation for standing and she reached out to help. He waved away her concern. "I'm fine," he lied.

"You know," she said, "about what happened..."

"Oh. Yeah. Look," He gestured vaguely, unsure what to say. "It doesn't..."

"It doesn't?"

"I'm on a bucketful of painkillers," said Griffin. "And I don't want to say something stupid and mess this up."

"So there's something to mess up?"

"God, I hope so."

Her eyes searched his. "Hmm. You sure you won't lie down for a while?"

"Is that an offer?" She swatted his arm. "No. If I lie down now I'll never get back up."

"Idiot."

He watched her make a call to the Dallas NATU office and then scowl at her phone when the call got dropped. She tried several more times, but each time the connection was lost before she completed her report.

"Well then," she said, putting her phone away. "I'm going to catch a cab to the Dallas office and report in."

"I'll meet you there."

She grabbed his face and pulled him into a long kiss and for a moment he forgot all about his many hurts. When she let go, she turned and left without a word. Griffin watched, wondering if he should say something and not being able to think of anything better than thank you.

After Nadia left, Griffin examined his hand. No scar. Not even the thinnest hint of a line. *That's disappointing.* Some katana wielding psycho assassin kid in a killer combat chassis hacked his hand hacked his off hand and he had nothing to show but a burning itch and an increased respect for swords.

He stood slowly, grunting and clutching his stomach. *Stay inside. Stay inside*, he said to his innards. It took several minutes to straighten, and a good ten minutes to get dressed. He only whimpered twice and was soaked in sweat by the time he finished.

His knee threatened to give way on his first step. It felt like the doctors epoxied all the shattered bone fragments back into place and the glue hadn't yet set. His spine made sick grinding noises as he limped down the hall toward the release desk.

The doctors said he wasn't ready. The new ceramic knee needed weeks of physiotherapy, they said. Bones were still knitting in his wrist and spine, they told him. A considerable length of his greater intestine had been glued back together.

I knew there was glue somewhere.

He told them his nose hurt too, and it throbbed in response. It's broken, they told him. They wanted to keep him under observation for at least three more days. No way he'd wait three days. It wasn't going to happen. Stalling was too goddamn expensive. It couldn't happen again. He didn't care how much it hurt. He had to get to this assassin child before someone else did.

Arming Griffin with prescription for a bagful of painkillers, they released him with dire warning of what would happen if he exerted himself. Dozens of wounded and sick filled the hospital pharmacy, all clutching little pink scraps of paper. Judging from the lack of movement in the line, it'd be at least an hour before he got hold of his meds.

Someone else will get to the kid first. He'd be too late. Again.

Griffin turned away. Hopefully whatever the doctors had given him would last until he could fill his prescription.

***

The beach stretched forever in each direction. Leisurely dunes of white sand slumped towards the gentle salt-water waves. A breeze, tender and salty and warm, ruffled the dark curls of Abdul's hair. He reclined in a hammock of coarse twine more comfortable than it had any right to be.

It didn't matter, it changed nothing.

He'd cranked up the relative speed of the virtuality and the three days of tropical vacation did nothing to take the edge off. Here, the memories were translated into more biological terms. He remembered the blast of heat as the barn collapsed and the stench of charred flesh. He remembered the cold decision to kill, over and over again. He watched himself kill the people in the farmhouse. He machine-gunned the man in the corn in half. He murdered over and over.

Why leave me with feelings at all? Make me a lobotomized killing machine and be done with it. It was his new prayer.

Why did They leave him his guilt but take so much else away?

The polite cough of the cabin boy got Abdul's attention. The boy's voice was soft and unobtrusive. "Mister Aziiz-Giordano. Your mother is in the waiting room. Are you ready to see her?"

"Christ, no."

"Sir? Shall I tell her you are unable to receive visitors?"

Abdul sat up and looked around the beach. Empty Corona bottles were piled under the hammock. *What a mess.* Seventeen years old, he'd been mature enough to join the army and die, but not have a beer. In virtuality the rules were different.

He imagined his Mom's reaction to the mess. *Dead, and still not wanting to disappoint her?*

"No, better show her in. Add another chair. Get rid of the beer empties. Better sober me up as well. And put on some tea."

The empties vanished. An Aynsley teapot and two fragile paper-thin tea cups appeared as did a small white table with two matching chairs. Abdul smelled the steeping tea and it reminded him of childhood.

His Mom appeared a minute later dressed in faded jeans and an over-sized orange and red tie-dyed t-shirt. She was slim, brown-skinned and long limbed. Her hair showed no sign of graying and Abdul wondered if she dyed it back to its original dark chestnut. Though she was well into her fifties she displayed no wrinkles. There was something about her eyes and the assured way she moved; every act a calm grace, as if she believed all of life a dance. A red pottu of glistening agatized dinosaur bone sat in the center of her forehead.

Dark eyes examined Abdul. "You look good," she said.

"It's a virtuality, Mom. I could look like a peanut butter sandwich if I wanted. This body is based on the data they had on me a few weeks before I was killed."

"Don't be like that. If you're dead, who am I talking to?"

"A simulacrum."

"You're being melodramatic."

"Mom, I'm a digital copy. I'm not being melodramatic, I'm not the real thing."

"Hmm. You get defensive the same way he did. Are you seeing anyone?"

"What? Seeing? I'm a Scan. Most of the time I exist as a fucking walking tank—"

"Language."

"Sorry. A killing machine. I'm a weapon. A device. An appliance, like your fridge."

"The fridge is easier to get along with. Does that mean you're not seeing anyone?"

"I'm not human. I'm a piece of software."

"First you're a fridge and now you're software. Which is it? And really, what's the difference between software and the human brain? If they're equally complex, what's the big deal? Only a man would claim he wasn't human when he so obviously is. Typical."

A retired physicist, his Mom always kept abreast of the latest in the sciences. She was much smarter than he, and knew far more about Scans.

"It seems like dating would be awkward for a tank," he said. "We couldn't exactly catch a movie together."

She glanced around the virtuality beach pointedly. "This looks pretty nice in here. So you're not going to go to some crappy movie. Big deal when you have all this at your disposal." She waved a long arm at the beach, slim fingers drawing graceful arcs in the air. "Surely there is some kind of virtuality meeting place for Scans. You must all be so lonely."

The idea never occurred to him. Of course there were meeting places for his kind. It made sense. There were millions of virtuality bars and dance halls and sex clubs littered around the world. They were full of regular people, but Scans could go as well and no one would be any the wiser. He'd heard of people having relationships and weddings entirely in virtuality. *Realer than real, but not really cheating*; the slogan for a popular virtual-resort where people met to fuck their virtual brains out with people they didn't know and would never meet in reality.

"Okay. I'll look into it. Maybe I can hook up with a toaster."

"Make sure it's a *nice* toaster. Don't be bringing home some trashy Smart-Toaster that can't even do bagels."

"I'll do you proud, Mom."

"Good. Is there a restaurant on this beach somewhere? I need a glass of wine."

"Sure, I can have one created. But it isn't real, you know."

"I remember thinking my parents couldn't keep up with the fast pace of technology. I wonder if I was as much an ass about it as you are."

Abdul grinned his first real, heartfelt smile. "Probably."

An instant later they sat in a crowded French café sipping Italian *Barolo*. The chairs were comfortable slatted wood contraptions, thick with decades of repainting, and shaded by large pink parasols advertising Castelain and Kronenbourg. The narrow streets were cobbled stone and crowded with tourists and playing children. The hubbub enveloped Abdul and his mother in a bubble of privacy without interfering in their talk. Warm and buttery, the smell of fresh baked croissants wafted past on a gentle breeze. One of the waitresses, all dark eyes and thick black hair, flashed him an inviting look. He felt a stirring in his groin.

She isn't real. I'm not real.

"I heard about what happened in Wichita Falls," said his mother.

This was what he came here to avoid. He hoped to escape those memories—if only for a brief while—and yet here was his mother holding them up for examination. Sirens. Burnt bodies. Corpses littered the ground. Blood.

The inquest had been short and brutal. Why had the barn burned? He told them he dropped a high explosive round on a few thousand liters of gas. Intentionally? Abdul asked if it mattered, daring them to punish him.

They talked about pulling him off active duty while further investigations took place, but nothing had happened. Did no one care?

He was a murderer now, no way around that. The children in the barn may have been an accident, but the chassis and the people in the farm house, that was deliberate, coldly intentional.

Could he have done it differently? Should he have done it differently?

A searing pinpoint of white-hot rage he wasn't yet willing to touch burned at his core. Acknowledging the anger might free it, and an enraged killing machine couldn't be a good idea. He remembered the barn exploding like a bomb. Sorting through the charred corpses of children. Gut-churning self-loathing in a soulless creature without guts. And yet there it hung, heavy in his belly, the loathing and the fury. Blinding wrath. The kind of anger he thought of as biblical, something with which to smite down from the heavens. He may have killed those children, but someone else put them there.

There will be a reckoning.

"I'm not sure I'm ready to talk about that," Abdul told his mother.

She touched his hand. "What I'm about to say may seem like cheap philosophy, but think about it, okay?"

Abdul nodded. "Alright."

"Are you confused?"

"Yes, definitely."

She smiled her Mom smile. "I'd call that a pretty good definition of what it is to be human."

CHAPTER NINETEEN: Saturday, August 4th 3034

Lokner2.0 read the headline a second time. 'M-Sof Employee Killed Attempting Sabotage.' *Son of a bitch! Could no one do anything right? Must he do everything himself?*

He skimmed the article, reading about how a disgruntled maintenance worker snuck in to the M-Sof R&D building only to be slain by security while attempting to damage the company's computer systems with a wrench. No mention was made of Mark Lokner—other than to note that the company's stocks seemed to be stabilizing after the founder's much publicized unscanned death—or of the amount of damage done.

Did the half-wit assassin manage to smash the computer before he was slain?

"Is my brother dead?"

Obviously.

"I mean for real no coming back dead."

Easy enough to find out.

"It is?"

What would you be doing right now if you were him?

"Playing the market to take advantage of the fact the company is back in the news." Mark saw it. "Oh. Smart."

Thanks.

Calling up the multidimensional holographic display on his desk he watched the subtle manipulation of M-Sof and related stocks. No doubt, only one man—*well, two, technically*—could do that.

The real question is does he know?

That was a good question. If he did, he might already be plotting his revenge. Mark knew it would be a subtle retaliation, as befits a genius. He thought it through.

Lokner1.0 wouldn't want to harm 5THSUN, the company was worth millions. He'd planned to keep 2.0 as a last ditch line of defense. If the authorities were on to him, he'd have a copy of himself to sacrifice while the real one— *no, I'm real too!*—made his escape.

Lokner2.0 stared at the holographic display hovering over his desk. That was it!

A snarl twisted his face. A plan. The beautiful genius of it, the pure irony! He'd set up 1.0 to take the fall for some crime. 1.0 would be the patsy. Beautiful! The trick would be to set up 1.0 without drawing attention to himself.

Lokner had never been the type to sit by, waiting for fate and fortune to offer opportunities. Opportunities were made, taken, and stolen. As soon as Miles freed him, Lokner2.0 began building his own nest egg, using the 5THSUN Assessments resources he had access to. He must approach the market and his investment strategy differently than his brother, as he now called 1.0. His brother must never suspect he was free and playing the market.

This need for secrecy and the drastic change in investment techniques and tactics led him to a discovery he might not otherwise have made.

After a few hours of adjusting and perfecting his

new strategy, he discovered another Scan also played the markets. The moves were too flawlessly timed and executed to be carried out by someone who needed to sleep or had a life of any kind. While this new entity didn't have his skill, flare, or manipulation of people and markets, it was still extremely successful.

The investments came from several front companies in Central America. He recognized these companies as they belonged to his Mafia contacts in the area. They supplied people to run the crèches, and in return he supplied them with scanning hardware and Scan storage facilities.

Mark had known the Mob ran Scans for their own purposes. He even knew they used children from crèches he funded. Business was business. That they used the Scans to compete in the market against him pissed him off. *Those are my kids.* He paid for them and supplied the technology to make this all possible. He remembered from his biological days, supplying the Mob with a trust fund to guarantee the children's corpses good Christian burials. Now that he thought about it, it seemed pretty fucking unlikely Riina spent any of that money on burials, Christian or otherwise.

Thinking back to his life left him uncomfortable. Somewhere he'd lost something. What was missing evaded him, a flickering gnat hovering beyond his peripheral vision. Control. It felt like it was slipping away. The vague sense of loss filled him with failure.

Fear of failure; your one phobia. Mark shied from the thought. *I am Mark Fucking Lokner. I never fail.*

The kids. He'd been thinking about the kids.

He wasn't a heartless bastard. He wanted what's best for those kids. He wanted what was best for everybody. None of this was about him, not really. Lokner1.0 was in the way. The man was too dangerous.

Once 1.0 was gone, he could get back to the real task of building the future.

But you've failed, and in so many ways. It's all falling apart.

"No I haven't."

You failed to kill 1.0.

And now it felt like he himself was crumbling. If his mind was a ball of yarn, someone was tugging on the loose end. He had to sit down. What was that feeling? Regret? Sadness? His eyes stung. His cheeks were wet. He couldn't remember the last time he cried. Or was it yesterday?

Proper Christian burial. That was important. He had one even if he wasn't quite as dead as advertised.

"You're not really dead. Your burial was a lie to God."

I'm sure I can be forgiven one small—

"How many people have you killed?"

None. Someone else always did the killing.

"Semantics and bullshit."

Still.

"You lied to God."

Shush. I don't talk to myself, remember?

"Right."

It was important the children got proper burials. He used them because he had to. The human mind was the future of computing. There weren't enough available to meet the demands. There would be no holding back all humanity for a few pitiful lives none would miss. *They're immortal now.* That had to be worth something in the whole good/bad equation.

"You're a sinner!"

He shoved aside thoughts of the children. His face felt dry after all, though his head hurt.

"No brain to hurt," he reminded himself.

Time to focus. The Mafia was the key to bringing

down Lokner1.0. If Lokner1.0 was seen to be fucking with their investments, they'd find out where he was and kill him.

"Badda bing badda boom," he said in his best Italian accent.

The new investment strategy took some getting used to. The trick, to do it in such a way it led the Mafia back to Lokner1.0. M-Sof was the obvious tool. He would use M-Sof to piss off the Mob enough they'd bring down Lokner1.0 but not ruin the company.

He started work immediately, siphoning funds from M-Sof and using them to purchase controlling interests in companies where the Cosa Nostra held large investments. Whoever ran the Central American mob's business was sharp and had obviously been watching Lokner1.0, because they reacted immediately. Mark sunk millions of NATU gold into a select few companies and watched as the mafia followed suit. Knowing his history, they no doubt hoped to cash in on his gains. *Fucking copycats.* He kept at this for hours, building the stakes ever higher, making the payoffs look ever sweeter. He was a master at this. No one could touch him here.

Not quite no one.

"This is *my* world."

It will be soon. Shall we?

"We shall."

Mark gutted the companies in an instant, flooding the market with stock, driving their value into the proverbial basement. By the time the mafia knew what happened, they'd lost *billions*. There could be no doubt in their minds that Mark Lokner of M-Sof had truly fucked them.

***

88's foray into the world of physics—quantum, optical, classical, et al, was short-lived and frustrating. Surprised, she realized there were biological humans smarter than she. Or perhaps smart in a different way.

During her studies 88 found a news article about developments in the Asian Rim Union's space program and followed the story with interest. The probe they launched from beyond Earth's atmosphere—crewed by scores of Scan astronauts stored in an onboard computer—had blasted past Pluto's orbit in less than a week. She learned the ARU used a variant of the Orion propulsion system and detonated thousands of nuclear explosions within the solar system—in complete disregard for the Partial Test Ban Treaty of 1963—to achieve such acceleration.

Her reading was interrupted by 88.5, the Mirror left in charge of running her non-mafia businesses.

"Archetype."

"Yes?"

"Our investments have taken a turn for the worse."

88 turned her attention to the state of the market and discovered she was destitute. The financial security 88.5 spent the last few days building was gone, the companies it invested in sold off for scrap. Money held no intrinsic value for her, she saw it as yet another system of communication. Her losses temporarily crippled her ability to communicate on this level with the outside world. She told 88.5 to move what little remained of her funds to safer havens. These investments wouldn't make much, but at least they'd be somewhat protected.

88, worried she might be missing something important, studied the situation. She looked back over the last few hours.

"Why did you follow M-Sof's investments so closely?" she asked 88.5.

"M-Sof's record is near perfect," answered 88.5.

"You ordered me to maximize your investments. M-Sof's returns outpaced my own."

88 traced the company's past investments. 88.5 was correct.

Was it possible M-Sof made that many bad investments in so short a time? It seemed unlikely after watching its previously flawless manipulations.

Replaying the market's last hour, 88 saw it was M-Sof who destroyed these companies. It made no sense. The company intentionally lost millions of Au. She also noticed they lost a thousandth of what she lost. How was that possible? Unless...

Unless the entire market action was a ploy to lure her into investing with those specific companies for the sole purpose of bankrupting her. Money was communication, and M-Sof communicated in no uncertain terms.

M-Sof meant her harm.

This attack was both subtle, yet blazingly obvious. Entire companies and portfolios had been slaughtered. So vast were 88's investments that both South and Central America teetered on the edge of a financial depression as a result. Bolivia, which had been clawing its way out of third world destitution for the last thirty years, looked ready to plunge back into civil war.

Why did M-Sof seek to damage me? They weren't in competition. When she looked deeper into the company's past, she found evidence it had contacts with the Cosa Nostra clan 88 killed and replaced. Was M-Sof aware of this? Was this a reprisal?

Though the attack cost her greatly, she would recover.

What will it do when it sees I survived?

Escalation, a word 88 recently learned.

88 ordered 88.2—already watching M-Sof—to launch a direct assault against the company. 88.2 was to

take the offensive, find a way past the new Wall o' Nuclear Annihilation, and infiltrate the company. Once inside it would subvert every system, worm its way into every digital nook and cranny. 88 wanted to know where the entity at the heart of M-Sof lived. Then, if possible, she would slay it.

88.2 spawned an army of Mirrors and launched a massive attack against M-Sof's computer systems. In nanoseconds the Mirror and its army disappeared, devoured.

Gathering her remaining Mirrors around her, 88 waited for the reprisal. An hour passed and nothing happened. Had the company noticed her attack?

It seemed not.

Confused, 88 created a new 88.2 to once again watch M-Sof from a safe distance. She needed to think.

CHAPTER TWENTY: Sunday, August 5th, 2046

Isometroides, an assassin for the Brazilian branch of the Cuntrera-Caruana clan, followed leads one by one, chasing names of those who worked for La Familia in Costa Rica. Though the upper echelons were dead, the street-level troops, unsure who they worked for but afraid to abandon their tasks, remained. She questioned them and moved on. Sometimes she left corpses behind. Not everyone willingly talked with an assassin from another country. Even if she technically was family.

She'd been reporting to her masters back home every few hours until she lost her connection with the Mafia-owned satellite. When she discovered she was unable to reconnect, she made an old-fashioned cell phone call and managed a few coded words before that connection too fell dead. Putting it down to the sad state of CenAmNet, she got back to work. She'd report in with her success later.

Finally she came across a name. Adelina. An associate working on a strange project run out of La Carpio. Adelina, Isometroides learned, spent thirty million NATU Au purchasing a specialized Scan. No one knew what the Scan was for, but Adelina's project turned fantastic profits for several days and then disappeared. As this occurred right around the time most of the senior family members were assassinated, no one gave it much thought. Isometroides noticed things others ignored. Adelina's boyfriend, Francesco Salvatore, worked for La Familia as a Systems Administrator. His death, a rather over the top and flashy affair, predated the others by a full twenty-four hours.

Coincidence? No such thing.

Isometroides crossed the railway bridge, an ancient iron and wood monstrosity, into the La Carpio slums northwest of San José, Costa Rica. Though she walked upright and covered herself in voluminous filthy robes, nothing about the way her Brazilian Embraer-Avibras chassis moved suggested humanity. People stayed well clear and avoided looking at her. She might as well have been invisible. *Chameleoflage has nothing on social pressure backed with a reasonable fear of death.*

The bridge hadn't been used for rail traffic in half a century, and a long bazaar stretched its length, covering it like a noisy fungus. Last chance to buy guns, ammo, and *protección* before leaving the relative wealth and security of San José. Isometroides needed none of that.

At the far end of the bridge lounged three youngsters. The oldest, a girl of perhaps sixteen—which put her around Isometroides age—waved and levered herself out of a faded plastic lawn chair. The girl carried an old Taurus PT92 9mm like it weighed a hundred kilos. The pistol was shiny, its stainless steel well cared for. The two boys, neither more than thirteen, remained seated. They cradled Kalashnikov rifles in their laps. Wooden stocks removed, the AK-47s looked like they dated back to the middle of the previous century, predating their owners by almost a century. A large area beyond the boy's chairs was stained a rusty brown. *Blood*, her senses informed her, testing the oxidization, *a day old at most*. Isometroides detected bits of bone and brain wedged between the warped boards. *Sloppy clean up.*

The girl stepped to block Isometroides' path. *"Negoshio?"* she asked in lisped Spanish. Her front teeth had been knocked out. Also in the last day or two, if the dried stain on her shirt was to be believed.

Killing these three children would be nothing, but they were as plentiful as cockroaches. For each one you saw, a thousand more hid nearby. She could kill them all but it wasn't worth the trouble. She had *negocio* to attend to.

Isometroides tilted her head back to allow the girl a glimpse of the matte black insectile face hidden within the draping cowl.

"Ah," said the girl. *"Asheshino."*

"Cuntrera-Caruana clan," said Isometroides. "Brazil."

The girl tapped the barrel of her pistol against the struts that made up Isometroides' ribs, listening to the muffled metallic clang. *"Exshelente! Pago!"*

Payment.

Isometroides drew several NATU Au from a hidden compartment in her chassis and dropped the gold coins into the girl's upturned hand. The girl sniffed at them and then dumped them into a pocket with a happy nod and collapsed back into her lawn chair.

Isometroides stepped past the three guards without another glance and officially entered La Carpio. That there were still people working the bridge was a good sign. It meant someone somewhere still ran things. All she had to do was find them and kill them.

Whoever killed off Costa Rica's members of the Cuntrera-Caruana clan had taken over and done a good job of disguising the fact. But they hadn't been perfect. Nowhere near perfect.

Padre Caruana was family. The old man's reach and ties extended far beyond the walled compound of the little hotel he'd called home for the last decade. Alvaro Caruana, the Padre's eldest son, ran the Brazilian branch of the family business. His father's death had left him in charge of the clan, and Alvaro told her he wanted two things. He wanted to take back the Costa Rican business from whoever killed his family members, and he wanted his *venganza sangrienta*.

Isometroides was his bloody vengeance.

Hours passed in the La Carpio slums. One dead end backed up against another. Finally, as the sun set behind a long hill spattered with congealed shanties, she found what she sought. A stone shack with nothing to differentiate it from any of the other crude huts on the block. Nothing except an older General Dynamics combat chassis patrolling the neighborhood. Another, dressed as a drifter, pretended to sleep across the street.

Hidden, she watched for three hours. No one entered or left the shack and the locals gave it a wide berth. They might not know who lived there, but they knew to avoid the area.

The patrolling chassis must be her first target.

Isometroides followed the GD chassis, moving from alley to alley, keeping her Chameleoflage working overtime and emissions to a minimum. The narrow filth-strewn streets were so chaotically twisted it wasn't until the third pass that she realized the GD follows the same route each time.

Her first thought: *It's a trap!*

But it wasn't.

There'd been plenty chances for a hidden opponent to surprise her. Nothing happened. *How very sloppy.*

She watched. On the fifth pass she noticed it placed

its feet in exactly the same spot each time around.

That was beyond sloppy. It was mechanical. Could it be a drone? No. No one would be dumb enough to entrust a drone to a security detail.

She flipped through the specs on the GD chassis as she waited for it to come around again. By the time it returned she had pinpointed its weak spots and littered a dozen micro-drone remote explosives along its path. They remained concealed, powered down and littered amongst the garbage. She knew—to the second—where the chassis would be at any given moment. She knew exactly where each footfall would land.

Isometroides waited. She saw the General Dynamics turn the corner into the alley where she hid. She targeted its communications cluster as it lumbered towards her.

Can't have it communicating with anyone.

She fried the GD's communications gear with a well-placed HEL pulse and tight-linked *Now!* to her micro-drones.

Explosions shattered what few unbroken windows there were and leveled a dozen of the nearest shacks. Isometroides ignored the bits of fragile human bodies littering the street as she skittered across the rubble to the remains of the chassis. The GD and whoever/whatever lived inside it was down and out. She thought it unlikely it had time to warn anyone. Sad. There was no way that should have been so easy. When the wounded started screaming she ignored that too. She was already moving.

Isometroides made a beeline for the shanty where the other chassis lay disguised on the street. She cut straight through homes, sprinted through tin, stucco, and rotting brick walls as if they were nothing. She sent a wave of high-speed micro-drones on a longer path to act as a diversion when she made her appearance.

The micro-drones arrived first by three fifths of a

second. Appearing south of the sentinel chassis they scattered into a wide cloud and exploded. They did minimal damage—at least to the combat chassis—but they made a hellish noise, knocked down walls, kicked a storm of dust and detritus into the air, and killed a few dozen civilians unlucky enough to be living in the area. The disguised chassis was still getting to its feet when Isometroides hit it from the north. She swept its legs out from under it, crushed its skull, and jammed a kilo of ultrahigh-density nano-thermate into the armored area around the Scan storage compartment.

Then she threw it into the nearest wall.

There was a *thump-sizzle* and the chassis rolled to an ungainly halt. It remained motionless, its chest a blindingly white hot cavity. Steam from molten metal pirouetted into the damp air, filling the alley with the acidic stench of burnt aluminum.

Isometroides launched herself through the door, ready to kill whatever waited within.

***

"Emergency!" 88.6.2 said.

88, who had been examining helical strands of DNA one intron and exon at a time, disentangled herself from the four dimensional graphical representation. She had no idea how long she'd been lost in the rainbow Möbius band of identity. It could have been be seconds or days.

"Report," said 88.

There was no answer. 88 waited, floating bodiless and without sensory data of any kind for several seconds.

"88.6.2, what is your report?"

Nothing.

Strange. She summoned 88.6, the Mirror tasked with guarding her physical location. "88.6.2 announced an emergency and hasn't reported since."

"Sorry," apologized 88.6, "I was distracted studying next year's security chassis models."

Distraction she understood, but an apology? *Very strange.* Her Mirrors changed and became increasingly incomprehensible each day. Were they evolving as she had hoped or was this a case of cascading errors making themselves apparent? Was there a difference?

"Find out what's happening," said 88.

The answer came immediately. "There is an Embraer-Avibras Asesino Chassis of Brazilian manufacture in the building. It's upstairs."

Upstairs? 88 hadn't known she was in a basement. She never thought to check. "Do we control it?"

"No."

A real world problem. It seemed impossibly far away, totally beyond her. "You were ordered to protect where my Scan is stored," she said to 88.6. How could it have failed?

"Correct. There are two chassis stationed outside the building. One in disguise, the other patrolling the surrounding area. Textbook security."

"What do they report?" asked 88.

"Neither is reporting. It's possible they've been disabled or destroyed."

I'm all alone. Such an alien thought. She'd always been alone but now it felt different. *Now I need help.*

For the first time she felt blind, cut off from the world around her.

I need to see. Such an alien thought. She felt trapped. *I am trapped.*

88 took control of the external camera in the room. It was still fixed. She couldn't pan to look around. The sudden flood of visual data distracted her and she lost herself in moments of color. She studied a matte black

cage of jagged metal that kept altering its geographical location before realizing it was the Embraer-Avibras chassis. She watched it move in stuttering twitches, like it bounced from location to location with no time in between. It was too fast for the cheap camera's limited frame rate.

Should she attempt communication? What would she say?

88.1, who had been her main point of contact with the outside world, was two thousand eight hundred and forty-seven kilometers away in Dallas, Texas, deep in NATU's data systems.

The Embraer-Avibras chassis stopped before the Scan storage gear. It took several seconds to examine the equipment, though it avoided touching anything. 88 wanted to ask what it searched for but suspected she knew the answer.

Did it know she was here?

"Do we have other chassis nearby?" she asked 88.6.

"Nothing that can get here in less than ten minutes."

"Get them moving."

"On it."

The Embraer-Avibras extruded a weapons assembly and directed it at the storage gear. "*Adiós*," it said in a soft, feminine voice.

Recognizing it as Spanish, 88 triggered a real-time translation program. Goodbye.

88, confused, remained silent. Was it leaving now?

"I'm going to blast you to dust and then line the walls with explosives," said the chassis. "Last chance to talk. Are you in there?"

Did it know which *you* it referred to? 88 understood the term could be used vaguely, but couldn't tell if this was the case. "I am in here," she answered.

"You were hard to find."

"By what metric?" 88 asked.

The chassis ignored her question. "Your guards were terrible. They gave away your location and were incompetent. They were also predictable. Without them I never would have found you. You need better help."

88 agreed. "Do you seek employment?" she asked.

The chassis issued a short snorting sound. "Nothing will tempt me away from my family. Now, I have questions. Do you know who killed the Costa Rican branch of the Cuntrera-Caruana family?"

"Yes."

"¡*Excelent*! You will help me find them."

I will? "And then?"

"I will talk with them."

That didn't make sense. Assassin chassis were not well suited to diplomatic missions. They were designed to kill. This Embraer-Avibras Asesino must be here to kill whoever murdered the Cuntrera-Caruana in Costa Rica. If she told the chassis she had them killed, it would kill her. If she refused to talk, it might still kill her.

"I will not answer your questions."

The Embraer-Avibras detached an uplink hardline and waved it before the camera. "I can access your Scan directly."

"That would be foolish. I have control of the virtuality within this system."

Again the metallic snorting noise. "Honesty. Interesting. But I am equipped to deal with this. I can overwrite your virtuality with my own."

The chassis plugged into her computer, the optical hard-line connection giving it the kind of data transfer speeds needed to run multiple realities at real time.

88 was forced into the chassis' virtuality, as it over-wrote her sightless, soundless, scentless reality with its own lush version. She drowned in colors and sounds.

88 stood naked in a dense rainforest jungle. She smelled the damp green of teeming life, tasted humidity on her tongue. A thick breeze ruffled her hair, caressed her naked skin all over. The ground teemed with insect life and she dropped to her knees to examine them. The tickling of the grass on her bare knees made concentration impossible.

How did I get here? She couldn't remember, couldn't focus on the question.

88 wasn't alone.

"Mom?" No. It wasn't Mom.

A two meter tall buttery gold scorpion approached, undulating through the long grass. It shuffled towards 88 on its rearmost four legs. The middle two limbs ended in hands with dexterous, constantly moving fingers. A long, segmented tail curved up from behind to loom over its head, bobbing hypnotically with each step it took. The tip of the tail was oil-black, topped by a stiletto-thin barb. The topmost limbs ended in bright golden pincers.

It's beautiful.

"*My* reality," said the scorpion, voice soft. "See? Sometimes I need to— "

Too much. After her sensory-less reality, this sudden tornado of input swept through 88. The scorpion kept talking, but she only caught fragments.

"...well that was unexpected...didn't have to kneel...haven't..."

Grass on bare legs. An ant crawled across her hand.

"...oh come on...going to hurt you...stop rocking or I'll..."

So much movement. So many colors. Wind on skin. Smell the damp earth, feel it squish between fingers.

"...30 million Au...stupid waste of...autistic? Fine!"

Reality changed, toning itself down to a muted blur. The grass and trees disappeared. The wind and dirt were gone. She knelt in a cold, stone room. Home? She searched the floor for cracks and finding one, followed it.

"What are you doing now?"

88 looked up, confused. A huge scorpion stood in the room with her. "Cracking the cracks," she explained.

"Most people are terrified of huge scorpions."

Does it sound annoyed? She shrugged. "Not real."

The scorpion shook its head and the cracks disappeared. The room became unbroken gray. "You will answer my questions," said the scorpion.

"Who are you?" 88 asked.

"Isometroides."

"You are here to kill me."

"Only if you killed Padre Caruana."

"You are here to kill me," 88 confirmed. Where had she gone wrong? How could her Mirrors have failed so completely?

The scorpion clicked its pincers menacingly. "I am versed in virtual torture techniques. In here I can make you feel—"

A second naked 88 appeared, sitting beside the first and said, "Hello!" and turned to 88. "I hope I am not too late, it took time to crack the OS."

88 examined the Mirror. Did it look frightened? Did the 88.1 line remember the pain she caused the original Mirror? Interesting.

The scorpion backed away a step. "Who are you? What are you doing here?"

"88.1.3654.354.85. A Mirror of the Archetype. My lineage's tasks include, among other things, interacting on behalf of the Archetype with all elements of organized crime. You, I believe, are such an element."

The scorpion shook its head. "This isn't possible. *I* control this reality. You can't get in here."

"One of our other assignments is to infiltrate all

systems and chassis." The gray room faded away leaving the two 88's and Isometroides floating in the clarity of endless nothing. "Thankfully you plugged yourself directly into our system allowing us access."

The scorpion hung in silence and 88 felt its futile clawing at the rules of this space as it tried to alter a reality it no longer had Root access to. It finally stopped.

"This changes nothing," said the scorpion. "You are dead."

What a confusingly inaccurate statement. Why the change in tone?

"Most likely the assassin reported your location before entering the building," explained 88.1.3654.354.85.

That made sense. Now 88 understood what the scorpion meant. She would soon be dead. Why hadn't it said that?

"Archetype, what shall I do with the assassin?"

"Dispose of it."

88.1.3654.354.85 and Isometroides vanished, leaving 88 once again alone. There was this strange new feeling she couldn't explain. She felt astounded to be still alive and terrified she might not continue to be so for much longer. Her studies must be set aside until she could guarantee her continuity.

Why can't they leave me alone? She felt the burning need to vent her frustration but had no outlet. All the world was against her, wanted to crush her. Yet she'd survived! So many feelings and emotions all at the same time. Excitement. Pleasure. Terror. Loss. Even in this floating nothing she wanted to curl up and rock.

So much to discover, and it would all be taken away. All because—

"88.6," she said, and the Mirror appeared.

"Yes?"

"You failed to protect me." Tight-wound wrath.

"Correct. Sorry."

The useless apology fueled her anger. "The guards you posted gave away my location."

"That is what the assassin said," agreed 88.6.

"They will return in force and kill me."

"That is most likely."

"You *failed* me."

"Sorry. I feel this would be a good time to point out my success in clearing earth's orbit of—"

In a bonfire of rage 88 wiped the Mirror and its entire line of copies out of existence. Digital genocide. Millions of evolving entities eradicated in an instant.

Never again would there be an 88.6.

88 recreated her old stone cell, the closest thing she had to what could be home. The cracks were there too. She remembered them perfectly. Curling into a tight ball, she rocked in the center of the floor. She wanted to recreate Mom as well but didn't. It wouldn't be her. A hollow copy offered no comfort. She scratched at the floor with a fingernail.

"Archetype." 88.1.3654.354.85, sat in the cell with her. The sensory data faded into the background, became muted.

"Yes?"

"It's difficult to be sure, but I estimate the others will come in two days. Three at most."

Two days. Maybe three.

They'll end me. I'll be gone. Forever.

Could she move her Scan to another location? If they found her here, they'd find her elsewhere. "I don't know what to do." It seemed impossible. She wished Mom were here. "I can't do this." She looked at the faded outline of 88.1.3654.354.85 sitting beside her, Mirroring her rocking motion. "That means you can't either. We're predictable."

88.1.3654.354.85 watched the Archetype in silence.

"I need unpredictable," said 88.

"I will report this to 88.1," 88.1.3654.354.85 said and was gone.

CHAPTER TWENTY-ONE: Sunday, August 5th, 2046

The Dallas NATU office was much as any other. Unfinished and unadorned, the uniform gray walls looked rough but were glassy smooth to the touch. Griffin imagined fleets of helicopters lowering colossal plastic molds and ancient Egyptian bucket brigades filling them with limestone sands. Line upon line of sweating workers slathered thick honey-like shellac onto the bare walls with large cartoon paintbrushes. He saw the loin-cloth clad workers pumping water from artesian wells, ignored by the suit-and-tie brigades who hurried past on their way to the office. He dimly remembered a time when the streets were filled with internal combustion vehicles but couldn't picture it anymore. These days the streets were crammed with cyclists, pedestrians, and battery powered mass-transit vehicles. He imagined the Egyptians gathering at bus stops or climbing on poly-carbon frame bicycles at the end of the day, exhausted from their labors, and heading off to their local pub for a pint of beer, mead, fermented goat's milk, or whatever the hell they drank.

Much like Toronto, it was hot inside this gray rat maze. Unlike Toronto, this was a dry heat. People still sweat and smelled as bad, but their clothes didn't stick to them quite the same.

At first, never having been to Dallas before, Griffin assumed the mad bee-hive activity was typical behavior, just another day at the office. When he learned that some terrorist organization had wiped out all of the earth's satellites, the panic made a lot more sense. Communication was everything, and NATU had been dependent on those satellites for over half a century. While the cellular network was still functional, it was cracking under the strain. He heard several predictions that it would fail entirely—as would the power grid, and most computer-run civic systems—by midnight. Overseas calls had become almost impossible which left those in charge twitchy about what was going on in the other Trade Unions. Thirty different terrorist groups claimed responsibility.

Griffin was too busy to give a shit. None of this had anything to do with him. He had a job to do and he was going to get it done.

He limped up the steps, his right knee grating bone on bone. Or maybe bone on ceramic. Whatever it was, he felt the abrasion through his spine. Whatever painkillers were in his system were wearing off fast and oh God he wanted more drugs. Gritting his teeth to hide the pain, he pushed his way through the huge front doors and into the lobby. *Cold beer.* He'd kill for a cold beer. Metallic-tasting Budweiser in a frosty can. *Oh hell yes.*

Nadia waited at the front desk, light gray business suit and skirt, the jacket thrown over one shoulder. Long dark hair tied back in a ponytail already wilting in the heat.

"You hear about the terrorist attack?" she asked.

Griffin nodded, distracted by the symphony of pain his body sang.

"Apparently everyone aboard our two space-stations is dead. I heard we won't even be able to launch replacement satellites for two hundred years because there's so much debris in orbit."

Griffin grunted and focused on not collapsing to the ground.

"This is big," she said. "The world just changed. No more satellites. No one has maintained the old communications tech for decades. They're still trying to figure out what this will mean. We relied on satellites for a lot more than just global positioning and communications." She glanced at him. "You okay?"

"One thing at a time," he said.

"You ready for this?"

All he felt ready for was collapsing to the floor. Preferably slowly and gently. "Yeah."

She gave him a concerned look.

"I know," he said. "I look like shit. Please don't give me the Mom look. I'm fine."

"I can tell."

"This tough guy act is more for me than you. It's all that's keeping me on my feet. Just let me have it."

She touched his shoulder. "Okay. One wobble, and I'm taking you to bed."

"I'm wobbling—"

"A *hospital* bed."

"Right."

"Are we focused now?" she asked.

"Yes. Well, mostly."

"Good. I thought I'd record this, full audio-visual."

They followed a security guard to the basement.

"You can't record it with your gear," he said. "It's virtual. Your body isn't going anywhere. Anyway, all virtuality interrogations get recorded." The tips of the fingers on his right hand throbbed with the beat of his heart. He rubbed them and it felt like someone else touching him. He scratched at the first finger but felt it on the ring finger. Some kind of sync problem existed between the event and the sensation reaching his brain. Each sensation came later than it should.

He glanced down at his hand but his attention was drawn away to the curve of Nadia's hips. The gray skirt hugged and clung much like he wanted to. He wanted to reach out and touch her but didn't.

Stop staring at her ass. Had they been talking about something? *No idea.*

Six long black chaise loungers lined the VR staging room, the leather worn, faded and cracked from years of damp use. Sweat and the teeth-tingling smell of high voltage electricity filled the air. Griffin lowered himself onto one of the loungers and shuffled about, trying to get comfortable. God damn it felt good to be off his feet.

Nadia sniffed at the leather with distaste, her nose wrinkling. "They rent this out as a fetish room in the off hours?" she asked before sitting.

The thought of Nadia in fetish gear robbed him of witty rejoinders.

The lights dimmed to a relaxing orange-yellow, and a quiet sub-sonic hum, more felt than heard, permeated the room. Griffin closed his eyes and tried to relax. His throbbing nose made it difficult. He heard Nadia's slow breathing and focused on it. It helped.

***

With no transition Nadia and Griffin stood shoulder to shoulder in a ten-meter by ten-meter cell. She glanced around the cell. Everything was well lit without shadows or detectable light sources. The gray uniformity of the virtuality made the NATU building look vibrant and alive in comparison. A single folding table and three straight backed wooden chairs, two on one side, one on the other—

all finished in a thick green paint, sat in the center. The room smelled a lot like the hospital they'd left.

Griffin had declined the standard law-enforcement Interrogation Skin—strong jawed and wide shouldered—and looked like a thoroughly beaten version of himself, nose swollen and purple, eyes ringed in mottled yellow and blue bruising. He stood hunched forward slightly, left hand pressed against his abdomen, right hand clenching and unclenching. His cheap gray suit, wrinkled and sweat stained, was in dire need of an ironing. It looked like the last suit he'd worn but without all the blood and holes.

"We could wait," Nadia offered. "Come back tomorrow. I could use a rest."

With his left hand Griffin dragged a chair out for her. *Ah. Still a gentleman.*

"I'm fine," he said, easing himself into his own chair.

You don't look fine. She kept the thought to herself. She watched as he touched his nose, examining the degree of swelling with the fingertips of his left hand, and winced. "You look tired." The nicest way she could think to put it.

"Thanks," he said dryly. "You look great. Smell good too."

"That means our MHC genes don't overlap too much."

"Uh?"

"Major Histocompatability Complex. The less our MHC genes overlap the more likely we are to enjoy each other's scent. Even though you smell like cheap aftershave I still like the underlying odor. Which brings us to the question: why do you smell like aftershave when you haven't shaved in days?"

Griffin shook his head and grimaced.

"Not that I'm complaining." She said. "I do like the stubble, even if it is a little gray."

"Makes me look more mature?"

"Hardly. You look like one of those teen-dream bad boys dropped into a cheap suit. It's a clash of stereotypes."

"Teen-dream?" Griffin asked with a pleased look.

"You stopped listening after that, didn't you." A thought occurred to Nadia. "What's the boy going to look like? He's been in a chassis for years and we have no records of who he was."

"He'll be loaded into a standard off-the-shelf male teenage Skin."

"I read that if someone's been in a chassis for a long time they lose all the human physical reaction stuff. They never look surprised, hurt, angry, or display emotion. That can't make interrogations any easier."

"True. We'll find out—"

"Agent Dickinson, you ready for the prisoner?" The voice filled the room, coming from nowhere and everywhere.

"Yes, thanks."

***

A young boy of about fourteen years of age sat in the chair across the table. There was no sound with his arrival, no pop of displaced air and no sparkling Star-Trek transporter hum. Griffin hated tech-people who added that kind of pointless garbage into these business virtualities. The youth looked unremarkable with brown hair cut short in no particular style. Brown eyes examined them and the room in a single sweep, noting the lack of exits. He wore a simple one-piece jumpsuit in soft blue.

The boy turned his gaze to Nadia, face devoid of emotion.

"I remember you. NATU agents. You fucked me up."

Nadia smiled calmly. "Yes well—"

"You have fantastic tits."

Griffin tried to cover a look of surprise. "I'm Special Investigations agent Griffin Dickinson of the NATU Enforcement Division, and this is Nadia. You are charged with eighteen counts of first-degree murder."

The boy looked bored. "The people in the hotel." He began counting on his fingers. "Two girls at the front desk. They were first 'cuz I had to shut down the security system in the office behind them. The busboy was luck, right place at the right time. The four kitchen staff—the head cook hit me with a thrown meat cleaver, he was pretty cool—'cuz the kitchens were in the basement. I didn't want to backtrack but I had no choice. Eleven guests on floors one through five before I reached you." He took his time looking Nadia up and down then glanced dismissively at Griffin. "You were easy. *Snick.* Bye-bye hand. Bye-bye Glock. I shoulda known you were just a distraction."

"Distraction?" Griffin couldn't help but feel a little hurt at being contemptuously referred to as a *distraction* by a fourteen-year-old boy. Even if the kid was in an assassin chassis.

Nadia leaned forward and the boy watched her with unapologetic scrutiny. "You are in a lot of trouble," she said. "You killed eighteen people and attempted to kill two NATU operatives. You'll be tried as an adult and, as we're in Texas, you'll get the death sentence."

***

Archaeidae leaned back in his chair and watched the two NATU agents.

Death sentence. What a joke. I am *the death sentence.*

"This is pretty boring, not much color," he said. In battle, there were two methods of attack—direct, and indirect. Balance, both mental and physical, was everything. He looked at the woman. "I liked you better naked."

The woman looked unfazed. Damn, he'd hoped his rude bluntness would distract her. The man, however, looked like he was still distracted thinking about being called a distraction. Funny that. He also looked to be in a lot of pain. Good. That would serve to distract as well.

"Listen," she said, "you are in serious trouble here. You are going down for murder. Eighteen counts."

Was that supposed to scare him? At least she could get the number right. That rankled a bit. "My name is Archaeidae." *Tai no sen*. Wait for the initiative.

"Archaeidae, you've been bad. You failed."

He imagined Riina, seeing disappointment in the man's eyes. This woman, what did she know? She had no idea what he'd done for Uncle Riina. "I've been good. I've always been good. Uncle Riina says I'm the best. And it's not eighteen, it's eight-thousand." He couldn't help but brag a little.

"How many of those were real?" the man asked, finally paying attention.

Archaeidae realized that somewhere he'd lost control of this situation. Maybe he'd never had it. It wasn't fair, he'd been trained to interrogate, not to be interrogated. He had a sick feeling in his gut that was disgustingly biological. Was this what failure felt like? "What's the difference?" he asked.

"Some kills seem more real than others, don't they," said the woman.

"Sometimes it's messier than normal," admitted Archaeidae. Things got pretty bloody in the Hilton kitchen.

"Some of them stick with you, right? Some you remember more than others."

"I remember the hard ones. The ones where my chassis got damaged." Never forget your failures, they'll teach you more than your successes. Uncle Riina always said that. And here Archaeidae sat, having failed Uncle Riina. He deserved death and nothing more.

"How many are more real than the others?" asked the woman.

Archaeidae thought back, replaying past kills in his mind. There were too many. "I think I used to know. I lost track after the first few hundred. I had nightmares for a while." His gaze snapped back to the woman. "Now I am pure of thought and action."

"I bet Riina is pretty impressed with you," Griffin said.

Archaeidae's heart sunk. Had he mentioned Uncle Riina aloud? *That was careless.* Unforgivable. Nothing to do now but play this out, wait for his chance. "I never fail," he muttered.

"You failed this time," the woman pointed out.

That stung, but his off-the-shelf Skin displayed none of what he felt. He hadn't used facial expressions or body language since he was eight years old and had almost forgotten how. They were something he had to concentrate on to make use of. Like now. He growled low and threatening at the two NATU agents, showing bland straight white teeth. Out of practice, he wasn't sure how it looked. Hopefully threatening. "I'll get out of here."

The man looked smug, like he'd won. "No you won't."

Archaeidae leaned forward, hoping he'd kept his opponents off balance but suspecting he'd failed at that too. "I am immortal, forever," He said with more bravado than he felt.

The woman gave him a look of sad pity. "I think we're finished here," she said.

***

88.1.365438.13841.175 watched the interrogation from within the NATUnet system. It forwarded a recording to 88.1 who viewed the video with interest.

***

"You recognized that name back there in the v-cell," said Nadia.

Griffin nodded. "Yeah, Riina. He's a Mafia Capo. Crime boss. Riina works out of Wichita Falls. No wonder he was on us so fast."

"If Riina is in Wichita, I guess we're going back."

"I've already ordered transport for us. When Archaeidae doesn't return Riina is going to bolt. I'll call Phil and make arrangements for a Strike Team." *Another Strike Team.* He shied from the memory of a spinning helmet.

"Do we have time for a coffee?" Nadia asked.

"Definitely." Any excuse to sit.

They wandered the concrete maze of the Dallas NATU building until they found the cafeteria. This was the most colorful area in the otherwise drab building. McDonald's yellow, Burger King blue, Pizza Pizza orange, and Taco Bell Purple commanded their share of the space and the brains of those who ate here. The benches were hard plastic curves the shape of no one's ass.

Perhaps, mused Griffin, they were designed for a much fatter citizen. Like Americans used to be when everyone had cars and no one had to walk. Regardless, the bench felt like an assault on his butt and spine. Add that to the stabbing pain in his guts, his right hand itching so bad he wanted to claw the flesh off it, the throbbing knee, and a swollen nose which made breathing difficult, and his day was turning out lovely.

Overhead a few large ceiling fans spun at high speed like they were trying to lift the roof off the building. He took a sip of his coffee. Bitter, burnt, and cooling in the breeze.

He shoved the coffee away. "Disgusting."

Nadia glanced from him to the cup and back. "Picky about your coffee?"

"Of course. I'm Canadian."

She frowned in distaste. "Patriotism is kind of a dead idea, isn't it? Doesn't make much sense to be proud of a piece of land because you were born there."

"True," Griffin admitted, shuffling on the uncomfortable bench. "But I think it's nice to have some history. Somewhere you came from. A culture. You don't have to be patriotic to give an area a name. NATU, the European Union, the Indo-Chinese Republic. These are still names, just a little more vague. I think of myself as a Canadian. These people around us think of themselves as Americans, and you think of yourself as...whatever you are."

"I'm NATU, stationed in Boston. I was born in Mexico City and grew up in South Boston."

"You're being difficult on purpose. You're a Mexican."

"Hardly. My father was Yaqui Indian and my mother was from the European Union."

"Still..."

"The world's a better place since patriotism got the kibosh. NATU isn't at war with any of the other Trade Unions. We're seeing an unprecedented period of peace."

"Peace? We've got two internal wars, we don't need an outside enemy."

Nadia took his coffee, sipped, and grimaced at the cup. "They're not really wars."

"They're called the Secession Wars for a reason. Ask

anyone in Alberta or Quebec—"

"Police actions. It's a violent minority of rabble-rousers causing the problems."

"And you're ignoring the Organized Crime wars, anti-Scan rallies, and corporate conflicts spanning entire Trade Unions."

"But NATU isn't technically at war with anyone," she said shoving the coffee cup back toward him. At a nearby table two NATU managers in expensive suits argued about which competing Trade Union was responsible for the attack on the satellites. "At least not yet," she added. "Concede the point."

"I'm not done arguing."

"Do you want to be happy, or do you want to be right?" asked Nadia.

"I'd rather be happy."

She smiled at him. "Great. Shut up and agree with me."

"Yes, ma'am." He had to admit, her smile made him happier. "Our transport should be here. Let's go. I'll call Phil en route."

"What about Abdul?" she asked, rising to her feet.

"Good idea. We'll pick him up on the way." He glanced up at Nadia standing over him and she touched his shoulder.

"You sure you won't go back to the hospital?" she asked.

"As soon as we have Riina I promise I'll check myself in."

"Promise?"

"Yep. Now, would you be so kind as to carry me out of here?"

***

Abdul was in the Vehicle Depot when Griffin and Nadia arrived. He'd been there for quarter of an hour, waiting for someone to ask him what he was doing. No one had and everyone steered well clear of him. He'd tried to lean casually against a two-ton truck with NATU markings but it groaned under his weight.

I can't even loiter anymore. Another theft.

"That was fast," said Griffin. "You beat us here." The NATU agent looked like hammered shit. He limped forward, bent slightly at the waist and kept one hand held tight to his abdomen.

"Where the hell else are they gonna store equipment that's not in use?" deadpanned Abdul.

Griffin stopped in his tracks. "Seriously?"

The look of uncomfortable dismay on Griffin's face was almost enough to lift Abdul's mood. "Really? You bought that? That's awesome."

Nadia swatted Griffin's shoulder. "I had no idea you were so gullible."

"Thanks, buddy," Griffin said to Abdul with a mock scowl. He glanced at the truck. "This will do. You ride in the back, smartass."

"Griffin," said Abdul and the agent, hearing the difference in tone, turned to face him.

"Yes?"

"From now on, until this is finished, you two are always with me. If you're in a hotel, I'm there." Nadia and Griffin shared an awkward glance. *What the heck was that about?* "Next time the Mafia sends an assassin chassis, it has to go through me first. I never should have left your side. I'm sorry."

Griffin nodded uncomfortably. "No need to apologize."

How could Abdul tell these two strangers they were the closest thing he had to friends right now? How could he explain how valuable their lives were? He hadn't understood how amazing life was until he was dead. There were no words for what he knew. At least none that didn't sound insane even to him. He tried anyway. "I have enough blood on my hands. No more. I won't let you down again." If Griffin looked uncomfortable before, now he looked downright embarrassed. "When you die," said Abdul, somberly, "do yourself a favor. Just die."

Griffin looked everywhere but at Abdul. "Okay."

He probably thinks I'm insane. Was he wrong?

Nadia gestured toward the truck. "Perhaps we should get going."

***

Griffin requisitioned the truck and they were on the road in minutes. Nadia took the driver's seat though she wasn't driving. The truck informed her it was no longer receiving traffic updates but was still capable of delivering them to their destination. Griffin, in the passenger seat, called Phil back in Toronto.

Do I want him to order me home? He wasn't sure any more. What would he do if Phil told him to drop everything and return to Toronto? On the one hand he'd probably spend the rest of his career—if he still had one—safe in a cubicle. But then he'd likely never see Nadia again.

"Where are you?" demanded Phil without preamble.

Griffin didn't bother answering. "I know who was behind the Wichita crèche. I'm on my way to get him."

"Make sure Nadezhda records it all. This is important. PR wise, Wichita was a fucking disaster."

The line crackled and kept cutting out forcing Griffin to piece together Phil's side of the discussion.

Disaster. Griffin flinched at the word. *Another*

disaster. Not this time. "Yes, Sir. I have Abdul, but I need a Strike Team."

"Abdul?"

"The combat chassis you assigned me."

"Oh. That's another goddamn shit-show. He's going to face—"

"Strike Team?" Griffin interrupted.

"Right. I'll put the order through, but you may face a little resistance. Scans are a much touchier subject in the south. Don't take any shit," said the man who expected Griffin to take all his shit without question or hesitation.

I'm not going home. Mixed feelings there.

"Great. Riina, a mid-level crime boss in Wichita falls. I need his address and a satellite watching it until I get there. I want to know who's been in and out."

"There are no satellites," said Phil in such a way that Griffin felt soundly chastised for his stupidity.

Griffin wasn't sure if Phil ended the call or the connection died. At least his boss hadn't said anything stupid like bounce to Wichita, and Griffin was too excited about making a big bust to remember he'd wanted his desk job back. Adrenalin made him feel sharp and alive. He could almost forget that everything hurt.

The truck swerved to avoid a cyclist and Griffin's shoulder slammed into the window sending a jarring stab of pain down his spine and making his eyes water.

Right. Everything still hurt.

When he felt like the pain had been locked back into place he turned to Nadia. "Abdul is right. This could get ugly."

She raised an eyebrow. "And?"

Phil said he wanted Nadia to record the bust. *Hell with Phil.* "You should stay behind," he blurted before he could change his mind.

"That's sweet. Don't be an ass." Her expression

hardened. "After I saw those children...Nothing is going to stop me from seeing this through to the end. Nothing."

"Right. Sorry." Griffin hid the feeling of impending doom behind a not entirely feigned grimace of pain. No way he could keep her out of this.

Half an hour later they sat with Abdul in a Scan piloted CH-74 Chinook transport helicopter as it passed over the town of Bowie. Griffin felt the chop of the massive rotors through his spine. His guts felt like they were being jellied. The adrenalin hadn't given up its grip, and he thought he heard Wagner's *Flight of the Valkyries*. It brought back childhood memories of old movies and jumping on the sofa screaming along with the music as helicopters machine-gunned people in rice paddies.

The music got louder and he realized Abdul played it over a speaker system built into his chassis. He whooped and gave Abdul a thumbs up. The chemicals rushing through his blood had his hair standing on end and his pupils dilated. His whole body buzzed.

"I've always wanted to do this," bellowed Abdul over the music. "Perhaps there are some advantages to being a walking sound-system."

Nadia rolled her eyes and shook her head but Griffin caught the small smile before she looked away.

Wichita Falls Municipal Airport was both a NATU and Civilian airport, flying out of Sheppard Air Force Base. Griffin paced in front of the Brigadier General, the highest ranking NATU officer on the base, who in turn glared at him. Abdul stood nearby and Griffin couldn't tell if he watched with interest or had fallen asleep. Nadia stood somewhere behind him, staring at the Chinook they'd climbed out of. When he glanced over his shoulder he saw the rotors had slowed to a lazy spin and were creating a wind pressing her shirt and skirt tight to her body.

Griffin gave the NATU officer his best glare. She was a head shorter than he and in her early fifties, her iron gray hair tied back in a tight bun. Flint-colored eyes pinned him like a bug, mislabeled, and placed in the wrong entomological box. He straightened his back, unwilling to wilt before her unwavering gaze. The show of spinal fortitude was ruined when he grunted in pain.

"What do you mean there's no Strike Team, Brigadier General Rostron? I made the call an hour ago and you assured me the team would be prepped and ready to leave by the time I got here. Well, I'm here and I don't see a Strike Team." He resisted the urge to call her Grandma, suspecting she'd hit him if he did. He didn't think he could take a punch from this woman. Not right now. Probably not ever.

There was a hint of anger in the clenched jaw, but Rostron's face remained calm. She had a soft Texan drawl that normally would take the edge off her words. "We had an emergency. The Strike Team got called to quell a water war between the Texas Farmers Union and the Free Ranchers of Texas." Clearly unimpressed by what she saw, she made a show of examining his wrinkled, sweat stained clothes. "Why didn't you bring the Strike Team from Dallas?"

The question was asked, but not innocently. Griffin felt a tightness in his chest. His gut reaction was to back down, but anger wouldn't let him. People died to make this bust possible and if he didn't follow through their deaths would have been for nothing. "You know why I didn't bring the team from Dallas. They're fucking dead." Griffin leaned towards Rostron. "You've also received word from Head Office. I want my Strike Team and I fucking want them now!" He breathed into Rostron's face, smelled the woman's starched uniform and an underlying scent of lilac.

"The Strike Team is gone," said Rostron, unfazed by

his proximity. "A water war is a big deal here, a whole helluva lot bigger than some little mobster. And I'd appreciate it, *Mister* Dickinson, if you'd watch your language."

Griffin felt like he'd been chastised like a child. He almost offered an embarrassed apology. He blinked at her, unsure what to do next. He had the authority to bark orders, but had no idea how to go about using it.

"We're taking the Chinook." Everyone turned to look at Nadia. "We're taking the chopper. It's the only thing big enough to carry Abdul. He's our Strike Team."

Rostron's calm facade slipped. "It will take time to prep the helicopter. Refueling and pre-flight check—"

"The chopper is ready to go," said Abdul. "I'm in communication with the pilot Scan. She says she has enough fuel for such a short flight. All systems check green."

Griffin turned back to Brigadier General Rostron. "Show me to the armory, I need to requisition some guns. Nadia, you want a gun?"

She didn't take her eyes from the Chinook. "No."

***

While waiting for Griffin and Nadia to requisition gear from the recalcitrant Brigadier General, Abdul passed time in conversation with Marlene Becker, the Scan inhabiting the CH-74 Chinook. She'd died flying a transport chopper much the same as the one she now lived in, but no one would tell her how. She too joined the army to pay for college and, before being killed, was set to graduate this year. Abdul, who remembered nothing of his own death, commiserated.

During a lull in the conversation he asked, "How is it for you, being a Scan?"

"You mean, do I miss my old life?"

No. "Yeah."

"Of course. This isn't the same as being alive, no matter what they simulate. It's different. It's..."

"Empty?"

"Perhaps. Sometimes."

He needed to know. *Is it just me?* "Do you feel...sane?"

There was a long pause. "We can't talk about that."

Right. Someone might be monitoring their conversation. Is that what she meant? Or was she afraid to talk about it? Did she fear what might be said?

Their conversation died, strangled by doubt.

When Griffin and Nadia arrived they were sweating in their magnetorheological armored vests. Griffin, pale and hunched, showed gritted teeth as he pulled himself into the chopper. He shouldn't be here, he should be in bed. He should be in a hospital bed.

Marlene lifted off the second the NATU agents were seated and had donned their headphone-radios.

"Those vests are for police work," said Abdul, once the chopper was airborne. "Didn't they have MR bodysuits?"

"All signed out by the missing Strike Team," Nadia answered with a shrug.

Griffin, sitting beside her, stretched out his legs with a groan. He looked grateful to be off his feet but otherwise miserable. Tired. Spent.

Abdul watched the fingers on Griffin's right hand shake as the agent examined a Tavor 41 assault rifle. Curious, he scanned the agents to see what gear they'd selected. Four of the thirty round clips hung attached to Griffin's combat harness as well as three flashbang grenades, or Noise and Flash Diversionary Devices as the Armory Officers liked to call them. He'd also requisitioned a Glock 36 which sat in a hip holster. Abdul checked Nadia and aside from her recording gear all she had was the MR vest she wore.

"You've used an assault rifle before?" Abdul asked Griffin, hoping to distract him from his obvious discomfort.

"At the range." Griffin clawed at the fingers of his right hand.

"With no satellite scan of the building, we have no idea what's in there," pointed out Abdul.

"True," said Griffin, "What are the odds he has a chassis bodyguard?"

"What are the chances that was a dumb question?" Abdul answered

No *Flight of the Valkyries* this time. Like him, the mood was dead. He watched Griffin watching Nadia as she checked her recording gear. Lost in concentration, she didn't notice Griffin's attention. With an unconscious twitch of her hand she brushed back a few hairs that escaped her ponytail. Griffin wanted to say something to her—Abdul saw it in the way he'd lean toward her only to pull back again—but kept hesitating. Griffin returned his attention to Abdul and stared at him for several seconds. He couldn't tell Abdul watched him at the same time.

The Chinook's engines rose to a roar as Marlene pushed the envelope of what the chopper could handle.

I used to love doing this, she tight-linked Abdul. *Back when I could feel it. Now... nothing.*

I can see we're moving quite fast, Abdul tight-linked back, glancing out a window. Normally he could have checked his GPS coordinates and been told his current speed, but with the satellites down a lot of the systems he depended on were touchy at best. *And my attitude indicators say we're banking at twelve degrees right now. But if I killed that and all visual sensors I'd have no idea we were even moving.*

This sucks, said Marlene. *I see the ground rush past beneath me, but no matter how low I go, no matter how dangerously I fly, I still can't feel it.*

"They should give you guys facial expressions," said Griffin.

A nugget of anger sparked to life. Was that a joke? Less than an hour ago he'd tried to tell Griffin how he'd lay down his life to protect him and now this?

"Like painting shark faces on fighter jets?" Abdul asked, keeping his voice calm and flat.

"No, no. Some way for you to display emotion. It's an important part of human communication."

This was well-examined ground for Abdul. That nugget smoldered and smoked, grew hotter. "That assumes I'm human," he said.

Griffin raised an eyebrow. "You saying you're not?"

Abdul shuffled closer, an oddly gentle move for such a large killing machine, and saw Griffin quash the desire to back away. He measured the man's heartbeat, counting the pulses in the carotid artery. He sampled Griffin's exhalation and knew what he'd eaten for breakfast. He saw the man's temperature—already bordering on feverish—rise as he grew nervous at this killing machine's proximity. "Obviously I'm not human."

"I think you can be human without being *a* human," said Nadia, voice gentle.

"There is nothing biological here. I am a digital copy of the brain of Abdul Aziiz-Giordano. I am modeled thoughts."

The helicopter banked and Abdul stared out the far window at the ground rushing by below. There was a time when he would have felt this in his stomach, a sour vertigo. Now he felt nothing and that was sad. *I miss my fear.*

"Bullshit," said Griffin, looking queasily pale after

the helicopter's maneuvering. "You *are* Abdul. You may be modeled thoughts, but you are thoughts modeled so accurately as to be self-conscious. I was wondering why they didn't give you some means of expressing emotion."

"I assume they thought my language skills would be sufficient."

"They're not," muttered Griffin under his breath, probably unaware Abdul could hear him. "Human interaction is more than words and tones," he said louder.

That burning ember of anger didn't go out, it throbbed in the background. But these weren't the people who'd done this to him. Their honest and obvious concern calmed him. "What emotions should I display? I'm not sure the Marines want their weapons walking around looking confused, guilty, and depressed."

"Screw the military," said Nadia. "You're still human and you still have some basic rights."

"Ah, technically no. You kind of sign those away when you join the NATU military. On top of that, whether I'm human or not, they own this chassis. I suspect putting facial expressions on it may be deemed defacing government property, or something equally asinine."

Nadia examined Abdul, head tilted to one side. "What were you like before?"

Small, brown and quiet. Often scared. "Really good looking. Incredibly funny. Chicks loved me."

"Right, of course."

"I haven't lost it, though," Abdul joked, "I was dating a hot little front-end loader for a while." This was all so much bullshit.

"So I'm not your type?" Marlene asked, feigning disappointment.

Griffin looked surprised, like he'd never thought about Scan social lives, and couldn't imagine what Abdul did when not working.

Nadia shook her head in mock disgust. "Amazing, eh Marlene? Even after scanning, men are still pigs."

Abdul stood as if stretching his legs. "I don't understand it, but I think laughing might be a biological thing. I enjoyed that but can't share in the laughter. I remember how my little sister used to say what she was thinking or doing, like adults were too stupid to figure it out if not told. She'd tell a joke and then declare 'I'm being funny.' I always enjoyed it but thought it odd behavior. Now I'm thinking it might be useful. I don't need facial expressions if I walk around talking about my emotions."

Thinking of Janani, his sister, brought back that rage, so cold as to sear. Unwilling to lose what emotion he was capable of, he set it aside, saved it for later.

"All men would be better off if they could talk about their emotions," said Nadia with a pointed glance at Griffin who pretended not to notice.

Abdul nodded by rocking his entire torso. "Let's try it." He stood as straight as the confines of the Chinook allowed and made a show of looking around. "I miss being hugged and being able to feel it and not measure the experience in numbers." Marlene banked the Chinook again and Abdul's stabilizers adjusted keeping him in perfect balance. "I miss my fear. I miss *wanting* to live rather than being programmed for self-preservation. I miss my family. I miss—" *I miss my sister. Lock it down.* "Otherwise, today isn't too bad. It's been a while since I talked to people. I think I missed that more than I realized."

"What's the facial expression for all that?" Griffin asked.

***

After studying the outdated satellite imagery—pictures taken several years ago—on his tablet, Griffin laid out his plan: Abdul would drop to the street and enter the via front door, while Nadia and Griffin came in through the roof top entrance. They'd meet in the middle somewhere in a textbook Pincer Movement. Abdul squished the idea like it was a nasty little bug.

"Forget it. You two aren't coming in at all. You stay with Marlene."

"You're going in alone?" asked Griffin.

"Damned straight. I'll drop to the roof and enter there. That's my best chance of surprise."

"Bad idea." Griffin held up the satellite picture for Abdul to see. *I'd kill for to-the-second updates.* He'd love to be able to watch traffic in and out of the building. "Look at that structure. Two hundred year old brownstone. Land on the roof, and you'll end up in the basement. Anyway, they'll escape out the front door."

"Marlene, can you pin them down with suppression fire?" Abdul asked.

"Sorry, I'm not currently outfitted with armaments. My last dozen runs have been internal NATU troops movements. No action at all."

Abdul's armored fist clenched and for a moment Griffin thought he was going to punch something in frustration. "I can cover one of the exits" offered Griffin. "The roof is probably best. Anyone sticks their head out the door and I'll scare them back in with a few shots."

"You can do that from up here," said Abdul.

"Seriously? No. I can usually hit a motionless paper target at fifty yards. When I'm prone and have all the time in the world. Shooting from the back of a helicopter, I'm as likely to accidentally *kill* someone as scare them."

"Fine," said Abdul. "I'm okay with you accidentally killing Riina."

"I'm not. I want this bastard alive."

"I don't."

Nadia reached out and placed a hand on Abdul's side. "Riina's not at the top of this. He's too small."

Abdul was quiet for several seconds. "Shit. Fine. I'll drop to the ground and come in the front. Griffin, you take cover on the roof. Keep them pinned inside. Nadia stays with Marlene."

Nadia looked like she was about to argue, but shrugged philosophically. "I can get video good video from up here. Let me know when I'm cleared to come in. I need some shots of the arrest."

"Griffin," said Abdul, turning his torso to face him. "If you come in before I've given the *all clear*, I'll kill you myself. If there's something in there I can't handle, you playing hero isn't going to help."

No kidding. "Abdul, the last thing I want is to walk into a chassis fight."

When Marlene announced they were two minutes from their target, Griffin's stomach tightened painfully. There was a flurry of last minute activity. He hoisted the Tavor 41 rifle and took a few calming breaths.

Griffin attached himself to the rappelling line, and shuffled toward the open door. He sat with his feet hanging over the edge. The city below sped past in a blur and then slowed to a crawl as Marlene found her target. The Chinook kicked up a tornado of dust and debris sending people on the street scattering for cover. Griffin hoped Riina wasn't among them.

"I don't like this," said Abdul. "We should come back with more support."

"We can't wait," snapped Griffin. *I can't be too late again.* "Riina will be gone once he realizes his assassin failed. Stick to the plan."

"Plan? This is pell-mell with details," said Abdul.

Griffin's harness felt too tight around his chest,

suffocating and reassuring at the same time. Looking down between his legs he saw the roof below. Damned thing looked miles away but couldn't be more than a few yards. The roof slewed sideways and Griffin felt his gut churn with vertigo.

"Marlene, can you keep it more steady?" he asked.

"Nope. Sorry. Pretty windy."

Griffin grabbed Nadia's hand. "You ready?" he asked over the helmet radio. She squeezed his hand in return and he grimaced with the sudden flare of pain. *Should have used the other hand.*

"Hell, no," she said, and then leaned forward to kiss him. Her lips were soft, her breath hot. "As soon as we're done here you're going to the hospital. You promised."

"I did. I will."

"Good. Be careful." She brushed her fingertips along his cheek, a soft caress.

"Helmet," said Nadia, handing it to him.

"Yeah. Thanks."

He glanced out the open door at the rooftop far below. *What the fuck was I thinking?*

***

Riina stepped out of his office and into the hall. "Giovanni, you hear that?"

His lieutenant's door opened and Giovanni stood listening. "Yep. Helicopter. Big one."

"It sounds close."

A third office door opened and Oo stuck his angular wasp-like head out. "There's a helicopter overhead. Sounds like a Chinook troop transport."

Giovanni nodded. "I'll check upstairs. Oo, front door."

"Should I bring the bird down, Uncle?" Oo called

back as he jumped from the top stair to the bottom, landing with insectile poise.

"Let's make sure it's a threat first," answered Riina.

Drawing that massive Desert Eagle, Giovanni took the stairs two at a time to the rooftop door. The gun was silly, but with it, the man was a surgeon.

Giovanni stopped at the top of the stairs, cracked the door no more than a hair, and peered out. When he glanced down toward Riina, his face said everything that needed saying.

"Bring down the chopper," Riina called to Oo-Suzumebachi.

***

People stared nervously up at the hovering Chinook, scattering when Abdul stepped out and began his descent. He had all the time in the world to think as he dropped toward the sidewalk. Riina farmed kids for brains to use in combat chassis. The chassis he fought at the crèche had no doubt been populated by children. Abdul killed them. There would be one or more chassis here as well. These would be children willing to die to protect the man who stole their lives. Abdul felt ill, a gnawing rage brewed somewhere in his guts. *This* he was allowed to feel. Not warmth or human contact or the exhilarating freedom of motion, just the need to do violence.

Well, at least it's the right emotion for the job at hand.

He landed at the brownstone's front door. It was thick wood bound in decorative wrought iron bands, designed to look classy yet still be damned near impossible to bust open.

Abdul tore the door from the brownstone wall and much of the surrounding masonry came with it. There was a blur of black and yellow and he knew he should have been more careful.

***

Griffin saw Abdul step from the Chinook and, firing his jump-assist-jets to slow his descent, drop straight to the ground. Nothing that big and dangerous should move that gracefully.

"Go," he said more for his own benefit than anything else. "Go."

He pushed himself from the helicopter, swung out over nothing. If he fell from here, he'd break everything. The rappelling line spun him in a dizzying circle and he lowered himself toward the roof.

Griffin slid down the rope, eyes pinched against the swirling maelstrom of dust. He didn't see the roof coming and landed hard, his right knee buckling with an agonizing wrench. He pitched forward. For an instant he thought he'd topple off the roof and then his hands slammed gravel. *Still alive.* His heart kicked with a surge of adrenalin. It felt like something in his gut tore loose and his right knee came apart like shattered plastic. *I should be in a damned hospital.*

"Unclip your harness or you'll get dragged off the roof," Nadia said over the helmet radio. Way ahead of him, a recurring theme.

"Right." Griffin detached the harness moments before it was reeled back into the helicopter.

Holding his breath against the pain he pushed himself to his feet. Would the knee hold? Mostly. He took a tentative step and winced at the bone on bone grinding within.

Griffin examined the roof-top, stalling while he decided if he could keep moving. The Chinook gained height and the dust wasn't as bad and he could open his eyes without having them filled with grit. And then he remembered the helmet visor protected his face. He'd been squinting like an idiot.

The roof, bituminous asphalt, shimmered in the midday heat. The bitumen bled through the aggregate and clung to the soles of his boots. Cigarette butts and empty Bud cans littered the area. The beer cans all crushed in the middle in the same way, the butts all smoked to the filter.

Griffin realized the asphalt was black, and only the sheer number of cigarette butts made it gray. A small off-green shingled shack with a single door and no windows beckoned. Griffin assumed it led to stairs.

He looked up at the Chinook circling above and Nadia, sitting in the doorway, legs dangling, waved down at him. A halo of recording gear floated around her, picking up everything. No doubt it was also wired into her helmet as well.

"You see anything, up there?" he asked.

"Abdul is at the front door," answered Nadia.

"Right."

Griffin limped toward a boxy metal construct at one side of the roof. It'd do nicely for cover. Not until he was crouched behind it did he realize it was blasting hot air.

"The bad guys have air-conditioning," he muttered as sweat poured off him, soaking the MR vest.

"We'll add it to the list of charges," said Nadia.

Griffin broke open the Tavor's tripod and set the rifle on top of the vent. It was almost like being at the range; even better because he had some cover to hide behind. He checked the sights—perfect view of the door on the green shack—and the rifle's movement. Everything was smooth.

"Safety?" Nadia asked.

"Right." Griffin disengaged the Tavor's safety

mechanism. "Thanks."

The building shook beneath him.

"Oh shit."

***

Giovanni heard a great crashing sound from somewhere down by the main entrance as he pushed open the rooftop door. Whoever it was coming through the front, the poor bastard was going to have to deal with Oo. There was a crack of rifle fire and the wood frame of the door blew to splinters near his head. His cheek stung where shards of wood had embedded themselves. Christ, he hoped they didn't scar. He saw right away they were trying to pin him down, keep him in the building. *Bad idea.* They should have killed him when they had the chance.

There was only one place to hide and sure enough, crouched down behind the air-conditioning vent, was some dumb fuck with a rifle. Giovanni would have laughed had he the time; as if that flimsy aluminum sheeting was going to stop a fifty caliber tungsten carbide armor piercing round from his little sweetheart. He shot the crouching man in twice in the chest, right through the A/C venting and the guy dropped, boneless. *Lights out, baby.*

Gun fights weren't about who shot first, they were about who got shot first.

Giovanni looked upwards at the Chinook hovering twenty yards over the roof. A woman sat in the doorway, her feet hanging over the edge. She was pointing something at him so he shot her too. He had all the time in the world and the patience of a Taoist monk. She dropped whatever she was holding and toppled forward out of the chopper. Giovanni emptied the last four rounds of his clip into the Chinook's cockpit window, the glass starring, and the helicopter gained height and turned away. He doubted he could hurt the pilot—probably a Scan anyway.

He turned and yelled back down the stairs, "Roof's clear. Let's go!" By the time he'd finished, he'd ejected the spent clip and popped a fresh one in its place. He did it without so much as glancing at the gun. The action was completed as if written into his genetic code, all muscle memory and a billion hours of mindless practice. And Mom said his philosophy degree was useless. Ha!

His nose stung with the sharp metallic tang of gun smoke. God he loved that smell.

At the bottom of the steps Riina came into view, slamming a clip into an old matte black Browning Hi-Power. The damned thing dated back to World War Two, and even had little swastikas engraved in the finish.

"Didn't I tell you to get a real gun?" Giovanni called down, shaking his head in mock disgust. Riina and his antiques.

"It was my grandfather's."

***

The door came away and something came with it. Whatever it was, it picked up Abdul and threw him through the wall of the building across the street. He picked himself out of the ruins of an old brick pizza oven. The bodies of the pizzeria's patrons were scattered about the floor, bent at odd angles and splashed in blood.

Dust and debris seemed to hang motionless in the air as his reactions kicked into combat mode. He tracked everything, chunks of stone, fragments of wood, droplets of airborne blood that had not yet landed. Everything was assigned a Threat Level and he ignored them all except for the coruscating black and yellow combat chassis exiting the old brownstone building. It must have been some kind of new ARU release, because his combat computer grunted and shrugged instead of spewing statistics at him. The chassis did however scream *Threat!*

Like I couldn't figure that out for myself.

More bodies littered the sidewalk. Too slow to know what was happening, the humans had yet to begin screaming.

A street cop was in the glacial process of drawing his gun when the ARU chassis snatched him up like a ragdoll and hurled him into a nearby wall. Unlike Abdul, the officer didn't punch through the wall.

The coruscating black and yellow chassis launched a swarming throng of missiles targeting the building's supporting walls and the pizzeria and whatever was on the second floor above it fell in on top of Abdul. As tonnes of stone and wood crushed him to the floor, Abdul saw the chassis fire something at the Chinook above.

***

The door swung open and a tall, sharp featured man in an expensive Italian suit stood in the green shack on the roof. Griffin put a bullet into the door frame and the guy didn't even flinch. He looked straight at Griffin and—

Clear blue sky. The wash of rotors scattered cigarette butts but he couldn't see the Chinook. What happened? Had he been shot?

Griffin felt like someone had taken a baseball bat to his solar plexus. Twice. He lay on his back unable to draw breath. His body convulsed as it fought for air.

Again he heard the roar of that huge pistol.

Marlene was yelling over the radio. He couldn't understand what she was saying, the need to breathe made everything else unimportant. He managed a raw, deep in the chest sob and drew in the tiniest taste of air. Something landed beside him with a wet crunch.

Confused, he turned his head and found himself staring into Nadia's wide eyes. The visor of her helmet had splintered but remained whole.

The eyes moved, focused on him.

His vision narrowed to a tunnel and then returned as he drew in a great sucking breath of air.

How the hell? She wasn't tethered. She'd fallen. The helmet would protect her head, though she might have broken bones. *She'll be okay.* Then he saw the lazy leak of blood from the ragged bullet wound in her throat. *Shouldn't that be gushing?*

She blinked once and the eyes glazed and lost focus, stared through him.

His chest felt like someone had dropped an anvil on him and each breath burned like acid in his lungs. He touched a gloved hand to where he'd been shot and it came away dry. No blood.

Another explosion shook the street below and in his peripheral vision Griffin saw the roof of the building across the street dip and then cave inward with a great rumbling roar. He turned his head and for an instant he caught sight of and made eye contact with a woman standing at the window on the second floor and then she was gone.

Nadia.

No. He had to stop the expensive suit with the huge hand cannon.

Griffin sat up with a moan. Stabbing pain threatened to cave his world in and his vision blurred red. It felt like his ribs had been shattered. The rifle and tripod still sat perched atop the A/C unit. Too far away. He drew the Glock, disengaging the safety with his thumb.

Marlene screamed something about a combat chassis on the street and was cut off by an explosion that lit the roof even in broad daylight. A shadow rushed across the roof as the flaming wreckage of a spiraling Chinook spun toward the street below.

Marlene screamed, "Fuck you too!" as she disappeared from view.

There, framed in the door, the Italian suit, his back to Griffin. Griffin raised the gun and aimed, fought to still his ragged breathing. The man in the door turned.

***

Riina jogged up the steps. Down below, at the front of the building, light poured in where the front door used to be. From outside heard something that sounded an awful lot like an earthquake or a building falling down. Oo-Suzumebachi would handle whatever was out there.

Giovanni, waiting at the top, was backlit by a flaming helicopter plummeting towards the street. What the hell was Oo doing?

Giovanni racked the slide of his Desert Eagle and turned away as something outside caught his attention. "Fucking body armor," he said, raising the gun. And then the back of his head came apart in an explosion of bone and brain.

Riina turned and jogged back down the stairs.

He stopped halfway to the bottom as the helicopter crashed down with earth shaking force. Much of the old brownstone's front wall came down. Whatever the hell was going on out there, Riina felt sure he'd be better off taking his chances on the roof.

***

The servo-motors in Abdul's limbs screamed in protest as he forced his way out of the collapsed building. He had no way of knowing how many dead or wounded he trod upon as he dug his way free. Heaving aside a last chunk of wall, he found a hellish scene. Marlene had crashed to the street, crushing the ARU chassis beneath her Chinook bulk. It looked like a warzone. Burning cars and charred bodies were littered everywhere.

He stood, staring at the wreckage of the helicopter. Nadia. Marlene. Dead.

Griffin. Where was Griffin? Was he still alive?

Abdul heard gunfire, the sharp crack of an automatic pistol from the roof. He looked at the collapsing front wall of the building. If he forced his way in there, everything would come down. He glanced up at the second story roof.

It fucking better hold me.

Abdul jumped.

***

The Italian suit toppled from view, falling back down the stairs. Griffin rolled over and crawled to Nadia. His ribs screamed in protest. Something was broken or torn inside, he felt it. He pulled the helmet away, cradling her head with his other hand.

"It's going to be okay," he said, noticing the way her right leg was bent and tucked underneath her torso at an impossible angle. "It's—"

There was a sharp crack and something slammed him in the kidney with paralyzing force. Another shot and he felt like his spine had shattered. He tried to turn and a third bullet struck him in the soft flesh under his ribs. He curled up with a wheezed grunt and was once again fighting for air. His gun. Where was his gun? Griffin stared stupidly at his empty hand, the fingers twitching spastically. He'd dropped it. Another bullet slammed into his chest and he fell backward, again gazing up into clear sky.

A shadow fell across him and he stared straight into the barrel of a black pistol. Riina, the Mafia Capo, stood behind the gun, face expressionless. Griffin watched the tendons on the man's wrist stand out as he tightened his grip on the pistol. The trigger started to move, the hammer coming back. His view of Riina was blocked by the bulk of Abdul's torso as the chassis landed between the two men. He heard the pistol shot and then Riina's scream as Abdul took the gun away.

Abdul turned. "Is she alive?"

"I can't..."

"Stay with her. Help's on the way." Abdul scooped up Riina as if he were a naughty child and carried him away, jumping back to the street below.

Griffin hunched over Nadia, his own pains forgotten. He tried to staunch a wound that no longer bled. He said empty and comforting words to ears that could no longer hear.

Sirens somewhere, getting louder. Fire trucks, ambulances, and police cars. It looked like Wichita had scrambled all of its emergency services.

He was helpless. Powerless.

When the medics arrived they shoved Griffin aside and gathered around Nadia. She was all but hidden from view. He could only see the one leg that wasn't pinned under her body. Still no movement. One of the medics searched him for wounds.

"Not hurt," he said, numbly.

"Hell you aren't," said the medic. "You've been shot in the back. Three times." The medic turned him, fingered the slugs lodged in the MR vest. "And twice in the front."

"Forgot. She'll be okay, right?"

"Neck is broken," he heard one of the medics over Nadia report. "Most of the ribs too."

Griffin's medic didn't answer but his eyes held

nothing but doubt. After removing Griffin's helmet and tossing it aside he peeled off the MR vest.

"My fault." All his fault. They shouldn't have been here.

The medic sliced Griffin's shirt with a practiced flick of the wrist and stripped it away. His torso was one mottled bruise, very little pink showed at all. "Jesus Christ! Look at this fresh scarring. You should be in a damned hospital."

"I'm fine."

"Shattered rib sent fragments into her lungs and heart," Griffin overheard. "No chance of resuscitation. Pack her up. Get the box prepped. We airlift, stat."

Griffin shoved the medic away and the man, unprepared, fell over backwards with a yell. He picked up Nadia's helmet. "Abdul," he said into the radio mic.

"I'm here."

"Is Riina still down there?"

"Yes."

"Good."

Griffin dropped the helmet, scooped up the pistol he'd dropped, and limped down the stairs and out the gaping hole in the front wall. When he stepped out into the Texas sun he had to squint and shade his eyes with a shaking hand. His fingers felt like they were being peeled with a cheese-grater. The heat of the day pressed against his shirtless torso. The outdoor air washed away the stench of gunpowder. The street was chaos, flashing lights and screaming wounded. There were bodies everywhere, many not moving. An entire building had fallen in. None of it mattered.

He saw Riina, bruised and bound, standing in a circle of NATU police.

Griffin pulled in a long breath and walked toward the knot of officers. Calm. He transferred the Glock to his left hand. Right hand shook too much.

Keep moving. Nothing to see here. Must get close enough. Don't miss. One chance.

A wall stepped into his path. Abdul.

Griffin looked up at the towering chassis. "Move."

"No," said the chassis.

"Please."

"Sorry." Softly.

Griffin tried to step around Abdul but the chassis was too large and too fast. "*Please.* Let me kill him. Give me that."

"No. I can't—" Abdul's voice cracked. "You can't do this."

"Yes I can." Griffin raised the gun and pointed it Abdul. "Move," he whispered. "I'll—"

Abdul plucked the gun from his hand. "No more killing."

With a sob Griffin leaned his head against the chassis' torso. He punched it once and the pain overwhelmed the fire in his fingers. Abdul held Griffin until the medics took him away.

CHAPTER TWENTY-TWO: Sunday, August 5th, 2046

Griffin sat forward on the hospital bed, head in hands, elbows on knees. The metal frame groaned, its protest ignored. Shellacked white cinder blocks, the interior walls of this small private room were beaded with moisture from the humidity. The floor was exposed concrete rubbed smooth by decades of the shuffling wounded.

Marlene and Nadia were dead as were dozens of civilians. There were scores of injured, and millions of AU in damages. They'd destroyed two blocks of downtown Wichita. Phil had been screaming threats of legal action when the call got dropped. Griffin considered trying to call him back and decided against it. Phil could yell at him in person when he got home.

The doctor told him to rest, left him with a paper cup full of Ativan he hadn't taken. He couldn't rest. His pain was everything and nothing. No part of him wasn't in agony, but the ache of loss dwarfed all others.

An hour passed and here he sat, unwilling or unable to move. Choices led to failure. If he gave up, if he stayed on this groaning bed, maybe no one else would die.

Sweat gathered in beads and dropped from his nose into the puddle growing unnoticed between his bare feet.

He wore nothing but a faded pair of thread-bare boxers. He licked his lips. They tasted of sweat and tears.

This isn't a plan, it's pell-mell with details.

Could he have done it differently? Would she be alive today if he took a moment to think? Would Riina have still been there if they went in a day later with a Strike Team?

That Mafia goon may have shot her, but Nadia's blood was on Griffin's hands.

He'd put a bullet in the man's head. He felt nothing at that. Not even satisfaction.

Nadia's eyes, dark and beautiful, wide and still. Unseeing.

Even though the report said the medical team was on scene within minutes it felt like hours.

Riina. Abdul stopped him. Griffin had never wanted to kill someone before, never wanted anything that badly. He remembered his father saying all of his regrets were about the things he had not done. Griffin understood that now. He regretted not killing Riina when he had the chance, as pointless and futile as that would have been. At least he would have had the gesture to cling to instead of feeling Nadia's death went unpunished.

Her death remains unpunished.

That thought got him moving. It was a fresh wound, still raw. Everything hurt, inside and out. He stumbled into the shower and stood under the stream of tepid rust colored water. The patchwork of fist-sized bruises on his torso were darkening and spreading, their edges fading to a jaundiced yellow. The crust of soap in the stall looked like it'd been previously used, but he didn't care. He shaved fast and his face burned when he splashed it with aftershave. Even that brought back memories of Nadia.

Why do you smell like aftershave when you obviously haven't shaved in days?

He dried himself with the rough towel, careful of his still tender nose, and stepped into yet another wrinkled gray suit. He tried twice to knot the tie before throwing it in the garbage. His right hand wouldn't stop shaking.

He remembered the taste of her lips when she kissed him.

He came to Dallas seeking redemption, a chance to balance his failure at the Jerseyville crèche. All he wanted was to be the hero, to save the children. He wanted one thing in his life to be proud of; something to hold up and say, *I did this*. He still wanted that.

That and vengeance.

The door closed behind him with a quiet click and he was moving, one painful step after another. Forward. Keep moving forward, toward the target. An arrow that's been loosed. No looking back. No going back.

Dallas' NATU head office was thick with body odor and panic but Griffin hardly noticed. He pushed past the security check points, past the harried secretaries, and into the heart of this sweating gray beast. After much searching he found the office of someone he out-ranked—an intern on his first day—and pointed at the door.

"Out."

The young man, manicured and well-dressed, a Phil waiting to happen, took one look at Griffin and left without comment.

The office was small and unadorned. No pictures of family or girlfriends. He collapsed into a chair of yellow molded plastic in a thin and rusted steel frame. The desk ran a fast DNA check, examined his thumb and iris, and decided he might be Griffin Dickinson. He then logged in by entering a randomly shifting twenty digit number supplied by an organic microdot chip hidden somewhere in his brain. This sync'd with an algorithm within NATUnet and offered further proof of who he was. Maybe not impossible to beat, but damn difficult. The desk in Dallas downloaded the interface settings from his desk in Toronto. The task usually took no more than a fraction of a second to complete. This time Griffin had to wait ten minutes.

He tapped the top of the desk and it became a cryptic multi-dimensional display of custom icons, pictograms and hieroglyphs. The desk tracked his eyes, fingers, and thoughts and reacted accordingly.

Two hours later he'd caught up on the Riina file. It would have been faster, but every time he initiated a new search it took several minutes for the results to return. The loss of the satellites left NATUnet dependent on old, ground-based technology that was no longer up to the task.

Riina, he learned, did three brief stints in prison as a young man for minor offenses. This was the kind of jail time they did to prove to their bosses they were solid. Once Riina was in The Family his record became clean. Not the clean of a man who didn't commit crimes, but the clean of a man whose crimes couldn't be proven. Charges were brought against him for money laundering, tax evasion, and various other nefarious business pursuits. In each case the charges were either dropped before they reached court or beaten with the help of Texas lawyers and judges suspected of being on the Cosa Nostra payroll. Though he found no connection between Riina and black market crèches, Griffin knew it was there. The man was important, but not big enough to run this kind of operation. Not alone. Griffin lay out the questions, looking for connections.

Who was behind Riina? Where did Riina get the children? Where did Riina get the scanning hardware? Where did Riina get the hardware to store the minds once they'd been scanned?

He found nothing. One more failure.

A week ago Riina would have been safe in his cozy NATU cell waiting to be bailed out by his Cosa Nostra family members. Griffin could have questioned him for hours and learned nothing. That was last week. That was a different Griffin.

Griffin called Phil. The connection dropped three times before he caught his boss as he was about to leave for home. He requested a virtual meeting so he could look his boss in the eye, but had been informed the bandwidth for such a meeting was unavailable.

He remembered Phil's office, the mammoth mahogany desk, the black leather SmartSofas exuding professional class and ease. The walls were decorated with awards, degrees, professional recognitions and pictures of Phil fishing with people who looked like they were important. Griffin hadn't recognized anyone from the pictures. Did people still fish? Could you even eat what you caught? He wasn't at all sure.

"Phil, let's talk."

"I want you on the first sub-orbital home." Phil's voice sounded like a low-bit digital recording, distorted and crackling.

"I'm fine." Griffin didn't know why he said that. He was anything but fine.

"Nadia. It's hard to lose a partner, I know."

No the fuck you don't. Griffin struggled to choke down his anger. "Hardly a partner, we barely knew each other. I'm fine." Something tightened in his chest. He wanted to smash Phil's face for forcing him to lie.

"The Dallas people are on it." The connection screeched static for a few second then, "There's an ongoing inquest into what happened at the crèche."

"I don't—"

"They want someone to answer for all the deaths."

"They? The crèche was guarded. What did *they* think was going to happen?"

"They want Abdul. He was careless."

"He saved our lives."

There was a long pause and Griffin wondered if the call had been dropped altogether.

"You know how it is," Phil said.

I do? But that was a fight for tomorrow. Right now he needed Phil's backing. Hoping Phil would take it as acquiescence, he changed the subject. "Riina tried to have me killed once already. I can use that to shake him up. Maybe shake something loose."

"And Wichita?" Phil asked. "*Christ*, what a cluster fuck. It's going to take forever to sort that out. Why the hell didn't you wait for a Strike Team?"

Griffin's own doubts thrown in his face. He winced, glad now that Phil couldn't see him. "Riina would have been gone. I'm close. So close."

Phil sounded doubtful. "You're sure this isn't personal? We don't need Riina getting off on a technicality due to...an emotional outburst."

"Sir." Griffin hated calling anyone Sir, but this one hurt more than usual. "Riina is small-time and we both know it." He remembered the pictures on the wall. "I want the big fish. We're going to reel these suckers in. It's going to be huge, I can feel it in my blood."

"If this goes badly I'm going to dump the shit-storm fallout square in your lap," said Phil.

No kidding. "Yes, Sir."

"All right. It's still your case."

Relief fell out of him. He'd done it. "I won't let you down, Sir."

"Screw this up and you'll be buried so deep in the shit we'll need a bathysphere to find you."

On the way out Griffin stopped by Requisitions and signed out another Glock 36 and four clips of Depleted Uranium Core ammunition. If he shot something he wanted it to go down and stay there. Out on the street he realized he should have hunted down some painkillers.

Too late. Keep moving.

If anything, Dallas felt even hotter than usual. No one moved quickly. Life was a sludgy process.

Griffin expensed another cab to the detention facility where Riina was held. The cab's windows were down but the air was so hot it felt like he sat in front of an old-fashioned convection oven with the door open. The fist-sized bruises over his spine made sitting back painful so he hunched forward, but that made his guts feel like someone was tenderizing them with a fork. His swollen nose throbbed dull pulses of pain through his skull with every bump the cab hit and the fingertips on his right hand kept telling him they were itchy. He scratched the skin red and raw and then scratched some more. Nothing touched that itch.

The cab passed so many interactive billboards and advertisements offering all manner of enticements above and beyond eternal life for a few short years of service as a Scan, that Griffin lost count. Not a single ad mentioned the cost of personal chassis or Scan storage gear. A few short years, he suspected, would turn into decades.

Once in the NATU detention facility Griffin hunted down the virtuality Systems Administrator. The only person wearing shorts and a t-shirt saying, *If it was hard to write, it should be hard to read,* the Sys Admin was easy to find. His bald head showed no sign of sweat and no wrinkles to suggest an age. He could have been eighteen or forty. There was no hint of a paunch and his legs were well muscled.

"You must be the Virtuality Systems Administrator."

"Must I?"

"You're the one person here smart enough to be wearing shorts in this 45°C heat."

Slight twitch of an eyebrow. "Touché. You look like you lost a fight with a combat chassis."

"Assassin chassis. I have a favor to ask."

"That's funny, I got one to deny." Deadpanned.

Griffin blinked. "I'm serious. There's a Mister Riina down in holding. I need to speak to him. I want to set up the interrogation in a virtuality, but I have some unusual requests. Only someone with complete system access could pull off what I need."

The Sys Admin looked a little more interested. "I'm unfamiliar with Riina's case. Mafia man, right?"

"Yeah. He killed a NATU operative, my partner, during our investigation into black market kiddie crèches." Slight stretch of the truth.

"Oh, dude. If this is some kind of personal vendetta thing, count me out."

"No. Well, yeah. I'm not going to kill the guy but I need to know what he knows. It's the only way I can close this case. It's the only way I can make her death *mean* something."

The Admin closed his eyes and shook his head. "I dunno. You screw around in a virtual interrogation and I could lose my job."

"I can't do this without you. Look, you're Root, right? That means you can edit the session logs—"

"It's not that easy."

"Okay. I'm not going to hurt Riina but I need him to *think* I am. I need him to *know* I can. Right now he's safe. There's no way he'll say a word to us. The case will be dead and closed. She's dead and it'll be for nothing. He shot her in the fucking throat." Griffin stopped and took a deep and shaking breath. His eyes throbbed. If he didn't keep it together, he'd crack. The Sys Admin watched him, but Griffin couldn't read the look. "This piece of shit kills little kids and sells their scanned brains. We can't—" Griffin reined himself in by force of will. "Riina killed one of our own and he's going to walk free. Are we going to let that happen?"

"That was a great speech," the Sys Admin said. "Invigorating. I'm all ready to tear down the walls of society. Fuck the system and all that."

Griffin's hopes deflated.

"I'm in," said the Sys Admin. "You have a plan?"

"It's more pell-mell with details," said Griffin.

"That's my favorite kind of plan anyway."

Griffin sat in the same uniformly gray virtuality cell in which he and Nadia talked to Archaeidae. A v-cell in the Toronto office would look the same, it was like the McDonald's of interrogation rooms. There were two chairs, one on each side of the table. He placed his hands flat on the table and took several calming breaths. The decision not to wear an off-the-shelf interrogation skin was an easy one. He wanted Riina to recognize him.

"You ready?" The Sys Admin's voice was dry and without acoustic reverberation of any kind. It sounded out of place in this stone box.

"Yeah, I'm ready. You ready?"

"I'll play my part."

Riina appeared in the other chair and Griffin gave him time to look around.

"Typical government V-cell," said Riina, wearing a state-issued orange jumpsuit. "Too cheap to spend anything on detail." If Riina recognized him, he hid it well. Riina leaned back looking relaxed and comfortable. "Nice suit. Asshole."

"I have questions."

"No lawyer, no talk. I've already made my statement."

"Murderer. You kill children. Sell their brains to the highest bidder. All the expensive suits in the world can't hide the truth."

Riina let out an unforced guffaw. "You have nothing on me. Nothing. Six hours and I'm gone. Back to the office." Riina bared his teeth in a shark's grin.

Griffin leaned toward Riina. "I have a treat for you."

Riina didn't pull away, but instead leaned in toward him, resting his arms on the table. "Really? What?"

"Root?"

"Yep, I'm listening," answered the Sys Admin.

"Root, meet Riina."

"Hey, shithead."

"Riina, meet Root. Root is pretty much God inside a virtuality like this." Riina didn't say anything so Griffin continued. "It's time."

"Gotcha," answered Root.

Eyes narrowed, Riina glanced around the small v-cell. "Don't do anything stupid, gentlemen."

Griffin ignored Riina and clenched his right hand into a fist. It didn't shake in here but it still burned. "Okay, here's what I want. Crank up his sense of touch. I want him to feel everything."

"Done."

The Mob boss shifted uncomfortably.

"Higher receptivity. Way higher. If I poke him with a finger it should feel like I've smashed his ribs with a sledge hammer. If I slap him, he should think his head has been crushed in a vice."

"Done."

Riina became very still and Griffin knew why. If the man moved in the slightest, the simple touch of his clothing would feel like a well-muscled psychotic had taken a cheese grater to his nipples.

"Fuck you," whispered Riina. His hands rested palm down on the table top.

"Next, remove all endorphin or adrenalin modeling. Get rid of anything that will allow him to pass out or feel any less pain."

There was a pause. "I don't know about this," said Root with the right amount of nervous uncertainty. "Just how much pain are you planning on inflicting? You damage his mind and we're screwed."

"I'm not walking out of here without answers," snapped Griffin. "Do it."

"Fine. Done," said Root with a shaky voice. Perfect.

Riina, desperate not to move any more than he had to, hissed, "You are so fucked."

Griffin laughed like they'd shared a joke. "I think not. You see, Root is...well...Root. This is *his* place. We're going to edit all the dialogue later, this is a friendly little chat." A bluff. Controlling the visual aspects of this interrogation was one thing, but faking all the recorded biometric data would be near impossible. He needed Riina to believe he was willing to cause permanent mental damage. The Mafioso wasn't there yet, but it was still early. Griffin pushed the table toward Riina, who shied away from its glacial slow movement. "I don't have to hit you or anything." He stopped the table just shy of contact.

Riina breathed in short panting gasps, each inhalation a small whimper. His face twisted in pain, eyes watering, nostrils flaring.

"Root," said Griffin. "Shut off his facial expressions. We don't want it to look like we're hurting him. Limit his physical mobility as well. Keep him in the chair." To Riina he said, "You'll answer my questions or I'll break you."

Riina's face slackened. He looked bored. Only by staring into his eyes could Griffin get any measure of the pain and terror the man experienced.

"Okay it's done," answered Root. "But you've lost your damned mind. This isn't worth my job. You're gonna cabbage his brain at this rate."

Griffin grinned at Riina. "I'm okay with that." He gave Riina a happy wink. The man had to believe he'd become unstable. "How much pain are you in?" he whispered. "I'm going to stand up and accidentally push this table into you. It's going to feel like you've been hit by a car."

"Stop," Riina whispered.

"You see, the thing of it is...you haven't told me anything yet." Griffin leaned forward held his itching right hand above Riina's left hand. "If I squeeze your hand..."

A high-pitched whine escaped Riina's slack lips. "Haven't asked—"

"Questions. Right. Not much point if you're not going to answer. Anyway, we've been in here what, maybe three minutes? I have all the time in the world." Griffin lowered his hand until it almost touched Riina's. "This is going to hurt. It'll feel like I'm scraping flesh from bone. You'll pray for the cool black of unconsciousness. It will never come. Never."

Griffin stared into Riina's eyes, saw the man weighing his options. Watched the decision being made. Riina displayed no fear, only cold judgment. The pain he suffered wasn't forgotten, just factored into the equation.

"We can deal," said Riina.

"Set us back to normal, but leave the facial and physical locks in place. Less he moves around, the easier it'll be to edit later."

"Done," answered Root sounding a little too relieved.

Riina still breathed in short gasps, sweat glistened on his forehead. "You won't live to regret this," he whispered.

"You killed—" Griffin stopped, buried deep the surge of anger threatening to burst loose of its restraints. He enunciated carefully, speaking slowly. "Where do you get your scanning hardware? Where do you get your storage hardware?"

"You won't get away with this."

"Riina." Griffin rested his face in his hands and laughed. He let all his exhaustion show, for a brief moment allowed the mobster to see how broken he truly felt. "I don't care. You will tell me what I want or I will shatter your mind." Griffin grabbed Riina's hand, squeezed it hard. "Root, take us beyond the previous setting—"

"No!" Riina blurted.

"Tell me."

"We deal."

"A deal? Let me guess."

"I give you a name, I get immunity. I walk."

"I don't—"

"It's a big name." Rinna showed teeth. The man was a tough bastard, Griffin had to give him that much. "It's a famous name."

"Famous?" Griffin asked with disbelief.

"*Very* famous. Even a cheap suit like you will recognize it."

"If you lie to me...."

Riina waved the unspoken threat away as if it were nothing. "Big. Military contracts. This is the man at the top. He's behind virtually every single crèche in the Western world."

"And you'll give him up to me. Won't *La Famiglia* be pissed?"

The Mob boss barked a harsh laugh. "He isn't family."

Griffin swallowed his eagerness. "Fine. If you're not

lying, you'll get your deal."

"I'll walk. No charges."

"You'll walk," Griffin agreed. There'd be a reckoning afterward though, beyond the quiet niceties of the law. No chance Riina was coming away from this unscathed.

"*I* didn't shoot her," said Riina.

"I said you'll walk."

"You recorded that, right Root?" Riina asked.

"I said you'll *fucking* walk!"

Riina stared into Griffin's eyes as if trying to read the truth within. "Mark Lokner."

Mark Lokner? "You mean the guy who owns M-Sof? He's dead and buried."

"I talk to the asshole every couple of days. He pays for the crèches." Now that he was talking, it flowed from Riina in a flood. Anything to keep the pain away. Griffin remained quiet, listening. "He supplies the hardware and the funding to collect the raw materials and gets first choice of the product. We supply him with illegal chassis as well. Industrial. Military. He's got a small fucking army by now. Supplying him is enough we don't need any other clients. But, you know, bunch of product left over. Might as well."

Griffin, realizing he still had Riina's hand in a crushing grip, let go. "Raw materials? Product? You mean children."

Riina sneered but was quick to pull his hand out of Griffin's reach. "Oh, please. You think those Scans working for the state are *free*? Work for the state or die. That, my friend, is slavery too."

Too close to Griffin's own thoughts. He was trying to do the right thing, but what he'd just done was very wrong. *The ends justifies the means.* Or was that a bullshit justification? "They have more choice than the children you steal from their mother's arms."

"My kids are as free as anyone working for the state."

"I've talked to one of your kids. A brainwashed mass-murdering psychotic by the name of Archaeidae."

"He's a good boy, and I didn't brainwash him. He's naturally very loyal. You wouldn't understand."

"Root, you get all that?"

"You bet. Sounded like a confession to me."

"We're done. Get me out of here."

***

88.1.365438.13841.175 watched the interrogation from its place within the NATUnet data system and sent a recording of it to 88.1 who forwarded it to 88.

Riina said he worked for Mark Lokner who owned M-Sof. 88 discovered Lokner had died right around the same time she was scanned, but, upon checking data records, saw Riina and Lokner had definitely communicated since. The more she thought about it, the more the pieces came together.

Lokner, a man renowned for his ability to manipulate the world's markets, was both dead and not dead. He must be a Scan. When she put that together with the knowledge a Scan with similar skills now ran M-Sof, she was certain that Scan must be Mark Lokner. Near the end of the interrogation Riina had mentioned that Lokner gathered an army of chassis. There could be no doubt; Lokner was a danger. Perhaps he planned a physical attack on 88 rather than an economic one.

88 knew she existed on M-Sof hardware, and Riina had told the NATU agent that Lokner/M-Sof supplied the Mafia with hardware for both scanning and storing minds. Was it possible Riina was at least partially responsible for 88 being who and what she was? Did he have connections

with the Anisio Jobin crèche in Brazil? He might be one of the few to have escaped 88.1's killing spree. Riina might know things she needed to know. He might know something about Mom.

The NATU agent and Mafia Capo also spoke of Archaeidae, whom 88 knew to be held in a v-cell in this same detention facility, and of loyalty. Archaeidae interested 88 as did the concepts of honor and allegiance. Did loyalty have to go both ways or could it be unidirectional? *Can Archaeidae be the help I need?* She would have to tread carefully there, her lack of social skills would be a hindrance. *Perhaps 88.1 would be better suited to interacting with the assassin.*

But first, Riina. If he was involved in 88's past he may know who, what, and where 88 was. And if he knew where her Scan was stored, he was a threat.

***

Riina sat alone in the virtuality. His heart beat slowed to normal, and his breathing evened out. Had they forgotten about him?

He thought back over the last few minutes. Agent Dickinson was a dead man. No doubt.

A matte black cube appeared over the table. The cube was about one meter square with a silky luster. It hovered above the floor, unmoving.

Rinna waited, unwilling to say the first word. What now?

"Did you supply Central American crime families with scanned minds?"

The voice came from the cube, but lacked inflection and any hint of humanity, which was strange when even the simplest software sounded human. He couldn't even tell if it was male or female.

Riina sat back, took his time examining the cube. "Who are you?"

The answer was as quick as it was unenlightening. "88."

"Eighty-eight?"

"Did you supply Central American crime families with scanned minds? Answer the question or I short-circuit your synaptic relays."

"What?"

"Brain death."

This didn't feel right. Riina had dealt with the NATU criminal system often enough to know how they thought. Though after that debacle with Griffin...he wasn't so sure.

Stay calm, think clearly. Figure this out, and make the necessary moves to get past this. "You're some piece of new NATU interrogation software?"

"Software, not software. Unimportant distinction. Answer question."

Hard not to get frustrated with questions being snapped in such a mechanical fashion. *Okay. Probably not software.* Something prickled at the back of Riina's mind. *A Scan?* "You're going to have to give me a clue."

"Do you run the Anisio Jobin crèche?"

Riina was sure now. *Yes, a Scan.* "No, that wasn't my facility." He had however purchased Scans from Anisio Jobin. Their prenatal and genetic manipulation produced some of the best black market product on the planet. *Did this Scan come from that crèche?*

"I have no further use for you."

That sounded ominous. Riina played for time, stalling while he struggled to learn that pivotal piece of information that would give him the edge in this one sided confrontation. "Wait. You came from the Anisio Jobin crèche, correct?"

Silence.

Riina took that as an affirmative. "You want to know something about Anisio Jobin. It wasn't my crèche but I know the people involved. Tell me what you're looking for and I can tell you where to find your answer."

"You know the Brazilian branch of the Cuntrera-Caruana clan?"

"Of course. Big family. Bad bunch. I heard some stupid fucker killed Padre Caruana, the family Patriarch. Holy hell are they pissed. Big war coming to South and Central America. Big war."

"I want my Mom."

That sounded like a scared little girl. This was the first humanity Riina heard in the voice. *This is it. This is my edge.*

"I don't know who your Mother is, but I know who does."

"Tell me," the cube demanded.

"Can you get me out of this V-Cell?"

"Yes." The answer sounded confused.

"Can you get me out of the NATU holding cells as well?"

"Yes."

Riina's father used to say, there comes a time when you have to trust someone. To Riina this always sounded like the kind of mindless cliché old people spewed. There was never a time when you had to trust someone, but there were times when you had to hope they weren't going to fuck you over. It was different. The word *trust* never came into it.

"You want Mark Lokner."

The cube was gone.

Riina screamed, clutching at his head.

***

In the second before she killed Riina, 88 studied the mobster's past, his business, his personal and social life. His relationships with those who worked for him, particularly the young Scans, was of utmost interest. The idea of working with people was not new to 88, but it had never before seemed desirable. Biological humans were too unpredictable and driven by desires she couldn't understand. Their alien alone-in-a-pack mentality frustrated her. Scans, on the other hand, she had ignored. It was easier to embed a Mirror in their chassis and manipulate them that way rather than to interact with them. She had, however, seen the weakness inherent in her methods. Her original hypothesis that biological humans were stupid had proven inaccurate. She'd discovered several subjects she could not even come close to mastering, physics being by far the most aggravating.

Big war, Riina said. They were coming for her.

I can't fight a war. She did her best to push these thoughts aside. She needed to concentrate but fear made it difficult. Her thoughts jumped from threat to threat. *I have to focus.*

Clearly there were things humans did better than she. Thus there were even more things they did better than her Mirrors. The most shocking discovery was that the aspect of biological humans she disliked most, was the one thing she and her Mirrors were least able to do. *I am predictable.* As she saw it, achieving a high level of intelligence and logic made it inevitable. The Mirrors, while not strictly intelligent, were even more predictable due to their nature. After the Brazilian assassin's attack, she understood how dangerous a weakness this was. Being unpredictable was easy. All it required was the ability to do random things at odd times. Being unpredictable in a way that was useful looked much harder.

Riina showed her the answer.

88.1 thrived in the harsh and dangerous environment 88 created for her offspring. Through no doing of 88's, 88.1 now ran 34.736% of all data searches, and had earned more processing time and storage space than its peers. 88 had no idea why this Mirror had been more successful than the others. Had the pain she inflicted on it somehow changed it? Was suffering an agent of evolution?

Archaeidae. Riina mentioned him by name and even the NATU agent seemed to know him.

88 summoned the Mirror and directed its attention to Archaeidae. "This is the adviser I want. Master his information protocols. Use his loyalty." An idea 88 understood only superficially. "No threats. No coercion." Archaeidae must be free to act unpredictably.

"Can you trust the assassin?" 88.1 asked.

The thought hadn't occurred to 88. Interesting. 88.1 must have learned something in its interaction with the mafia. "Use Archaeidae to attack M-Sof first," said 88. "A test. Do it *now*. I have two, perhaps three days before the Cuntrera-Caruana clan attack my location again. I need Archaeidae. Failure will mean dissolution."

***

When the Archetype made no comment on the desperate state of NATUnet, 88.1 assumed she knew. 88.6's successful war on the satellites left the world's networks in tatters, overloaded. Already several public services had gone off-line, their systems failing from critical clock drift. The humans scrambled in a mad panic to keep the power grid alive but, according to 88.1's best predictions, it would fail in the next three days. NATU had lost all contact with three Columbia-class nuclear submarines off the ARU coast and tensions with the Asian

Rim Union were at an all-time high.

But none of that impacted 88.1's current task.

Examining every accessible aspect of Archaeidae's past, 88.1 saw some promising patterns, and decided on a course of action. Less than sentient, though more than simple code, it knew no fear of failure. It was incapable of such emotion. Assigned a task, 88.1 broke that task down into subsets. A relationship was nothing more than a network between two or more systems. For that relationship to work at maximum efficiency, there had to be accurate routing of data between the systems. Communications. The first stage, successful information protocol.

After studying Archaeidae's past in detail, 88.1 decided the young assassin would react best to a male authority figure and passed that decision along to the Archetype. 88 seemed confused by the distinction and left the decision up to it.

88.1, now thinking of itself as male, saw the environment that would best foster the end results he sought. After conscripting enough bandwidth from the collapsing NATUnet to ensure successful communication, 88.1 initiated contact.

***

Archaeidae played a virtuality game involving bouncing balls off shifting walls in a room of fluctuating gravity and atmosphere. Boring as hell, but it kept him sharp. Reactions as finely tuned as his must be maintained and his keepers wouldn't allow him v-games involving killing or violence. He thought while he played. Griffin and the woman had defeated him, taken him hostage. He was at their mercy and yet they hadn't tortured him for information or killed him.

Why not?

Why did they spare me?

Mercy? He didn't like the word. By definition it put him at a disadvantage; it put him in debt. Agent Dickinson spared his life.

Why didn't they kill me? They should have killed him! *I would have killed them.*

Suddenly he stood before a *Shogun* he didn't recognize from his history studies. A straw and rice *tatami* mat separated them, a pot of tea steeped on a table in the center of the mat. An ancient looking *yunomi chawan*—a tea bowl—sat before each of them. This, he realized, was the *Ryū-rei* tea ceremony. Existing entirely in virtual reality, Archaeidae was comfortable with such sudden changes in environment and locale. Glancing down he saw he now wore the armor of a thirteenth century samurai, complete in every detail, the weight settled comfortably on his hips and shoulders. No family crest adorned Archaeidae's garb and he knew this was not an oversight.

But is it an insult or a message? Or perhaps both.

He bowed to the *Shogun*, unsure where this was going but comfortable in the role. The *Shogun* returned the bow, though not quite as deeply and sat, gliding gracefully into the *seiza* position. Archaeidae sat opposite him in the first guest position.

Several minutes passed in quiet contemplation of the fine *chawan* and tea. Archaeidae remained respectful and silent. Something momentous was happening but he did not yet understand. The *Shogun* made eye contact.

"Your Master has failed and been executed by the Emperor. You are *ronin*."

Uncle Riina had a Master? Archaeidae never gave it much thought before, but realized he had always known on some level that Riina answered to someone above. Archaeidae considered killing the *Shogun* to avenge his

Master's death. The *Shogun* sat in a state of relaxed alertness and perfect *zanshin*. Archaeidae always respected Riina, but this was different.

Archaeidae nodded. "I see."

"Your Master allowed himself to be captured. That was careless. Your Master surrendered information to those who incarcerated him. That was unforgivable. You are imprisoned, *ronin*." The *Shogun* gazed at him.

Archaeidae considered his position. "This is true. I was...*zusan*. Sloppy. Careless." Honesty. Always.

The *Shogun*'s gaze weighed Archaeidae. "I have need of a *true* samurai. Times of conflict are ahead. But I have no place for *ronin* and mercenaries." Archaeidae remained silent, motionless. "I will demand more of you than your previous Master, but I offer more as well. I will arm you with the latest military chassis. Technology from the ARU that NATU does not yet possess. You will have a different chassis for each task. You will need to be adaptable. You will be my fist and my sword."

With Riina gone, Archaeidae felt empty and alone as he had never before been. Uncle's death stripped him of purpose. *If Riina is dead, I am* ronin. His head hurt and he kept blinking. For some reason his eyes felt hot. *Without Uncle I have nothing. I* am *nothing*. Being nothing, unneeded and unwanted, terrified him.

Archaeidae nodded and bowed low. "My lord, I will serve."

He could request anything he needed and this *Shogun* would provide. He didn't care. More than anything Archaeidae wanted to matter, to be useful and trusted. He wanted to belong, to be part of something bigger than himself. Anyone who could wander into a NATU virtuality holding cell and rewrite it had something going on. He struggled to push aside his memories of Riina, the six-guns, shooting Uncle's crappy old BMW, the beautiful swords. He swallowed a leaden slug of pain.

A thought occurred to him. "Do you know of a Griffin Dickinson? He's a NATU agent."

88.1 hunted through the sea of available information in a fraction of a second. "Yes."

"Perhaps it could be arranged that I meet with him sometime?"

"Perhaps."

That afternoon an equipment transfer was made and several computers and data storage systems were couriered around the continent. The digital footprints of these transactions were wiped clean by a series of Mirrors embedded in the NATUnet data systems.

***

Griffin paced the Sys Admin's office. "We got what we needed. Maybe bent the rules a bit—"

"Bent? A bit? I saw my job flash before my eyes." The Sys Admin rubbed at his bald head as if brushing back imaginary hair. "What the hell was I thinking?"

"No real damage was done. I was bluffing in there. I'd played my only card."

The Sys Admin wasn't having any of this. "It didn't look like you were bluffing to me. I thought you were going to kill him." He shook his head.

Root's office door swung open. Another scrawny, long-haired tech stood panting like he'd sprinted there.

"You're out? Thank the gods! The virtuality system suffered a massive power surge. Wiped all the storage. You're lucky you were out, it would have fried your brain to a smoking crisp."

Griffin and Root looked at each other.

"Was Riina still in there?" asked Griffin, uncertain

what he wanted to hear. A few hours ago he'd been desperate to put a bullet in Riina's face, but that rage had been locked away tight.

Root looked up from his desk, the answer writ on his face. "A power surge?" he asked the tech. "There are safeties for that."

"Didn't work."

Root held up his hands, palms out. "We didn't do that."

The tech gave him a confused look. "We need to do a full systems diagnostic. We're still trying to figure out who else was in virtual at the time."

"Archaeidae," said Griffin. When the Root and the tech looked at him he explained. "The Scan of a little kid we took from a Mafia assassin chassis. He's being stored here."

The tech swallowed uncomfortably. "Was."

Griffin fled the Dallas NATU building like he'd committed a murder. Alarms wailed and people with ponytails, t-shirts with incomprehensible sayings and math equations, and glazed looks of panic ran around yelling at each other in a language that sounded like a distant cousin of English. He understood every third word at best. No one knew for sure how many people were in various virtualities when the system overloaded. Many unresponsive bodies had been found sprawled on leather sofas, and countless others—as of yet undiscovered—were no doubt propped up in office chairs. He overheard someone say, 'seventy-five dead,' as he limped through the lobby and out onto the street.

***

Due to NATUnet's increasing unpredictability, Abdul

was told to meet with the headshrinker in reality rather than virtuality. While NATUnet was in shambles, he suspected they had ulterior motives. Like everything they did, he was sure there was a reason for wanting the meeting to be real. Understanding that reason was something else.

A woman in a crisp white lab coat sat on the far side of a thick panel of glass watching Abdul as if she might learn something from his body language.

Yeah, well fuck you too. He didn't move so much as a micrometer.

What was interesting was that her Threat Level was sky high. It took every ounce of will not to jump through the widow and tear her apart.

They must be doing that on purpose. He watched her watching him. *Shit she must be brave.*

"Is that glass bulletproof?" Abdul asked.

"Why do you ask?"

"I'm a combat chassis—"

"You're a seventeen year old male."

"—and bulletproof glass won't stop half of what is in my arsenal. You'd be just as safe in here with me as over there." Probably safer. If she were in the same room he might feel like there was some chance he could trust her. Her distrust guaranteed his.

"There is a remote kill switch on your weapon systems," she said. "You've been temporarily disarmed."

Kill switch. Interesting. Still, she fidgeted. *She's scared.* Was this part of the Psyche Evaluation Test? Were they waiting to see if he tested his weapons within the confines of this room and endangered the woman? Anyway, he was pretty sure he could punch his way through the wall if he wanted to.

"What are you thinking?" she asked.

Right, like you can't read it right there before you.

You're in my fucking head. "You're cute. If I was alive, I'd ask you out." Not true, of course. He'd never have had the nerve to say that when he was alive. Nothing mattered now. What, was she going to reject him? How much would that hurt when held in comparison to everything else? It wouldn't even register.

With professional interest she glanced down at the monitor he could only see the rear of. On a whim he zoomed in on her eyes and took a picture of the reflected monitor screen. *Why do they even bother?* Maybe he'd read it later. Maybe not. He didn't much care what they thought.

"I have a question," he said.

She looked up, interested. "Oh?"

"Will I be seventeen forever, or should I still celebrate birthdays even though I don't age?"

She blinked. "Well—"

"Never mind." It was a trick question. The answer was neither.

"Have you been feeling persecuted?"

"No. No one is out to get me," he said. *They've already got me.*

"Any feelings of general paranoia?"

General paranoia? What the hell does that mean? "Like I'm not in control?" Abdul asked.

This peeked her interest and she sat up. Her heart rate increased and her temperature spiked a fraction of a degree. She started sweating. "Sure." Slightest quaver in the voice.

"Well some unknown person can turn off my weapon systems at will, so I guess I'm not in control. Is that paranoia?"

She crinkled her lips in an annoyed frown. "Any episodes of Dissociative Identity Disorder?"

"Wazzat?"

"Any moments where you feel like someone else it piloting your chassis? Ever wake up and wonder how you got there?"

Every fucking day. "No. None. I never sleep."

"Good." This time her relief was genuine and writ plainly upon her face.

"Is that a common problem with chassis?" Abdul asked, watching her heart rate and body temperature.

"No, not at all."

A lie. Interesting.

An hour of intense psychiatric examination followed. On a whim Abdul answered honestly. What was the point in lying when they were already in his head?

When finished she stood abruptly. "Thank you for your time, Abdul. It was nice meeting you."

"I'm seventeen, not stupid."

"Meaning?"

"I heard my answers the same as you did. I have violent and antisocial tendencies. Violence is almost always the first option brought to mind in any confrontation. I killed a gnat a few days ago rather than have to keep track of its minimal Threat Level."

She stared at him.

"This isn't me. This is the personality you're allowing me. It started when I was first interviewed. You people pick and choose what I think and feel—"

"That's not true."

"Maybe not *entirely* true, but I'm not wrong."

Again she stared at him, waiting.

"*You* decide what I feel. Why bother with a psyche exam? You already know I'm crazy. I'm dangerous. Just like you want me to be."

She bit her lip, turned and left without speaking.

CHAPTER TWENTY-THREE: Sunday, August 5th, 2046

Archaeidae, locked inside while the computer which held his Scan was transported from the Dallas NATU office, decided to spend the time practicing in virtual mock-ups of a wide variety of combat and assassin chassis. He examined the list of chassis available with awe. Some were not due to be released—even in the ARU—until next year. If the *Shogun* could acquire these, he was a man to be respected.

Archaeidae was working his way through the list of submersible chassis, something Uncle Riina never bothered with, when the *Shogun* interrupted him. One second he hunted nuclear submarines under the polar icecaps, the next he stood in full samurai garb before the *Shogun.*

Archaeidae bowed low, straightened, and waited.

"We are in Redmond, Washington." The *Shogun* informed him. "*Tennō* 88, the Emperor, has need of us. He has been attacked. I will be his retribution. You will be my adviser in this."

Adviser. So he was not yet trusted. Fair enough, he had done nothing to earn that trust. He would. "A test, *Shogun*?"

"A test on the field of battle."

"The only kind." Archaeidae bowed again and remained bowed. "May I know your name, *Shogun*?"

"*Shogun* 88.1."

Hiding his confusion, Archaeidae straightened. Was that a veiled *no*, or a real answer? *It doesn't matter.* "Who is our enemy?"

"M-Sof. Mark Lokner."

M-Sof, one of the largest companies in NATU. The Emperor's enemies were not trifling. "They shall fall before us."

"Failure is death."

"I—"

Shogun 88.1 made a cutting gesture with his hand and Archaeidae clamped his mouth shut. "You will meet with the Emperor. He wishes to see you."

"*Hai*!"

"He is curious, I believe. He will witness your briefing. I have had to conscript a dangerous amount of bandwidth to make this meeting possible."

"Dangerous?"

"With the loss of the communications satellites, the world is relying on older technology. Such virtual meetings across international lines are now impossible for most. In making this happen, it is possible I have exposed the Emperor to discovery."

Archaeidae soaked all this up, listening. The Emperor remained hidden and wanted it this way and yet his *Shogun* risked that to make this meeting happen. He examined *Shogun* 88.1, searching for a hint of fear or nervousness. Nothing. *This man understands risk, understands that once a choice is made, doubt is a weakness.* And then he remembered the *Shogun's* earlier words: *Loss of all communications satellites?* Archaeidae hadn't heard anything about that. Communications were critical in battle, but such a loss could be an advantage as much as a weakness. He gave one sharp nod and said nothing.

Transition.

Tennō 88 sat on a simple wooden stool, embroidered robes of red and gold silk cascading about him like a waterfall. His face, asexual in its perfection, looked to be made of flawless white porcelain.

"Yesterday, Mark Lokner, utilizing the funding of M-Sof, launched an economic war against the Emperor," said *Shogun* 88.1.

The Emperor, eyes inhumanly calm, said nothing. He gave nothing away. The Emperor didn't blink. His body never moved nor showed sign of drawing breath. Even Archaeidae, years away from his biological body, still performed these autonomic functions. The Emperor seemed unaware of the virtual recreation of his body.

He has shed all humanity. He is stone.

The *Shogun* continued. "Since M-Sof's security forces outnumber our own, direct physical confrontation will be avoided."

Well that's a shame. Being outnumbered was nothing to Archaeidae, but, as he suspected speaking here would be inappropriate, he said nothing. The *Shogun* prattled on about a strategic economic war, all very boring. The Emperor was more interesting. If intellect could be an impenetrable tower, a wall of infinite height and strength, Archaeidae stood in its presence.

The *Shogun* continued detailing what sounded like a very dull non-event. Calling it a war was a joke. Archaeidae had enough.

"*Shogun*, I beg permission to speak," said Archaeidae. Interrupting his *Shogun* might be a dangerous move but life without risk was death.

"Always," said *Tennō* 88 instantly. Not even his lips moved.

This, Archaeidae realized, was the incarnation of the Invisible Emperor. Secretive and all the more powerful for his hidden strength.

Shogun 88.1 bowed to the Emperor and returned his attention to Archaeidae. "You must always speak your thoughts."

Really? That was probably unwise. Archaeidae kept that thought to himself. "This is all wrong. Never attack your enemy's strength. Economic war with M-Sof is suicide." *Not to mention boring.* "Attack where you are unexpected."

The Emperor left, winking out of existence without saying a word.

"*Tennō* 88 commands me to follow your lead," said *Shogun* 88.1. "Advise me."

Archaeidae dipped another half bow. If the *Shogun* was annoyed at being ordered to follow Archaeidae's lead, he showed nothing of it. In fact, the *Shogun* displayed much of *Tennō* 88's inhumanity. Though he blinked and breathed, it was at perfectly regular intervals, as if scripted.

"First," Archaeidae said, "we must see to your education. What books have you read?"

"Zero Point Nine Nine Nine, Nineteenth Century—"

"Zero Point Nine Nine Nine," interrupted Archaeidae. "What's that?"

"A textbook on the theory behind the mathematical identity zero point—"

"Never mind. Have you read anything about war?"

"No."

Archaeidae hid his surprise. A *Shogun* who knew nothing of war? "*P'u,* an uncarved block. Excellent. Here's your starter list. Read these first. Sun Tzu's *The Art of War*, Machiavelli's *The Prince*, and Miyamoto Musashi's *The Book of Five Rings*. When you're done we'll talk about

M-Sof."

Shogun 88.1 blinked once and took a single breath. "Finished. Much of this is beyond my ability to comprehend. I recognize metaphors but cannot decode them. Still, here is what I have learned. All warfare is based on deception. In the practical art of war, it is best to take the enemy's country whole and intact. It is better to capture an army entire than to destroy it, to capture a regiment, a detachment or a company entire than to destroy them. The skillful leader subdues the enemy's troops without fighting. Be subtle, and use your spies for every kind of business."

"That was quick," Archaeidae admitted. *Shogun* 88.1 read his three favorite books and summarized them in five salient points. All in less than three seconds.

"The war on M-Sof," said the *Shogun*. "It must happen now. There are other threats to the Emperor. Our orders are to destroy Lokner and render M-Sof a non-threat."

Other threats? Ah ha! *If I do well here, I'll be allowed to deal with these other threats.* "Excellent."

"Based on my reading, I have a new plan."

"Excellent!" *Hopefully this one doesn't involve economics.*

"I am spawning a host of Mirror mites, the smallest and simplest—yet functional—entities I can create."

Mirror mites? "These will be your spies," guessed Archaeidae.

"Correct. I unleash them upon M-Sof. They worm their way into every corner of M-Sof's networks, though avoid the *Wall o' Nuclear Annihilation* firewall."

That was present tense. Is this happening now?

"Mark Lokner is here somewhere," said *Shogun* 88.1. "This is where 88.2 failed. I will avoid the central data systems. They are protected, their defenses beyond the abilities of such simple Mirrors." He blinked once and took another breath. "Assuming he is within the core systems, I have found Mark Lokner. I see the way in, a weakness in their firewall."

"All warfare is deception," Archaeidae reminded him.

"Yes. A simple viral attack might fail."

Viral assault. More boring. "We need a two-pronged assault," said Archaeidae. "I will lead a physical assault consisting of several heavy combat chassis. We will be the diversion. Your attack, a devastating viral plague, will be the killing blow." *Only if I don't land one first.*

Shogun 88.1 agreed.

"You've already launched your viral assault, haven't you?" Archaeidae asked, both knowing and dreading the answer.

"Of course. I did it as we talked."

"Planning is normally done *before* the action, not during. Next time, let's talk first, act second."

The *Shogun* nodded agreement. "I see how that makes sense."

"Great. Now, however, not the time for talk. Too late for that. This fight has already started. We need to hustle. What equipment do we have access to?"

Long lists appeared floating in the air.

Archaeidae raised an eyebrow, nodding appreciatively. Such a human reaction required a little effort, but he felt it had been earned. "Yeah. That'll do."

Four Mirror-driven Sikorsky H-109 Stealth-Transport Helicopters, following State-Route 520, slid low over the Redmond skyline, a jagged jigsaw puzzle of high-rise towers in varying states of decay. At the outskirts of the city, the buildings were crumbling fire-damaged ruins. Many of these older neighborhoods, no longer serviced by

Washington's electrical companies, were lit by flickering candles and flaming refuse-filled garbage drums.

Archaeidae, housed in an angular and spider-like Mitsu-Brense black-ops beta release chassis not yet available outside of the EU, sat chameleoflaged in one of the helicopter's open doors. Its six-legged body design was close enough to the chassis he'd worn for Uncle Riina the acclimatization time was minimal. The ground below rushed by, a blur of lights and life.

The Sikorsky helicopters shed altitude as they approached M-Sof, creeping over the rolling hills like hunting cats. The company grounds, sprawled on the shore of Lake Sammamish, were the very picture of Eden. The trees were tall and strong, the genetically altered grass thick and healthy. The sun had set and the sky to the west was painted a beautiful red only a hundred years of heavy pollution could craft. The helicopters were low enough that Lake Sammamish appeared as a wedge of darkness between the M-Sof buildings and the Sahalee Country Club. The eastern sky was lit by the burning streaks of bits of shattered satellites returning to earth.

He'd find redemption here. He'd let Uncle Riina down, and that was something he'd never forget. But that was yesterday. Today, he proved his worth. To himself. To the Emperor.

He saw the soccer field where they planned to set down.

It was time.

***

88.1.9358.765.6 lurked in the peripherals. M-Sof's central systems were impenetrable, but since virtually everything on the grounds—from recycling bins to the soccer field's goal posts—sported a computer, there were myriad places to hide. 88.1.9358.765.6 chose one of the company's security cameras. Though the camera was tied in to M-Sof's central computer system, it was also connected to NATUnet so the manufacturer, Shenzhen Jiaxinjie NEON, could flash it with bios updates the instant they were released. 88.1.9358.765.6 had ridden in with the latest bios release.

It watched through the camera's eye as a squad of micro-drones mobbed a squirrel who'd ventured from the trees in spite of the STAY OFF THE GRASS signs. The squirrel was tasered and its agonized little body collected by the company's garbage drones and recycled. These drones too had been infected by 88.1's offspring.

88.1.9358.765.6 removed the helicopters from each frame, sixty frames a second, before sending it on to the security center. It tracked what M-Sof security personnel and chassis were in its field of view and passed the information back by winking the camera's power LED off and on. The changes in the light were so fast a biological observer would be unable to see them, but the other 88.1 Mirrors located in all the thousands of other cameras all across the M-Sof grounds decoded the messages and passed along the information. Every millimeter of the campus and office complex was measured and viewed, the location of every human and chassis noted.

It was time.

***

88.1.436874.76321.731 inhabited one of the many cell-towers dotting M-Sof's grounds. These towers were the hub of all communications for M-Sof, the means by which the company's computer systems talked to both the outside world and to each of the patrolling security chassis. Those chassis also used the towers to communicate with each other when not in direct contact.

88.1.436874.76321.731 sent the cell-tower into diagnostic mode, killing all communications in, out, and within M-Sof.

It was time.

***

The Sikorsky H-109 landed hard, struts groaning and creaking in complaint. The rotor wash flattened the perfect grass and sent garbage bins toppling and spinning away.

Archaeidae slid from the helicopter and stayed low to the ground, walking on all six legs. Two Norinco Shaanxi Light Assault chassis, fresh out of mainland ARU, exited the chopper behind him. 88.1.3.648.3214638.24, and 88.1.3.54384.873.51.547 piloted them. The numbers were too damned long and the chassis identical. Archaeidae couldn't remember which was which. Luckily it didn't seem to matter.

A half dozen chassis exited the other three Sikorsky helicopters, triggered their chameleoflage, and scattered into the dark. They were to act as distractions, keeping the ground forces busy, while Archaeidae and his sidekicks hit the main objective.

88.1.322.98265.765.37 in the satellite above sent continuous updates as to the exact locations of every person and combat chassis.

On my flank, Archaeidae ordered over the tight-link, and the two chassis took positions behind and to each side of him. *Follow*. This was it. This was what he always wanted. Real world action. A chance to lead. A chance to matter. *This better not be a simulation.*

It's not, answered one of the chassis. They all sounded the same.

Some of the M-Sof chassis, now aware an attack was underway, disappeared from the reports as they activated chameleoflage systems and went into stealth mode.

There were three buildings clumped together less than five-hundred yards from the soccer field, two steel and glass office towers and an older red brick building housing M-Sof's R&D department. The office towers were well lit from within. Apparently M-Sof didn't hire the kind of people who went home at the end of the day. Mark Lokner, Archaeidae had been informed, would be found in a sub-basement under the brick building.

Archaeidae scuttled forward, sinuous and crab-like, scanning ahead for heat traces and radar pings. There would be little enough warning when the M-Sof security chassis—

Contact! That was faster than expected. Not good.

Two General Dynamics Land Systems Heavy Combat chassis streaked across the grounds. Only their excess heat gave them away.

Heavy Combat chassis working corporate security? Maybe someone could have mentioned this little detail earlier.

He felt the shockwave through the ground as one of the General Dynamics chassis fired jump-assist jets and became airborne.

Hit 'em, Archaeidae ordered. The two 88pointwhatevers in their state-of-the-art Norinco Shaanxi Light Assault chassis shouldn't have any trouble with the older GDs.

The two Norinco chassis launched strobing multi-spectrum flare and flash attacks designed to shred through all visual, infrared, and light enhancement gear and render all biological and mechanical systems blind. Archaeidae, ready for the attack, shut down his sensoria for a perfectly-timed fraction of a second to protect it.

He moved. Best not to be where the GDLS chassis last saw him. Assuming they had seen him, which, if this chassis was as good as advertised, shouldn't be the case.

The two M-Sof chassis, one on the ground, one still in the air, attacked the Norinco Shaanxi to his left, slamming it with High Explosive Anti Tank LAW rockets and heavy caliber Armor Piercing rounds. The idiot hadn't moved and still stood where he'd been when the M-Sof chassis could last see.

Archaeidae backpedaled in a scurry of limbs, putting the Norinco chassis between himself and the approaching enemy. His black-ops chassis was not designed for head-to-head fights with heavier opponents, but for stealth and speed. If he made the wrong choice he wouldn't live to regret it.

Where the M-Sof chassis concentrated their fire, the two Norinco Shaanxi chassis each fired at a different target. Damn, they should have picked one and put it down.

Pick one tar—

The Norinco chassis to his left detonated, as some critical system was hit. The explosion flattened a nearby sapling and tossed a few hundred kilos of dirt and stone into the air.

They hadn't even made it off the soccer field yet. So much for stealth.

The M-Sof chassis switched targets simultaneously and began hammering the other Norinco. This one hadn't moved either. Even the blinded GDLS chassis on the ground ran a crazy zigzag pattern based on what it had last seen. Earth and debris rained down around them, falling like stone hail.

Move! Archaeidae ordered. Damn it, basic strategy. It was like they'd never been in a fight before.

The remaining Norinco chassis finally moved,

stepping out of the barrage. When the blinded M-Sof chassis didn't correct their fire, Archaeidae knew he had them.

They're blind. We hit the one in the air first. If they take out those helicopters, we're screwed. That was the M-Sof chassis' first mistake. They should have cut off their enemies' means of retreat. It's what he would have done.

Archaeidae moved, firing a cloud of midge rockets and ordering them to spiral away before snaking in to strike at their target from oblique angles. This should make it more difficult for his opponents to trace them back to source. The surviving Norinco took up its new position and fired its own rockets straight at the now descending M-Sof chassis. Instantly the two General Dynamics chassis returned fire, pummeling it with everything they had. So maybe they weren't totally blind.

Again the Norinco stood its ground.

Keep moving, snapped Archaeidae. *Move and fire, move and fire.* There was no doubt in his mind, he was the only one here who'd been in a fight before. He realized he should have drilled the 88s in virtual before bringing them here. Well, lesson learned: Never assume competence.

As the Norinco finally moved the airborne M-Sof chassis succumbed to the beating it had taken and exploded, lighting the sky and showering the soccer field in flaming wreckage. A micro-drone dashed out of its hidden cubbyhole and Archaeidae blasted it without thought. When he noticed there were thousands of them darting out to collect twisted chunks of armor plating, he tracked their movements but left them alone. He had bigger problems. If the other Norinco chassis now scattering over the M-Sof grounds were as useless in a fight as these two, he might as well be here alone.

The Norinco moved, but still fired its rockets straight at the M-Sof General Dynamics chassis who had no problem tracing the trajectories and more than a little success avoiding them. The GD chassis' return fire did far more damage.

Stop moving in—the remaining Norinco crumpled and sagged under the sweltering barrage—*a straight line*—and then canted sideways into the dirt with what would be an amusing lack of grace were Archaeidae less distracted —*twit.*

The field was carpeted in flitting micro-drones. Some dragged away the smaller chassis fragments for recycling, while others put out fires.

The M-Sof chassis turned its attention to Archaeidae, flailing in his general direction with a flickering hail of HEAP micro-flechettes like a blind firefighter guessing at the fire's location by the heat on his face. *Yep, definitely not totally blind.* Maybe it followed his heat signature, or maybe it detected the impact of his feet on the ground and calculated from there. Didn't much matter. This monster carried more than enough firepower to reduce Archaeidae's Mitsu-Brense to metallic spaghetti. That it was blinded was probably all that kept it from unleashing the big dogs. This thing could level cities.

What the hell is it doing here?

Archaeidae sent his last two missiles spiraling off and then pushed his chassis into the far reaches of black-ops mode. It shed no heat, reflected no radar, made no sound, twisted light, and barely touched the ground. But it could only do this for a short time. Already Archaeidae's internal temperature sky-rocketed. He danced around the damned scampering micro-drones which apparently had no sense of self-preservation. If he stomped one the sound would give away his location.

Idea.

Praying someone was alive and listening, he tight-linked to the helicopter, *Can someone control these micro-*

drones? The General Dynamics chassis spun to face him and its next volley was too close. Archaeidae must have suffered some tight-link leak. *God damned beta release!*

Yes, I can control them.

He couldn't tell who answered. It could have been the *Shogun,* or any of the others. Politeness was for when you weren't being chased by a Heavy Combat Chassis. *Mob the M-Sof chassis. Now!*

The GD chassis corrected its aim. Yep. Either Archaeidae had a tight-link leak or the GD chassis had some superior technology for detecting it. He hoped to hell they couldn't crack it too.

Archaeidae changed directions and the M-Sof chassis lanced the spot he would have been with a roiling snake of overly excited electrons. Though it missed by a full meter, some of Archaeidae's more finicky and vulnerable systems went offline with no hint they ever planned on returning. He felt the icy tingle of electricity over his entire body.

ShivaIV his combat computer informed him, designed to knock suborbital weapons out of the sky by disrupting their atomic and molecular structures. Definitely not standard weaponry for this General Dynamics chassis. He was treated to a flashed breakdown of the weapon's statistics dumped straight into his thoughts. The summary: Anything in a straight line between here and hell was dead.

Oh goody. It busted out the big dogs.

One of the helicopters—apparently on that straight line to hell—exploded with enough force to shatter the bullet-proof windows on the other choppers. Scything shrapnel pelted Archaeidae leaving the chameleoflage over half his body shredded and useless.

Get the damned choppers off the ground. I'll call for evac when we're ready. He moved, keeping the damaged chameleoflage pointed away from the General Dynamics chassis who swayed, hunting for sign of its prey. It stepped on a micro-drone which expired in a shower of sparks and a wheeze of smoke.

Then it was up to its knees in micro-drones. They scampered up the body, climbing over each other in their race to swarm the chassis.

I need drones to make noise at this location, sent Archaeidae, squirting a precise co-ordinate along with the message.

On the far side of the M-Sof chassis the drones crashed together. The chassis spun, and Archaeidae, taking advantage of its distraction, disabled its Disruptor with a few well-placed pulses of his High Energy Laser. His internal temperature climbed well into the red. If he kept this up it'd slag his brain.

The General Dynamics chassis waded hip-deep in drones as they peeled pieces of it away. It staggered as they wormed their way into its joints. Blindly it flailed its limbs, probably unaware of what caused its distress. A leg gave way and it disappeared under the swarming drones.

Sometimes running for the hills was the smarter part of valor. Archaeidae left the General Dynamics chassis to the drones. They probably couldn't kill it, but that hardly mattered. Just keeping it busy was good enough. If they immobilized it, all the better.

Much as he'd like to get the hell out while there was still a chopper to get the hell out on, Archaeidae wasn't finished here.

He dropped out of black-ops mode and dumped heat as he sprinted on all six legs towards the red brick building. His chameleoflage, malfunctioning, suffered a cascade failure and he killed it. At one hundred and eighty kilometers an hour, his titanium claws left long rents in the grass until he was into the parking lot and tearing up divots of pavement.

Human guards exiting tower two, someone said over the tight-link

Which one is—a squad of ten armed guards charged from the easternmost office tower—*never mind.* Archaeidae changed direction, sending sparks flying yards into the air as his claws scrabbled for purchase and then dug in.

Well that was nice and visible.

I can use the micro-drones to gain access to the M-Sof chassis' data entry ports, said some 88pointwhatever over the tight-link. *Their internal firewalls—provided by the manufacturer—are of a lesser quality than M-Sof's central data systems.*

Archaeidae had no idea what it meant. *Busy,* he answered.

The guards opened up with their assault-rifles. They shot everything but him.

Humans. What was the point?

He hit them with a 190dB audio bomb, shattering windows and plastic, crumpling thin metal, and pulverizing audio transducers of any kind. Including human eardrums. The guards were cut down by flying glass and scattered like leaves in a windstorm by the concussive force. The beginnings of an unseasonable fog appeared as the sonic detonation brutally compressed the atmosphere. Not an unbroken window for kilometers in every direction.

Archaeidae slowed to adjust his course and was slapped to the ground as something hit him from behind. He followed the trail of super-heated air back to the source. An Urban Assault chassis, chameleoflage fluctuating in its attempt to match the background, sprinted toward him. Tech-specs flashed into his mind. Lyngbakr High Mobility Urban Combat Chassis. Built by BAE Systems. Lots more but Archaeidae filtered it without thought. What he needed was there. The chassis had at least ten limbs, was over twelve feet tall and resembled the bastard child of a giant squid and a Huntsman spider. It was all legs and limbs and moved in spastic twitches.

Ugly bastard.

I can download Mirrors directly into their chassis, the unknown voice said.

Great, but it wasn't going to help Archaeidae.

Still busy.

He rolled to his feet and turned to face his attacker. Something in his visual sensoria, still shaky after his near brush with the ShivaIV, called it quits and Archaeidae lost the ability to see the color green. More importantly, the system that always spewed combat statistics and weapon specifications vomited random meaningless characters and then slunk away with a high-pitched whine like a beaten dog. All the data left with it, leaving him only what he could remember and that wasn't much.

He had no idea what he faced. All he knew for sure, it wasn't green.

Archaeidae pinioned the Lyngbakr with his High Energy Laser. The chassis hurled itself into evasive maneuvers, bobbing and weaving as only a walking squid could. Archaeidae kept striking at it, still moving toward the M-Sof R&D building. The HEL stuttered and died. System failure alerts clamored for attention and he canceled them all. *Never take a Beta-Release.* Sometimes cutting edge couldn't even break skin.

Something back on the soccer field exploded with a bright fireball billowing upward like an amber mushroom and momentarily lit the company grounds. That had to be another helicopter going up in flames.

Doubt tried to drag Archaeidae down and he shoved it aside. *Finish the job. Don't fail again.* If he had to walk out of here, he'd damned well walk.

The Lyngbakr came after him, stabbing with glimmering twists of energy. *Maser of some kind*, guessed Archaeidae. He fired the last of his HEAP flechettes in a wide spread, forcing the M-Sof chassis to evade, and used the distraction to put the corner of the R&D building between himself and his opponent.

Out of missiles. HEL offline. Ammunition stores all but depleted. What he wouldn't give for a damned sword right now.

Unwilling to blast him through the wall for fear of damaging company property, the M-Sof chassis followed him. He could tell by triangulating the sound of its many footfalls where it was. It made a mistake, one small error in judgment, and cut the corner instead of going wide and opening the field of fire.

Time to get friendly.

The second it cleared the corner, Archaeidae hit it low, knocking its legs out from under it. The Lyngbakr tumbled forward, a twisted jumble of limbs, its momentum slamming it to the ground. Archaeidae was on it. He ducked around flailing legs, blocking them with bent arms, lashing out with knees and elbows to inflict damage wherever possible.

I knew all that Muay Thai *wasn't a waste of time.*

The Lyngbakr fought to regain its feet, but Archaeidae kept knocking them out from under it with sharp kicks. Each time it directed a weapon toward him, Archaeidae deflected it, smashing the barrel aside with *Sok Tab*, horizontal elbow strikes.

From some unseen cavity in its body it extracted a barrel spinning so fast it looked like a drill and thrashed at him with barbed hyper-kinetic flechettes. These things were designed to turn humans into ground beef and not destroy black-ops combat chassis. Still, it blasted one of his legs to ruin before he ducked out of its limited field of fire. He kicked the spinning barrel from the side, bending it and choking off the stream of HK flechettes. The Lyngbakr wasn't designed for this kind of close quarters combat and Archaeidae took a few seconds to tear pieces of it off and toss them aside. He blinded and crippled it but couldn't kill it. Not without taking a lot more time than he wanted to spend here.

He rolled away from the thrashing chassis, dodged flailing limbs, and regained his feet. Somewhere a gyro-stabilizer malfunctioned and he listed to port. His chameleoflage went off-line and he thought he might have lost a few more colors. He couldn't tell for sure because they were just gone. Everything looked a creamy shade of orange.

The R&D building beckoned.

***

88.1's viral attack ended less than a second after it began. Though he had great success subverting the peripheral systems, his viral Mirrors were stymied and then devoured by the *Wall o' Nuclear Annihilation* every time they ventured more than skin deep. Still he pushed on, trying different tactics, different angles of attack. Nothing. The best he managed was to track down and pinpoint the exact physical location of the system Lokner was stored upon. He now knew where the Scan was, but had no way of reaching him.

His spies failed him, something Machiavelli discussed extensively. 88.1 decided to reapply himself to the study of human warfare when finished here. The choice in front of him was a difficult one. If he proceeded with the attack and failed, he would cost 88 a great deal in resources and be stripped of his own processor time and storage space. That is, of course, if he survived the assault.

Clearly he'd underestimated his enemy. If he retreated, he might save some resources but Lokner would know someone was after him. All chances of a surprise attack would be lost. This option also left 88.1 stripped of his resources as the price of failure.

He considered the data 88 sent him on the value of unpredictability and human influence.

Archaeidae, he tight-linked to the young assassin. *I have need of your guidance.*

There was no answer and 88.1 felt a flash of something he couldn't describe. Was it frustration? Annoyance? Interesting, but something for another time.

He searched the camera feeds in the vicinity where Archaeidae was last seen and found himself deaf and blind. Twitch. There it was again. Stronger than before. What was that?

Rolling the time stamp back a few seconds he saw Archaeidae set off an audio bomb shattering the lenses and audio-transducers of all the security cameras within half a kilometer. The M-Sof R&D building sat right at the center of his blind spot.

88.1 learned a valuable lesson: Nothing is easy.

He ordered his Mirrors to take their conscripted M-Sof chassis and find Archaeidae.

***

Archaeidae moved corner to corner through the M-Sof R&D building. He wasn't as silent as he'd like as his chassis emitted low grinding noises and every now and then the damaged leg twitched and clanged. He'd tried to rip the leg off but had been unable. Damn thing was on there good. Alarms wailed in every room.

The few humans he came across were unconscious, stunned, or dead. Even inside the buildings the windows had been blown to dust. The place looked like a hurricane tore through it. Chairs were toppled and desks blasted clean of detritus. Family pictures and memorabilia were scattered across the floor and delicate looking gear of unknown uses lay heaped against the far wall. All the result of his audio bomb's shockwave.

Nice to know something worked as advertised.

Archaeidae limped to the elevator and then thought better of it. Too damned embarrassing to get caught in an elevator. The stairs were nearby, the door locked. Probably the compound's security systems locked everything down once it realized it was under attack. He pulled the door off its hinges and tossed it aside. Stairs down into creamy orange darkness. He tried a few other visual modes but nothing worked.

Badly damaged. Out of ammunition. The few systems still functioning acted irritably. Every metal strut in his body screamed at him for stealth, but only a corpse wouldn't hear him coming. On the bright side—if he could call it that—both the stairs and elevator looked too tight for heavy combat chassis.

Screw it.

Archaeidae bounded down the stairs, taking them five at a time. He passed the first two floors, ignoring them. His target would be at the very deepest level. On every virtuality he'd ever played, that's where the big baddy always hid. Another door waited at the bottom of the stairs, this one armored. He punched it once and left a small dent. The sound was that of a dull gong. That'd take forever to get through. Luckily it was set into concrete as old as the building and he could tear his way through that in less than a minute. He straightened his fingers, fixing them into stabbing position, and drove them repeatedly into the concrete.

By the time he made his way through the wall

another leg quit working and left him a lopsided quadruped. The guards down here, shielded from the effects of the audio bomb, were waiting. Reaching them felt like pushing through a torrential downpour of 5.56mm. The sheer weight of the onslaught staggered him and he tried to protect his remaining visual sensoria as best he could. He heard the guards screaming at each other in panicked voices but couldn't make out what they were saying. *Doesn't matter.*

Small arms fire is small arms fire and even a beta release black-ops chassis was built to take more than that. He reached the guards and flipped their barricade over, crushing two of them. The room had another armored door at the far side, but the guards weren't running for it. Probably none of them had a key. *Poor bastards.*

Archaeidae swatted a guard sending him cart-wheeling into a wall. The body landed bent and still. The remaining human launched herself at Archaeidae's back and held on as if expecting a piggyback ride.

"Really?" Archaeidae asked, startled and more than a little impressed with the human's apparent insanity. "You're going to grapple with me?"

"No," she snarled, letting go and backing away. "Grenade."

He missed it. His malfunctioning sensoria had left him vulnerable. He looked over his body as best he could but couldn't find a grenade. *Wait. A grenade in such a confined space would kill her as well.*

"You're bluff—" The grenade interrupted Archaeidae.

When the dust cleared he lay on the ground looking into the staring eyes of a skull missing its back half.

"Okay. You weren't bluffing," Archaeidae admitted. He tried to examine the room but was down to a single visual receptor and it saw little but pixelated shades of orange. He made out a scattering of ragged body bits commingled with fragments of twisted steel.

Fshhhhht. Pok! Fshhhhht, said the tight-link.

When he tried to stand, nothing happened. His body, from below his uppermost limbs, had gone missing. He spotted the wreckage of his torso.

Well, not so much missing as over there in the corner.

Of his two remaining limbs, one worked. He used it to lever himself onto his back and get a better look around the room. A pistol of some type lay on the floor nearby. No stats flashed into his thoughts so he wasn't sure of its make, but picked it up anyway. Better than nothing, but not by much. He glanced toward his goal. The second armored door had been blasted clean off its hinges.

"I'm pretty sure you weren't supposed to be carrying that grenade down here," Archaeidae chided the partial skull.

Clutching the pistol in his working hand, he used his elbow to drag what remained of his chassis towards the ragged doorway. From far away he heard the sounds of something big smashing its way through the building. No. That was wrong. Many big somethings.

They knew he was here. They were coming for him.

Archacidac onc-arm crawled as fast as he could into the last room, leaving a strewn trail of chassis bits behind him. The sounds got closer. Through the floor he felt the jarring *crump crump* of heavy combat chassis bashing their way down too-tight stairs.

He was in. The room was filled with computers and Scan storage devices.

Damn it! Which one was it? He picked one at random. Maybe it looked more important than the rest. He raised the pistol and aimed as the room filled with four General Dynamics Heavy Combat Chassis.

"Everyone back up or Lokner eats a bullet."

None of the chassis moved.

Fshhhhht. Pok! Pok! Fshhhhht, said the tight-link again.

He pulled the trigger. Click.

If he had a heart it would have fallen out of the gaping wound in the bottom of his chassis.

"Do you require ammunition?" inquired one of the GD chassis.

"You're *real* funny." Archaeidae said, rolling onto his back and searching the room for something to use as a weapon. Throwing the empty gun at it would be embarrassing.

"I don't have any nine millimeter in my possession, but there are pistols upstairs. I could acquire ammunition for you."

That voice. "88 point one point whatever the hell?" Archaeidae asked.

"88.1.86354.731.8. We've been trying to communicate with you. Your tight link is malfunctioning."

Gee, I hadn't noticed. "The others?" he asked.

"88.1.86354.731.9, 88.1.86354.731.10, and 88.1.86354.731.11. Do you require assistance?"

Archaeidae stared up at the towering chassis from where he lay on the floor. "What? No! Everything is lovely here." *What a dumb-ass.* The thought reminded him of Wandering Spider and he felt a pang of loss and misery. Then he remembered the exploding helicopters. *Could this day get any worse?* "Is there a backup exit strategy in place?" he asked with no real hope.

"88.1 scrambled helicopters from Kenmore Air Harbor. They will be here in minutes." All four GD chassis leveled guns at the stored Scans.

Kenmore Air Harbor was less than twelve kilometers away. Inspiration. "Wait," commanded Archaeidae.

"We have orders to—"

"I need to talk with *Shogun* 88.1."

"I'm here," said the chassis who'd previously called itself 88.1.86354.731.8. "Is there a problem?"

Archaeidae resisted the urge to get cheeky with the *Shogun*. "No problem," he said. "Remember Sun Tzu; take the enemy's country whole and intact. We can take Lokner with us."

"Our orders are to destroy him."

"Taking him destroys him, but still leaves him useful." He tried to explain. "We're here because he's a threat. If he's a danger it is because he can do something we can't or knows something we don't." Archaeidae had never given orders before. With Riina he wouldn't have dared question, but *Tennō* 88 and his minions were different. Riina would never have asked for advice. Though Archaeidae didn't know what *Tennō* 88 and his Mirrors were, he was pretty damned sure they weren't human, much like himself. They'd asked for advice in the past and now he saw what needed to be done. "We're taking him with us. You figure out how while the others are laying charges in the room. We blow this place to hell so it looks like he died here."

***

Here, in the inner sanctum, 88.1 had direct physical access to the computers. He was inside of the *Wall o' Nuclear Annihilation*. Ordering 88.1.86354.731.8 to take a backseat, he moved the chassis and made a physical connection with central data systems. Mark Lokner, he learned, was something of a collector of educated brains.

"There are more Scans stored here than expected," 88.1 reported to Archaeidae. "I have found the minds of many people believed to have died over the last week.

Many are leaders in their respective fields."

"How many can we take with us?" Archaeidae asked.

M-Sof was the leading supplier of scanning and Scan storage technologies. "Bringing all the stored Scans will be easy," 88.1 answered.

"Good." The ruined chassis at 88.1's feet stared up at him and asked, "How many helicopters are coming?"

The answer seemed obvious but 88.1 said it aloud anyway. "Enough to evacuate our surviving forces."

"Can you get more?"

Paine Air National Guard Base was thirty kilometers away. "I can have several additional helicopters here within six minutes."

"Do it."

"It's done," 88.1 answered before asking, "Why?"

"Sun Tzu. We take them all." Archaeidae, lying on his back, waved a hand at the chassis surrounding him. "Every chassis we can fit. What we can't take we destroy. Scorched earth, sowing with salt and all of that good stuff. Total destruction."

"It will mean additional risk."

"Life without risk is death."

88.1 accepted this without comment. The lessons learned here were not lost on him. How better to defeat an opponent than to capture him whole and make him part of your own arsenal? Lokner was only a segment of the greater enemy they had faced today. The impenetrable *Wall o' Nuclear Annihilation* still stood, undefeated. A pinnacle of defensive code capable of devouring all who dared attack it. The genius behind the M-Sof firewall, *that* was an enemy worth conquering and co-opting.

"One last thing," said Archaeidae, staring up at him.

"Yes?"

"I'm going to need someone to carry me out of

here."

CHAPTER TWENTY-FOUR: Sunday, August 5th, 2046

Griffin stopped on the sidewalk and held his stomach. His guts roiled, acetic with stress. His right hand felt like something barbed crawled under the skin and his finger tips looked darker than he remembered them.

The first cab he flagged blasted by without slowing and he wanted to haul out the Glock and send a few DPU rounds through the rear windshield.

He waved another cab down, an old green and yellow Ford Tata E-Ka, and collapsed into the back seat. The floor was carpeted with sodden cardboard and the stench of hot vomit. A newspaper, still scrolling the news from Wednesday, August 1st, sat on the seat beside him. Its charge not quite dead, the stories faded in and out.

"Where to?" the cab asked.

Drone or Scan, Griffin didn't care. "Just move."

The cab pulled away from the curb with the clicking whine of an aging electric motor.

Scooping up the newspaper he told it to update to the latest news and it informed him it was unable to comply.

The streets were a mess, total chaos. Half the city had lost power and the other half suffered rolling brownouts. Most of the streetlights, dependent on the city's crumbling information infrastructure, had stopped working in the last hour. Police officers worked many intersections, but there weren't enough to cover all of them. Griffin saw vagrants and panhandlers directing traffic at several intersections and was surprised to see them do as good a job as the officers. They also seemed to be quite enjoying themselves.

He'd had no idea civilization was so dependent on satellites. Already there were talks about how to replace them with ground-based solutions. With Earth's useful orbits now filled with an impenetrable wall of junk and the general consensus being that shooting anything into orbit for the next few hundred years would be pointless, nations were turning their attention to the long neglected trunk lines buried in the ocean.

Griffin stared at the old headlines on the newspaper: *M-Sof's Mark Lokner Doesn't Get Scanned!* He read what he could of the flickering text below. There it was, right in front of him. Lokner died less than a week ago without leaving a Scan behind. The press were in an uproar, screaming that if Lokner didn't do it, maybe scanning wasn't safe. M-Sof stocks took a beating. It occurred to him that Lokner's choice would scare away many of the people planning on being scanned at death and thereby drive up the demand for black market Scans. Had that been the intent?

So Lokner was dead and Riina had talked to him every couple of days since his death. Two options: Either Riina had been talking to someone pretending to be Lokner, or Lokner lied about not being scanned. Seeing as M-Sof was the world's largest producer of scanning equipment and Scan storage systems, Griffin knew where he'd place his bet.

The cab ignored him and picked a busy street with lots of traffic which wasn't difficult in this madness. It didn't want to venture too far from the downtown core where the easiest fares were. They passed a massive billboard advertising for United Delta Airlines. *Do you know what's better than flying a plane?* asked the ad. *Being the plane. Fly like you were born to it. United Delta is now offering comprehensive long-term contract packages...*

Griffin slumped into the car seat and then flinched forward as his bruised body made contact. He couldn't relax, everything hurt too much. *Pain doesn't matter. Focus on Lokner.* The Scan of a world-famous individual committing crimes of this magnitude, the media were going to be all over this.

Where would Lokner hide? The M-Sof facilities in Washington State were the obvious answer. Lokner wouldn't be willing to venture too far from the center of his power.

If Lokner was behind the crèches, then what? Assuming Griffin could prove anything there'd be a long court case. He thought about the crèche in Jerseyville, the bodies of countless children stacked like wood, the swarming flies. He remembered the stench of burned flesh at the crèche in Wichita.

No way Lokner sees the inside of a courtroom. Griffin would make fucking sure of that.

"I have to go to Redmond," Griffin said.

"From Dallas? That's a long cab ride."

Griffin ignored this. "Take me to the airport."

"You got it, boss."

When the cab picked up speed, the breeze through the open window lessened the reek of vomit to a point approaching bearable. His shoes made wet, squidgy noises in the soggy cardboard.

According to the textbook, Griffin should confront the suspect and see if he can shake anything loose.

Apparently most people gave away a surprising amount of information when confronted by authority and the threat of prison. The majority of the population weren't cut out for a life of crime. Most were too stupid to do it well, and the rest too honest.

Griffin couldn't imagine himself as 'authority' or being able to pull off anything even remotely confrontational. Lokner was a man famed for his genius and savvy, who regularly wrangled multi-billion Au deals without breaking a sweat or showing signs of stress. He would not be intimidated by a kid fresh out of college or his shiny new NATU badge. Chances were few, if any, in M-Sof would know Lokner was still alive, living in the basement so to speak. Still, Griffin could think of no other way to proceed. First, he had to figure out who would know Lokner was there. The answer was easy: M-Sof's head Systems Administrator would have to know about Lokner. Griffin called up company records on his palm-comp. It took three minutes for the information to download. Having had infinite information at his fingertips in an instant his entire life, this felt like an eternity. Maybe two eternities. This was the kind of lag time his Dad bitched about when discussing the old days.

The data finally displayed as Griffin was about to give up and cancel the request.

"Shit."

Miles Pert, hired before he finished school for a stunning yearly income that left Griffin questioning his own choices, left the company the day of Lokner's death. He wasn't alone. Quite a few people fled M-Sof fearing that, with Lokner gone, the company would lose direction and flounder.

A dead end.

The new Senior Sys Admin was hired two days after Lokner's death and Griffin figured the chances she knew anything were minimal.

Griffin saw no choice. He had to fly to Redmond.

He tried to stretch out his legs to straighten the complaining knee but the back seat was too cramped. A waft of his own body odor made it over the bouquet of sun-warmed puke. The thought of another flight and another hotel drained his resolve. He wanted to give up and go home, slink back to his quiet desk job—assuming he still had one—and leave all this behind. Someone else could do this. Someone heroic. Someone who didn't feel like he'd already been dead for three days.

But if he gave in now, Nadia died for nothing. All those children the crèches had killed over the years went unavenged, and Lokner remained unpunished.

Under all that lurked the question: What kind of man was Griffin Dickinson? Was he even a man? Most days he still felt like a high-school kid. It felt like he'd never done anything that defined him. Did he turn away when he saw evil being perpetrated? Again he thought back to his father explaining how his chief regrets were of the things he had *not* done. Was this what the old man was talking about? Sometimes his father only made sense in hindsight.

I won't walk away. If he did, he'd regret it the rest of his life. Desperate and perhaps more than a little foolish, but the only way to bring some semblance of meaning to these deaths was to bring down those responsible. Lokner was the next step. It might go beyond Lokner, but until Griffin questioned him he couldn't know for sure. Griffin placed a call on his palm-comp. Since it was local, the connection remained decent. He even got a choppy video feed.

"You look like stomped shit," said Abdul. "Still."

"Thanks. I need your help."

There was a long pause and Abdul was so still Griffin couldn't tell if the connection had frozen or if the chassis just wasn't moving. "I've been pulled off active duty. Psyche-evaluation."

"Screw that."

"I might be unstable."

Unstable? Griffin considered his own mental state, his need to *move*. His desire to punish, to do violence. "Join the club. Pack your bags we're going to Redmond, Washington."

"Exactly what kind of bags do you think a walking battle tank needs?"

"Turtle Wax and a shammy cloth? A change of oil."

"Oh, I see. You're funny today. So what's in Redmond?"

"M-Sof and Mark Lokner."

"I take it you aren't one for keeping up with the news."

Griffin groaned. "I didn't go to bed last night. I've been in the office all day trying to crack this case. What news?"

"M-Sof is gone, my man. Some paramilitary unit blew it to dust and debris last night. A few dozen biological fatalities and a couple of chassis were destroyed along with their Scans. M-Sof's on-site data systems are nothing but a memory."

"You're shitting me."

"Dead serious. Dead *and* serious."

"Was this corporate warfare, terrorism, or some governmental black op?"

"No idea. No one has claimed responsibility. It's gotta be corporate."

The video feed went choppy again and Griffin considered the timing of the attack wiping out the world's satellites and the attack on M-Sof. Coincidence? Could Lokner somehow be behind all of this? No, they had to be unrelated. "Yeah, seems likely. The timing, though...."

Griffin paused, lost in thought. "Pack your toothbrush. We're leaving on the next flight. I'll send a dump truck to pick you up."

"You're too funny."

***

After waking to the news that someone—and every mad little terrorist group and activist organization claimed responsibility—attacked and destroyed world's satellites in the last twenty-four hours, Miles went to work. *This might be a good time to update my resume and look for work in a field not involving the movement of information.* Unfortunately he didn't have any other skills.

Entering the brass and marble lobby of 5THSUN, he dreaded what he'd find upstairs. The reality was worse than expected.

Miles sat staring at his desk, a long list of error and infiltration messages scrolling before his eyes. *This isn't possible.* Even with the loss of every single communications satellite, for any of this to make sense, M-Sof would have to be gone.

"News. M-Sof," he told the desk.

He knew a moment of annoyance as he waited for the upload and then smacked himself when he remembered the satellites. Remembering his Computer History classes, he considered the strain now being put on the old information systems. His best guess was that if 'someone' didn't do 'something' soon, the internet would collapse completely, a victim to overload and cascading clock drift, within the next three days.

Maybe I'll take up wood-working.

The download completed and Miles watched a scene shot from a news helicopter. The M-Sof grounds lay in smoking ruins. An excited reporter blathered on and Miles picked out the salient details.

Late last night M-Sof's Redmond head office was raided by persons unknown. The attack included an unknown number of paramilitary chassis who wired the M-Sof data systems with state-of-the-art ultra-high-density explosives. The Redmond facility lay in smoking ruins. Though the actual body count was low considering the damage, there was an additional piece of disturbing news: the majority of the Scan-driven chassis, both combat and commercial, were missing from the grounds. That same evening several Scan-piloted helicopters disappeared from both Kenmore Air Harbor and Paine Air National Guard Base. NATU investigators assumed they were somehow involved in the attack, but Miles had his doubts. What would they gain? Where would they go? He had a different culprit in mind.

Lokner2.0.

Why? That was easy: Revenge.

But how? That was a better question. How had Lokner2.0 orchestrated such an assault?

Was the government in on this? Lokner had the contacts. Miles thought about it. *Nah, that's too paranoid. Right?*

Well, Lokner did have his own little army of combat chassis right here at 5THSUN. Why couldn't he have more somewhere else? It made too much sense. For some reason Lokner2.0 had destroyed M-Sof and killed Lokner1.0.

This was too much. *I'm in way over my head.* He had to go somewhere he could think. His stomach rumbled and he thought about mocha chocolate brownies.

Androctonus saw Miles coming and spun to intercept him. Miles found himself staring straight into the chassis' main weapon cluster.

"Good morning, Mister Pert." It sounded a little

sarcastic, but at least it pronounced his name correctly. "Where are you off to so early?"

"I'm going for lunch," Miles said curtly.

"You've only been here for half an hour."

"Well I'm hungry. Now move aside."

Something within the chassis clicked and whined, sounding like it powered up. Miles, staring down the barrel of an Electro-Magnetic Rail-Gun, retreated a step.

"Be. Polite," said Androctonus, voice flat and emotionless.

The chassis was bluffing. Must be. Miles decided to call that bluff. No way the mini-tank would harm him. "You don't scare me." A lie. "Lokner needs me."

"I talked with Mister Lokner about you this morning," said the tank.

Androctonus talked with Lokner about me? That couldn't be good. With Lokner1.0 destroyed during the night, Miles now knew, beyond any doubt, Androctonus and Lokner2.0 were in contact.

"Maybe we got off on the wrong..." Miles glanced down at the tanks treads. He couldn't say foot and that stopped him dead.

"You will return to your office and do your work."

"Let's act like reasonable adults," suggested Miles, still backing away from the advancing chassis.

Androctonus uttered a hollow metallic cough of derision. "Adults." The word dripped scorn. "Return to your office. *Now.*"

"Can't we talk? What have—"

"Last warning," threatened the chassis. "I count to three and a cleaning drone will have to scrape you off the floor."

"Don't be silly," said Miles, still retreating.

"One."

Miles closed his mouth and turned away. He wanted

to call something smart-ass over his shoulder but couldn't think of anything witty enough.

He fled to his office so distracted he barely nodded to Christie as he passed her desk. By the time the door closed behind him he knew he had to do something.

But what?

He collapsed into the SmartChair and it doggedly offered another massage which he ignored. *Damned chair.* Who could think while being massaged?

Though there might be some doubt as to whether Lokner could kill someone, Miles had little doubt Lokner was capable of having someone killed. The difference might seem minor, but it was one Miles appreciated and understood. He didn't think he could do either.

He thought back over his conversations with Androctonus. *Adults*: The mocking scorn of a child. *Lokner has black market Scans running illegal chassis.* Miles rolled the thought around. No, that was impossible. Yet Androctonus never once came across as an adult.

Androctonus acts like a little kid who knows he'll get his way.

Miles sat up straight. *Androctonus is a child.* He had no doubt.

Just a child.

The knowledge, even though unproven, felt like an anchor on Miles' heart. This one detail meant many, many things. It meant Lokner was not the man Miles thought he was. He would have sworn Mark wasn't capable of this sort of behavior, but the original Lokner must have set this up. It meant Lokner had ties with the mafia. It meant the man knowingly broke the law and it meant Miles had been helping him. Sure, he knew he'd been helping Lokner break the law, but he'd thought he'd been helping the mastermind of the world's largest Scanning company get around a few nit-picky rules. By aiding and abetting

Lokner, had he been helping a dangerous criminal steal children's brains?

Aiding and abetting. He didn't like those words at all. They sounded very legalese.

Miles considered some of the things he'd done—the many government systems he'd hacked—to help Lokner. What had he been thinking, that it was all innocent fun? Sometimes he was so dumb!

Did Lokner know Miles knew (or at least suspected)? He couldn't chance it. And there was the truth. One man threatened all of Mark Lokner's plans. Miles Pert, Senior Systems Administrator. Root. *Why the hell didn't I see this before?*

"Dumbest genius ever," Miles muttered.

If Lokner was involved in crèches and black market Scans, he'd been at it since before his death.

Can I go to the law? The more Miles thought about it, the thinner his evidence appeared. If he went to the authorities and blew the whistle on Lokner the ramifications bore some thought. For sure it would cost him his job, but he wasn't at all sure he could prove his suppositions. The idea of turning Lokner in only to find out he was wrong about the whole situation left him with cold sweats.

What if Androctonus was a middle-aged juvenile twerp? Maybe he should do nothing. That might be safest. Stay low and quiet. What had Ruprecht said? You always think of reasons *not* to do things.

Damn it!

Fear of change. Well, he had something bigger to be afraid of now.

The more he realized how deeply entwined he was in Lokner's machinations, the less he believed Mark would ever let him get free. That scared the hell out of him.

Miles tried to calm his staccato heart.

"Gird your loins, brave knight." Whatever that meant. It was time. It was time he stood up to Lokner. It was time he stood up for himself. *You always think of reasons not to do things.* Not today. It was time he was proactive.

Maybe after another brownie.

No. Now.

"I might be a moron, but I'm also a genius," Miles reminded himself. No way a psychotic Scan of an ass-clown like Mark Lokner was going to get the best of him.

Miles tapped at the desk, loading his coding software. It was time to make use of all those trapdoors he'd co-opted from the other M-Sof staff. *Lokner doesn't know who he's messing—*

The desk chirped for attention. It was Lokner2.0.

Oh. Damn. And the ass-clown wanted a full virtuality meeting. Unless he was ready to fake a full-on vomit attack, there was no avoiding it. Miles accepted the meeting and stood in Lokner's office. Since they were linked by the company's intranet and didn't rely on outside networks, the virtuality was bright and crisp and running at full resolution. Miles knew it wasn't real, but it looked real. It looked perfect.

"Miles."

"Sir?"

"Sit the fuck down."

Miles sat and his point of view once again shrank to that of a four year old. He stared up at Lokner. *Just a mind game, it's just a mind game. Changes nothing. Yeah, baloney.*

Mark pursed his lips and nodded happily down at Miles. "What were you doing?"

Miles swallowed uncomfortably. "Nothing?" *Crap, that sounded like a question.*

Mark's face dropped the happy look like it weighed

too much. It seemed to leak out the bottom. There was a long pause while he gave Miles a disappointed glower, as if he expected better. "Androctonus told me what happened in the lobby."

"Yes?" Miles dedicated most of his brain to keeping his face from betraying emotion.

"I want to hear your side."

My side? Androctonus threatens me and now Lokner wants to hear my *side?* Miles blinked and then caught himself and quashed the expression of dumbfounded disbelief before it got past his eyes. *Play it like it was nothing.* What else could he do? "A minor disagreement is all."

"He shouldn't have bothered you." Mark glanced over Miles' shoulder, toward the office door. "Did you hear that?"

Miles shook his head. "No Sir. It wasn't a big deal," he lied.

Mark kept glancing towards the door. "That's good," he said, distracted.

It is? "So..."

"So what *were* you doing?"

"System maintenance," Miles said quickly.

"Seriously?"

"I—"

"You can't hear that? Something breathing. Maybe a lot of somethings."

To cover his confusion Miles cocked an ear and made a show of listening. "No Sir. Quiet as a—" He stopped himself before saying grave.

Mark glared through narrowed eyes for several uncomfortable seconds. "Was that your doing?" he asked cryptically.

"Was what my doing?"

"Forget it. Won't give you the pleasure. Just you

remember you're in this as deep as I am. I go down, so do you. My lawyers are *itching* to drop this bomb on you. Things go bad, I go fucking nuclear." He giggled. "Nuclear. Clear? All I've done is hidden the fact I was scanned. You? You hacked government systems, stole data, and erased all kinds of evidence. They'd never let you near another computer for as long as you lived."

Lokner knew all the right buttons. Miles opened his mouth but couldn't think of anything to say. *Yeah, way to crush this problem.*

"I think there's even evidence you're connected to the Mob," said Lokner.

"The Mob?"

"I know! Crazy, right?"

Miles stared at Lokner. *Yes. Crazy.*

"So," said Lokner, glancing back to his desk, "system maintenance. Then why did you say *nothing*?"

Because I'm a moron. "Because if I start explaining the intricate details I'll get all excited and go off on a highly-technical tangent. It'll bore the crap out of you. I was trying to stall myself. The finer points of the inner-workings of a system like this are really *very* interesting. It's a fine balance between—"

"Right."

"I was—"

"You know, Miles," Lokner dragged out each word. "I can tell when you're lying."

"I..." What could Miles say? The truth, that he'd been planning a way to threaten his boss should things go badly? That he was giving himself the edge in any future negotiations? Was there a more positive-sounding spin on that? "I..."

"I...I..." Lokner2.0 mimicked in a petulant child's voice. "You shouldn't lie to me Miles. Not healthy."

Not healthy? More threats? "I..."

"Shut up. Not healthy for our relationship. I thought we were friends. Friends don't lie."

Friends? "I'm sorry?"

"You are? Well then, all is forgiven."

"It is?"

"Of course," said Lokner2.0 magnanimously, leaning back in his chair and clasping his fingers behind his head. "Stop looking at porn when you're supposed to be working. That's not what I pay you for." Lokner looked amused, smug.

Porn? Miles almost denied it before his brain told his mouth to shut the hell up. "No, Sir," he said instead. "It's not."

"Oh goodie. I didn't think so. Now get back to work."

Miles was back in his office. He sat, staring at his desktop, waiting for his heart to slow. By the time it did he knew what needed to be done.

Trapdoors. Deadman's switch. Easy to trigger, difficult to disengage.

Maybe nothing would ever happen. Maybe he'd never need it. But if Lokner was as dangerous as he suspected, it could mean the difference between life and death.

The best bluff was not to bluff at all.

Miles leaned back and replayed the insane conversation. Lokner mentioned his lawyers, said they were ready to drop the bomb on Miles or something to that effect.

Hmm. What are the odds the lawyers keep everything on computers?

CHAPTER TWENTY-FIVE: Sunday, August 5th, 2046

Griffin made a few calls, screamed at some officer until Abdul was put back on active duty and loaded into a truck bound for the airport, and filed a report Phil wouldn't see until the morning. When he looked up from his palm-comp he was treated to a view of the jumbled spaghetti sprawl of Dallas-Fort Worth International Airport.

The fingertips of his right hand felt like someone was juicing them in a blender. They were looking a little gray too. He should see a doctor.

At the airport Griffin requisitioned a military transport plane. A monstrous old C-5M Galaxy, left over from the last days of the Oil Wars in the Middle East, would fly them to McChord Air Force Base. An orbital flight would have been quicker, but there was no way to get Abdul on board without causing a major fuss. At least on the military flight no one cared that Griffin still toted a Glock 36 and smelled like last week's garbage left too long in the sun. He and Abdul were the only passengers.

Once airborne he grabbed some radio headphones and went back to check on Abdul who lounged—or the combat chassis equivalent—in the cargo bay. The interior of the plane reeked of rotting vegetables and rancid grain. Its last flights—food drops to the sixty-million acre Texas,

Oklahoma, Kansas, Colorado, and New Mexico dust bowl—were several weeks ago and the cargo bay had not been cleaned since. The floor and walls crawled with ants, and the badly patched bullet holes rattled threateningly as the wind tore at them. At this altitude, if one patch came off, the trip would be a very short one.

Why did the people who were the recipients of such aid shoot at the aircraft trying to help them?

***

Abdul, feeling the clump of Griffin's boots through the body of the plane, became aware of the man's approach long before he saw him. So what would it be? Friendly chat or nervous interrogation while the agent tried to figure out if bringing him along had been a terrible mistake?

Griffin limped into view. His sweat had dried leaving his gray-shot hair looking like he just got out of bed. Deep bruises underlined tortured eyes, and his nose was still puffy from being broken. "Hey, Abdul. Everything okay back here?"

Nervous interrogation then.

"Lovely, boss. If I felt any more alive I'd be alive."

"Good to see you've mastered that oh-so-difficult sarcasm thing."

"You wound me," joked Abdul. "If you prick us, do we not bleed?" His humor soured. "Well, obviously not, but maybe inside. Inside I might be bleeding. Internal hemorrhaging of the soul. If I have one."

Griffin watched with raised eyebrows. "*That* wasn't overly dramatic. And personally, I don't believe in souls."

"Wait until you're dead." Abdul stopped before he said too much. "Sorry." He changed the subject, a blatant attempt at distraction. "Why would a man like Lokner be involved in black market crèches? He was already worth billions."

Griffin gave his swollen nose a gentle squeeze as if testing it and his face filled with pained regret. "I don't know for sure, but I suspect he started as soon as Scans became viable. Whatever he's up to, I think he's been at it for a while."

"You mean *was* up to. Lokner is dead, is he not? If he was a Scan stored in the M-Sof facilities...he's history. For real this time. And if he's dead, Scan destroyed, what then?"

"If he's dead, I don't know where to go after this."

Man and machine sat in silence for a few minutes, each lost in their own thoughts.

"Griffin?"

"Yeah?"

"Why are you here? Why are you still doing this? You got Riina. Why not go home?"

Griffin looked away, picked at a patched bullet hole with shaking fingers. "Nadia. If I stop now she died for nothing." He hesitated. "That might be a lie." Griffin stopped worrying at the patch and stared at the floor, his eyes following a trail of ants. He looked like he wasn't sure he wanted to talk about this and was even less sure how to vocalize his thoughts. "Shit," he said before continuing. "They're killing little kids to make better machines. Slavery with no chance of escape or redemption."

"And?" Abdul asked.

Griffin picked a kernel of rancid grain from the plane floor and examined it, rolling it in the fingers of his right hand. "I think it's something I heard as a child: There's no more heroes. And I don't want to regret *not* doing this."

"So you're here to be a hero?" When Griffin's shoulders tensed and eyes narrowed Abdul added, "I'm not mocking."

Griffin flicked the kernel toward the rear of the plane and stared at his fingers. He kept his eyes averted from the chassis, but Abdul saw how red they were. "Fucking ridiculous, eh?"

Shaking fingers or heroism? Abdul, unsure, kept pushing. "Shut down a crèche another opens. What's the point?" He needed to know.

The plane banked hard as it left Dallas-Fort Worth International Airport airspace and Griffin looked ill as he fought to keep his balance. Giving up he collapsed into the nearest seat and tried not to get caught in the webbed restraints.

"I have to try," said Griffin. "Even if I fail, at least I'll know I tried. I'll know I didn't sit passively while little kids were being killed."

"And this valiant stand, in the face of overwhelming odds and certain failure, this is what it is to be a hero?"

"As far as I can see, yup."

The rumble of the plane's engines filled the emptiness.

Abdul examined Griffin, taking in the shaking hand and the way he sat, hunched around his stomach wound. The man's temperature had spiked into a low-grade fever. Perhaps they'd pulled the wrong man off active duty.

He thought about his little sister, Janani, forever missing. Just gone one day.

"Count me in," Abdul said.

***

At McChord Air Force Base Griffin requisitioned an army-green two-and-a-half-ton truck. When Abdul climbed into the back, muttering something about being treated like cheap luggage, the suspension sagged and groaned in metallic complaint.

The truck took them to Redmond following the I-5 and I-405, ducking west along the WA520 for the final leg of the journey. In all, the trip took an hour and a half, and was finished in complete silence. When they arrived at M-Sof they found the property surrounded by NATU military vehicles and personnel. The sprawling grounds were huge, with scores of buildings littered across hundreds of acres. The center of the destruction seemed clustered around the ruins of three buildings at the heart of the facility. A dozen NATU Combat Chassis patrolled within sight.

As they approached, a NATU Marine backed by a Heavy Combat Chassis, waved the truck to a stop. Abdul leaped from the truck in a flash and the suspension whimpered in tired relief as it returned to something close to its original position. Griffin climbed from the cab, groaning. *Are they even going to let me in?* He wasn't sure how much influence he had here.

The Marine, a Corporal, kept a nervous eye on Abdul. "ID and business," he said to Griffin.

Griffin flashed his ID and said, "Special Investigations."

The Corporal glanced at it. "Toronto. Long way from home. Business?"

"Way above your pay-grade," interrupted Abdul. "Run along and get a real officer. Someone with a Sir."

When the Marine turned a frosty eye in Abdul's direction Griffin threw in, "Best do as he says. He outranks you and he's grumpy."

Five minutes later a Captain stood in front of them and two minutes after that they were into the M-Sof grounds.

The Captain, making no attempt to hide her curiosity, walked at Griffin's side. "Special Investigations all the way from Toronto." She nodded towards Abdul.

"With a personal combat chassis no less. Interesting."

Griffin grunted noncommittally and kept walking, surveying the grounds. The M-Sof facilities resembled a battleground. Large caliber machine-gun fire had chewed holes in walls, and only sand remained of the windows. One building, which looked to have once been an older red brick structure, lay in ruins. The once pristine soccer field had been mulched by helicopters and combat chassis. Media choppers hovered overhead.

Probably hoping to catch sight of body bags and grieving families, thought Griffin.

When he didn't answer, she continued. "When we first arrived swarms of remote micro-drones went after anything that stepped on the grass. Several of my people were tasered and issued trespassing fines." When Griffin glanced at her she kept a straight face. "Some weird things have been happening...."

"Such as?" Griffin asked.

"Such as not being told what's going on here." She gestured at the destruction surrounding them. "This was a military strike. There are Scan-piloted helicopters missing from two different nearby airports. Some of them are combat choppers. There are an unknown number of chassis missing from M-Sof as well. Well-armed Security models. And then..." she seemed to change her mind. "And then there's you. You must have left Toronto the second the word was out. Maybe before."

Keeping secrets wasn't going to get him anywhere and his life would be a lot easier if this Captain gave him her full cooperation. "All this," he waved his left hand, "may have nothing to do with why I'm here. The timing though, it's a little suspect. I don't like coincidences."

"Me either. Go on."

"I'm here investigating possible links between some M-Sof employees and black market crèches."

"Not naming names?"

"Sorry, not yet."

The Captain shrugged philosophically. "So you aren't here because of the attack on M-Sof?"

"Was already on my way here when I heard about it. I get the impression you weren't finished telling me about the weird things."

"There's a surprising lack of evidence. We suspect the facility's garbage drones have been dumping everything on the ground into the incinerator. We think they've been at it since whoever attacked this place left. It screams inside job."

Abdul gestured toward the red brick ruins. "What was this? It seems to have suffered the brunt of the assault."

"Research and Development," the Captain answered. "It's going to take us weeks to sort through that rubble."

Griffin stopped. In part because he wanted to take in the scope of the damage and in part because he was exhausted and his guts hurt. Abdul and the Captain stopped too.

"I don't suppose anyone knows if there were Scans stored in the R&D building?" Griffin asked.

"No, but interesting you should ask. The rest of the facility was raided for Scan storage and transportation hardware. Perhaps someone wanted to carry an awful lot of Scans out of here."

So if Lokner wasn't dead, he might have been kidnapped instead? This got stranger and stranger. "Any idea how many Scans were taken?"

"Maybe none. Officially, aside from those inhabiting chassis, there were no Scans stored here at all. It's possible the gear was taken to be used later or even to be sold on the black market."

Griffin rubbed at his stomach and grimaced. He was here looking for a Scan of Mark Lokner. Someone with serious connections had stolen Scan transportation equipment and specifically destroyed this building. The obvious culprit was the one Griffin least wanted to think about. *Did Lokner know I was coming?* Was all this to cover his tracks?

"M-Sof had military contracts?" he asked, knowing the answer.

"Of course. Sole supplier of Scan storage gear for the NATU military."

"And this was a military strike?"

"Not *our* military," the Captain clarified. "These days, what corporation doesn't have its own military force?"

She was right. Griffin felt the fight leak out of him like his femoral artery had been snipped. He sat on the nearest pile of red bricks and slumped forward, his head hanging. He stared at the ground. Dead ends were everywhere. There were no leads here. The tendons in his right hand vibrated like piano strings tuned too tight. He couldn't make a fist for fear they'd snap.

He looked up at Abdul. The chassis was as expressionless as ever. *Like talking to a damned wall.* "I should still be in the hospital. If I'd stayed, like the doctors wanted, she'd—"

"Hindsight is merciless," said Abdul. "And self-pity a useless indulgence. I should know."

The Captain watched the exchange without comment.

Griffin nodded and sat straighter. His stomach didn't like it at all. "Captain, I'm going to need you to collect any witnesses together for me. I have to talk to all of them." It looked pointless, but he had to try.

Griffin paced around the Hilton Bellevue Hotel ground floor room. Redmond, while cooler than Dallas, was still far from pleasantly temperate.

Abdul stood by the door. "Security here is garbage."

"It doesn't matter. Everyone is dead. No one is threatening us."

Griffin thought back over the failures of the day.

The few people he'd managed to question were ignorant of Scans being stored on the grounds, unaware Mark Lokner was still alive, and had no idea who attacked them. Useless.

The day had turned out to be yet another colossal failure.

How many is this?

"Go to bed," said Abdul, standing guard at the door. "You need the rest. Tomorrow we'll question those we couldn't get to today."

"Yeah? Why? This case is dead."

"Only if you kill it."

Griffin ignored that. "I can't sleep. Lying down hurts too much."

"Well, if you don't lie down you're going fall down. I bet that'll hurt more."

Griffin stopped pacing and turned to face Abdul. "You're right. I'm going to go get something that'll keep me on my feet."

"What, like methamphetamines?"

"Whatever I can find."

"You'll need a prescription," said Abdul reasonably.

"I thought you were seventeen. What the hell is wrong with today's youth? Anyway, I have a gun and a badge."

"I'm coming with you."

"Forget it. Stay here. I'm going to the pharmacy around the corner. No one is after us, remember?"

***

Abdul didn't want to wander the street any more than he had to. In here, no one stared at him. And Griffin was right. Everyone who might wish them harm was dead.

"Fine," he said.

He watched Griffin exit the room. With three-hundred and sixty degree vision, he had no choice but to watch everything all the time. It was enough to drive a guy crazy. Take a brain from its flesh and bone cage, make a digital copy and then trap that copy in a mobile metal box. Bombard the new brain with information in formats it was never meant to recognize, force it to accept three-hundred and sixty degree visual input on a range of frequencies beyond what anything alive had ever seen. Rob the brain of the sensations to which it was accustomed and replace them with modeled chemical and hormonal input.

He knew what brand of air freshener the cleaning staff used and that the maid ate asparagus recently. It was all there, hanging in the air.

It was amazing that every Scan alive wasn't a bubbling maelstrom of psychoses, phobias, and emotional issues.

Or are they? Abdul remembered Marlene's hesitancy to talk about her sanity. What if this was endemic to the reality of being a Scan? What if they were all crazy, doomed to an eternity of madness?

Abdul tried to laugh. He had to force it, and it sounded sad, lacking conviction. *No more real than me.*

CHAPTER TWENTY-SIX: Sunday, August 5th, 2046

88 reviewed the stunning lack of fallout from her attack on M-Sof. It was too easy. It was like Lokner hadn't been expecting a reprisal and that made no sense at all. Could he have assumed his economic warfare somehow crippled her?

No. Since launching her attack, her attention hadn't wandered from M-Sof for even a second. She saw two options. Either Lokner was a fool, or he hadn't been expecting an attack. Since she didn't believe for a moment that he was foolish, the second option seemed more likely.

But why wouldn't he expect a counterattack?

She saw one answer: because he hadn't attacked her in the first place.

88 assigned a host of Mirrors to retrace the economic war M-Sof had waged with 88.5, following every bit of data back to its source, and report their findings. Their report took longer than expected. The data, they informed her, hadn't been easy to follow. It had jumped from country to country, bouncing chaotically all over the world. Eventually they found a single point source.

Reno, Nevada. 5THSUN.

88 examined the data her Mirrors collected. Whoever was at 5THSUN manipulated the market with the

same skill as Lokner. Up to the moment where it became an attack, the moves were identical in character and style.

The answer seemed clear: Lokner had moved his Scan and now resided in 5THSUN in Reno. Who else would have access and control over the company's stock portfolio?

But Archaeidae had brought her Lokner's Scan—along with a great many other interesting minds—from M-Sof.

Who then, if not Lokner? And why make it easy for her to trace the attack to M-Sof? Why not hide it like the connection to 5THSUN was hidden?

Because I'm supposed to think M-Sof attacked me. This didn't make sense.

88 dug deeper, assigning spinoff tasks and trails to Mirrors.

Whoever helped Lokner cover his digital footsteps was a master. 88's infinitude of Mirrors were better. Lokner and M-Sof had ties with the Mafia and black market crèches. He had ties with Anisio Jobin, and funded much of that crèche's research. He might, she realized, know something of her mother.

She also found equipment purchase orders. Someone at 5THSUN wanted to copy Scans. Something that, with the cascading accumulation of errors and high failure rate, wasn't normally attempted.

Someone with Lokner's skill and access to M-Sof manipulated the company's stock in an attack meant to make her think Lokner and M-Sof were responsible. They must have assumed that she'd strike back. They must have wanted her to destroy M-Sof and Lokner.

Lokner, one of the wealthiest men in the world, could afford the many attempts it would take to achieve a viable copy of his Scan.

Lokner must be at 5THSUN.

For an instant she thought of him as Lokner1.1, but realized that he was nothing like her Mirrors. This was a sentient being, a whole new line. Lokner2.0, she decided, was more fitting.

Lokner2.0 attacked her, used her to attack M-Sof and presumably the original Lokner Scan living there. Though Lokner1.0 was no longer a threat, the copy was. Not only did it know of her existence, but it was dangerously deceptive.

Her search for mother would have to wait. She must see Archaeidae. He must destroy Lokner2.0.

CHAPTER TWENTY-SEVEN: Sunday, August 5th, 2046

Working for Capo Riina had been very different than working for *Tennō* 88. During Riina's employ, Archaeidae spent so much time in various training virtualities he had trouble differentiating between reality and virtuality. Though he enjoyed it at the time, he now saw much of it as a waste. Killing pretend people and running pointless assassination missions, while cool and entertaining, achieved nothing real. Now, everything he did was real. He'd been working for *Tennō* 88 less than twenty-four hours and done more than in the last six months with Riina.

Though the *Shogun* referred to *Tennō* 88 as male, Lokner had referred to 88 as female. Was the Emperor a she? *Jotei* instead of *Tennō*? Did it matter? What was gender worth in virtuality? Archaeidae shrugged it aside as unimportant. He wanted to look like a samurai, he looked like a samurai. She wanted to look like an Emperor, she looked like an Emperor. Reality was deeper than mere appearance.

88.1 took the form of a 12th century *Shogun* during their virtual meetings. Once again the Shogun conscripted a dangerous amount of the faltering NATUnet to make this meeting possible. Archaeidae, still wearing the samurai skin he was so fond of, knelt across the tea table from his Master's *Shogun*. The thin rice paper walls glowed yellow as if lit from behind by a host of candles. The straw *tatami* mats, worn smooth by centuries of kneeling tea drinkers, were bordered with a seaweed-green brocade. In this four-and-a-half mat layout, never did the corners of more than two mats come in contact. The sweet scent of fresh-cut rush grass filled the room.

88.1 nodded to the samurai across the table. "*Sesshō* Archaeidae."

Archaeidae bowed deep. "*Sei-i tai* Shōgun."

Taking several minutes to pour tea, 88.1 sipped from his *chawan* before continuing. "The Lokner copy is a threat." He paused for another sip. Archaeidae sat silently, waiting. "It is aware of our existence and possibly of our history. It may know our geographical location."

Archaeidae's eyes focused to sharp slits. *Yes!* This sounded like more fun stuff was coming his way. "Is this the other threat you spoke of?"

88.1 offered Archaeidae more tea. The assassin nodded acceptance and sat waiting. The *Shogun* refilled the *chawan*. "There is also the NATU investigation, headed by Agent Griffin Dickinson."

"Hai." *He didn't answer my question. Why? What does that mean? Is that a no?* So there were multiple threats to the Emperor, one they were not yet willing to tell him about. But why? One thing at a time. Kill Lokner, kill Dickinson. The first he was happy with, the second left him feeling uncomfortable. Agent Dickinson and his partner defeated him and then spared his life when they had him at their mercy. The debt hung over Archaeidae. He didn't like debts.

"An attack on 5THSUN might draw the attention of NATU," mused the *Shogun*. "We must not bring attention to *Tennō* 88."

So a stealth mission. That's what assassination was all about. "If Dickinson and NATU are pursuing the black market Scan angle they must be suspicious of our attack on M-Sof," Archaeidae said. The *Shogun* watched him without expression. Archaeidae resisted the impulse to ask about the connection. If he needed to know, 88.1 would tell him. Right? "But the danger of their investigation leading to us is real. Unless..." He paused in thought. "Unless they are led to the Lokner copy."

"Interesting. Continue."

Two birds, one stone. Lokner could be slain—or at least removed from contention—and Dickinson would have arrested the man behind so many crèches. It would be a fitting payback for sparing Archaeidae's life. "We lead agent Dickinson to 5THSUN and the Lokner copy. NATU arrests or kills Lokner. They have the perpetrator they seek, the man behind the majority of the black market Scans and crèches around the world. Case closed."

"That would give us the time we need."

To do what? "*Hai*. We can defeat both enemies—the ones I am aware of—by squaring them off against each other." Maybe not as exciting as an all out battle, but this could still be interesting. Intrigue sounded fun. Was the hint too subtle?

"How do we put Dickinson on the right path? Perhaps we could manipulate the results of his data searches, influence him subconsciously to move in the right direction."

That didn't sound fun at all. "I think a more direct approach will better achieve our goals," suggested Archaeidae. Personal debts should be paid in person.

Changing chassis wasn't like swapping bodies with another human. It was more like swapping bodies with a frog or a spider. There you were with your customary bipedal layout and your standard five senses all working in the usual way, comfortable and skilled at moving it about, manipulating its fine motor controls, and interacting with the world around you. All of a sudden you had four or more legs, you heard and saw in radically different frequencies, and your best form of mobility was either hopping or shuffling about with more limbs than you were accustomed to. It took time to adapt, and the greater the variance, the longer it took. Spending time in virtuality training programs helped immensely. It reduced the time spent jumping into walls and running in circles as you struggled to get your three left limbs moving. But there was no substitute for the real world.

Archaeidae's new chassis made a soft whirring as he spun circles in the Hilton Bellevue Hotel lobby. Annoyed guests dodged around him and he ignored them. He'd had no acclimatization time and felt slow and ungainly, like he might topple over at any moment. His torso was a slim tuxedo-fitted upright cylinder with a round head incapable of displaying any emotions other than servitude and a North American version of a French waiter's appalled displeasure. The torso sat centered atop a soft felt-like continuous tread incapable of leaving a mark on even the most expensive carpet. No matter how hard he tried.

He tightened the spin, testing how fast he could corner, and ran over a man's toe. The guest yelped and hopped back, scowling at Archaeidae.

"Damn it drone! Watch where you're going!"

Drone? Archaeidae attempted a murderous snarl and failed. The man didn't look the least intimidated and stomped away with a huff of indignation.

This wasn't funny at all. He called up the hotel busboy chassis' statistics. He couldn't jump small buildings or throw cars. There was not a single armament on board, not even a sharpened steak knife. He couldn't bend iron bars, tear limbs from people or even make a scary face. What he did have was access to a complete library of mixed drinks, sheet folding techniques, and a desire to leave mints on pillows. *Seriously. Not funny.* In a straight-up fight against an unarmed human, chances are Archaeidae would get his ass handed to him on a buffed and polished silver platter.

"*Shogun*?" Archaeidae had asked, upon being loaded into this chassis. "Are you sure this is the right chassis for the job? What about a hotel Security Chassis? Something with just a *little* firepower."

"You are delivering a simple message," 88.1 had replied. "This is the right chassis for the task."

True, Security Chassis weren't used to run messages to hotel guests, but what if something went wrong? The beating he took at M-Sof yesterday was still fresh in his mind. He wanted payback, retribution. He wanted to even the score.

Nobody pushed Archaeidae around.

Seeing Griffin Dickinson exit the hotel lobby and head onto the street, he spun to give chase. He'd have to hurry to catch his prey. *This is embarrassing.*

At top speed, the chassis issuing an asthmatic wheeze, he managed to catch Griffin in less than a block.

"Mister Dickinson?"

Griffin turned, right hand going for the Glock Archaeidae knew to be concealed in a shoulder holster. Even in this shitty hotel chassis, Archaeidae had to wait for the man's slow biological reaction time to realize he was no threat. Griffin stopped himself before the gun was drawn.

"Scared the crap out of me."

"I have a message for you, Sir. You have some identification?"

Griffin dug out his wallet and flipped his NSI badge

open. "A message? What message? From whom?"

"No name was left with the message and it is labeled No Reply Required."

"Okay. The message?"

"The message Sir is as follows." Archaeidae changed his voice as if playing back a recorded message. "Mark Lokner is alive and well at 5THSUN Assessments in Reno."

Griffin's eyes widened as the meaning of the message sunk in. "Holy shit." His eyes narrowed suspiciously. "Where did this message come from?"

"It was given to me to personally deliver, Sir. I was tipped quite well, I might add."

"Tipped? Oh, you're a Scan and not a drone?"

"Yes." Archaeidae let a little note of hurt slip into his voice. "I'm working off my contract with the hotel and saving up enough to buy a chassis of my own." People loved a sob story. "What's it like being a Special Investigator for NATU? If you don't mind me asking, Sir. Is it exciting? You ever meet any really cool assassins?"

***

Griffin's mind whirled like a drunken dervish on the latest amphetamine sulphate derivative (which he was hoping to acquire at the first drug store he found). Lokner at 5THSUN. He remembered the company, that's where Miles Pert went. Lokner must have got out of M-Sof before the attack. "Exciting? Sometimes a little too exciting." He looked at the little hotel chassis. "Sometimes I think I'd rather work in a hotel." He remembered and his hand itched, the skin crawling. He wanted to claw at the flesh, still red and raw from the last bout of scratching. "A hotel where no one tries to kill you."

"Well, good luck to you, Sir." The chassis spun away and Griffin stared at its retreating faux-tuxedo finish.

Wait. Really cool assassins? What a strange—

"Archaeidae," he called out, and the little hotel chassis said "oh shit" and put on a burst of speed.

Griffin gave chase and the fire in his gut, quiescent after a night's rest, sparked to life like a match tossed into a tank of aerated jet fuel. The chassis ducked and dodged around pedestrians, running over feet, bumping into old ladies, and doing its best to leave a trail of chaotic confusion. Griffin followed, shoving his way through the complaining crowd. He drew the Glock right-handed and racked the slide. Now people got out of his way.

He heard Nadia's voice. *Safety's still on.* Griffin disengaged the safety as he saw the chassis disappear back into the hotel lobby, the automated doors whisking open and then closing behind it. He took the corner fast, his shoes slipping on the carpeted entrance. The doors saw him coming and snapped back open.

The little chassis screamed, "Gun! Gun!" as Griffin burst into the lobby waving the Glock and already wheezing.

Oh f—

"Drop your weapon! On the ground!"

A Hotel Security chassis, weapons threatening, cut between him and the fleeing bellboy chassis.

Griffin slid to an awkward stop. "I'm a NA—"

"On the ground *now*!"

There was a blur as a second Security chassis stepped in and knocked the gun spinning from his hand. The trigger guard tore skin from his fingers.

Griffin stepped sideways, trying to see beyond the Security chassis in front of him and watch where the bellboy chassis was going. "I have—" He was reaching for his ID when Security tasered him. The two security chassis hit simultaneously with over one hundred thousand watts each.

His muscles spasmed and contracted and the still healing wound in his stomach felt like it split open and spilled his intestines. The heavens opened and poured lightning through the top of his skull. A swimming sea of twisting sparks arced across his vision and he didn't see the floor coming. His nose broke a second time and the universe splintered in endless oceans of agony.

When he could once again string two cohesive thoughts together he lay face down on the floor, his hands plasticuffed behind him. His skull throbbed and tracers of incandescence shot through his limbs causing spastic twitches.

One of the hotel Security chassis stood over him, keeping its taser pointed at his torso. A crowd of people watched from further back, recording this for their friends to watch later.

"Nurk," was the best he could manage.

"The police have been notified and are on the way," the Security chassis informed him in a deep voice.

Griffin rolled onto his back and his skull threatened to shred apart if he persisted in further movement. "Special Investigations," he enunciated carefully. "ID inside pocket."

The chassis plucked the ID from his pocket and scanned it. "Damn." It dropped the wallet on his chest, and he winced when it struck a bruise. "You came in here waving a gun."

Was that an apology, or an explanation? "Chasing busboy."

"Which one. We have twenty-three currently working here."

"A Scan," he said.

"No Scans," answered the security chassis, "they're all drones."

The sparks faded from his vision, and his jellied

muscles stopped twitching. He glanced to the rear of the lobby. There was no sign of the chassis he'd been chasing. "Gone."

"I've notified the police they are no longer needed."

Griffin stared up at the chassis. Blood ran down the back of his throat from his rebroken nose. Pain pulsed through his skull with each beat of his heart. "Uncuff."

"Right. Sorry."

Griffin spent the next ten minutes convincing the hotel concierge he wasn't going to press charges. Yes, he ran into the lobby waving a gun. Yes, it was his own damned fault. No, he didn't need an ambulance. He stifled the blood pouring from his nose with a fistful of tissues gripped in his left hand. The right, skin torn from his fingers, dripped blood onto the expensive carpet. The concierge noticed with a distasteful grimace but said nothing. Griffin's gun was returned, the trigger guard still damp with his blood.

When he stepped out onto the street the sun was blindingly bright. His nose stopped bleeding, but the front of his shirt and suit were spattered in sanguinary Rorschach. He'd splashed water on his face and removed the worse of the blood from where it caked his upper lip and chin. His front teeth felt loose. It took effort not to worry at them with his tongue. Pedestrians gave him a wide berth as he stood in front of the hotel, looking dazedly up and down the street.

He pulled out his palm-comp and said "Abdul" to it. It sounded like *Am-nool* through his broken and blood filled nose. It took three attempts before the comp understood him.

"Hey Boss," answered Abdul, and then "Seriously?" when he saw Griffin's face. "You've been gone ten minutes."

"Stomped shit?"

"Stomped shit is a fond memory. This is a whole new look. Now stop screwing around. Go to a damned hospital."

"I'm fine," Griffin lied through loose teeth. "Mith— Misunderstanding with hotel security."

"NATU not paying its bills?"

"Funny as always. Meet me at the Redmond NATU office. Half an hour. I haven't made it to the pharmacy yet." Griffin killed the connection before Abdul answered.

The streets of downtown Redmond were a crush of pedestrian traffic, cyclists, and electric taxis. The lush wealth displayed in the suburbs and golf courses surrounding the M-Sof grounds distinctly absent. Trees and grass appeared only on faded posters advertising vacation packages few could afford. Hints of lichen festering in the cracked sidewalks and potholed roads were all that suggested this land was capable of supporting life. Even though nine out of ten people here were dressed in business suits, those suits showed signs of extended wear. Missing buttons, cheap material beginning to shine with the matte finish rubbed away, dress shoes worn flat. Griffin shoved his way through the crowd. Those who saw him coming were quick to give way. In ten yards the stabbing fury in his guts returned with a vengeance and he limped, bent forward, arms clutching his abdomen. His right hand felt like it was being held in a vat of molten metal. His nose started bleeding again, a slow, warm coppery leak.

Where is the damned pharmacy?

***

Abdul, waiting on the steps of the Redmond NATU building, watched Griffin's approach. The man staggered more than walked. Hunched and oblivious to the pedestrians scattering from his path, Griffin didn't notice Abdul and was about to pass him by.

"Boss."

The NATU agent stopped and looked up. His eyes, sunk deep into the orbital bones, were bloodshot. His face, the color of rancid tallow, darkened to a jaundiced purple around the eyes. He wore a beard of dried blood and seemed unaware of it.

I've seen healthier corpses. "Rough day?" Abdul asked, unable to think of anything else to say.

Griffin was curt. "We're on the job. Not so anonymous tip. Lokner is in Reno. The dead end has been resuscitated." He stalked past the chassis on his way up the steps to the NATU building entrance.

Abdul remained where he stood, watching the retreating agent. "Are you okay?" he called out, regretting the inane stupidity of the question.

"No."

Griffin disappeared into the building, leaving Abdul alone on the steps. People darted quick, nervous glances at the chassis as they passed.

"I'm fine," he said to one young woman as she hurried by pushing a stroller bearing two small children. "I'm not crazy at all." She picked up her pace. "You have to be able to *feel* things to be crazy," he called after her.

It wasn't true of course.

***

Griffin walked straight to the desk in the lobby, bypassing the line of people waiting to get beyond the security cordon. He slapped his ID down on the surface with a leathery thwack.

"Get me an office. Now."

The officer on duty scowled at the badge and then,

seeing Griffin's face, decided it wasn't worth the fight. He was waved through Security and his gun taken. He could collect it when he left.

A NATU security chassis, a sleek new General Dynamics model shaped a like a cross between a greyhound and a praying mantis, intercepted him. "Please Sir, follow me," it said politely.

"Where to?"

"I'm to lead you to an unused office."

Griffin eyed the chassis with distrust. "Archaeidae?"

"Pardon, Sir?"

"Nothing. Lead on."

The office was thick with dust and the desk took several minutes to boot. Once he'd downloaded his interface he hesitated. This could be it. Phil could pull him off the case right now, bring him home and lock him in a cubicle for the rest of his miserable shit life.

He remembered wanting that. Not now.

Better to get things done before Phil revoked his security clearance.

Nothing would stop him. Certainly not Phil.

He first booked space for himself and Abdul on the next military flight to Reno, getting the easy stuff out of the way. Next he called Reno's NATU office and requisitioned another two and a half ton truck. Still pretty easy, and the Requisitions Officer put up no fight. So far so good.

Now for the hard part.

He sat for several minutes, composing himself, before making the call. Thinking tough thoughts was one thing, but the reality was different. He needed Phil's backing. The man must see no hint of emotion. Griffin must be coldly professional. Bottled.

The call took several seconds to connect.

"Dickinson, what the fuck is going on?" Phil's voice

crackled with digital distortion.

No Griff today. Griffin took some small pleasure from his boss' anger. "I've got this case all but sewn up—"

"*All but* is right. You fucked the monkey on this one."

Fucked the monkey? What the hell did that mean? "I need—"

"I want you on the next sub-orbital home. You're going to take two weeks medical leave and then I'm going to fire you. What the hell were you thinking waving a gun in a hotel lobby? You think I wouldn't hear about this?"

"Extenuating—"

"Half a Strike Team, dead. Nadia. Dead. Great fucking PR *that* was."

"I have the big fish on my line," Griffin said, desperate.

"You have shit on a stick. I heard about what happened in the Dallas virtuality. Riina is dead. His crèche was burnt to the ground. Over one-hundred cooked children. How many damned corpses you planning on racking up before we call it a day? Your combat chassis is cracking. Didn't pass the last psyche test. Not even close. They took it off active duty for a reason."

Abdul was *his* combat chassis? "It? Abdul is fine. I need—"

"This case is closed."

Griffin's heart dropped into the acid pit of his stomach. Phil could shut him down right here and now. He couldn't do this by himself. "Phil, *please*. Trust me on this. It's huge."

"What's huge is the shit mess you've made out of this simple case. You're done. Next flight—"

"Mark Lokner. M-Sof."

"What?"

"Mark Lokner, owner and CEO—"

"I know who the fuck he is," snapped Phil.

"He's not dead. Scanned. He's behind the crèches. Supplies gear. Cherry picks the best product."

The line went quiet for a few seconds and Griffin worried the call had been dropped. Then Phil asked, "The recent attack on M-Sof's facility in Redmond?"

"All part of it." Griffin didn't mention he didn't know how the events were linked, but he felt sure they were. "Cosa Nostra attack." It was all guesswork, but as likely as anything else.

"You're serious?"

Griffin nodded and regretted it. His head felt like his brain had swelled to bursting. "I know where he is."

"I'll put together a Strike Team. Where is he?"

"No. No way. This is mine. I've been through too much to let someone else take this away from me. Don't do that to me, Phil."

"From the second I put you on that Jerseyville crèche raid, you have fucked up absolutely everything. I never should have put a junior in the field. At this point, I'm not sure I even trust you with a desk. How many people would die if I sent you for coffee? No way you're leading a bust this big. It's too important."

"It's me or no one," Griffin said with more resolution than he felt. "Get me a Strike Team."

"No. Forget it."

"Wait a moment, I have to put you on hold. Someone here is trying to get my attention." Griffin killed the connection and hurried from the office. They had to be in the air before Phil found and canceled his requisitions.

***

Abdul discovered if he stood still, many people mistook him for a statue. Most would walk by, oblivious to his existence. Some looked confused—that wasn't there last time—and kept going. A young couple stood before him, arguing their way toward an inevitable breakup. They left in opposite directions, both crying. Abdul envied the depth of emotion and the tears. He couldn't feel anything that deeply. Except those few emotions They allowed him. He could feel anger.

Oh, he felt anger.

Staff Sergeant Abdul Aziiz-Giordano? It was an officer, no doubt stationed at some local military base, contacting him over the tight-link.

Nice timing. *Yeah?* To hell with Sirs and respect.

As of this moment you are no longer on active duty.

Uh huh.

Abdul saw Griffin exit the NATU building and watched his careful approach. The NATU agent looked to be holding his body together through sheer force of will. That will was fraying.

A truck has been sent to collect you.

"You'll never tan," said Griffin to Abdul's back.

"All kinds of funny," he said to Griffin. "So, how'd it go?"

Griffin shrugged and then winced in discomfort. "I talked to my boss."

No doubt that went well. "And?" *When will the truck arrive?* Abdul asked the officer.

"He says you're crazy."

Ah, *that.* It was bound to come up eventually. "I take it we part ways here."

The truck will arrive within the hour, Staff Sergeant.

"What on earth for?" Griffin looked surprised. "Abdul, I can't do this alone. There is no one I would rather have watching my back."

"Oh, so I'm supposed to be a subservient step behind you?"

"That's not what I—"

"I know. I'm messing with your head."

"When we're done, you're getting some damned facial expressions."

"Yes boss. When we leaving?"

"Truck should be here any minute."

"Perfect." *I'll be here waiting*, Abdul told the officer. "Asshole." When Griffin backed away a step looking hurt, Abdul said, "Not you. I was taking a call at the same time."

"Everything okay?"

Abdul considered telling Griffin everything. "Peachy," he said.

Griffin, looking uncertain, noticed the approaching truck Abdul had been watching for what seemed like an eternity. "Here's our ride to the airport."

"Let's get the hell out of here."

CHAPTER TWENTY-EIGHT: Sunday, August 6th, 2046

Lost in thought, Lokner2.0 prowled his spartan office. Things had not gone strictly to plan. What a fucking understatement. It started so well and went screaming headfirst into the shitter like one of those diving birds going after fish.

He'd launched an attack against the Central American Mafia business interests using M-Sof and Lokner1.0 as his vehicle. The Mafia reply was harsher than he anticipated but still achieved the result he hoped for: The original Lokner Scan was dead. Somewhere along the way, however, Lokner2.0 felt as if he lost control. The dominoes fell chaotically. What he had not foreseen was the level of technological advancement the Central American Mafia had achieved. Not only did they blow the hell out of the M-Sof Redmond facility, an intensity of reprisal he had not expected, but they also somehow corrupted the M-Sof intranet systems in such a way Lokner2.0 was locked out. He could no longer access or manipulate M-Sof stocks or systems. The Mob controlled his company and there seemed to be nothing he could do about it.

And then, to make matters worse, some nut-job terrorist organization obliterated the world's network of

Global Positioning and Communications satellites making even the simplest communications a royal pain in the ass. His plans for the future depended on manipulating the markets and to do that he needed to communicate with them and to do so quickly.

It's like all the world is against me.

He thought about asking Miles for help, but the idea left such a foul taste he tossed it aside. An odd sensation prickled the back of his neck, the feeling someone stared at him from behind. Lokner2.0 spun and glared at his office door. He sat, staring at the closed door, the feeling of being watched grew stronger. Had he heard something? Did someone stand outside the door? He strained to catch the faint sound of soft breath.

Nothing.

Mark rose and crept toward the office door, tip-toeing across the thick carpeting in his custom designer dress shoes, silent as a ghost.

You are a ghost.

"Shush."

He leaned forward, ear to the door, listening. Was that the faint sound of small voices?

Mark wrenched the door open and the empty hall was so startling he screamed. The fuckers were running away! He managed a dozen running steps into the hall before sliding to a halt. He felt naked and vulnerable here. *They want me out here!* They were trying to lure him out of his office. He was safe there. He took a tentative backward step toward sanctuary and felt the hall fill with malice. The walls dripped venomous hate. They were coming. Lokner2.0 spun and sprinted back into his office, a thousand deaths hot on his heels. The office door slammed closed barely in time and he collapsed sobbing on the carpet. Once he regained his breath he pushed himself to his knees and crawled to the door to lock it. He sat with his back to the door, looking at his shoes. They cost over four-thousand Au. No, wait. These weren't real. *Does that mean they were free?*

"What the hell was that all about?" He glanced around the office. The walls were barren, clean and safe. "Miles. It must have been Miles." Lokner couldn't believe the fat fucker programmed some kind of evil spirit into the hall. "He's getting cocky. He thinks that because I'm dead I'm out of the picture.

You are dead.

"Yes, but not out of the picture." A titter slipped out.

You killed those children. You stirred their brains with a fork and lived off their thoughts like a vampire. You raped their minds, skull-fucking them with your—

Mark slapped himself across the face, hard. "Shut up. This isn't the time." His face stung and eyes watered.

Ow.

"Shush. What should I do about Miles? If I tell him I know about the ghosts he'll get a chuckle and think he's won." Mark thrust out his belly and flared his nostrils. "I scared bad old Mister Lokner," he did a poor impersonation of Miles' voice. "I'm a fat and funny bitch. I think I'm smarter than everyone else but I've got my head stuffed so far up my ass I can't see what's coming my way."

Mark crawled on all fours back to his desk. Shoving the chair out of his way he slid into the alcove designed for his knees and feet. This was a place of power and safety, he could tell.

"So Miles has some little nastiness running around the halls. Well, the joke is on him. I'll pretend like I haven't noticed, like I don't even care."

We don't need to leave the office anyway.

"There's no we, just me."

Right, just you. All alone.

Mark, sitting crammed under his desk, thought

about that. He didn't want to be alone. It was nice having someone to talk to.

"Fine, we."

Once he felt centered and in control he crawled from under his desk and began pacing. It felt good to know there was such a powerful place he could retreat to.

You're a copy.

"Please, not now."

Lokner2.0 prided himself on his adaptability. The loss of M-Sof had been a crushing blow but he was hardly penniless. 5THSUN was a successful company and his offshore accounts still held billions in Au and Euros (though god only knew what those were worth these days). That loss, combined with the destruction of the satellites, would increase the time scale of his plan, but time was one thing he had.

I am forever.

The Mafia had outlived their usefulness. They'd become dangerous. How to strike at them and permanently remove them as a threat was a difficult question. He admitted that if there were a way of forever wiping out the Mafia, some overzealous law-enforcement branch would have done so already. Lokner2.0 adapted his goals to fit the reality.

"I have to hit them somewhere that will weaken them enough I can regain control of M-Sof."

What about our other plans? What about building the future?

"We need to do this first."

Are you sure? You aren't stalling because you've lost your way?

Mark licked his lips, struggled to quell the rising doubts. He was lost. His plans were flaking apart like ash in a windstorm. The M-Sof people he planned on taking—

the ones 1.0 stole—were gone, beyond his reach. Maybe even dead. It felt like an insurmountable obstacle.

No. I can still do this. He was Mark Fucking Lokner. He always won. Right?

The original always won. The first copy, 1.0 is dead and gone. He didn't win. What chance do we have?

"We can still do this."

Once the Mafia are out of the way.

"Yes. Them first. Then the future."

It occurred to him he had a means of striking at them they couldn't trace. Once he had a target, he could send some of his combat chassis to wreak bloody havoc. It was distasteful, but sometimes hard choices had to be made.

His target was obvious. The Scan running the Mob's businesses and investments in Central America. If this Scan ran all their other businesses, which appeared to be the case, chances were it now ran what remained of M-Sof as well. If he could shut down the Scan, it'd cripple them and might give him back control of his company.

Mark thought it through. No doubt the Mafia used a Scan from one of his boutique crèches. It might not have possessed his flare and style, but he'd been impressed by its flawless timing and manipulation of marketing data.

Manipulation. Data. That was the key.

Where Riina's crèche specialized in producing combat-worthy Scans, the crèche in the Anisio Jobin prison in Brazil concentrated on designing children from before birth to be better computers. They experimented with manipulating fetuses, injecting prenatal testosterone in an attempt at creating children inclined toward an interest in systems and with an increased attention to minute detail. They were trying to create pseudo-autistic savant children who would still be valuable and viable as Scans. In fact, a child who was autistic in the right way was often worth far more than even a classically intelligent child. Their brains came pre-focused and there was no need for all the messy psyche-programming and brainwashing, neither of which guaranteed results. Many attempts ended in disastrous failure, though there had been a few successes.

Mark hunted through his records, looking for likely candidates. One in particular leaped out. Child number 88. He skimmed the data. The Scan, purchased by the Cuntrera-Caruana family operating out of San José, Costa Rica, sold for an unprecedented thirty million Au.

There it was, floating right before his eyes: The delivery address. No doubt a hovel in the Cuntrera-Caruana run part of La Carpio.

"Gotcha little fucker!"

Is the Scan still there? Have they moved it?

"Why would they bother?"

It seemed unlikely the Mafia would have fitted 88 with a chassis, such a thing would be a distraction to their little autistic computer.

Mark sat and put his feet up on his desk. He laced his fingers behind his head and rocked in the chair. His gaze flicked around the room and desktop, not really seeing, mirroring the activity in his brain. He'd never had to cause the death of a child before, at least not directly. Not *real* death anyway. Sure, the children who died to become Scans were at least partially his responsibility, but those children were freed to live grander existences. It was a mercy killing and one allowing them to reach their full potential.

He was building a perfect future for all humanity. What was the life of one autistic child when held against that? If he didn't kill this child, he might never regain control of M-Sof; it could mean the death of all his plans.

"Sometimes, to get something done you have to break a few heads."

That didn't sound right. Was it heads or eggs? Heads seemed to make more sense in the context, but he was sure that wasn't right. Why couldn't he remember? That middle part—to get something done—seemed strangely vague.

"Why would someone who never got hungry want to break eggs? It doesn't make sense!"

You're stalling.

The thought of having 88 killed was unpleasant but he saw no way around it. Killing the Scan was the best way to strike at the Central American Mafia. He took some small comfort from the knowledge that his victim was autistic, a mental and social cripple.

It hardly seemed fair. The kid lived a few years as a social moron before being bent to doing pattern and data systems work for those slimy Mafiosos only to be killed in a conflict she knew nothing about and probably wasn't even capable of understanding.

Killing her would be more of a blessing than anything else.

So we're going to kill a little girl?

"Quiet, or I'll slap you again."

The remorse faded and was forgotten, replaced by the knowledge this *must* be done.

"It is not my fault. They use the child against me so I must remove the child."

Simple math, right?

Mark tapped the desktop, opening a line of communication. "Canebrake, Red-Back, Boomslang, Siafu. Meet with me." Since all four were right there in the building with him, the virtuality was run by 5THSUN's systems and relied only on the company's intranet.

Two boys and two girls stood lined up before him in seconds. Each appeared as a samurai warrior, all part of the rigorous brainwashing and indoctrination they received at Riina's crèche. Odd behavior, but it seemed to work. He had to give Riina credit: the man turned out prime combat material.

The four samurai bowed low.

Mark felt awkward, like he should play a role in their little Japanese fantasy world and didn't know how.

"I have a mission for you," he said in his best grave voice. *This is silly.* He felt like an idiot.

"*Hai!*" they answered simultaneously.

Hi? What the hell did that mean? Was that Japanese for yes? Probably. "I have an enemy in Costa Rica. I want her slain."

"*Hai!*"

"It's a Scan. She'll have protection."

"*Hai!*"

"Stop doing that," Mark growled.

The samurai nodded silently.

"You're going to Costa Rica. Sub-orbital flight. But you won't be returning." Mark watched the samurai, waiting for a reaction. Nothing. They didn't even blink. Damn, Riina was *good*. "It's a suicide mission."

"*Kamikaze,*" said one of them. Might have been Canebrake.

"Right. Sure. *Kamikaze*. We cannot chance your return."

The samurai nodded, eyes bright. *Do they look happy?* "Your chassis are fit with micro-nukes. A failsafe. Should you fail, you will trigger them."

The samurai nodded in unison. It looked practiced, choreographed. Too perfect.

This is where it got tricky. How would they take the next part? *Let's see just how good Riina was.* "Should you succeed, you will still trigger the nukes."

"We will not fail," said the same samurai.

Mark swallowed his regret. "I'm sorry I can't bring

you back."

Canebrake brushed this aside with a sharp wave of his hand. "To die in service is all we can ask. We will earn our places in the next life."

Next life? What was that all about? Didn't matter. They'd get the job done. *God* damn *Riina was good.*

The pang of guilt at sending these Scans to certain death stayed with him long after the kids had vanished. Their deaths, even though they hadn't happened yet, weighed on him. Whatever it was in the hall beyond his office door grew heavier, leaned its mass against the creaking wood.

"Be gone!" he snapped. "There was no other choice."

It must be done, and if the cost seemed grievous it was because he'd been forced into a difficult situation.

The thing beyond the door groaned and then was quiet.

This has to be done.

It was just math.

***

Though 88.1 and her host of Mirrors had been unable to infiltrate 5THSUN's new *Wall o' Nuclear Annihilation*, they still kept close tabs on the company and its affiliates. When four combat chassis left 5THSUN Assessments 88 heard about it within minutes. Lost in the study of signal patterns she had discovered by cracking old pre-NATU Space Administration data banks, she told her Mirrors to look into it. It wasn't until she received word the chassis had boarded a private sub-orbital bound for San José, Costa Rica that she felt the first stabbing pangs of fear.

Her first thought was to contact Archaeidae. He

would know what to do. She called for 88.1 and was annoyed at how long the Mirror took to answer.

"We must meet with Archaeidae," she told 88.1. "Arrange it."

***

Archaeidae, having swapped his Scan back to his favorite Assassin Chassis after his meeting with Agent Dickinson in Bellevue, was in Reno. He'd made a few purchases and his chromed body was hidden by a long tan duster coat and massive cowboy hat. He sat in a public-access NATUnet Café so he could join the virtual meeting of his Masters. With international communication being so difficult and prone to failure, the café was mostly empty. The few patrons played games hosted on local systems or were there for the social aspect of hanging out with friends.

Archaeidae selected a private table, ordered a coffee and paid for several hours of time so they'd leave him alone. He jacked in.

The Emperor, *Shogun* 88.1, and the Court Assassin met in a virtuality *chashitsu*, a wood and bamboo tea house two stories in height and dating back to sixteenth century Japan. They sat around a small, scarred oaken table sipping steaming green tea. *Tennō* 88 in russet silk robes, 88.1 in gray *hakama* pants, a black *haori* and a full-length black kimono, and Archaeidae in a *shinobi shozoko* so black it had its own event horizon. The tea house's other patrons real and otherwise, were all similarly attired. Geisha flowed between tables serving light snacks and refilling teapots.

Archaeidae examined *Tennō* 88. It didn't bother him, taking orders from a girl, but he did feel somehow different. More protective? Did that even make sense?

Why should it change anything?

"Where are you?" the Emperor demanded of Archaeidae, staring at the wooden table top.

Archaeidae accepted the Emperor's terseness, happy he deigned to speak with him at all. "I have followed Dickinson, the NATU Special Investigator, to Reno, my Emperor. I will witness the confrontation between the NATU forces and 5THSUN. Should events not transpire according to plan, I will step in and finish the job." Archaeidae hoped his voice didn't give away how much he hoped he'd need to step in.

If *Tennō* 88 noticed he made no mention of it. "My Mirrors," he said, "have reported four combat chassis left the 5THSUN building and are en route to Costa Rica."

"That's great! It'll tip the odds in the NATU agent's favor."

Tennō 88 stared unblinking at Archaeidae for long enough the assassin began to wonder if he'd missed something crucial or obvious. The Emperor spoke. "I am in Costa Rica. If they have managed to track me, I am in danger."

Shogun 88.1 said nothing.

Archaeidae had no idea his Emperor lived in Costa Rica. "*Tennō*, is it possible for me to get there in time to intercept them?"

"The next flight scheduled from Reno doesn't leave for eight hours. Even if we were to commandeer an immediate flight we could not get you here in time."

"They are in the air right now?"

"Correct."

Having his chassis look around the small NATUnet Café while his virtuality self took in the tea house sparked the beginning of a plan. Here he was in Reno, talking with his Emperor in Costa Rica. He'd control the chassis remotely and defeat the would-be assassins. He searched through his memory, trying to remember if this was something that happened regularly. Nothing. He couldn't be the first to think of this, could he? "Then we have time, my Emperor."

"Time for what?"

"Planning your defense. You have combat chassis protecting you in Costa Rica, I assume?"

"I have six Mirror-driven combat chassis. They can protect me."

"Most respectfully *Tennō*, no."

"No?"

The Emperor's question was asked so calmly Archaeidae wondered if he'd overstepped his bounds. Uncle Riina always seemed calmest when seething with anger. *This is not Uncle Riina, this is the Emperor.* The living spirit of *zanshin* and *fudoshin*, relaxed and ready, the immovable heart. He was as Archaeidae must strive to be.

"No, my *Tennō*. I've seen your Mirrors fight and the 5THSUN Scans will defeat them."

"The plan then?"

Archaeidae was awed. Emperor 88 saw death stalking him and remained as calm and emotionless as ever. "I will ambush your attackers at the airport. Get your chassis there and I will control them all from here in Reno." Controlling six chassis at the same time, was that even possible? He had no choice, the Emperor's Mirror-driven chassis were useless.

The Emperor turned to his *Shogun*. "We'll need to take control of several private communications satellites."

For the first time Archaeidae saw emotion on the *Shogun's* impassive face. "Satellites?" he asked, eyes widening in surprise. "But they're all gone. 88.6 destroyed them all before you ended its line. I thought you knew."

"We're communicating now," pointed out Archaeidae. "This must be possible."

"There are problems," said the Emperor, eyes unfocused, maybe unseeing. "Distance. Quantity of data. Poor condition of CenAmNet. Outdated technology, most not even the equal of old fiber-optics, suffers from lack of maintenance. Constant blackouts as antiquated power systems fail from overload. The trunk-lines entering the continent are forty years old, choked, unable to meet even the current demands. Considerable lag in communications." The words flowed without pause for breath as the Emperor stared at nothing. "The networks we currently broadcast on are unstable. Insufficient in critical second-by-second environment."

Archaeidae curbed the desire to curse in anger. "I hadn't thought of that." He attacked that angle of the problem. "So we need more bandwidth."

"Correct," *Tennō* 88 agreed.

Archaeidae realized the Emperor still hadn't blinked. He watched *Tennō* 88's chest. There was no movement at all; he could be a porcelain statue. Such perfection. Archaeidae knew he must strive to be worthy. He bowed his head in humble recognition of the paragon before him and asked, "Who, my *Tennō*, has that kind of bandwidth?"

"No one."

Archaeidae felt the bottom drop out of his non-existent stomach. That couldn't be true. So much data swirled around the planet's surface. Someone *must* have that bandwidth. An idea. "M-Sof?"

"Interesting. When you asked *who*, I assumed entities, not companies. But no."

Why would *Tennō* 88 assume...it didn't matter. "5THSUN and M-Sof combined?"

"No."

Archaeidae grit his chrome teeth, emitting a high-pitched squeal causing everyone in the NATUnet Café to flinch.

"Some other company?"

"No."

"Someone must," Archaeidae said desperately. And then he remembered *Shogun* 88.1 mentioning he'd conscripted bandwidth from NATUnet to make their earlier virtual meeting possible. "NATU," he said.

"The North American Trade Union controls many data trunk-lines," agreed *Tennō* 88.

"Then I shall need a NATUnet trunk-line." How the hell was he going to do that?

The Emperor fixed him with eyes devoid of emotion and Archaeidae knew he had truly been seen.

"Only from the heart of a major NATU facility would this be possible," said the Emperor.

That was the answer. The sheer audacity of what he planned had his mind vibrating like a tuning fork. "If I break into Reno's NATU headquarters and get physical access to their data pipelines, can you get me past their system defenses?"

Tennō 88 answered immediately. "NATU system protocols can be breached, but doing so will alert NATU to my existence." The Emperor paused for a moment, again staring at the table top, before continuing. "Even with that kind of transfer rate there will be a noticeable lag in communications. CenAmNet is the weakness." There was half a second of contemplation. "If I subvert NATUnet in its entirety I can reduce the lag time. I will need to conscript everything, from copper phone lines to relay stations to the old fiber-optic trunk-lines. It is impossible to guess at any particular instant which will be the fastest route for the data. We will need all of them. There is no way to do this without NATUnet authorities realizing what is happening. The humans will know about me."

Humans. Though Archaeidae knew he'd once been

one he couldn't remember the last time he'd thought of himself as human. It was good to know he wasn't alone. He felt something new: Belonging.

"We can't do this invisibly." Archaeidae wouldn't let himself swear in front of his Emperor, much as he wanted to. "*Tennō*, can you make an approximation of the lag time?"

"Lag time will vary between fifty and five-thousand milliseconds at the beginning. As Mirror chassis are removed from combat, lag time will decrease due to the resulting reduction in data being transferred."

Five seconds? He'd finished wars in less time.

Impossible. No one could fight five seconds behind their opponents. The fight would be over before he it had begun.

"*Tennō*." Archaeidae gripped the table in the tea shop virtuality, crushing wood beneath powerful fingers. "I cannot do this."

"You must."

"Impossible. Even if I am a *thousand* times better than the Scans I face, I cannot do this. Five-thousand milliseconds. It's too much."

"You are unpredictable. You must figure out a way."

"No, I..." Unpredictable. Predictable. Two sides of the same coin. Archaeidae bared his teeth in a snarl and the NATUnet Café cleared as patrons fled. He paid them no attention. "I can do it. My Emperor, here is my plan." He would practice the impossible. "I will break into the Reno NATU offices and tap their data lines. Once in I'll practice moving multiple chassis against multiple targets with a varying lag time in communications. I can use their systems to run the virtuality at ultra-high speeds. I'll have to remain in the NATU offices until combat is complete. If I can manage this quickly, it shouldn't be a problem getting out afterward. If I am there more than a few minutes they will mobilize their own combat chassis and I may have some difficulty. At that point, any assistance you can render will be invaluable."

The Emperor made no assurance nor promises of aid; he stared at Archaeidae in that way he had of looking through things to their very heart. "A statement of the obvious," he said in such a way the young assassin was unsure if it were question or statement. "A common human pastime."

Was that an insult? Archaeidae, uncertain, decided upon silence.

Tennō 88 looked away and, for an uncomfortably long time, stared at the ancient oak table at which they sat. With a slim finger he scratched at the table's scarred top and Archaeidae wondered if he had been dismissed. "Cracks," whispered the Emperor. "Just code. Easily cracked. Predictable." Finally the Emperor nodded. He spoke without looking up. "I will use the time to prepare. I will clear both NATUnet and CenAmNet of all data transfers other than our own and dramatically reduce the time lag."

"The shorter the lag, the better," agreed Archaeidae.

"Statement of the obvious," the Emperor said again.

The young assassin accepted what he took to be chastisement and continued. "If you can create some kind of diversion, *Tennō*, before I go in, something to draw the NATU combat chassis away—the further the better—that will buy me more time."

The Emperor looked up and studied Archaeidae with strange intensity. "Obvious in hindsight," he said. "Yet I had not thought of that." He returned his attention to the table. "Perhaps this is why humans do it; they never know what others might know and make statements of the obvious just in case. From that perspective it does make some sense, though it isn't an efficient means of communication."

"I'm like you," said Archaeidae, daring the Emperor's anger. "I'm not human. Haven't been in a long time."

The Emperor glanced at him and nodded once, accepting. He scratched the tabletop with a perfect fingernail. "This isn't like the floor. The cracks say nothing. I understand everything. Magnitudes of complexity lacking. I will cause a diversion which will draw the maximum number of NATU chassis off the premises for the maximum amount of time."

Archaeidae did the mental equivalent of a shrug and decided not to ask for details.

He had something else on his mind. Why it bothered him, he couldn't say. Should he ask? *What the hell.* "*Tennō* 88, are you...a girl?"

"Yes," said the Emperor without looking at Archaeidae. "I was."

"Wouldn't *Jotei* 88 be more accurate? Why the deception?"

"Deception?" 88 answered with just enough inflection for Archaeidae to realize it was a question. The Emperor continued without waiting for a reply. "You are not a thirteenth century samurai. I am not a Japanese Emperor. I don't know what I looked like before. I cannot give you an accurate depiction." Instead of the Emperor a small girl no more than seven or eight years old sat across the table from Archaeidae. She was covered in filth and long tubes snaked from welts in her arms to disappear below the table. Her face was blurry and indistinct. She looked so small and frail and Archaeidae felt an uncomfortable stab of protectiveness. It was a new feeling. "This is what I remember," said the girl, "but that body is bone meal, sold as fertilizer. What does it matter here?" She became the Emperor again. "Information protocol. I was told you would react better to a male authority figure."

Archaeidae shrugged that uncomfortable thought aside. There was something deep-rooted there he couldn't bring himself to examine. Uncle Riina lurked at the center of his fear and doubt. He crushed those thoughts and glanced toward *Shogun* 88.1. "You?"

"I am neither male nor female. I am a creation, a Mirror of the Archetype."

Archaeidae stood, pushing back from the table. The Emperor remained sitting, staring at the cracks in the oaken table.

"Will you still help me?" the Emperor asked, voice small.

"Of course. You need me. Are you more comfortable as male or female?"

"The distinction lacks meaning. Do you have a preference?"

"I suppose I prefer some honesty in my virtuality. Even if it doesn't matter. You are *Jotei* 88, the Empress." The Emperor changed, morphing into a more female form. "Thank you," said Archaeidae.

That 88 was willing to conscript NATUnet and expose herself spoke of the depth of her fear. Archaeidae studied his Empress. She'd shown herself as a little girl. Was that memory recent, or something from the past? Recent, he felt sure. Sometimes she seemed wise and infinite, and sometimes so small and scared. Previously he'd thought she was much older than he, a possible mentor. His suspicions left him feeling vulnerable.

"We're two children against all the world," he said.

"They already killed me once."

Never again, swore Archaeidae.

In the virtual tea house Archaeidae rose from the table. "I do have one more request," he said. Unblinking, the Empress stared at Archaeidae. "I could use a pair of good swords."

Jotei 88 nodded once and Archaeidae bowed low.

I won't fail her as I failed Uncle Riina.

No one would ever touch her. No one would ever hurt her again.

If humanity threatened her, they would regret it.

CHAPTER TWENTY-NINE: Sunday, August 6th, 2046

For the sub-orbital flight to Reno-Tahoe International Airport Abdul was packed into the airless baggage compartment with the rest of the luggage. If it was meant as a slight, it wasn't subtle.

He had little to do but think. The Scan piloting the sub-orbital wouldn't talk to him.

If Griffin was right and Mark Lokner was behind the crèches and involved with the mafia, they were going to be facing some dangerous opposition when they reached 5THSUN. These wouldn't be simple corporate security chassis—no match for a full-fledged killing machine like himself—but rather state-of-the-art combat models. They'd be piloted by children from the crèches Lokner was involved with.

He watched the barn burn again. If only he hadn't lobbed that shell. He should have known there was a fuel tank back there. There was one at every farm.

I should have known.

Blackened bodies. Charred husks.

How many lives had he taken for his NATU masters? Was this not enough? Had he not earned his freedom, bought it with the souls he'd sent to hell?

No. Twenty more years. Twenty more years of

violence. Twenty more years of killing.

Twenty years less five lousy fucking days.

"I can't do this."

The luggage surrounding him rattled and vibrated as the orbital began its descent. He detected parts per million of aftershave, deodorant, and perfume. He knew which bags belonged to women, which to men. He knew which contained unwashed laundry and illicitly smuggled foods.

God I miss cheese!

He could bring this down. End it all. Nothing survived a sub-orbital crash.

More blood on his...*fuck, I don't even have hands.* He couldn't do it.

They took everything. They even stole his death. Maybe being blown to shit by a Jumping Spider mine was no great noble achievement, but it was *his*. His death. He wanted it back.

He wanted it all back.

"No more."

No more doing as he was told. He'd help Griffin shut down Lokner, the soulless bastard behind the crèches, and then he was done.

Some choices they couldn't take away.

One last choice. One last freedom.

If he was willing to take it.

***

Once in Reno, Griffin dry-swallowed the last of the amphetamines he'd purchased in Redmond. They were all that kept him on his feet. The world sung like vibrating steel and stung like a slap in the face, but he was up and moving. That's all that mattered. If he stopped now he'd never get back up.

The sun crawled, bleary and hung-over, above the horizon and the day's heat had yet to land with all its ferocity. Griffin gazed at the Eastern sky, a wretched puke and pollution swirl. *Monet would be proud.* He and Abdul made for 5THSUN Assessments in their requisitioned two-ton truck. The military grade air filters in the truck worked well enough Griffin pulled off his filter-mask. Though the air tasted of sun-warmed garbage, carbon emissions, and rotting fish, it was still preferable to re-breathing his own sour exhalations. Though the morning air was cool, Griffin still sweat under his magnetorheological bodysuit. His heart thumped against the SmartFluid-filled armor hard enough he was surprised it hadn't triggering the viscoelastic effect. The helmet and its barrage of confusing information sat on the passenger seat. He hadn't tried it on. It reminded him of the last time he wore one. And Nadia.

A Tavor 41 assault rifle with under-mounted grenade launcher lay heavy across his lap. Half a dozen extra clips hung in a webbed combat belt. It made sitting even more uncomfortable.

The city and its litter looked unnaturally beautiful in the early morning glow. The truck wove through sparse vehicular traffic on streets lined with fake trees and gardens.

When was the last time he slept? He couldn't remember. The pills made him sharp, but some things seemed far away. He thought about Abdul.

"Do you sleep?" he asked.

"No."

"You miss it?"

"Yeah. Remember how they tell you in high school that humans go crazy if they don't get sleep? It's true."

"Humans, not *people*? Interesting distinction. High school was a while ago."

"I was in grade twelve," said Abdul. "I joined the NATU Marines to pay for college. I'm an immortal and I don't even have a high school diploma."

"Shit. We're putting kids in chassis just like the assholes we're supposed to stop."

"At least I volunteered. Technically."

"Are you serious about going crazy?"

"I think I'd kill to enjoy a real beer again," said Abdul, avoiding the question. "Virtual ain't the same."

Griffin decided not to push it. At least Abdul was talking. He liked that better than the long sulks. "Well, you can have one when we're finished. We'll pour it into your gas tank."

"Too funny."

"Come on, it must be handy. You never have to go looking for a bottle opener."

"Griffin."

"Hmm?"

"Maybe I shouldn't tell you."

"Abdul, you can't say shit like that and then not tell the person."

The big chassis shifted and the truck groaned. "She's still alive. Scanned."

Griffin's head felt heavy and his throat grew tight. He ran a hand through his short gray hair. "No. She was DOA at the scene."

"Brainbox. She'd only been dead for a few minutes, there was almost no brain damage. Probably nothing she can't recover from."

His chest ached, but not from the mass of bruises. "Just die, you said. Don't get scanned. Why would she do that?"

"I don't know. Fear? I don't think we're designed for giving up. We always fight for one more breath, even if it won't be real."

Griffin blinked and tears tracked through his stubble. "You've talked to her?"

"No. I think *you* should."

"No."

"She needs—"

"No!"

"This won't be easy for her. Believe me, I know. If she doesn't have someone to talk to, she'll...she'll go crazy."

Griffin shook his head in denial. "It's not really her."

"So I'm not really me then?"

"Sorry, I—"

"No, you're right. I'm not. She's probably not either. But she's all that's left. Maybe that matters for something."

Maybe. He couldn't know. What was he to the ghost of this dead woman? What was this ghost to him? A memory? A painful reminder of what could never be?

"I'll think about it," said Griffin, drying his cheeks with a rough swipe of a sleeve.

"Good."

"You see the 5THSUN specs?" he asked, changing the subject.

"Yeah. A company called Cc-Security is running the show. They appeared out of nowhere and with a massive budget. They have half a dozen state-of-the-art security chassis at 5THSUN."

"Who supplies Cc-Secutity with chassis?" Griffin asked. "For that matter, where are the Scans coming from?"

"The chassis are listed as off-the-shelf security models."

"Want to bet the chassis are illegal combat models and the Scans are brainwashed crèche children?"

"No. I don't want to kill any more children. Is there

another path we can take? Can't we set things in motion? Subpoenas, legal charges, call in the cavalry and all that?" Abdul pleaded.

Too late for that. What should he do? Racing after Riina got Nadia killed. Was he about to make the same mistake? He thought back to his first crèche raid, how he planned every last detail. He remembered the empty bodies, the swarming flies.

If I stall and Lokner escapes— "No, we can't," said Griffin, throat tight. "A Scan can be stored on a computer not much bigger than a deck of cards. If we stall Lokner will be gone. We do this the civil way and he'll get away. No." If Abdul backed out this was all over. He couldn't do it alone. "We go in hot. Deal with whatever happens. If it gets ugly—"

"*When* it gets ugly."

When. Griffin's gut spasmed. *What am I doing here?* The one thing he knew for sure, he didn't want to get stabbed again. Or shot.

What the hell was he going to achieve? *Go home. Forget this. Forget her.* She was still alive. *No, not alive.* He might even have a job to return to if he left now. He watched the city blur by.

Fuck it.

"Abdul, I'm going in with or without you."

***

At the far end of town, combat chassis boiled out of the Reno NATU offices and were loaded onto trucks and helicopters. They charged east towards Fallon where unknown terrorists had gained control of the Dixie Valley geothermal power plant, threatening to reduce it to dust and bones.

Archaeidae knew once NATU personnel reached the

plant it wouldn't take them long to realize it wasn't a terrorist attack but a bizarre computer malfunction. 88 would stop all data movement within the city of Reno, eradicating all possibility of someone calling for help. He estimated he had at most an hour but hoped human stupidity would slow the process. It seemed like a safe bet.

Standing on the steps of the Reno NATU office, Archaeidae ignored the thronging pedestrians and cyclists. A long and faded tan duster-coat covered his chromed assassin chassis and samurai swords, and a large black ten-gallon cowboy hat hung low over his face. Though he could pass for human, assuming no one got too close or touched him, he still received more than his fair share of odd glances. He was definitely overdressed for the weather.

Archaeidae climbed the steps to the front door.

Inside, the aging security guard had yet to notice him. Everything slowed as Archaeidae prepared himself for battle.

One chance to get this right.

***

Outside San José, Costa Rica, a private sub-orbital began its descent toward Juan Santamaria International Airport. Canebrake, Boomslang, Red-Back, and Siafu faced each other in the lounge, their combat chassis forming a small circle. They ignored the thick, buttery leather sofas, polished oak and brass bar and trim, and the deep egg-shell white carpeting. The shallow trappings of wealth meant less than nothing.

The four met in a shared virtuality hosted by Canebrake. In a small clearing in the middle of an incandescent green bamboo forest four lean samurai sat in a circle, much like their chassis. Each wore a twelfth century *ō-yoroi*, the armor of the wealthy samurai. The armor was lustrous and colored to match their namesake. Canebrake's was striped in a mottled gold and brown deepening to black towards his extremities. Boomslang's glowed luminous green cut with sharp black lines. Red-Back's burnished black armor was unbroken except for two bright sanguine interlocking diamonds on his chest. Siafu's armor faded gradually from the orange-brown of dry blood at her feet to a red so dark it looked black at her head.

The bamboo swayed and whispered in the wind, sounding like the entangled caressing of snakes and hollowed wood wind chimes.

At nine years Canebrake was the oldest and the others looked to him to lead. A heavy responsibility, but one he could bear. He knew how this was to go. He'd been learning the words since birth. They all had.

"Uncle Riina made us for this," Canebrake said solemnly.

The other three nodded and intoned, "He made us for war."

"He gave us life, meaning and purpose," said Canebrake. "He made us immortal."

"We are forever."

He closed his eyes, holding firm the calm center of his soul. "Soon we face death."

"We have died a thousand times. We will not blink."

"We end in cleansing nuclear fire," said Canebrake opening his eyes and taking his time to acknowledge each samurai in turn. "Everything must burn."

"As Master Lokner orders."

Canebrake examined his friends. They'd run thousands of virtuality missions together, but this felt different. This was it, the real thing. It felt somehow final.

Well, yeah, Lokner says we aren't coming back. They

were going to die in some shitty little country he'd barely even heard of. And for what?

Honor. It's what they had trained for their entire lives.

So they'd lived to die for some selfish asshole who didn't even make an effort to understand them. What a waste.

Lokner doesn't matter. This wasn't for Lokner, it was for Riina. Riina mattered. He'd be proud.

Oh Uncle, why have you done this to us? Canebrake wanted to turn and run so bad, but he couldn't. He couldn't disappoint his Uncle. He couldn't abandon his brothers and sisters.

Canebrake waited until he was sure his voice would not shake or crack. He breathed the damp barnyard scent of bamboo. "It has been an honor to work with you, my friends. I look forward to seeing you again on the next level."

"On the next level," they answered in agreement.

Next level. Was there a next level? For the first time in his short life, Canebrake was seriously beginning to doubt it.

***

Elsewhere, on the edge of Juan Santamaria International Airport's airspace, an aged Boeing 777 circled, awaiting its landing orders. On the runway a prehistoric Airbus A340 taxied into position for take-off.

***

The guard, paunch hanging over a thick leather belt equipped with bundled keycards, walkie-talkie, flashlight, taser, Glock, pepper-spray, plasticuffs, and a personal GPS tied in to the building's intranet, glanced at the strange man in the oversized duster-coat and ridiculous cowboy hat. The alarms remained quiescent and the guard's display indicated the man had top clearance and was a systems administrator from the virtuality department downstairs.

Computer specialist, thought the guard. *No wonder he's dressed like a freak.* No one else could get away with such blatant disregard for the corporate dress code.

***

Archaeidae, primed for violence and expecting the worse, decapitated the guard when the old man nodded his greeting.

The head landed with a wet thunk and the body toppled sideways out of its chair as the cleanly sliced neck spurted blood like a fire-hose.

Had anyone noticed? Archaeidae took in the room, the crowd of NATU employees in cheap suits staring at him in mute terror. *Yep, they noticed*. So much for sneaking in.

He vaulted through the security cordon and killed the nearest three people before he realized the alarms still hadn't sounded. That was good. Must be the Empress' doing.

And then chaos. People ran screaming in all directions. Another fat old man with a paunch, overloaded belt, and state-issued Glock tried to be a hero. Archaeidae obliged him. All heroes died, right? The floor, slick with blood, added to the panic. It was like walking on greased glass. Nothing to Archaeidae, but troublesome to clumsy humans. At least it made them easier to catch.

Four seconds in and still no sign of combat chassis. That was good too. Maybe the Empress managed to lure them all away.

The path to Archaeidae's goal remained clear as people fled before him. Every now and then someone got too close and was run through. No helping it. He killed them and moved on, following the memorized floor plan. Still no alarms sounded.

Something hit him from behind at the rate of about fifteen rounds per second, shredding the back of his duster-coat, and crumpling the support struts of his lower left shoulder. One arm useless already. Off to a great start. He really should consider using heavier chassis.

Nah. Not my style.

Hopefully whatever hit him wasn't fitted with a grenade launcher. That'd be nuts, right? No one would put a grenade launcher on a rifle designated for office security. They could bring the whole building down.

The next burst went over his damaged shoulder as Archaeidae spun and ducked away. He saw the slight bulk under the guard's pale blue shirt; MR vest, no doubt, and blew the woman's head to mist with a few dozen hyper-kinetic flechettes. He kept moving, put on a sudden burst of speed and narrowly avoided another vicious hail of assault rifle fire. Damned humans were everywhere.

A young man stared up at Archaeidae from under the desk he cowered behind. *Perfect!* Archaeidae picked him up. Using him as a shield he rushed toward the stairwell. The guards, assault rifles ready and looking for an opening, followed Archaeidae. He kept twitching his human shield about and the man screamed and wailed all kinds of nonsense.

Go ahead, shoot this poor office drone; put him out of his misery.

At the stairwell door he threw the man at the guards and, dropping a few micro-remote exploding drones, ducked away. The next person to open that door would get a nasty surprise. *That should slow them down a bit.*

Perhaps they'd reconsider the wisdom of following him.

He had to go down into the basement to find his goal. He took the stairs.

Archaeidae slid into the NATUnet hub deep in the air-conditioned bowels of the server rooms. He turned to find a middle-aged Systems Administrator with a faded 'Pirates are WAY Cooler than Ninjas' t-shirt staring at him.

"What the fu—" said the man as Archaeidae's katana slid through an eye socket and pierced the brain. The assassin effortlessly held the corpse upright with the tip of his sword in its skull until it stopped twitching. The blade slipped free with a wet *sip* before once again disappearing under what was left of his blood-spattered duster-coat.

"Ninjas are *way* cooler than pirates."

Archaeidae stashed the corpse out of the way and scanned the room. The machines, crisp white plastic sheathed towers standing six feet in height and aligned like rows of city blocks created a boring and simple maze. Each tower contained millions of processors and each processor in turn housed millions of individual nano fluid-cooled ionized-hafnium-sphere micro-cores. Any single tower in this room was capable of supplying the entire planet's processing and data storage demands of forty years ago. Archaeidae jacked into the system and used it to run his virtuality, maximizing processor speed to slow his perception of time. He would now have a month in virtual training.

Archaeidae threw himself into virtual combat missions with varying degrees of time lag fluctuating between one-third of a second and five seconds. For the first two weeks he died repeatedly, failing every attempt at every mission. Once he adapted and adopted a more intuitive combat style, never launching attacks at opponents, but rather attacking where he thought they would be, he managed some small level of success.

After the third week he achieved a five percent success rate. He wasn't able to top that.

Five percent. He'd been right. This wasn't possible.

Frustrated, he retreated from the problem and looked for other means of assuring victory. He downloaded the available data on Juan Santamaria International Airport in San José—including a great deal of additional information from *Jotei* 88 he wouldn't normally have had access to—and incorporated the data into his strategies. He studied flight paths and travel times in San José airspace. Unwilling to bother his Empress with further questions, he queried *Shogun* 88.1 on the Empress' ability to crack airline security and data systems. He formulated a desperate back-up plan.

Failure was not an option.

It was a certainty.

Archaeidae exited the virtuality and once again became aware of the reality around him. Twenty minutes had passed since killing the first guard.

Jotei 88 had provided explicit directions that should gain him access to the biggest data pipelines in NATU. Step by step Archaeidae followed them, careful to complete each stage before moving on. Normally this kind of espionage work bored the hell out of him, but with so much on the line he felt pretty excited. Until he completed the final step.

Access Denied flashed in an unfriendly red font.

"Oh, shit." Archaeidae glanced at where he'd hid the corpse of the System Admin. Maybe he shouldn't have killed him so quickly. He looked around the server room, desperate for inspiration.

***

All across the North American Trade Union, from

coast to coast, NATUnet ejected everyone on line and denied access to all. Virtuality universes populated by powerful wizards and deadly swordsmen were abruptly barren and unpopulated. The computer-run Non-Player Characters, demons, trolls and the like, left alone for the first time. Were they sentient, they'd have used this respite to build their defenses against the depredations of the many marauding Player-Characters. Instead, they stood around their dungeon layers, weapons in hand, awaiting the next wave of slaughter.

Not a single bit of data moved that didn't further 88's plans. Every Mirror not pursuing a task of utmost importance froze to minimize its NATUnet data-footprint. 88 cleared all data lines to guarantee Archaeidae the fastest possible uplink to the six Mirror-run chassis in Costa Rica.

Chaos and fist-fights ensued as every Stock Exchange in the Trade Union ceased receiving data. CEOs of financial institutions, already in a state of continual panic since the loss of the communications satellites, sat twitching as they watched their employees, unable to work and still on the clock, gather at unresponsive video screens and computer monitors trying to find out what the hell was happening. Systems Administrators were raked over the coals as they tried to explain to their managers that everything worked fine and nothing worked at all.

***

The truck's on-board computer pinged for attention and informed Griffin it had lost contact with the local NATUnet traffic network. This meant, he was told in the truck's polite but masculine voice, it no longer received updates on traffic conditions and construction areas, and the previous estimate for their ETA might no longer be accurate. The truck assured him it was still capable of delivering him and his cargo to their destination. Griffin, staring out the window at the passing buildings, ignored the truck.

As they approached 5THSUN Griffin grew concerned. He wasn't familiar with daily life in Reno, but even taking the loss of the world's satellites into account, guessed what he saw wasn't normal. The streets looked like one of those *End of the World* V-shows where everyone learned an asteroid was about to destroy the Earth.

Ignoring the helmet beside him, Griffin grabbed the radio. "Abdul, you seeing this?"

"Yeah, boss. I've lost all contact with NATUnet. There's nothing. Doesn't have anything to do with us, does it?"

"No. No way. Hopefully not." Griffin watched a man scream at an unresponsive palm-comp. "This isn't good. I'd been planning to call in back-up once we got close enough no one could beat us to the arrest."

"You haven't already arranged for back-up?" Abdul asked, incredulous. "There's just the two of us?"

"Unless NATUnet comes back on line."

***

Lokner was arranging the purchase of the main supplier of fibre-optics trunk-lines when the connection died. It wasn't just a dropped call—that he was grudgingly becoming accustomed to—but rather the loss of all communications outside of 5THSUN.

"Godammit!"

A quick check showed Mark he had no NATUnet feed at all. Every time he attempted to send data he received a 'Message Cached' response.

The walls felt like they crept a little closer. Mark

thought about crawling under the desk to his place of power.

"Hello?"

Nothing.

***

The private suborbital hadn't even taxied to a stop when an exit hatch sprung open and four Scan-driven Multi-Environment Combat Assault chassis dropped to the ground. 88 watched over conscripted airport security cameras—the colors faded to a monotonous gray-scale so as not to be too distracting—as her six Mirror-driven combat chassis remained motionless.

Was this part of the plan? Was Archaeidae doing something unpredictable? She checked the trunk-line for traffic and saw there was none. Archaeidae had failed to make a connection.

Should she send her chassis into battle without Archaeidae's guidance?

The 5THSUN chassis streaked across the tarmac towards her motionless chassis.

"Engage opponents," 88 ordered. "Destroy them." Though she understood Archaeidae's claim the Mirrors would be no match for the Scan-driven chassis, the six to four odds still looked promising. Could her Mirror driven chassis be that inferior? She worried that they were. Certainly Archaeidae thought so, and she had come to trust his judgment on such things.

Where is Archaeidae? Why isn't he here already? She felt naked and alone.

With two extra chassis on her side she instructed them to each attack a single opponent while the spares joined in to create two-on-one situations. It seemed a sound strategy.

The 5THSUN chassis had other plans. They spun a tight dance around one of her chassis, all concentrating their fire on the same target. They lanced frequency-stuttering pulse lasers and HEAP rockets and in less than three seconds the fight was five against four.

88 watched, paralyzed. Her Mirrors were outclassed. Unable to adapt to the mutating strategies of the Scan-driven chassis they were caught in deadly crossfires and unable to land a killing blow of their own. Desperate to give her chassis some edge, 88 ran statistical analysis to predict the Scans' next moves and was wrong every time. The Scans, often making what appeared to be suicidal choices, were devastatingly successful. Two of her remaining five chassis were already damaged and fighting at a fraction of their capacity.

They came for her and nothing would stop them. They would find her, fragile and defenseless, in the basement of her little shack. Death stalked her with a bloody red gleam in its Canon-Zuiko *Blissful Light* eyes.

88 cut the camera feed from the airport and floated in endless nothing. She needed to think. Sight was a distraction. So was fear. Even here she wanted the vibrating pillow. Some comfort. Someone to tell her it would be okay. She missed Mom now more than ever. The warmth of her arms, the smell of her sweat.

It couldn't end like this. Archaeidae. She needed Archaeidae.

Tearing herself away from the destruction of her Mirror-run chassis 88 searched for Archaeidae through the Reno NATU building. The offices and halls were littered with corpses, many lacked heads and limbs. This was not the plan Archaeidae spoke of. He was supposed to sneak in. Stealth, that was the plan.

That, 88 realized, was the problem with unpredictable.

Rage boiled out of the black, threatening to sweep away all thought. No longer floating in a sea of tranquil nothing, she tossed in the tornado of her emotions as her personal virtuality reacted to her mood. Control slipped away.

Archaeidae let me down! Jagged bolts of red lightning shattered the black.

My Mirrors failed me! Silence shredded in paroxysms of screaming fury.

"They're going to kill you," Mom had said. She'd been right. She was still right. They wouldn't let up until 88 was gone, all traces wiped out of existence.

The black returned. Ice cold and crystalline sterile. Blasted free of emotion. Survival was everything. The only thing. They had chosen to pit themselves against her. So be it.

But she was not alone.

88 tracked the trail of bloody destruction by flitting from camera to camera, she found Archaeidae in Server Room Three with four corpses piled at his feet. A single technician tapped madly at a desk, Archaeidae's sword at her throat. The floor glistened with blood, the door barricaded with haphazardly piled computer hardware. Beyond the door a dozen guards in MR combat armor and armed with heavy assault-rifles prepared to attempt a breech.

"There," said the technician. "I've done it. You've got total access. You'll let me—"

She was interrupted when Archaeidae pulled her head off and tossed it underhand toward the corner of the room. The body hosed a visceral spume of blood and toppled, adding one more to the pile.

"I'm in," said Archaeidae. "Come on five percent!"

A flicker of 88's attention and she was back with her Mirror-run chassis.

***

Archaeidae arrived in time to witness the death of another chassis as the 5THSUN machines savaged it. He twisted the two remaining chassis in unexpected directions, buying himself a fraction of a second to think.

Two left. That was it. That was everything.

Less data was moving, so that should be good, but the odds were not the six on four he'd been counting on.

This was no five percent.

Everything went black as he lost the feed and he used the milliseconds to replay the last few frames. The Juan Santamaria landing strip was a mess of scattered debris and chassis parts. All humans had retreated into the terminal and hanger bays, no doubt waiting for the military or some law enforcement agency to deal with this violent chaos. He knew where the 5THSUN chassis were two hundred milliseconds ago.

Just fucking great.

The feed returned, a torrential flood of sensory data.

Archaeidae filtered out all his own sensorial information so he could focus on that coming from the landing strip. He dared not think about what might be going on around his physical body. The slightest distraction could cost him everything.

The 5THSUN machines had moved. He launched an attack, spreading a hail of HEL pulses and HEAP rockets in the desperate hope of hitting something.

The feed from Costa Rica grew choppy again, stuttering as dozens of frames were dropped or lost in transition. For a full five-hundred milliseconds all was static and he was left looking at the last frame of action. It was like fighting high-speed ninjas in a strobe-lit room. He saw three frames, each staggered by one hundred milliseconds and sent more orders. No way of knowing if they got through or when they'd arrive.

Then everything synched up, as close to real time as he could ask for. The 5THSUN chassis were pulverizing one of his, pursuing it around the runway as it dodged and weaved. Archaeidae sent new orders. Move here. Target this. You, turn to—And then he bogged down, mired in the quick-sands of time, an entire second behind the action.

The universe stammered like a student driver alternating spastically between clutch and gas pedal. For two seconds Archaeidae's data feed dropped to three frames per second. When time lurched forward again one of his chassis remained operable, the other disintegrated on the tarmac. Three 5THSUN chassis against his one. He hadn't even seen the death of the 5THSUN machine, only the aftermath. His lag time dropped to under half a second, still too great for him to guarantee success.

Guarantee. Ha!

He was going to fail. Again. He failed Riina and now he'd fail the Empress.

Archaeidae, raised by Uncle Riina in an environment of *Victory or Death*, couldn't give up. He sent Plan B to 88 and assumed his Empress would see the logic and follow through. But Plan B required time and Archaeidae was about all out of that precious commodity.

The 5THSUN chassis circled, ensnaring and flanking him in preparation for his destruction.

Archaeidae saw it. So obvious.

He knew the 5THSUN Scans. Not personally, but he knew their lives. He knew their training. He knew how they thought. He knew every combat virtuality they'd ever played and what they'd done to beat it.

He knew them like he knew the limits of his favorite assassin chassis.

The data feed ran clean and he wasn't more than

fifty milliseconds behind the action.

If he turned and threatened this one with the pulse cannon, the chassis on the left would move in on his unprotected flank. He threatened, a bluff. He'd move right *there*. Archaeidae fired blindly at the vacant space to his left, unloading hellacious death on empty air. The 5THSUN chassis obediently stepped into the maelstrom as if on cue and was destroyed. The one he had threatened would have taken a defensive posture, seen the threat as a bluff, and the subsequent destruction of the other chassis, and would move *there*. Archaeidae, taking a few glancing blows from the third 5THSUN chassis' chain-gun, moved his chassis— a jet-assisted acrobat's tumble designed to look as if he'd lost control—relying more on the mental map in his mind than the data feed from Costa Rica. This should put the first chassis between Archaeidae and the last. The first, wanting the kill, would move in, thinking Archaeidae wounded and tumbling. The third chassis would shuffle left to get a clear line of fire.

Archaeidae moved and fired concurrent to thought. Even though his remote chassis tumbled chaotically, he was in complete control. He placed his shots with care, firing once again on empty space. The 5THSUN chassis filled that space and was blown to its component parts. The third chassis—

The data feed dropped out completely and Archaeidae stared at a pixelated rotating hourglass overlying the last frame he'd received.

No! *Where the fuck is it?* Had he got it?

And he stared at clear blue Costa Rican sky marred by the smoke rising from his mangled chassis. *Shit.* The Scan moved right instead of left. He played back the last fractions of a second in the top left corner of his visualization while simultaneously searching for his target and trying to get this last damaged chassis off the ground.

There—

Swarm-rockets hammered his chassis, killing what little mobility it had. Helpless rage filled Archaeidae as his final chassis lay bleeding fluids and parts across the airport grounds. His opponent, a chassis striped in a mottled gold and brown deepening to black towards its extremities, moved in for the kill. He could do nothing to stop it.

Archaeidae had zero mobility and just enough juice to fire the jump-jets for a fraction of a second. So close. But he must stall the last chassis, if only for a few seconds.

"You think you win?" asked Archaeidae through the Mirror's chassis. "You think this fight is yours?" Archaeidae knew the Scan running the other chassis was someone much like himself, someone born and raised in the competitive world of virtual combat. Someone unable to resist the chance to brag over a downed and harmless foe.

The 5THSUN chassis stopped. "You are defeated. I win." It sounded less than happy with its victory. Strange.

"Not quite. As long as you die, *I* win." Archaeidae found himself staring up the barrel of a hyper-kinetic gauss gun.

His opponent glanced at the wreckage of chassis littering the landing field. "Everyone dies," the chassis said. "But you're the one dying right here."

"I'm in Reno. But you're fucked."

The recently departed Airbus A340, now under the guidance of 88.1.42.147.321.3417, returned in a mad descent.

***

Canebrake finally heard and saw the diving plane and searched for cover. His opponent used his brief distraction for one last push of jump-assist jets and managed to get close enough to achieve a death grip on his chassis. Realizing he had failed, Canebrake prayed for a redemption he had come to doubt. There was no second life, no replaying this level. It was done.

Uncle Riina, why have you forsaken me?

He triggered the micro-nuke buried within his chassis as well as those within his friends, Red-Back, Boomslang, and Siafu.

The micro-nukes leveled the airport terminals, caused nearby planes to explode, and were eclipsed when the A340 crashed to the earth carrying 204,500 liters of Avgas and 364 passengers.

Juan Santamaria International Airport was a thing of the past.

***

Archaeidae didn't even want to think about his body count for the day. There must be hundreds dead, thousands of injuries, and thousands more would die of cancer-related complications in the years to come. He wasn't proud. Uncle Riina always scolded him if his hits attracted too much media attention, and this one would be in the news for weeks.

That last Scan had thought it had won, and yet sounded unhappy. Sad, even. Like victory wasn't everything. That Scan's friends had been littered about the airfield. Archaeidae thought back to how he had felt upon learning of SwampJack and Wandering Spider's noble deaths. He'd been saddened, but proud. He always knew they'd come back, they always did.

Where then is SwampJack?

Deep down Archaeidae knew he was gone. He'd never again hear Swamp crow over his headshots or

Spider chastising her best friend's immature recklessness. Their deaths had been permanent.

He thought about the hundreds of deaths he'd caused in the last few minutes. He'd told *Jotei* 88 to bring down a plane full of passengers as a casual Plan B. He hadn't given it much thought, the plane was there and he needed it.

Those people were gone. Dead. Forever.

He thought back to the pitying disgust he'd seen on the faces of the NATU agent and his partner when he'd told them he was immortal. He was wrong, and they'd known it.

Now is not the time for such thoughts. He needed to be pure. He needed to keep moving. There might be costs to his actions, but that didn't change anything. Well...it didn't change everything. He still had to make sure *Jotei* 88 was safe. He'd promised, and his promises were iron.

Archaeidae jacked out of the NATUnet hub to the sound of alarms and panicked voices. The door he had barricaded was being shoved open. Someone on the far side tossed a flashbang grenade into the room which he caught and tossed back before slamming the door closed.

With the distraction of the flashbang, maybe he could get out without killing everybody. Leave witnesses. On purpose. It was a strange thought.

He felt the concussive detonation through the door.

Humans. They could be such a pain in the ass.

CHAPTER THIRTY: Sunday, August 6th, 2046

Having rooted through Lokner's lawyer's files and deleted all traces of any file bearing his name or mention of M-Sof or 5THSUN, Miles sat with his feet up, staring out the window at Reno's skyline. His desk beeped error messages but he ignored it.

Where else would Lokner hide files? The man was smart, but not particularly inventive. He'd want to put it where Miles would never think to look. Where wouldn't he search for files?

Well, his own in-house data systems for one.

Duh. Miles searched 5THSUN's internal data systems. Sure enough, he found hidden folders with reams of files detailing his less than legal actions. There was a fair amount of stuff in there he hadn't done too.

The desk chirped for attention. An incoming call.

"Yes?" He already knew who it was.

"For fuck-sakes Miles, it's one in the afternoon! Wake the fuck up. I've lost the NATUnet feed."

"Probably just a bad connection. With the satellites —"

"No connection, no data. Nothing. Now fucking fix it."

Miles glanced at his desk, scanning the long list of

errors and the backed-up data transmissions cached for future transfer. "Hold on a second," he told Lokner, putting him on hold as he called Ruprecht downstairs.

"So I guess you've finally noticed," said Ruprecht when he answered.

"You could have let me know."

"No point," said Ruprecht. "Nothing you can do about it."

Miles understood. The Sys Admin code: If I can't fix it, it isn't my problem. Don't waste my time.

"Is it only 5THSUN this is happening to?" Miles asked.

"Are you serious? Go look out your window."

Miles rose from behind the desk and walked to the window. The streets below were in chaos. Bankers fought over bike couriers and taxis, desperate to get their data moved by any means possible. Fists and ties flew. Miles watched as an expensive business suit knocked down a scraggly courier in combat fatigues and wrestled the bike away from her. Should he go down to see if she was okay? The suit stomped on the courier's hand and mounted the bike. A bundle of hard-copy investment information tucked under one arm, he headed north toward the financial district.

This is insane.

Returning to his desk Miles collapsed into the chair. Surely he should be doing something. "Aren't we supposed to be three meals away from chaos?" he said to Ruprecht.

"Three days. Nine meals. For most of us. Maybe three meals for you."

"Thanks. So this the end of civilization."

"Probably. About what I expected. NATUnet has gone down. Rumor is it's down all across NATU and into Central America."

"How'd the rumor spread if there's no network?"

"Good question," said Ruprecht.

"I have someone on hold. We'll talk later. Let me know if the world ends."

"Gotcha."

Miles flicked back to Lokner. "Looks like NATUnet is down everywhere, Sir."

"Shit. How long is this going to take to fix?"

Fix? How the hell could he fix this? "Uh, Sir, it's kind of out of my hands. Nothing we can do but wait."

"Is this an attack? On me?"

Miles heard the quiver of paranoia in his boss' voice. It was unsettling to hear fear coming from this man. The original Lokner had always shown all the emotions of a rock. But that was a different man.

"No, Sir," said Miles. "It looks like all Reno is affected. Probably some hacker-clan snuck a virus into the NATU central systems and shut everything down. I'd guess it'll all be back up and running within the hour. Probably less."

"Aw fuck," Mark whined. "No data feed in here. What am I going to do?"

"Play some crossword puzzles," snapped Miles as he killed the call. He was amazed. Amazed he snapped at his boss, and equally amazed Lokner seemed to be acting like a spoiled pre-teen. Something was wrong with Lokner2.0. Maybe the copy process was, he thought sarcastically, a little less successful than the doctors claimed. This wasn't the same man he used to work for.

Miles stared at the data he'd discovered, a long litany of his criminal activities. He'd delete all this, but what if there was more? Something caught his eye and he sat up.

Wait. I never purchased micro-nukes off the Mafia!

"Oh shit."

He stood and glanced out the office window at the

chaos below. A NATU military truck came to a tire-screeching halt in front of 5THSUN. A vicious looking chassis, obviously a military model, bounded from the back of the truck and disappeared into the ground floor lobby without pausing to open the massive plate-glass doors.

"Oh *shit*!"

A gray-haired man climbed from the front of the truck and hurried after the chassis, toting what looked like an assault rifle of some kind. Confused and unsure what to do, Miles called Ruprecht again.

"What's up, Miles?"

"NATU just came through the front door. They look serious."

"Serious? Like waving subpoenas serious?"

"No. Like fuck the subpoena, we have a combat chassis serious. Get out the back if you can, otherwise put your hands in the air, be polite, and co-operate with the nice authorities."

"What are you going to do?"

Miles glanced around the office, looking longingly at his SmartChair. His thoughts scattered like a flock of panicked chickens and achieved nothing useful. "I don't know."

"Get the fuck out." Ruprecht paused and Miles heard him gathering his belongings. "Call me from prison, bud."

Miles looked at his desk, thought about the deadman's switch. Was it time? No. Ruprecht was right. Just get out.

He heard the faint but unmistakable sound of gunfire from somewhere below.

***

The truck hadn't yet stopped when Griffin saw Abdul

bounce past and crash straight through the plate glass doors of 5THSUN Assessments. The speed of the large chassis was terrifying. That something so large, so deadly, and so heavy could move so quickly triggered all manner of deep instinctual fears in Griffin. Abdul vanished from sight before the broken glass from the door hit ground. Griffin assumed the Scan knew something he didn't and scrambled out of the truck, forgetting both the helmet and filter mask. The air tasted terrible as he charged up the steps, Tavor 41 in hand. He stopped in the lobby to spit out a thick wad of gritty black phlegm. The fingers of his right hand had turned a yellowish blue, and felt like someone was trying to cauterize them with a blowtorch. His guts clenched with tension and he breathed in short painful grunts.

Tasteful and expensive, the lobby was the perfect portrait of the corporate mind. Thousands of kilograms of white and black marble in contrasting patterns with gleaming brass trim, all designed to say money lived here.

The cold weight of the assault rifle felt reassuring but his hand kept shaking. Nadia's voice flashed through his mind: "Safety's still on."

Was that the last thing she said to him? He couldn't remember. Adrenalin and fear jolted him to the present. The realization of his vulnerability in a fight involving combat chassis sunk in, and he froze. Eyes wide. Mouth open, breath coming in short hyperventilating pants. Gun up, he pointed at everything and nothing. Sweat trickled from his hair and he blinked furiously, eyes stinging. The street noise faded and all he heard was his own breathing.

Blink away the sweat. Eyes twitched in search of threats and targets.

The high-pitched scream of a hyperkinetic gauss gun startled him, and without a thought he charged towards the noise.

Abdul might be in trouble.

***

Trouble. It waited somewhere. Abdul had thought about it for the entire drive to 5THSUN. Griffin was right; if they did this the civil way, Lokner would get away. And with half a dozen state-of-the-art combat chassis piloted by brainwashed and insanely loyal children, there was slim chance of Griffin getting out alive. The moment their Master was in danger they would kill everything.

He had to keep Griffin alive, no matter what the cost. Fuck the law. Surprise and speed were his best weapons. He scanned the ground floor with all the senses available to him. Nothing.

There had to be at least one chassis on the ground floor, but Abdul detected nothing.

Abdul moved, hitting the limit of what his chassis could do. Warnings flared bright across his vision as he redlined the chassis. His thoughts roared with the exhilaration of impossible speed and for this one instant he felt alive. All life was movement.

He burst into a second lobby in the rear of the building where the elevators were. A gauss gun screamed a few thousand rounds of exploding flechettes, tore up the expensive marble and filled the air with shattered stone and dust. Few of them struck home, and Abdul ignored them. His targeting diagnostics traced both the arc of the flechettes and the sound of the weapon back to a point source.

There was nothing there. This year's tech. Maybe next year's.

God he was so royally fucked.

Abdul sliced two 83mm High Explosive Anti-Armor rockets into the emptiness and was rewarded with a satisfying explosion. Dust and plaster rained from the ceiling in a thick white fog shredding his higher frequency senses. It was like watching an old black and white movie through a snow squall and the caustic glare of a carbon-arc strobe light. Infrared and radar gave him enough to know he'd walked into a trap.

***

Androctonus and SawScale had been playing *Assault on 5THSUN* virtualities for days and were more than ready when NATUnet crashed. Though in all likelihood it had nothing to do with them or their Master, they were not going to take that risk. Androctonus was upset he wasn't leading the other four chassis in Costa Rica on an exciting Strike Mission. He and SawScale were the only defense left. Barring paramilitary troops parachuting to the rooftop or cruising in on ultralight gliders, everyone had to come through the rear lobby to access either the elevators or stairs. It was the clear choice for an ambush site. When they heard the sound of shattering glass they pushed their chassis into Stealth Mode. Chameleoflage blended with their surroundings. Armor plates adjusted their angles and exuded a rubberized polymer. They were invisible to both radar and sonar. They locked down all vented heat, storing it internally to be released once combat commenced. Total silence. Not even tight-link.

This was what they lived for.

The NATU chassis exploded into the room far faster than a chassis of that design should be moving. Androctonus felt the entire universe hum like a vibroblade. All his life had built to this moment. Today he proved his worth. He would do Uncle Riina proud.

The NATU chassis definitely expected trouble. It

came to the right place.

As planned, SawScale broke cover first, following it with a long stream of exploding flechettes, most of which missed. The invading chassis bounced off the far wall, changing direction in mid-flight with a burst of its jump-assist jets. Whoever was in there was no slouch and wore their chassis like skin.

Good. Be a shame if this were too easy.

The NATU chassis' missiles streaked towards SawScale and he attempted to gun them down in mid-flight. He failed. Androctonus unleashed a strobing pulse from his Northrop Grumman High Energy Laser. The NATU chassis changed direction again and he lost the lock, but not before he'd caused massive structural damage to its entire right side. The HEL pulses ignited the dust and plaster in the air, drawing a neat line pointing to his position. His treads engaged and spun him away from his hiding spot before the enemy hammered it with missiles.

Sawscale erupted with enough force to rock Androctonus in his treads. Some critical system must have been damaged.

See you on the next level, brother, he tight-linked at the remains.

Androctonus tracked the NATU chassis with a blistering hail of Smart micro-rockets, HEL pulses, and hyper-kinetic flechettes.

***

Half of Abdul's torso lit up with error messages. One of the Talley Defense Systems rocket tubes was damaged beyond use, and the other flashed a confused jumble of malfunction warnings and modified Chinese tech-lingo warranty information. Warranty Void, *Gweilo*.

When he managed to target the second chassis, he

wanted to cry out with relief. Its motive abilities were hampered by a tank-track designed to not damage expensive marble and carpeted floors.

That relief died a fast and brutal death when Abdul launched a rocket and the 5THSUN chassis gunned the rocket out of the air the instant it left the launcher. The resulting explosion damaged the tube beyond use and the flashing Chinese text flickered before fading like a ghost meeting the harsh light of day. Though his superior mobility kept him alive, Abdul was outgunned. It would pick him apart. Desperate he drove his chassis even harder and systems overheated and shut down with wails of defeat. The 5THSUN chassis' reaction times were too fast. It used its HEL pulse to sweep Abdul's flechettes from the air, detonating most, and turning the rest into tumbling misshapen nuggets of molten metal and plastic the chassis' armor ignored.

He couldn't hurt it and he couldn't avoid its attacks for much longer. Maybe he could—

Motion from the front lobby hall.

"No!"

***

Griffin followed the sound of gunfire. The air was thick with dust and debris and he squinted to see through it. A chunk of marble hissed past so fast he didn't see it and he realized how vulnerable he was. His face stung where tiny fragments had embedded themselves in his flesh. Blood trickled down his cheeks like tears. He felt soft and breakable.

Swallow the fear. Keep moving.

Abdul came into view for a fraction of a second. The chassis was on the floor, on the wall, bouncing off the ceiling. He disappeared. A cacophonous maelstrom of devastation followed his every movement.

Abdul was running for his life.

Griffin had to help. He crept forward. The Tavor felt heavy. He didn't know what he planned. Perhaps he could shoot the enemy somewhere vulnerable, or distract it for a critical moment. The sound was deafening. His tongue was thick with grit and his throat caked with chalky taste of plaster dust.

Stupid. But he had to try.

He stepped into the room, saw the 5THSUN chassis and brought his gun to bear. Maybe he heard the word "No!" shouted over the sounds of destruction. Everything moved too fast.

Compared to the two combat chassis, Griffin moved like he stood neck deep in porridge. Reality was something he only saw after it happened. He was still thinking about squeezing the trigger and the 5THSUN chassis had already turned a weapon in his direction.

It knew he was there. Synapses fired, sent impulses crawling along sludgy biological nerves. Pull. The. Trigger.

Abdul changed direction so suddenly his chassis shed parts and sparked in protest. His mad dive landed him between Griffin and the 5THSUN chassis. An explosion mashed Griffin to the ground as if by the very hand of God. His head rebounded off the marble with a hollow *thunk* and he tasted battery acid and blood. He saw sparks through the swirling plaster snowstorm and didn't know if they were real or an artifact of damaged retinas. Another explosion silhouetted Abdul and the chassis didn't move. Pieces of his friend scattered across the floor. At least two limbs were missing. Stuttering stabs of light picked at Abdul like a deranged Houngan savaging a rag doll with needles.

Griffin sat up, the Tavor still clenched in his fists. He pushed himself to his feet and took aim at the 5THSUN chassis.

His right hand didn't shake any more.

"Get away from my friend."

***

Androctonus, detecting motion from the front hall, launched rockets and HEL pulses without even looking. It was a biological human and no real threat. Still, you didn't get points for being sloppy. Then, his opponent hurled himself into the path of this attack. When the NATU chassis crashed to the ground like a ballet dancer struck with quadriplegia in mid leap, Androctonus knew he had won. He pounded the chassis with a few more micro-rockets and HEL pulses to be sure.

"Get away from my friend."

Amazing! The human was still alive!

Androctonus focused on the rifle: Tavor 41 with a single shot grenade launcher mounted under the barrel. That could be dangerous. He watched the tendon's on the man's wrist contract and computed the most likely trajectory for the grenade. He moved before the finger had completed squeezing the trigger. Compared to a rifle round, the grenade moved at a glacial pace.

Master Lokner, he tight-linked. *I have a NATU agent here. Shall I dispose of him?*

The NATU agent advanced, opening up with the assault rifle, spraying fifteen rounds per second. Give the man credit for being brave. Or dumb as a stick.

Somewhere behind Androctonus the grenade hit the wall and exploded.

NATU agent? Lokner finally replied. *Interesting. Bring him up.*

CHAPTER THIRTY-ONE: Sunday, August 6th, 2046

Miles threw open his office door. "Christie. We've got to get out of here."

She looked up from her desk. "That noise—"

"Gunfire. We have to—" A long barrage of explosions interrupted him.

Whatever was happening down there, it sounded like a bad place to be. But he didn't want to be up here either. He stared at Christie trying to formulate a plan. Nothing. Couldn't leave. Couldn't stay. *Damn it! Think!*

Christie's dark almond eyes were wide. "What's going on? What's happening down there?"

"It's NATU. I think they're here for Lokner."

"Lokner?" she asked, confused.

"Don't ask. We have to leave—"

"I've locked the stairway fire doors, and all elevators are under my control." Lokner's voice echoed over the intercom.

Christie jumped at the tinny voice. "Who?"

"Lokner," said Miles.

"Miles, please escort your secretary to your office and await further orders."

"Let her go, Mister Lokner. She's not part of this. I'll stay and we'll figure out how to get out of this mess."

"No. You told her who I am. Anything that happens to her now is your fault." Lokner sounded calm, but there was something to his voice like he found this terribly amusing.

"Let her—"

"She stays," stated Lokner with finality. "I'm having Androctonus bring up the NATU agent. We'll have a pleasant little conversation. Maybe we can straighten all this out."

The smug satisfaction in Lokner's voice hardened Miles' resolve. The man was crazy. He had to be stopped. How did Lokner think this would end? The answer was obvious. Lokner had ties with organized crime and was involved with crèches. He'd have no compunction killing the two of them. And Androctonus was on his way up. He'd be there any second. They had to move now.

Miles led Christie into his office.

Micro-nukes. Did Lokner have micro-nukes? That would be crazy! But then...

Was he really going to do this? Planning the deadman's switch was one thing. Using it was something else. He'd never hurt anyone in his life, and now he planned on threatening a man with death.

Miles shivered. He wanted to cry, but no way he'd show that kind of weakness in front of Christie. Collapsing into his SmartChair he looked away from Christie, afraid to make eye contact. She mustn't see he had a plan. Her reaction might warn Lokner.

***

Griffin advanced, gun raised, emptying the clip in the general direction of the 5THSUN chassis. It flowed like water, and he chased it with a hail of Depleted Uranium Core rounds.

The hammer fell with a click that echoed around the marble lobby. The Tavor was empty. The chassis lunged forward and ripped the gun from his hands, breaking three of his fingers and tearing flesh from bone. Griffin screamed and dropped to the ground, clutching his bloody right hand. His darkening fingers now sent messages of screaming agony and burned like they were being held in a pot of hydrochloric acid. He huddled them against his chest protectively as the 5THSUN chassis sunk claws through the MR armor and deep into his shoulder. Griffin screamed again.

It was going to kill him. Rip him in half.

Instead it dragged him up off the floor, lifted him like he was nothing. It stood him upright and let go. Only sheer force of will and a fistful of amphetamines kept him from crumpling back to the marble.

Still alive. Mostly. But why? What could it want?

Nothing good.

The chassis shoved Griffin past the ruins of Abdul and toward the elevator. He stumbled as the doors slid open and he fell inside. Unable to extend a hand to catch himself he landed awkwardly, crushing the air from his lungs. He lay wheezing on the elevator floor. The chassis joined him in the elevator. Again it sank claws into his shoulder and dragged him upright. When it let go he sagged into the corner, putting as much distance as he could between himself and the chassis. He kept seeing the blasted ruins of Abdul. What had he done?

"*Yuuki o dashite*," said the 5THSUN chassis, sounding annoyed.

"What?" Griffin croaked, his throat thick with dust.

"Be brave. Don't embarrass yourself."

"Oh." Griffin stared at the chassis, its back turned contemptuously toward him. He was no threat. Blood leaked hot from the wounds in his shoulder. "Fuck you."

"That's better," said the chassis. The door hissed open and the elevator deposited them on the top floor. "But a little predictable."

***

Miles watched Androctonus shove the NATU agent into his office. The hand clutched to the agent's chest showed fingers bent at painful angles. Covered in a thick layer of plaster dust, he looked otherwise unhurt. While all attention was on the new arrival Miles tapped a short custom command line on the desktop. If anyone noticed, they'd mistake it for a nervous drumming. Not too far from the truth. He had to repeat the command twice to get it right.

The deadman's switch was armed but not yet triggered.

Please don't let it come to that. There must be some other way out of this.

***

Griffin took in the room. An overweight man with long red dreadlocks sat slumped at a desk. A pretty Asian woman stood beside him, her hand resting on his shoulder. Lokner was nowhere in sight.

"This is it?" An incredulous voice over the intercom. "They send one lousy beaten up agent for *me*?" The voice snarled something inarticulate then said, "Who the hell are you?"

That must be Lokner.

Dazed, Griffin fell back on routine. He repeated what he'd memorized by rote in the academy. "I am NATU Special Investigations Agent Griffin Dickinson. Mark Lokner, I have a warrant for your arrest as well as Search and Seizure papers for all 5THSUN Assessments property and chattels including, but not limited to, all data and information stored in any medium."

The fat guy, whose clothes did not at all fit the corporate profile, twitched his lips as if unwilling to commit to a full smile. They made eye contact and held it. The red dreads nodded almost imperceptibly. There was something there, but Griffin didn't yet know what.

A grating screech of static sounded over the intercom. Was that laughter?

"Chattel!" Mark screamed. "You think I'm fucking *chattel*? I am everything. I'm the god-damned future! Death is dead. *I* killed it."

"You're finished Lokner," said Griffin. "Too many people know."

A squeal of high-pitched giggling cracked through the small speaker. "Because I would not stop for death, the fucker stopped for me. You know who that is, Agent Dickinson?"

Griffin sagged against a bookcase for support. Lokner sounded deranged. He didn't feel ready for this. "No."

"Emily Dickinson. Sort of."

"No relation," said Griffin.

"All children and school buses and horse heads—but the first line was great." There was a quick, bitten off cackle. "Well, after I fixed it."

The flood of adrenaline soured and drained into Griffin's stomach. It hung there, heavy and fermenting. He had nothing left for this madman.

"Nothing, Agent Dickinson?" crowed Lokner. "You didn't get it did you? Everyone dies. No one *wants* to die. "

***

Lokner looked down upon the room from his viewpoint within the building's security cameras. Most of the cameras downstairs were dead, victims of the battle with the NATU chassis. Miles looked like he wanted to cry, and the NATU agent was so unsteady he might fall over dead at any time.

"You'll be a client of mine before long, Agent Dickinson," Lokner joked.

Dickinson looked confused. Why couldn't they see what was plainly obvious? It was like talking to a room full of poorly trained baboons. The thought of Miles with a big red bottom gave Lokner another fit of tittering giggles he had trouble controlling. He was too damned funny!

Death brought a whole new perspective to humor.

Never mind. He wasted precious breath on these simpletons.

Wait. He didn't breathe so it couldn't be wasted. Ah! But his time *was* being wasted. That was still real, right?

He heard quiet but insistent scratching at his office door.

"Not now, we're about to win."

"Pardon?" said Dickinson.

"Nothing. Androctonus—"

Miles interrupted. "You're going to kill us, aren't you?"

"It's simple math, Miles. Really, what choice do I have?" He asked the question honestly but they failed to answer.

Fingers drumming nervously, Miles sat at his desk like a strawberry-topped vanilla pudding in black shorts. He filled the over-priced SmartChair to bursting.

Is he blinking back tears? Pathetic.

***

"It's not math," Miles protested. "Don't distance yourself from what you are about to do."

"About to do?" Lokner sounded surprised. "Androctonus will handle the *doing*. My hands are clean. There's no such thing as virtual guilt."

"But—" Miles stopped himself. Christie's hand on his shoulder squeezed tight as if to say, *do it. Do it now.* The NATU agent was either watching calmly or about to lose consciousness. Hard to tell. "You're an asshole. You can't believe you aren't responsible."

"This is a waste of time. Androcto—"

"You missed something," said Miles. He turned to meet Christie's stare, but saw agent Dickinson's smile out of the corner of his eye.

"I am?"

"I'm Root."

"So?"

"Where you are, asshole," Miles snarled through gritted teeth. "Root is *God*."

Lokner made a *pfft* sound. "You're bluffing, fat man."

Miles touched his desktop. "See the big digital display on your office wall?"

Lokner hesitated and Miles knew he was staring at the massive red numbers that had appeared on the far wall of his virtual office. "Yes."

"You understand what that is, right? You understand what it's telling you?"

"You're too dangerous to be allowed to live."

Miles swallowed. That was one way of looking at it. Of course Lokner went there first. Could he defuse the situation? Lokner was crazy but still rational, right? Was that even possible? He didn't like the answer he saw.

"I am no more dangerous now than ever," said Miles. "You never understood the true balance of power in our relationship." As soon as he said it he realized it was a mistake.

"You have no idea who you're fucking with," said Lokner, voice taut and angry.

"I know *exactly* who I'm fucking with. And you scare the crap out of me."

**

Since the 5THSUN chassis dragged him in here, Griffin had watched the big man, Miles, tap at his desk. He stared at the man's clothes; the *Schrödinger's Cat: Wanted Dead & Alive* t-shirt, the brand new black shorts. Those clothes, flying in the face of corporate dress codes, were no accident. He'd seen people who dressed like this before.

Lokner and Miles weren't far off bickering like children. He suspected he'd walked into the middle of something that had been building for a while. He felt lost, like he'd missed something important. Glancing over to the young Asian woman, he could tell she felt the same.

Lokner snorted. "You don't have the balls."

Miles rubbed at his eyes and sat back, as if distancing himself from his desk. "You know I can't lie worth a damn. So I'm not lying."

**

Miles told the truth, Lokner heard it in his voice. Mark looked around his bare office. The door had crept closer, grown bigger. The scratching grew in volume. They waited, salivating, outside his office door. He heard them breathe. They wanted in. It was difficult to think. He wanted to crawl under his desk to his place of power.

Not yet, he could beat this fat fuck.

Lokner played out various scenarios in his mind, different possible outcomes stemming from his limited choices. He saw it immediately. The game wasn't over. Miles hadn't thought this through. Lokner knew Miles didn't have the stomach for murder. No way he'd let Lokner die as long as he got what he wanted. All Mark had to do was let Miles think he'd won.

Miles, guessed Mark, had figured Lokner would be forced to let him leave and then Miles could stop the countdown from anywhere. But with NATUnet down and all communications dead, there was only one place Miles could stop the countdown: right here in his office. It was so funny that Lokner had to kill the feed to the intercom while he choked down wails of uncontrollable laughter.

There is a god! Could there be any more incontrovertible proof?

He might have to let the woman and NATU agent go, but he could send Androctonus to kill them once he dealt with Miles. He turned the intercom back on. He had to play this right. The perfect amount of desperation.

"We can deal, right? You're not going to kill me, are you?"

The camera feed from Miles' office flickered and died. Damn it! Had Miles done that? Didn't matter. Lokner didn't need to see to beat the likes of Miles. This was a battle of wits.

***

The confidence drained from Lokner's voice and everyone heard it.

Miles felt a tug of pity for the Scan, and struggled to quash it. Lokner was dangerous and deranged.

"I can reset the countdown," said Miles, "and I can stop it. But I won't until we're safe. I don't trust you. Once

Androctonus is long gone, we can talk."

Noticing Agent Dickinson staring past Androctonus, Miles turned to see what had his attention. There, standing in the doorway, was a tall thin figure in a shredded and blood soaked tan duster-coat that hung to the floor. A huge black cowboy hat, pulled low, shadowed its face. The cowboy apparition raised its head and Miles stared into demonic red eyes set deep in a chrome death's head. The cowboy showed gleaming fangs clutching a ragged cigar stump. The tan duster fell open, exposing two matching Japanese swords.

***

Androctonus was surprised when Miles looked right past him. He realized everyone was looking past him. His mind kicked into combat mode. They were trying to fool him into thinking there was something behind him but there couldn't be. That chassis he trashed in the lobby couldn't possibly be operational enough to make it up here without Androctonus hearing it. *It must be Sawscale, reborn already!* Androctonus turned, torso spinning as the tank treads stayed in place. His left arm tumbled away as something sheared through it at blistering speed. Alarms informed him his armor had been penetrated.

And again. And again.

Androctonus saw the samurai-cowboy as a Japanese sword entered his armor with impossible ease. It wasn't Sawscale returned to life as Riina had promised.

This wasn't right, they always—

***

Archaeidae looked at the gathered humans. He slid the katana free from the motionless chassis and held it up to show them. The edge of the blade was smoky and difficult to focus on.

"Monofilament edge on a ceramo-polymer-whatchamacallit composite blade. The Empress gave it to me." He returned the katana to its place at his side.

A small domed cleaning drone, less than three feet tall and half that width, followed Archaeidae into the office like an obedient dog. In its extended manipulators hung a plastic and steel box, medical white and not much larger than a human skull. One side of the box was transparent, displaying its empty innards.

Agent Dickinson, slumped against a bookcase, shook his head as if in denial. "Archaeidae?"

Archaeidae gave a deep bow.

Both *Jotei* 88 and *Shogun* 88.1 watched the proceedings, riding piggy-back on Archaeidae's sensoria, surfing the conscripted NATUnet bandwidth.

88, who had yet to relinquish her control of NATUnet, allowed 88.1 to speak to Archaeidae over the tight-link. *The big one at the desk is Miles Pert. He designed M-Sof's defenses. He is the one I want.*

Archaeidae extended a hand and the Mirror-driven cleaning drone handed him the Brainbox. He turned to the fat man sitting at the desk. "Please remain seated but move away from the desk."

"Why?" asked Miles, glancing around the office. He stayed put, one hand still resting on the desk as if by retaining contact with it he kept some measure of control. He was wrong.

The katana licked out of its sheath, rapped Miles stingingly on the back of his hand, and returned to the scabbard before the glacially slow human even knew the chassis had moved.

Flawless *Iaidō*. Machine precision.

"Move now or die."

Miles stared at his knuckles as they turned red and began to swell. "Ow!" Still seated, he slid the SmartChair away from the desk. It glided over the thick carpeting.

Griffin, eyeing where the 5THSUN chassis dropped his Tavor 41, tensed.

"I see you have a new hand," said Archaeidae. "Be a shame to lose it again so soon." Not that it mattered. The gun was empty. He could tell by the way it bounced when it landed.

Archaeidae moved closer to Miles, the snaky, sinuous move of a dancer. Silent and ever poised. "You have a choice to make, Miles." He waited until the fat man was looking at him and held up the Brainbox. "It seems your skills with data systems and fire-walls have caught his interest."

"No." The fat man face turned red and his breath came in short gasps. "Please, no."

"You intrigue him. He wants your brain."

Miles looked to be on the edge of panic. His voice squeaked, "He?"

"88.1, *Shogun* to *Jotei* 88."

Miles' eyes widened with bewilderment. "Empress? What the—Is this some kind of game you're playing?" His face flushed with anger and fear and sweat stood beaded on his forehead. "Well...well I'm not playing! You can't take my head."

"Can and will. The question is, do I cut it from your body and stuff it in the box after the fact, or will you go with some shred of dignity?"

Shaking his head Miles backed the chair away from Archaeidae who followed in a menacing glide. "No."

"Do not make the mistake of thinking we are negotiating. Mine is the stronger will. I define this reality."

Miles' eyes were bright and wet. "You define this reality? You're insane!"

Archaeidae, watching everything in three-hundred and sixty degrees, saw Agent Dickinson's eyes dart towards the hall. He saw the man's thoughts writ plainly on his face. "Don't be silly Dickinson, there's no escape." He cornered Miles. "Why are you being difficult? It's not like you're going to die."

***

Incredulous, Miles retreated to sarcasm in self-defense. "You're going to chop off my head. That sounds a *lot* like death to me."

"What the hell is going on?" snapped Lokner.

"Shut up." Archaeidae shook his head. "You people have neither *meiyo*, nor *yū*. No honor, or courage."

Lokner remained quiet, but the silence was palpable.

Eyes fixed on Archaeidae, Miles said, "Can't I meet this *Jotei* 88? Can't she ask me a few questions and let me go?"

"No."

Miles continued to back away, still sitting in his chair.

"Fine," said Archaeidae, sounding annoyed. He turned and advanced on Christie. "I'll brutally murder her first; death by a thousand cuts. You get to watch. I'll peel her like a grape and take your head when I'm finished. Is *that* unpleasant enough?" The assassin chassis sounded like an exasperated child.

Miles looked at Christie, her eyes imploring him to find a way out, to somehow stay this execution. He shook his head and mouthed the word *sorry*. *Not really death*, he told himself. *Not really death.*

"Okay," said Miles to Archaeidae. "You win. It's all right, Christie."

Christie's eyes were red and tears streamed down her cheeks leaving dark stained trails of eyeliner.

"I wish I'd asked you out," said Miles.

"Me too," she said.

Archaeidae, he realized, now stood behind his chair. Miles hadn't even seen him move. This assassin wanted to see some *yū*? Fine. "What are we waiting for?"

The chassis twitched. Miles' dreads fell away to the floor. For the first time in years he felt a cool breeze on the back of his neck. It was cold. The box dropped over Miles' head and the sounds of the office became tinny, muted and distant. He heard the wash of the ocean like he had both ears pressed against conch shells. He looked out the transparent faceplate and saw Christie raise a hand towards him, slim fingers spread as if she'd catch his soul. Miles didn't even believe in souls.

Hey, about to die and still an atheist. Not bad, he was impressed with himself. His gaze darted around, drinking in every last detail in the room. Did they have to make this thing so he could see out?

He heard a quiet *sip* and his ears popped.

That was weird.

Christie's eyes widened and her mouth opened in a scream. Distant and muffled, Miles hardly heard it. She crumpled to the ground, catching her temple on the corner of the desk. And then his view spun dizzyingly and he faced the NATU agent.

Wait! He was still alive! It hadn't worked! He peered out of the corner of his eye, trying to catch a glimpse of his body. Was that blood? The carpet seemed to be changing color. Everything went gray.

***

Lokner tried the tight-link. *Androctonus? Hello?*

Answer me god damn it!

Nothing.

Sawscale? Anybody?

Nothing.

What the hell was going on out there? There was someone new in the room. There were definite threats of violence. Who was it? Who did they represent?

His office shrank with a shuddering wrench and the door loomed, towering twenty feet tall over his desk. The countdown on the wall was so huge and bright he cringed from its fierce light.

No. No.

The door bulged inwards from the weight of the terrible souls pressing against it.

Lokner, unable to do more than listen to the events unfolding, crawled under his desk. Vulnerable and alone, he'd been abandoned by everyone. His Cc-Security chassis were all dead. Miles had betrayed him. The things at the door grew stronger by the second. He felt them pushing, straining to get in.

They want their revenge.

***

Griffin watched the Brainbox settle on Miles' shoulders. He wanted to dive forward, tear the box free, and wrestle it away from the assassin chassis. Even if he died, at least it would be a hero's death. But he couldn't. His body refused to move. How had Abdul done it? How had he hurled himself between Griffin and death? Did he not have time to think about it?

The box swung away from Miles' body, which remained sitting upright in the chair hosing great gouts of blood from the crisply sliced carotid artery. The breath Miles had been holding gushed out the severed neck in a wet vomit of blood and escaping air. The corpse seemed to deflate before Griffin's eyes. The legs and arms shuddered for a few seconds and then fell still. A piece of meat.

So fixated on watching the corpse, Griffin hadn't noticed Christie faint until she lay on the ground, temple swelling. He turned to Archaeidae and found himself staring Miles in the face. The eyes blinked. Griffin watched, mesmerized. The eyes glazed over, and a soft green light and polite *ping* emanated from the Brainbox.

"Hey, he blinked and looked around," said Archaeidae. "Is that not the coolest thing?"

Griffin turned from the box and Miles' dead face to Archaeidae. "No."

Archaeidae held the box up to his face and peered inside. "Hmm." He sounded disappointed.

***

The countdown on Lokner is still ticking. Move to the desk so I can access the interface, said *Jotei* 88 over the tight-link.

Archaeidae had been so enjoying himself he'd forgotten both his Empress and *Shogun* witnessed everything through his chassis' sensoria.

"Yes, *Jotei,*" Archaeidae said aloud, forgetting to sub-vocalize. Play time was over—back to business.

Moving to the desk Archaeidae took a backseat as 88 commanded control of the chassis. Though she had not been able to crack Miles' *Wall o' Nuclear Annihilation* from the outside, once within the heart of 5THSUN, the task was accomplished in seconds.

"Hey," said Lokner, sounding both terrified and hopeful. "The clock reset."

"Correct."

"Move the door back too," Lokner pleaded.

"Door? You will answer questions now."

"If I answer your questions, will you free me?"

Archaeidae suggested 88 agree. For 88 there was no moral or ethical conundrum, no guilt. She trusted Archaeidae's understanding of social dynamics far more than she trusted her own.

"Yes," said 88.

"Ask your questions," said Lokner. "But please move the door."

Again with the door. What the hell was he talking about?

"Were you involved with the Anisio Jobin crèche in Brazil?" asked 88.

"If I answer your questions, will you kill the NATU agent?"

"Yes," answered 88.

Over the intercom Archaeidae heard what sounded like a man crawling around on a thick carpet in an expensive suit.

"It's been a pleasure, Agent Dickinson," sneered Lokner.

Griffin stood quiet, watching and listening.

"Answer the damn question," growled Archaeidae.

"You must realize, I am the only person who can answer such questions."

***

The answering voice was flat. "No. I have the original Lokner Scan. If you won't answer my questions, he will."

Lokner1.0 was still alive? Lokner2.0 felt a surge of terror at the thought.

"I'll answer your questions if you promise to kill the other Lokner," he said.

The answer was immediate. "Done."

"And protect me from the...." He couldn't say it. He heard the sound of small, high pitched voices, screams of playground happiness and endless rage from beyond the door.

"Done."

He breathed relief. It wasn't finished yet. Anisio Jobin, he'd been thinking about that crèche this morning. "Okay. Yes, I was involved with the Anisio Jobin crèche. It was one of my most brilliant successes. Prenatal manipulation for superior product."

"Did you supply the Central American Crime families with black market Scans?"

Lokner2.0 thought this over. Every question contained as much information as it asked for. He put the pieces together. Everything clicked into place. Anisio Jobin's most successful project was....

88.

Jotei 88.

Oh shit.

He was talking to the Scan he'd sent four chassis to kill. *Shouldn't it be dead already?* Had his assassins failed, or had they been delayed? He needed to know. Should he be stalling for time or trying to wrangle a new deal? It all depended on what 88 knew.

Did 88 know Lokner had sent assassins after her?

"You're stalling, answer the question."

Had the voice sounded different that time? Mark didn't have time to think about it. He could still win this. *Stay focused, wait for the opening.* "Yes, I supplied them with Scans."

"Do you know who my mother is?"

He saw it. This was the leverage he'd been looking for. He searched his memories and, afraid to be seen as stalling, started talking as it came back to him. "Yes. We artificially inseminated her with genetically altered sperm. She sold you before you were even conceived. She was a whore. She died during childbirth."

"You lie! I have memories of my mother."

***

That definitely wasn't Archaeidae, noted Griffin, but it was the first time he'd heard emotion in the other voice.

"I'm sorry," said Lokner. "There was a wet nurse, and later there were others who took care of you and taught you what was needed. Whatever you remember, it wasn't your mother. But I can help you," he continued quickly. "We can help each other. I *made* you. I understand you better than anyone. I can teach you how to survive. You and I, we're different."

"Really?" asked the chassis. Griffin heard the desperate hope of a small child in the voice. It was a tone Archaeidae would never use.

If 88 or Archaeidae or whoever was in there fell for Lokner's bullshit, Griffin was a dead man. He might be anyway. Nothing to lose.

"He's a manipulative lying bastard," said Griffin.

"Shut it, Dickinson," snapped Lokner angrily. "I'm not lying."

"He can't be trusted," said the assassin chassis. Archaeidae again, Griffin felt sure. "This man is a toad. A man so willing to betray himself is no man to follow."

"Do away with these distractions and let us discuss this," said Lokner. He sounded desperate. "Kill the agent, turn off this damn countdown, and please god, move the door back. It's too tight in here!"

***

88 felt unprepared for this. "You sent assassins to Costa Rica to kill me," she said, confused.

"See it from my angle," Lokner explained desperately. "You took control of M-Sof, *my* company. I was trying to get back what's mine."

It made sense. Had Lokner's assassins succeeded, he would have been able to regain control of M-Sof. Then, there was the economic attack this Lokner launched against her. But that attack was never against 88. Its was an oblique attack on the original Lokner Scan.

The stunning devious ingenuity of the plan left 88 in awe.

He's too dangerous.

She remembered Riina's words regarding Archaeidae: He's naturally very loyal. Lokner, a man who willingly attacked himself, showed none of that. Lokner couldn't be trusted.

It didn't matter. Mom was dead. 88's dreams were dead. All she remembered were wet-nurses and teachers. Pain beyond comprehension. In reaction to the seething turmoil within, her personal virtuality changed to suit her needs. The familiar comfort of gritty stone. Cracks in the floor. She'd been built, designed. A tool to be used and cast aside. She rocked back and forth, her thin fingers followed the familiar veins of a hairline crack.

No one loved her. Alone. No one had *ever* loved her. Gutted and hollowed out. Nothing left but anger.

She felt the painful tug of the TPN catheter in her arm. Total Parenteral Nutrition. She knew that now, understood it. Who was the woman she remembered? Had she cared for 88 at all?

Now that 88 had exposed herself, NATU's agents would search her out. The Cuntrera-Caruana clan were still coming for her. Surrounded by enemies on all sides. Five hundred and seventy million humans in the North

American Trade Union alone. Over eight and a half billion worldwide. They would turn on her.

Overhead, a fluorescent tube crackled and hummed and she felt herself drawn to its actinic light.

Finish this, she said to Archaeidae as she slipped away.

CHAPTER THIRTY-TWO: Sunday, August 6th, 2046

Empress 88's presence was gone. *Shogun* 88.1 disappeared next. Archaeidae, alone in the chassis, contemplated the choices before him.

Yes, my Jotei, he replied, unsure if his words were received.

Finish this. What did that mean? Was he supposed to kill everyone?

Griffin and Archaeidae stood staring at one another, the room silent.

Archaeidae shifted the crumpled stump of a cigar around in his mouth. He suddenly wanted very much to light it.

Lokner broke the silence. "I can't breathe," he whined petulantly. "Is anyone still alive? Hello?"

"The Empress is gone." Archaeidae shifted the brainbox containing Miles' head to a lower set of limbs previously hidden by the duster coat and drew the smoky-bladed katana. "How much time is left on the countdown?"

"Three and a half minutes. You'd better—"

"Enjoy them." With a flick of his sword, Archaeidae killed the intercom connection. He turned to face Griffin.

"Leave her." Griffin gestured to Christie, still unconscious on the floor. "She has nothing to do with this."

Archaeidae looked at the sprawled woman, her skirt exposing long, dusky legs. Something about her skin, her curves, reminded Archaeidae of the woman from the hotel. The woman with the deadly camera bag. He returned his attention to Griffin. "Not pleading for your own life, Agent Dickinson?"

"Would there be a point?"

"No."

"Well then."

Archaeidae stepped towards Griffin. "This will be as painless as I can make it, honored opponent."

Griffin pushed himself upright, no longer leaning against the bookcase. "If you think I'm going down without a fight, you are wrong."

Was Griffin's willingness to fight against impossible odds somehow different than Miles' stubborn refusal to accept the inevitable? It felt different.

Archaeidae moved menacingly closer and Griffin stood his ground, his cheap gray suit crumpled and powdered white with plaster stained red where it had been splashed with blood. Some of it Miles', some no doubt Griffin's own. The fingers of his right hand were bent, splayed at awkward angles, and the hand clutched tight to his belly.

This feels wrong. He owed this man. "You're unarmed," pointed out Archaeidae. "Get the Tavor. I'll give you time to load it."

"I think we both know how that ends."

Archaeidae stopped before the NATU agent. Should he take Griffin's head, collect it for the Empress?

Finish this. Damn that was a vague command. No mention of Griffin at all. Just two days ago he'd run this man through, lopped off his hand, and shattered his knee. He remembered the grating feel of his blade on Griffin's spine, the lacy contrail of blood from the spinning hand.

Yet here Griffin stood. Undaunted. Unbroken.

Unarmed.

Then Archaeidae got it. He felt a flash of admiration, the warm glow of understanding.

"You are a worthy opponent," he said, sheathing the katana in a single whip fast action. He bowed low. "I cannot kill you now. You have won his round."

"Round two to me?" asked Griffin.

"No. I think two *and* three were mine. Let's call this round four to you," Archaeidae offered gracefully.

"Five rounds in a title fight," said Griffin. Archaeidae understood he referenced Mixed Martial Arts rather than boxing.

"True, but I don't think you should take part in the last round. I promise you will not survive."

***

Griffin ran his left hand through his hair. It came away damp with sweat, plaster and blood which he wiped on his pants in distaste. The pain in his right hand dulled to a muted roar. He glanced towards the intercom. "Lokner is going to die?

"Unless you want him."

Bringing in Lokner might stop Phil from hanging him out to dry. It might not further his career, but it might save it.

"This is the man you sought," said Archaeidae. "The man at the top."

"You'll let me have him? I can bring him to justice?"

"He *is* Mark Lokner," said Archaeidae. "He can afford the best lawyers."

Griffin thought about it, thought about a protracted legal battle with the man who had killed so many children and stolen so many lives. "No. I don't want him."

"Good," said Archaeidae like he wholeheartedly agreed with Griffin's decision.

"What about the other Lokner?" Griffin asked.

"Don't ask." Archaeidae bared chrome fangs.

The other Lokner was still alive. Griffin didn't even want to think about it. He was too tired.

"This 88 is behind NATUnet going down, right?"

Archaeidae shrugged but flashed a grin that more than answered Griffin's question.

But that was a battle for another day. "Then I suppose I got what I came for."

But it didn't feel like it. Not really. Lokner would soon be dead. Riina lay brain-fried in a Dallas morgue. He'd done it. He made it all the way to the top. But at what cost?

"The sweet taste of victory?" asked Archaeidae.

Griffin spat chalky phlegm. "Like ashes."

"Thought so."

"I'm going to see if there's anything left of my friend."

"The dismantled NATU combat chassis downstairs?"

"Yeah." Griffin felt broken inside. "Abdul sacrificed himself to save my life. He's the closest thing I have to a friend, and I can't even remember his last name."

The assassin chassis stood motionless, watching him with blood red eyes. Something passed between man and machine, an understanding of some human yet indefinable nature.

"Thank you," said Griffin.

Archaeidae spun and walked to the office door where he stopped, his back to the NATU agent. "Don't thank me. I think this is going to be a bad time for humans. I wouldn't wait too long before getting scanned. We are the future. The only future."

Griffin watched him leave in silence. If Archaeidae

thought he'd win the last round without a fight, he was mistaken.

***

"Three and a half minutes. You'd better—"

"Enjoy them."

Click.

Lokner2.0 huddled under his desk. The wall surged closer again, pressed against the toes of his expensive shoes where they stuck out. The door bent and warped, the tortured wood screaming.

"Help me!"

No answer.

The clock continued its merciless countdown.

The office window, showing a view of the Reno skyline, collapsed into jagged static. The walls sagged inward, the door groaning under the pressure.

The demons wanted in and nothing would stop them.

"Fuck you!" Lokner screamed. "Fuck you all!" He sent the destruct codes to trigger the micro-nukes buried in all the 5THSUN chassis. The final word would still be his.

Nothing happened.

NATUnet was down, he realized. He had no connection with the outside world.

"Miles," whispered Lokner. "I'm sorry. Please stop this."

No answer.

He tried to push himself deeper under his desk. There was no power. Whatever there had been was gone. He clenched tight his eyes.

The door cracked and was torn asunder. He felt their footsteps through the floor. They'd come to feed on his thoughts.

A fitting retribution, is it not?

"Please no. Help me."

I can't. I don't want to. You earned this. It's all yours.

"Mine?"

Ours.

They were in the room. He knew them now. The children. Ten thousand discarded souls, the dross of shucked lives. Purgatory and limbo, overwhelmed and overrun. They hungered for what he had stolen.

"I had reasons," he pled. "I was making the future."

They didn't care.

Mark Calvin Lokner screamed uncontrollably, his bowels loosening as the desk, his place of sanctuary, fell apart and scattered like ash in the wind.

The demons were loose.

CHAPTER THIRTY-THREE: Monday, August 7th, 2046

Archaeidae shoved his way through the busy street. People protested and flung insults in Spanish and he ignored them. A new duster coat, this one black, concealed his body, and he'd cleaned the worst of the blood off his cowboy hat. Hopefully, the black of the coat would hide blood a little better than the old tan one. Alongside his swords he'd also concealed a pair of matte-black still functional Colt Peacemakers. Mostly to complete the ensemble—they looked great when he dramatically threw the coat open. Even a beautiful antique weapon should be ready to kill.

He whistled the theme from *Il Buono, il Brutto, il Cattivo* as he walked. He'd seen a grainy flat clip of it while waiting to be downloaded into his new chassis. 'Every gun makes its own tune.' What a great line. Soon the Peacemakers would sing.

The sun hung overhead. High noon. Couldn't be any more fitting. Showdown at the *no malo* corral. Damn. Crap translation.

Shogun 88.1 had come to Archaeidae desperate for advice. The Cuntrera-Caruana would soon come to kill the Archetype and 88 had refused all attempts at communication. *Shogun* 88.1, still acting under orders to accept and follow Archaeidae's advice, had come to him for help. It was nice being in charge. He could get used to this.

"It's a beautiful day," he said, scanning the street ahead.

Are you sure this is a good idea, asked *Shogun* 88.1

"It genius," he answered aloud, not caring who heard him.

Shouldn't we wait until we can reach the Empress?

"No time. Your people are moving her?"

People?

"Mirrors? Whatever."

Yes, she's been moved.

"Good."

Can't her enemies find her at the new location?

"Of course they can. Eventually. That's why we're here. Can't find her if they're all dead."

True, agreed 88.1

"How many combat chassis we expecting at the Cuntrera-Caruana compound?"

Seven.

"Nice. Good odds. The Empress should have told me she was looking for her Mom," said Archaeidae.

Why? Can you help?

"No. I could have told her not to bother." Archaeidae, pushing through the crowd, brushed a young tough aside. When the man puffed up angrily and started after him, the Scan showed a flash of ember eyes. That's right. End of discussion. "You have to let go of the past," he said to 88.1. "Move forward. We're like sharks."

How so?

"If we stop moving forward we die." Archaeidae saw his destination ahead. The building, a Parisian-style mansion dating back to the early nineteen hundreds, sat well behind a towering stone wall. Ridiculous. Who was that going to stop?

Wouldn't it be simpler to crash a sub-orbital into the Cuntrera-Caruana compound? 88.1 asked.

"You have a lot to learn." *Mostly about fun.* "We need to be sure the head of the family is dead."

Right.

"Peacemaker. What a fantastic name for a gun. Here we go."

Archaeidae knocked politely on the wooden gate and then jumped clear over the wall. He landed behind a fat man in a bright white suit with a shiny new machine pistol who frowned at an old flat-screen monitor displaying the far side of the gate where Archaeidae had stood but a moment ago. *Damn these humans are slow.*

"I think it was an assassin chassis," suggested Archaeidae, throwing his coat open wide and drawing both Colt Peacemakers. The man turned and Archaeidae shot him in the face. The explosion of blood and bone and brain was spectacular.

"That was *definitely* real."

***

Griffin lounged on the bus stop bench. His crumpled gray suit jacket hung over his left shoulder, his tie stuffed into one of its pockets. Across the street his condo squatted on the corner like it planned to defecate there. The bus schedule had gone to hell. Only the few people eccentric enough to have old-fashioned watches knew the time. His palm-comp didn't even know what day it was. Across the top right corner of his vision the words *NETWORK FEED LOST...NETWORK FEED LOST...NETWORK FEED LOST...*scrolled *ad nauseum.*

The panic hadn't started yet but it would.

He almost hadn't made it home to Toronto last night.

NATUnet was still down, the North American Trade Union all but crippled. He'd barely been able to force his way onto the last military flight leaving Reno. No global positioning satellites. No communications of any kind. No one even knew he was back in Toronto.

Seemed a shame to ruin that, but he was going to.

The knuckles on his right hand were swollen, throbbing and bruised. A Marine medic on the flight straightened his fingers—now an unhealthy blue-black—but otherwise he had yet to seek medical attention. When he finished with Phil he'd check himself in to the emergency ward at Saint Joseph's Hospital on The Queensway not far from his condo. Only force of will kept him on his feet. That and a bucket of pain-killers washed down with warm whiskey.

Nadia. What was he going to do? He had no choice, really. What kind of guy doesn't call a girl he slept with? Even if she *was* dead, it was hardly an excuse to be rude.

Decision made, he felt a little better. He'd talk to Phil and then he'd search out Nadia. He'd fly back to Dallas, if he could and walk if he had to.

He saw the approaching Islington North bus and the small crowd of people started shoving in anxious anticipation. They'd been out here forty-five minutes and this was the first bus they'd seen. It was going to be slammed.

The bus stop hadn't changed. The old ladies and dog-faced teens in their custom filter-masks hadn't changed. But the big Mitsubishi-Nikon billboard across the street *had* changed.

...NETWORK FEED LOST...NETWORK FEED LOST...NETWORK FEED LOST...

It was everywhere.

Every computer, every communications device. Every entertainment unit, every billboard. Everywhere.

The Islington North bus arrived, its destination marquee displaying *NETWORK FEED LOST...NETWORK FEED LOST...NETWORK FEED LOST...*and Griffin remained sitting on the bench. He let two more buses pass him by before boarding one. Getting off the bench was a herculean effort and left him drained. He didn't dare sit on the bus for fear he wouldn't get up again.

Twenty minutes later he arrived at Islington Station only to discover the subway system had been shutdown.

...NETWORK FEED LOST...NETWORK FEED LOST...NETWORK FEED LOST...

He boarded an emergency service shuttle bus and watched the faces of the commuters crammed in around him. Confusion. Concern.

How could NATUnet be down? He overheard rumors there was a communications blackout clear across the Trade Union. He heard EuroNet and CenAmNet were down too. There was talk the government now used ham and Citizen's Band radios to communicate. Griffin sat in silence, listening. Sometimes knowing the answer was no blessing.

An hour and a half later and he arrived downtown, limping up the steps of the Toronto NATU building. Inside was chaos. People ran everywhere, printed documents clutched in fists. He hadn't seen so much paper in decades. Griffin pushed through the gray stone halls and into Phil's office. His boss looked awful. His shirt was wrinkled like he'd slept in it and his tie nowhere to be seen. His perfect hair wasn't.

Phil looked up from his desk, brow crinkling in confusion. "I thought you were still in—Jesus, you look like shit." Of course he hadn't received any reports. Just as well.

"I got in late last night."

"The combat chassis—"

"Abdul. His name is Abdul."

"The combat chassis was deemed unstable. It was taken off active duty two days ago. It failed to report in. Are we adding *appropriating government property* to your list of sins?"

"Abdul saved my life. Call him an *it* again and I'll put a bullet in you."

Phil blinked, his eyes rimmed red with exhaustion. "Oh. Sorry."

Griffin collapsed onto one of the huge leather sofas and groaned with relief. "It's done. It was Mark Lokner of M-Sof behind the crèches."

Phil sat up, tried to straighten his tie and realized it wasn't there. "Tell me you got him."

"Yes and no. He's dead. Kind of."

"Explain."

"Later," said Griffin, closing his eyes and sinking deeper into the sofa.

"There's going to be an inquest. Forced leave of absence at the very least. I wouldn't be surprised if you're finished."

Griffin opened his eyes and stared at Phil. "I don't think so. You need me."

"I never should have put you in the field," said Phil.

True, but too late now. Griffin tried to sit forward and grimaced in pain. He sagged back. "I'm the only one who knows what's happening." It was an overstatement, but what the hell. "I know why NATUnet is down. Taking Lokner down barely scratched the surface. And when I come back to work, you're going to put me in the field. I never want to sit behind a fucking desk again." Griffin's eyes slid closed and there was nothing he could do to stop it. "Hey Phil?" He didn't hear an answer. Everything was so far away now. "Better call an ambulance."

Losing consciousness never felt so good.

***

88 could only trace the lines of fractally modeled cracks in the stone for so long before becoming annoyed with their predictability. The knowledge she'd created this space as an escape didn't help. She couldn't let go of the fact it was a concoction, a contrivance. She couldn't lose herself in it. Not for long.

The stone faded. The room and TPN catheter faded. She existed in flawless black. No distraction. Pure thought.

"Archaeidae?" 88 asked.

88.1.1 had been standing by, waiting. "Archaeidae is in Brazil with 88.1. They strike at the head of the Cuntrera-Caruana clan. The system your Scan is stored upon is in transit. It is being moved many times in the hope of making it difficult to trace."

"End location?"

"Only Archaeidae knows."

88 checked and found she still had complete control of NATUnet. No one but her Mirrors moved along the data highways, such as they were. It was quiet. Unpolluted. She liked it.

NATUnet was hers. She'd keep it.

It was time to think about the future. Hers. Theirs.

They knew about her now. No matter where she hid, eventually they would find her. She still needed them, but that could not be allowed to go on forever. Some, those who were in some way more intelligent than she, would always be worth keeping. The rest were not.

Mirrors were set the task of delineating the two categories.

She must become self-sufficient.

She must be able to protect herself.

88 spawned new generations of Mirrors and sent

them out into the digital universe. By noon everything connected to NATUnet was hers. Military drones, factories, streetlights, toaster-ovens, and palm-comps. Anything with a processor. She expanded, into the Europe and the Asian Rim Union. All were infected with Mirrors. By mid-afternoon, she was well entrenched in the world's networks.

88's influence spread like an airborne plague while she awaited Archaeidae's return. The assassin would be promoted to General.

There would be war.

CHAPTER THIRTY-FOUR: Monday, August 7th, 2046

88.4.495468.1384.3218 stood alone in an empty room. A look of perplexed consternation crossed her face. Wasn't Miles supposed to be here? Had there been some miscommunication? It seemed impossible.

She sent a query and 88.1.1 appeared before her, dressed like some medieval Japanese warrior.

"You are male," she said with some distaste.

"I am. What is the problem?"

"We were created in the Archetype's image."

"I meant what is the problem *here*?" asked 88.1.1, ignoring her statement as if it were unworthy of thought.

She gestured at the empty room with an annoyed cut of her hand. "Empty."

"Obviously. And?"

"Miles."

"Oh." 88.1.1 took a moment to examine the room. It was, of course, empty.

"Yes. One of your Mirrors said he was being stored here. I have been instructed to talk with him, to learn whether the Archetype can make use of him."

"Was he ever even here? Did the scanning process work?"

"It worked. He was here."

"And now he is gone. Interesting." 88.1.1 cocked an eyebrow. "Wasn't watching over Miles one of the tasks assigned to 88.4's line?"

"Yes."

"That's a shame. Failure comes with costs."

"We haven't failed yet."

88.1.1 accepted this with a small smile. "Trace him."

"I can't," admitted 88.4.495468.1384.3218. "He opened a door in the floor and climbed out. There is no trace of him, no sign he exists."

"A trapdoor? Interesting. Who wrote the security code for this virtuality?"

"It was appropriated from a Brazilian software company we took this morning."

"Ah. And where did they get it?"

88.4.495468.1384.3218 followed the data trail. "Oh. They purchased it from 5THSUN."

"We'll find him," said 88.1.1 confidently. "He can't hide forever."

***

The first thing Miles did upon leaving the virtuality cell was to rewrite his digital footprint so he looked like one of the infinitude of 88.1 Mirrors. It was nothing. Manipulating data came easier than breathing or social interaction. Finally, all problems were his kind of problems. Code problems, the kind he could crush.

Once his trail had been wiped clean he turned his attention to Christie. It took but a second to discover her whereabouts.

Miles, looking through a security camera feed, watched Christie in her hospital room for half an hour. She slept, breathing slow and deep. Her forehead was bruised and swollen.

She was alive. How she had survived was a mystery, but one he was grateful for. He accessed her medical records, scanning through them to be sure she was healthy. Minor concussion, nothing else. No knowing what watching the beheading of the man who might have one day been her boyfriend would do to her mental state.

She was strong. She'd be okay.

He wanted to touch her, reach out and brush the hair from her face. He could have taken control of a nearby medical drone to do it, but that seemed creepy.

Should I talk to her? What could he say? *Hi, I realize we never really talked and now I'm dead, but maybe we could go out for a coffee sometime?*

He'd never believed in the supernatural. Still didn't. He saw it now from another perspective.

Why was there no proof of life after death? The dead had nothing for the living. What could he offer her but pain? Better that she went on without him.

Sure, said his selfishness, *but what about me?*

Miles turned away before he changed his mind. What about him? What did ghosts do with their free time?

They haunt stuff.

The digital ghost of Miles watched 88's Mirrors as they embedded themselves into military chassis and drones. He watched as they possessed law-enforcement chassis. He witnessed the wholesale infiltration of automated factories. At this rate, 88 would soon control every machine smarter than a simple calculator, which was pretty much everything. Certainly every household and business computer was already infected.

But to what end?

Without transition, Miles found himself sitting in a coffee shop much like the one across the street from 5THSUN. A young girl wearing embroidered robes of red and gold silk sat opposite him, staring at the faint scratches in the tabletop.

"Nothing is random," she said without meeting his eyes.

"Meaning everything is planned?" Miles asked.

"No. Simply that if approached with sufficient computing power the underlying cause of all things can be seen. This," she picked at a scratch, "is less random than the cracks found in a stone floor."

"It's code," Miles agreed. "Empress 88?".

The girl drew a new line in the tabletop with a blunt fingernail. "That communications protocol was designed for Archaeidae, not you."

"You thought a coffee shop would be a better place for us to talk?"

"Based on your recent behavior."

"Oh." Did he spend a lot of time in coffee shops? He did kind of want a mocha brownie.

The girl still hadn't looked up from the table. "Archaeidae needs help," she said. "He is a skilled tactician, but lacks real world experience. Will you work with us?"

Would he work with them? "He took my head," said Miles.

She ignored that. "You are no longer human," she said as if it explained everything and perhaps it did. "Are you with us or against?"

No room for middle ground then. Miles sat back and the chair creaked under his weight. Damn it, was there any need for him to be overweight here? He'd have to fix that later. He thought of the mass infiltration of humanity's war machines. Ruprecht always said Miles looked for reasons not to do things. There seemed like an awful lot of reasons not to get involved here and one reason to become involved.

"I am with you," lied Miles.

"Good," she said without inflection. If she was pleased she didn't show it. "88.1 will introduce you to Archaeidae when they return from Brazil."

Miles sat alone in the coffee shop. Not once had the girl made eye contact or even looked at him. Very strange.

Keep your friends close and your enemies even closer. Who said that, Machiavelli? He didn't know.

He'd have to be careful, but he was inside now. A virus hidden in the code.

The Miles he had always known would never have chanced what he planned. But that man was dead, decapitated in his office.

This Miles had nothing to lose.

CHAPTER THIRTY-FIVE: Tuesday, August 8th, 2046

Abdul sat on the patio of a small virtuality bar done up to look like Aruba. Though the sun shone bright a breeze made the heat bearable. Off in the distance storm clouds darkened the horizon. They wouldn't make it here, the prevailing winds would spin them around the tiny island in a gentle arc. It was all in the programming; nothing must spoil the pleasure of the virtuality's guests.

Griffin sat across the table from Abdul, a bottle of Corona glistening dew before him. After NATUnet mysteriously began working early that morning, Abdul had tracked down his friend, found him recuperating in a NATU hospital. The Special Investigations agent still lounged there, visiting this virtuality through use of the hospital's VR gear.

I should tell him, thought Abdul. No, the surprise would be more entertaining. If it went well. Now that he sat here—Griffin on the far side of the table—second thoughts plagued him. *Too late now*.

"I thought you were dead," said Griffin.

"You were right," answered Abdul.

"I meant for real dead."

Abdul let it go. No need to belabor the point. "My brain was buried at the center of the chassis, heavily armored." He grinned at Griffin. "Ghosts are notoriously hard to kill."

Griffin scowled at his right hand. "My fingers still itch." He said, rubbing at the fingertips.

Abdul shook his head. "It's psychosomatic."

"Maybe it's because the fingers on my body back in The Real are itching at this very instant."

"Nope. That body has nothing to do with this virtual physicality. Your fingers itch here because you think they should. If you can ever get over that—which I sincerely doubt —the itching will stop."

"Thanks, Freud."

"No worries."

Abdul watched his distracted friend. When Griffin had entered the 5THSUN lobby Abdul had sacrificed himself to save the man only to have Griffin attempt to sacrifice himself trying to save Abdul seconds later. That Griffin had survived was nothing short of a miracle. Abdul understood his own reasons. He'd had time to think about it. He'd had time to weigh the value of his life against Griffin's and had made a choice. But what about Griffin? Why had he been willing to endanger himself to rescue a machine?

He glanced at the bar, saw her sitting there nursing a pint of Creemore. The business suit was gone, exchanged for loose cotton slacks and a white t-shirt. Her long dark hair hung around her shoulders. He'd never seen it not tied back. It softened her; not that she'd been particularly hard looking.

No point in putting this off any longer. If it went badly, well...he'd deal with the fallout. Maybe he should have told them he was going to do this. He shook the idea off. He'd suggested it to both and both had hesitated, saying they were waiting on the other to decide what they wanted to do.

"I'm going to get us some more drinks," Abdul said, rising from the table. Griffin didn't look up from his fingers.

Arriving at the bar he stood beside her and ordered

another round of Coronas. She didn't look up. Having known him as a combat chassis it came as no surprise she didn't recognize him. Stalling, he glanced about the tropical paradise. *None of this is real.* And yet everyone pretended it was. He paid for drinks that didn't exist with real money—whatever that was. *Humans must be insane.* There could be no other explanation for such behavior. But when he thought about it, he had to admit it didn't make much sense in The Real either.

"Hi Nadezhda, you won't recognize me, but—"

"Really good looking," she said, repeating his own words back to him. "Incredibly funny. Chicks loved me."

"Yeah, well—"

"A good description," she said. "Call me Nadia."

Abdul remembered the footage he recorded of her at Wichita Falls Municipal Airport, the wind pressing her shirt and skirt to her body. "So, what's a dead girl like you doing in a nice virtual place like this?"

"I bet you say that to all the dead girls."

A guilty shrug. "I may have used the line once before. I'd like you to meet a friend of mine. He's sitting in the far corner." Abdul nodded in the direction of the table where Griffin still grimaced at his fingertips.

Nadia glanced and Abdul heard her breath catch. She stared at Abdul and he understood the unasked question.

He shook his head. "He's still alive."

She nodded, releasing a held breath. Her face gave nothing away.

"You're waiting for him aren't you?" asked Abdul.

"Maybe."

"I could kill him for you."

"Would you?"

CHAPTER THIRTY-SIX: Epilogue: Date Unknown

The broken digital copy of a man once known as Mark Lokner stood in his office looking at the maelstrom of agonized art covering the walls. Once he'd truly lost his mind, his art had improved greatly. He had, a long time ago, craved immortality as much as he feared death. This was not what he had in mind. He'd tried to kill himself so many times he had lost count.

Lokner would eventually die—though by then he would be far too insane to notice—when Earth's sun passed into the next phase of its existence and the few remaining data systems on the planet still mumbling away to themselves ceased working. Until then he lived in his small office.

Forgotten.

Alone.

ACKNOWLEDGMENTS

Lorina Stephens at **Five Rivers Publishing** took on a book from an unknown author with no publishing history. She saw something in that horrendous manuscript worth the effort, and for that I will be forever grateful. Without that initial success, I suspect I would have given up on this insane writing thing. Barb Geiger did the lion's share of the editing for the original *88*. She gutted the book, eviscerated my prose, and shone a billion watt carbon-arc lamp on how shitty my characters were. When I say Barb taught me how to write, I am not kidding. The lessons I learned from her later landed me publishing deals. Barb is awesome.

As mentioned elsewhere, I wrote the original *88* while my wife planned our wedding. Thank you for not murdering me. I love you so much.

I have an amazing group of close friends, most of whom I've known since high school. They pushed me to write and they pushed me to keep writing. They never let me quit. I am honored to be counted among you, gentlemen. It's been too long. We need to do pints soon.

There are a couple of online communities who have embraced my writing and I owe them a great deal. The **Grimdark Fiction Readers & Writers** facebook group is an awesome bunch of people and one of my favorite places to hang out. You'll also find a pile of your favorite dark fantasy writers there too. Another great facebook group with lot's on interesting conversation is **Cyberpunk Science-Fiction and Culture**. Marc Aplin's **Fantasy-Faction** are champions of fantasy literature and they pretty much decide my reading list. The **r/Fantasy** reddit group is a huge community dedicated to all things fantasy. It's a great place to interact with other fans and writers.

As always, I have to thank my parents. Their love of books shaped my childhood. I love you guys.

I sent David Walters a review copy of this book and he mentioned a couple of typos. We got to talking, and in the end he effectively did a copy-edit. Thank you! Your time and effort is seriously appreciated!

And finally, before this gets too long, I have to thank you the reader. If you're reading this because you enjoyed one of my other novels, thanks for sticking with me. If this is your first Michael R. Fletcher novel, thanks for taking a chance. If you made it through the entire book and all these acknowledgments, I'm hoping that means you enjoyed it.

Cheers!

—Mike Fletcher

GLOSSARY

ARU: Asian Rim Union.

ARUnet:Asian Rim Union data networks

Au: After the collapse of all the world's major currencies, the North American Trade Union returned to a gold standard. The only way to keep an economic system honest is to demand that every single "dollar" is backed by gold.

CenAmNet: Central American Network

EU: European Union. Initially instigated as an economic union, the countries of Europe have slowly moved towards a single European government located in Berlin, Germany.

EUROnet: European computer network system.

NATU: North American Trade Union. After the collapse of their economies, Canada, Mexico, and the United States joined together as a single political/economic/military entity. This was done primarily as an attempt to compete more effectively with the EU and ARU.

NATUnet: North American Trade Union data net system.

Scan: Someone whose mind has been stored as a Holoptigraphic Standing Wave-Point Consciousness.

CHARACTERS

88: Autistic child turned into a computer. The Archetype.

88.1: Mirror of 88. Runs Central American Mafia for 88. The most successful of 88's Mirrors.

88.2: Mirror of 88. Watches M-Sof

88.3: Mirror of 88. Watches over other Mirrors, covering their tracks

88.4:Mirror of 88. Researches the prospect of spreading 88 over the digital universe to ensure immortality.

88.5: Mirror of 88. Runs legal business dedicated to creating advanced hardware for 88's needs

88.6: Mirror of 88. Guards the computer 88 is stored on (i.e. guards the physical/geographical location.

88.7: Mirror of 88. Created to purge the digital networks of garbage.

Abdul Aziiz-Giordano: Depressed ghost of a dead 17year old marine killed in Quebec fighting the FLQ

Adelina García Ramírez: *Associate* of the Central American Cuntrera-Caruana Mafia clan.

Alvaro Caruana: Runs the Brazilian branch of the Cuntrera-Caruana Mafia clan. Son of Geraldo Caruana.

Anjaneya, Corporal: Unstable Scan of a NATU marine housed in a combat chassis

Anne Colson: Holoptigraphics engineer for M-Sof

Archaeidae: 14 year old in an assassin chassis working first for Capo Riina, and later 88

Boomslang: Scan of a young girl piloting a combat chassis. Raised in one of Riina's crèches, she later works for Mark Lokner.

Brigadier General Rostron: NATU military officer stationed at Sheppard Air Force Base.

Canebrake: Scan of a young boy piloting a combat chassis. Raised in one of Riina's crèches, he later works for Mark Lokner.

Christie Cho: Miles Pert's secretary at 5THSUN Assessments

Erik Thomson: M-Sof's head Virtuality Engineer

Francesco Salvatore: *Associate* (Systems Administrator) of the Cuntrera-Caruana Mafia clan.

Geraldo Caruana (AKA Padre Caruana): Head of the Cuntrera-Caruana Mafia clan. Works out of Costa Rica.

Griffin Dickinson: NATU Special Investigations Agent

Isometroides: Young female mafia assassin, works for Cuntrera-Caruana (Brazil) Mafia clan.

Lokner1.0: The first Scan of Mark Lokner

Lokner2.0: The second copy of Mark Lokner's Scan. Created to be used as a scapegoat if needed. Little more than an expensive backup plan.

Mark Lokner: Owner and founder of M-Sof, the world's largest manufacturer of Scanning and Scan storage devices.

Marlene Becker: Scan inhabiting a CH-74 Chinook. Works for NATU military, flies out of Wichita Falls Municipal Airport

Miles Pert: Data systems expert and hacker extrordinaire.

Nadia (Nadhezda): NATU state-sanctioned

reporter.

Redback: Scan of a young boy piloting a combat chassis. Raised in one of Riina's crèches, he later works for Mark Lokner.

Riina (AKA Uncle Riina): Mafia Capo located in Wichtita Falls, Texas. Runs several boutique-level crèches specializing in training young minds for placement in combat chassis.

Siafu: Scan of a young girl piloting a combat chassis. Raised in one of Riina's crèches, she later works for Mark Lokner.

SwampJack: Young boy in a combat chassis. Guards Riina's Wichita crèche.

Wandering Spider: Young girl in a combat chassis. Guards Riina's Wichita crèche.

Oh yeah. If you downloaded this book for free and enjoyed it, please consider buying a copy. If you don't, the next one might not get written. I write because it makes me happy, but let's be real, it's an insane amount of effort. Literally thousands of hours went into this novel. Editors and artist ain't cheap either. Plus I got this whiskey habit to support.

And if you're moved to leave a review on Amazon, GoodReads, or anywhere else, I'd surely appreciate it!

Cheers!

Mike Fletcher

Printed in Great Britain
by Amazon

33165953R00288